PRAISE FOR

In the Garden of Spite

"Riveting! Camilla, high-five! Amazing work!"
—Karen Kilgariff and Georgia Hardstark,
#1 *New York Times* bestselling authors of *Stay Sexy & Don't Get Murdered*

"*In the Garden of Spite* is a chilling, pitch-perfect novel that should finally make Belle Gunness a household name. A superb and unforgettable read."
—Deanna Raybourn,
New York Times bestselling author of *A Murderous Relation*

"Mesmerizing. . . . Fans of fictionalized treatments of notorious murderers will be fascinated."
—*Publishers Weekly* (starred review)

"Bruce uses a framework of fact to create fiction that horrifies . . . [a] grisly historical thriller."
—*Booklist*

IN THE GARDEN OF SPITE

A NOVEL OF

The Black Widow of La Porte

CAMILLA BRUCE

BERKLEY

New York

BERKLEY
An imprint of Penguin Random House LLC
penguinrandomhouse.com

Copyright © 2021 by Camilla Bruce
Readers Guide copyright © 2021 by Camilla Bruce
Penguin Random House supports copyright. Copyright fuels creativity,
encourages diverse voices, promotes free speech, and creates a vibrant culture.
Thank you for buying an authorized edition of this book and for complying
with copyright laws by not reproducing, scanning, or distributing any part of it
in any form without permission. You are supporting writers and allowing
Penguin Random House to continue to publish books for every reader.

BERKLEY and the BERKLEY & B colophon are registered
trademarks of Penguin Random House LLC.

ISBN: 9780593102572

The Library of Congress has catalogued the Berkley hardcover edition of this
book as follows:

Library of Congress Cataloging-in-Publication Data

Names: Bruce, Camilla, author.
Title: In the garden of spite: a novel of the black widow of La Porte /
Camilla Bruce.
Description: First Edition. | New York: Berkley, 2021.
Identifiers: LCCN 2020029193 (print) | LCCN 2020029194 (ebook) |
ISBN 9780593102565 (hardback) | ISBN 9780593102589 (ebook)
Subjects: LCSH: Gunness, Belle, 1859-1908—Fiction. |
GSAFD: Biographical fiction.
Classification: LCC PR9144.9.B78 I5 2021 (print) | LCC PR9144.9.B78 (ebook) |
DDC 823/.92—dc23
LC record available at https://lccn.loc.gov/2020029193
LC ebook record available at https://lccn.loc.gov/2020029194

Berkley hardcover edition / January 2021
Berkley trade paperback edition / December 2021

Printed in the United States of America
1st Printing

PERSONAL—comely widow who owns a large farm in one of the finest districts in LaPorte County, Indiana, desires to make the acquaintance of a gentleman equally well provided, with view of joining fortunes. No replies by letter considered unless sender is willing to follow answer with personal visit. Triflers need not apply.

—Popularly attributed to
BELLE GUNNESS

La Porte, Indiana, 1907

This happened many years ago, in the valley where I grew up." My children crowded around me on the bed; their hands were sticky with porridge and the empty china was stacked on the floor, where Prince, our collie dog, huffed and rolled over in his sleep. I had turned the kerosene lamp on the bedside table down, and the little flame cast the room in a soft, warm glow.

Outside the window, it was dark.

"A man was out in the woods chopping wood," I said, "when his wife suddenly came out from among the trees. She looked just as she had that same morning when the man set out from home. She was carrying a bowl of sour-cream porridge, which she offered him to eat. 'This is for you, dear husband, for working so hard in the woods,' she said. The man took the porridge from her hands, and it smelled *so* good and looked even better. Then he noticed that his wife wasn't sitting on the log with him but was crouching down in the underbrush, and he suddenly got suspicious that his wife was not really his wife at all but a hulder from beneath the earth!" At this my children chuckled and shuddered, and crept even closer to me under the knitted blanket.

"'I think you are fooling me!' The man cast the food aside. 'I think you are a hulder,' he cried. And up she went, and now he could see the long tail trailing under her skirt, and she ran off, screaming and cursing and neighing like a horse!"

The girls giggled with delight, but my son's eyes were large with fear. He was not yet four and a little too young for such terrible tales.

"Why did she give him food?" asked Lucy, her little face upturned.

"Because that's how they cast a spell, the hulder people. If you eat or drink something of theirs, they can catch you." I widened my eyes and twisted my lips. Lucy whined and squirmed beside me, and I could not help but chuckle.

"What happens then?" Myrtle's soft mouth hung open. She was easier to scare than her younger sister was, and I saw just as much fear as delight in her expression.

"Oh, they take you with them into the earth—and you can never come back then, or see your family again." I shook my head with a solemn expression.

"Why?" Lucy asked. I could see a trace of porridge on her round cheek.

"They always want a human bride or groom." I reached out with a finger to wipe off the smear.

"But she looked like his wife." Lucy's clear brow furrowed as she struggled to understand.

"That's right. The hulder can look like anyone you know."

"But how will we know then?" Lucy suddenly sat up straight. "How will we know that you are you?"

"Well, that's easy. If I am kind, I am myself. If I'm not . . . then I'm a hulder." I suddenly felt hot. A tightening in my chest made it hard to breathe.

"And you'll take us underground?" Myrtle shuddered beside me. Her dark eyes glistened in the dim light. "Never to come back?"

"Just that." I reached over to the bedside table for some of the silver-wrapped caramels I kept in a bowl. The story had suddenly soured on me.

I did not want to speak more of it.

PART ONE

Brynhild
Paulsdatter Størset

I.

Brynhild

Selbu, Norway, 1877

The smell of meat drove me out of the storehouse to rest against the timbered wall. My head was spinning and I felt sick. It had happened often lately.

"You should be careful, Little Brynhild." Gurine came outside as well, climbing slowly down the stone steps while wiping her hands on her apron. She was chewing on something: a piece of mutton. The old woman had become scrawny over the winter; age had sucked all the fat away, leaving her a bony frame and wisps of white-gray hair. She followed my gaze across the farmyard to the six men who stood by the barn. It was a cold but sunny morning in May; the birches in the yard were budding and the horses grazed in the pasture. One of the men, a farmhand called Ivar, told a story while gesturing wildly with his hands. All the others laughed. They were far enough away that we could not hear what he said, but we could certainly hear the laughter: hard peals of mirth hauled through the air. For a moment, I thought they were looking at me, but if they did, their gazes shifted away before I could be certain.

"They are not to be trusted, the young ones," said Gurine. "Like bucks in heat, the lot of them." She spat gray gristle down on the grass.

"He can't deny me forever," I said, although I was not so sure about that. I could not make myself stop looking at him, standing there laughing with his head thrown back. His dark, thick hair curled out from under his knitted cap, he looked healthy and strong, and his cheeks blushed red in the chill morning air. His hands were buried deep in his pockets. I knew those hands well, could feel the ghost of them on my skin even as I spoke. "I can make him do it, even if he says no." Even if things had changed between us, I still held out hope that I would know those hands once more. I found it hard to believe that all was lost.

"You put too much trust in the priest, Little Brynhild. He was never a friend to women like us," Gurine said.

"Women like us?" I glanced at her.

"Women with nothing to their names."

"Well, he doesn't much like sinners either. I will talk to the priest about Anders. If the priest says he must, he will." I lifted my chin just a little.

"Oh, Little Brynhild." The old woman shook her head. "I don't think it will be that easy . . . Anders has a farm to his name, and money too. Who do you think the priest will believe?"

My hand fluttered to my belly, caressing it through the worn fabric of my apron. "I have the child as proof."

Gurine clucked with her tongue. "You could have gotten that child anywhere."

I nodded. Anders had said that as well when I went to his room and told him what had happened. He laughed even, as if I should have known better than to come to *him* with my plight. "I haven't been with anyone else," I told Gurine, although she already knew that. We shared work and a bed at the farm six days a week, and it had become too hard to lie about the changes in me. We often toiled alone in the kitchen, stirring porridge and carving meat, so it was better that she knew in case I became faint. The fumes from the food did not agree with me since the child took hold. I was often tired and sick. The price I paid for my candidness was Gurine's constant warnings and a quiet offer to solve my problem with a knitting needle. She had seen this before, she said. It never ended well for the girl.

I did not believe that to be true, though. I would make him do what was right, even if I had to force him. It was the two of us together, after all, who had caused this to happen in the first place. I had not been alone in the barn after dark, deep in the musty hay. He had been there too, and I said as much to Gurine, who had sunk down on a stone slab that served as a step to the storehouse.

"Oh, but the world doesn't work like that," she said as another peal of laughter rose from the group of men by the barn. "You know it doesn't, Little Brynhild. If he were a lesser man he might do you right, but *that* one"—she nodded in the barn's direction—"he is heir to all of this and won't bother with a girl like you." She paused to spit gristle down in the grass. "If you are lucky, he will slip you some money or set you up with a tenant, but I don't think he'll do even that." Her face took on a thoughtful expression. "He is spoiled, that one . . . he won't care."

I could tell that she felt sorry for me, and that hurt more than any words. I never did well with pity.

"Hansteen will set it right," I insisted as a pounding at my temples warned me that a headache was coming on.

"The priest won't lift a finger." Gurine squinted up at me as I stood there beside her, wringing the gray, worn apron between my clammy hands. I hated how sure she sounded. I hated that she might be right. Cold sweat broke out all over my body and my heart raced when I thought that I might not get my way. This was a long departure from the giddiness I had felt when I first caught his eyes after Christmas. I had thought it all so easy then. I had thought it was the beginning of something. I always believed I could do better than porridge and toil, that my hard work and diligence would earn me a reward. And for a while, I had thought that he might come to care for me, and that one day, I would cross the yard in front of me not as a maid in threadbare shoes but as the mistress of it all—and him.

I never told Gurine about those hopes of love, but I did tell her about my plan to force him. I confided in her the same night that I knocked on Anders's door and found him drunk in his room. I had prepared every word I was to say to him. I had meant for him to feel remorseful of how our time together had left me in such trouble.

"How do you know it's mine?" he asked instead, sitting on the lip of his red pullout bed. His eyes were glassy from drinking. "I'm not the first man you have tricked into the barn."

"But you are," I protested. "There hasn't been anyone else."

"No?" He emptied the tin cup in his hand. "That's not what they say."

I felt confused. Who were *they* and what did they say? "Well, they lie. There never was anyone else."

He shrugged. The light from the candle he kept on the table chased shadows across his handsome face, and on the timbered walls. "I don't see what you want from me." His gaze met mine across the small room; the air was stale in there, warm and musty. I could hear the crackling of fire coming from the small black oven in the corner. There was no warmth in his eyes, though; they were much like dark pebbles in the flickering light. "Why are you telling me this?"

"Why?" I could not believe my own ears. "Because you should do right by me. We ought to go to the priest."

The corner of his mouth lifted in a smirk. "What for, Brynhild? Why should you and I go to the priest?"

"To marry," I replied, and my voice did not quiver when I said it. It was the right thing to do, after all. He might not care for me as I hoped he would, but he *had* gotten me with child. Outside the window, between the plaid curtains, I could see the birch trees moving with the wind, black silhouettes against a dark blue sky. I felt like they laughed at me all of a sudden, as if they were chuckling so hard they could not stand still.

"Marry you?" Anders laughed as well. "Are you mad or slow, or as shrewd as your father? Do you really think you can trick me like that?" Anders's brow glistened when he lifted the bottle from the floor and filled his cup to the brim. "I should never have sullied my hands with the likes of you." He put down the bottle and lay back on the bed, still with the cup. I had changed that bed just the other day, beaten the pillows and smoothed down the sheets while saying a quick little prayer. Not that it seemed to do me much good.

"You are drunk," I decided, and straightened my pose. "You aren't thinking clearly. Tomorrow you will see things differently."

"Oh Brynhild." He flung his arm across his eyes and gave a little laugh; the liquor in his cup danced and escaped, landed on his shirt, and created dark stains. "Don't you see? I would never, ever marry *you*." He spat the last word as if it were repulsive.

"I will go if you're with me or not." I forced my voice not to quiver. "Hansteen will see to it that things are set right between us."

He removed his arm so I could see his face. Something hard had settled on his features. He did not look so handsome just then but reminded me of my father. "Are you threatening me, Brynhild?"

"I just want what's right—and I'm sure the priest will agree. He never liked a sinner." This was not how I had wanted things to go between us, but what else could I do but stand my ground? The child was *there*, in my belly, growing and thriving. "Surely it's God's will for us to marry now," I tried. "He wouldn't have sent me this child if it weren't."

He glanced at me. "I think it's your *will* that's at work here, and that has nothing to do with the Lord."

"The priest might see it differently."

He chuckled down in the bed. "Oh, you wouldn't dare."

"I would! And then the shame would be all on you."

"Oh, I think some shame would drip on you as well, and Hansteen can't make me do anything." His lips twisted up and made him look ugly. Outside the birches laughed and laughed.

"You wouldn't like it if he banned you from church—your father wouldn't be happy, that's for sure. Maybe he'd even take the farm." I tried my very best to come up with things to change his mind.

"Go!" he suddenly shouted from the bed, so loud that I was sure his parents would hear it. He had dropped the cup down in the bed, and the rest of the liquor soaked through the hay.

It scared me, though, that outcry. Enough that I tiptoed back downstairs to the bed I shared with Gurine behind the kitchen. I crawled in under the woolen blankets, shivering from it all. Her arms came to hold me then, fragile as they were. "There, there, Little Brynhild." She made soothing sounds in the darkness. "Why is the young master shouting at you in the middle of the night?"

"It doesn't matter," I said. "I will see the priest about it."

She sighed when she realized what I meant. "So that's how it is, then?"

"It is." I stared up at the ceiling through the darkness.

"And now he won't—"

"No."

Her voice dropped to a whisper. "You know I can help you get rid of it—"

"No!" Even in my wretched state, I was not about to let this opportunity slip. "I can make him—I'm sure of it."

Gurine, however, was not so sure, and nothing I had said since could make her feel any different. She did not think I could make the marriage happen—but I could! I *had* to believe that I could. Hansteen liked me, and I had always been diligent at church. He would put the blame where it belonged for sure. Anders should have known better than to kiss a young maid in the barn. Hansteen would make him—and then he had to—and then I would never eat gruel again.

The men by the barn were moving now, carrying heavy tools. Anders carried an axe. They were to work on the western field today, mending fences.

"They are headed up," Gurine observed with a warning in her voice. It meant they had to pass us by and she wanted me to slip inside the storehouse. I did no such thing. I stayed put, righted my headscarf, and tilted my chin up as they drew closer: a gaggle of filthy men, hair greasy and shirts stained. I could see their muscles working as they walked toward us, how they bulged and strained under their clothes. Their lips were all drawn out in hard smiles.

"What is wrong with you, Little Brynhild?" Ivar said, mocking me. "You look like you just licked a lemon."

"What would you know about that?" I replied. "I'm sure you've never even tasted one yourself."

Ivar laughed. "They're fine enough with a little sugar, or so I've heard. You should try some of that."

Before I had time to reply, a man called Gunnar spoke. "I think she's gotten enough sugar for a while. Enough that she has started to swell." He kept his eyes on the ground in front of his feet; a smile played on his lips.

I drew my breath to reply to him when I noticed that Anders had fallen behind the others. His gaze met mine, as cold as before, but at least he approached me and that was something. "Leave us alone, Gurine," he said. The old woman got to her feet and gave me a worried glance before she shuffled across the yard with her head bent, leaving the two of us alone outside the storehouse. The men had continued up the hill, though a couple of them looked back over their shoulders. Gunnar was still smiling.

Anders let his hand with the axe drop down by his side. His brow looked slick despite the chill in the air. His eyes did not meet my gaze. "Have you come to your senses yet, Brynhild?" The axe swung slowly back and forth. "It's bad enough that everyone knows—"

"I didn't say a thing," I said quickly. I wanted to stay on his good side if I could. I wanted him to be my husband, after all.

"Women talk." He shrugged.

"I don't." And neither did Gurine. "I think it's you who have told them." I looked after the men.

Another shrug then. "Be as it might, I didn't come to talk about slippery tongues."

"No?"

"I wanted to know if you still think it's mine, that child you carry—"

"It is! There hasn't been any other."

He swallowed hard and would still not meet my gaze. "I suppose you still think we should marry, then."

"I do!" Could it be that he had come around? My heart beat faster in my chest.

He shifted on the ground before me; the axe still swung back and forth. "Why don't you come to the dance on Saturday night? We can talk then, down by the lake." He did not smile, did not look me in the eye. "It will be easier then, when there aren't so many people around. We can sneak away, just the two of us."

I nodded while all sorts of feelings battled inside me: some worry, some hope, and a bottomless want.

He lifted his gaze; it lingered on my belly, although there was not much to see yet. "I'll see you on Saturday, Brynhild. Alone." His gaze slid away from me. He heaved the axe over his shoulder and walked on fast to catch up with the rest, leaving me behind by the storehouse.

Gurine appeared in the open door to the farmhouse; she had heard every word, of course. She used her bony hand to shield her eyes from the sun as she stepped outside and came toward me while slowly shaking her head.

"What is it now?" I was annoyed. "Things are finally going my way. He wants to meet me—you heard what he said!"

"Yes, and I don't like it . . . Be careful, Little Brynhild." She took hold of my arm. "I don't trust that man at all."

Even before my skirt turned wet, I knew that I was bleeding. Though I had never felt it before, I knew what that pain at the bottom of my spine meant. I knew that the child would leave me.

I do not know if I already bled when he left me by the water's edge, or if the bleeding began when I slowly tried to rise. I knew I could not faint down there. It was May and the nights were still cold. I had to stand up and move my feet, get myself back home. I would *not* die, I told myself. I would not die—I would survive. I would survive if only to spite him. He wanted me dead; well, look: I was walking, if slowly and on shivering legs. I was walking in pain, away from the lake and across the dirt track to the safety of the woods. I wiped blood off my face with the hem of my skirt; tears and snot soaked the dark fabric too. A sharp edge was the only thing left where my tooth used to be; another tooth was clean split in half.

I did not feel that pain yet.

I could not stop the violent shivers, or the deep sobs that came ripping from my chest. Hoarse noises poured from my throat as I lumbered along like a wounded bear. The nosebleed stopped, so perhaps it was not broken, but my jaw was swollen and tender to the touch. Then it was the real pain—the only one that mattered. Before long, it came in ripples and aches as my belly convulsed to rid itself of the damaged cargo. I leaned against a spruce, pressed my shoulders to the rough bark, and tried to breathe through the contractions like women in labor do, although this was no birth. When it eased up some, I stumbled on and lifted my gaze, but there was nothing to see except for more trees, heavy branches crowded with lichen, ghostly white in the pale night light. The thick moss that covered the ground looked blue and the air smelt of wet soil and sap. Størsetgjerdet was still miles off, the way home steep and hard. I thought I might die before I made it that far.

I held on to trunks as I walked, careful to keep out of sight from the farms. No one was to see me like that. I would not let anyone laugh at me, even if it meant I perished in there, hidden by the trees. I paused again as more pain ripped through me, and my thighs were slick with fresh blood. I lay down on the mossy ground, folded my elbows under my chest, and spread my legs. Perspiration washed the blood from my brow, hot and thick, as I lay there panting, bleeding. The convulsions lasted for hours, maybe—minutes, I could not tell. It was fast, though, as births go. Anders had been thorough in beating the child out of me. When the cramping finally stopped, I fell over to my side and lay there for a while, gazing skyward. Every breath I took was a struggle as my ribs ached and burned. When I had gathered enough courage, I looked down on the mess on the ground. I could not tell it with my eyes, but I felt it was a girl, curled up in the hot blood.

The beginning of a daughter of mine.

Now it had come to nothing.

I used my hands to rip away moss and dig a hole in the soft, cool dirt. I was not sure how much good it would do, but I wanted to protect her from scavenging foxes. It did not get very deep, as I had no strength to give. I pulled off one of my woolen stockings, the cleanest piece of cloth on my body, and wrapped my daughter in it. My belly had just started to curve so there was not much to wrap. It felt slippery in my hands, though. Slippery and warm. The scent of iron was strong and fresh—it was animal scent, the scent of slaughter.

Down in the hole she went. Into the fragrant soil, next to a coiling root. As I pushed the damp dirt back on top of the remains, I marveled at the way it covered her up, smooth and soft, as if the girl were erased by blackness.

As if nothing were down there at all.

I smoothed the earth on top of the grave, but I did not weep, oh no—he had kicked all the tears out of me too. "If I put it there, I better get it out again," he had said before his foot hit my belly. Then he grabbed hold of the little bit of lace I had on my blouse—the very best I had—and yanked me from the ground to plant a fist in my jaw.

No, I would not weep for that man.

After I buried my daughter, I lay still for a little while longer, bleeding, while I looked up at the tall pines moving uneasy against the pale sky. Clouds came drifting with the dawn: wisps of slate gray that chased one another and snapped at one another's tails. Like wolves, those clouds, rushing across the sky, waiting for the red sun to rise. I waited for it too, down on the ground, curled up, ruined and empty inside.

This was what we were worth, the dead child and I. We could be torn asunder, cast away and laughed at while we bled. We were nothing but vermin and stains to those people. I wanted to be a wolf too, to snarl and bite and tear apart, and taste the blood of those who laughed.

Instead, I staggered to my feet and stumbled on. I did not even look back.

I would rise, if only to spite.

Vermin always survive.

DAYLIGHT HAD LONG since arrived when I finally made the last, slow climb up to Størsetgjerdet, my father's small tenant farm. A sour smell of wood smoke greeted me, and the bleating of our single goat.

Just a few steps left and I barely made it—it felt like crossing a mountain. Crusted blood striped my calves, my clothes were stiff with it, and yet I was still bleeding.

The single room inside the small house was dark, the ceiling low. Mother was out, but Father was there, sitting by the stove. He had his knife in his hand and whittled chips of wood into the flames. The scent of thin coffee reached me by the door and made my aching stomach convulse.

My father looked up, his gray beard thick and tangled. He took me in, top to bottom. "What mess have you gotten yourself into now?"

I found the pail by the door and threw up, heaved and sputtered into it.

"Looks like she's *rid* herself of the mess." Olina's voice sounded behind me. I could hear her uneven steps on the floor as she came to gloat. Her fingers grasped my stiff skirt, tugged at it almost gently. "Not so haughty now, are you?" Her voice was not as spiteful as I had expected. She was tall like me but slender and spindly; her left leg was stiff as a twig. There was nothing to do for that. My sister would never leave home.

Bright light flooded the dark, smoky room when Mother arrived, carrying water. My head was still curved over the pail as I did not trust the heaving to be over, but I heard her familiar shuffle behind me and my shoulders sagged with relief. The floor shook when she set down her heavy load, and then I felt her fingers splayed on my back. "Can't you see she's sick, you fools?" She pushed Olina back and my sister made a complaining sound. "Standing there like a cow," Mother snapped at her. "And you"—to my father—"is that all you can do? Sit there whittling while your daughter is bleeding?"

"She's no child of mine," he said, as he always did when displeased.

"Olina, help me get her on the bed." Mother did not hear him. I cried out when their hands came to touch me and force me away from the pail.

"Good God, child, who did that to you?" Mother paled when she saw the state of my face. Even Olina's eyes widened and she bit her lower lip. I tried to answer, but fresh pain was throbbing at my temples, and my swollen jaw made it hard to speak.

"Get her on the bed, on the bed, bring the pail." Mother barked orders while she and Olina forced me to move my legs and cross the floor. They took me to the bed in the corner, the one I shared with Olina. I slumped down on top of it, smelled the musty hay and sour sweat, blood—always the blood. Mother went to heat water; Olina sat on the three-legged spinning chair, staring at me, her mouth hung open as if she had never seen an uglier animal than me. Then suddenly there was a thudding sound and the quiet hum of steel.

My father had risen from the chair and thrown his knife across the room. It was embedded in the timber above my head, stood there, quivering. A curse.

Father had made his opinion known.

THE FIRST FEW days were a haze. I remember wet cloth on my face and an aching all over, a searing pain in my back and belly. Something was wrong in me. I could taste it as a bitter cloying on my tongue; I was festering from within. The blood on the rags Mother brought me turned from red and black to pink and yellow, and it reeked.

I often lay awake, too weak to talk but not to listen, staring at the ceiling. I knew the patterns and swirls of the timber by heart, just as I knew every inch of that room. The awkward angle of the small cooking stove, haphazardly installed. The open shelves on the wall above the table with cups, plates, and tins filled with printed psalms and letters. A large chest under a window for storage. The narrow stairs to the loft where we slept as children. The rickety spinning wheel placed in a corner. The four mismatched chairs with flaking paint. There were three clotheslines strung across the ceiling, heavy with musty garments. Two beds. One bench. Oh, how I loathed that place, and even more so when I found myself trapped there, too sick to move an inch.

Listening in on my family did nothing to soothe my pain.

"She won't last," Father said from his place by the stove.

"Don't you have any work to do?" Mother was sitting by the table, preparing moss for drying. It would help soak up the blood. "She will or she won't. It's up to God now."

"Will he hang if she dies?" Olina was stirring the pot of gruel. She would want me to taste it later. The thought of it made my stomach churn.

"No one will hang." Father sucked his pipe.

"Maybe we *should* tell someone," Mother muttered.

"Tell them what?" The pipe came away. "That she has made a fool of herself and gotten herself in trouble? We reap what we sow in this world."

"What did you sow then, to have such a grand life?" The bitterness coiled like smoke in the room.

"You knew what I had when you took me. If it's not good enough you're free to go elsewhere." He spat on the floor. "You and the changeling both."

Mother laughed then, loud and shrill. "Oh Paul, you can't talk your way out of that one." She would be nodding in my direction. "She is yours; just look at that nose."

"The changelings can look like anything they want; what do I know if you've been seeing some troll?"

"When would I have had time for that with your brood hanging in my skirts?"

It was Father's turn to laugh, a hard-edged chuckle. "Too late for regrets now, isn't it?"

"You *should* talk to someone, though." Mother's voice again. "If she dies, someone will have to answer."

He took a while, seemed to consider it. "We're losing income, that's for sure."

Mother sighed. "You should let her keep what she earns or she'll never get far."

"We feed her, don't we? Clothe her?"

"Barely. She saved up for that lace with what little you left her. Now I don't see how I can get the blood out."

"They say she was beaten by Selbu Lake." Olina had been out then, down in the valley. "They say it was *he* who did it—he who put that child in her."

Mother gave another sigh. "I'm just glad he didn't drown her, then."

"He was about to"—Olina's voice rose with glee—"but then someone came and he lost his nerve."

Do you want to sleep in the lake tonight, Brynhild? That was what he had said to me down by the lapping water. *I'll help you get in there, don't you worry. You and your bastard both!*

"They have never been very good to us, the people down in the valley." Mother's voice was hard as rock. "They always looked down on us, even those with little to their name." This was an old and worn complaint. I knew what she would say next: "We ought to keep ourselves to ourselves."

"If Father weren't so mad all the time—" Olina stopped midsentence; there was a scratching sound and a loud smack. He had gotten off his chair and stopped her foul mouth.

I heard him sit back down again, the creaking of his chair. "Perhaps it's better if this is the end."

Mother sucked in her breath. "Shame on you for saying such a thing. She is your own flesh and blood, and a blessing."

"Doesn't look much like a blessing to me, lying there bleeding in the hay."

"Have you no heart?"

I heard Father filling his cup from the bottle; strong fumes mingled with the smoke and sickness in the air. "The Lord gives and the Lord takes."

"And we ought to be *grateful* for every small gift he gives."

I opened my mouth then. Lips dry and split, and spoke my very first words since that night: "Or I could leave."

The room fell quiet; only the flames crackled and sputtered. Then there was a flurry of motion as my mother and sister crossed the floor and came into my vision, Olina with an angry red mark on her cheek.

Mother's dry hand landed on my forehead. "I think the fever has broken." She sounded surprised. I was not. I had sworn to live, if only to spite—and that was what I would do.

MY BROTHERS PEDER and Ole came by, delivering letters. They had already heard about me; I could see it on their faces when they entered. None of my siblings but poor Olina with her limp lived at Størsetgjerdet anymore. All had thought Peder would take over when Father grew old, and perhaps he would, but not yet. He was a tenant on another farm where he got more land to work for himself. Ole, far younger, stayed with him. Father complained about that; he would rather have Ole at home. My brother was happy to escape, though. Peder was not an easy man either, but he had a wife and young children. It was livelier there.

Peder nodded in my direction when he saw me. I was no longer in bed but sitting on the spinning chair with a cushion of moss between my legs. It did not smell as bad as it had. The blood had cleared up some, trickling pink.

"So you're up then." He delivered a small wad of letters to my mother. She took a quick look at them and noted the handwriting. Then she gave them to me.

"She is just sitting there," Olina complained, looking my way. "She can't *do* anything."

"She'll be back to work in no time, I'm sure." Peder's gaze avoided mine and he turned to serve himself coffee from the kettle. Ole was still lingering by the door, tall and broad-necked, a little simple. He did not look at me at all but stared down at the floor instead.

"Are they talking in the valley?" Mother asked Peder. Father was out, so we could chat freely.

"Some." Peder sat down and tasted his coffee, grimaced at the heat. His beard was dark and full, as Father's used to be, his face tanned and worn from long hours in the sun. "When will you go back to work, Little Brynhild? I'm afraid they'll find another maid if you—"

"She won't." Mother cut him off. "Not if I have any say in it."

He took a moment, thought about it. "Father won't be pleased if she stays at home."

"She could go elsewhere, like Marit did." My sister had served outside Selbu before she got married. I could see her crooked scribblings on one of the letters in my hands. Another envelope beckoned me, though, shone like a moon on a starless night. I knew that slanted handwriting, that poor spelling, as well as my own. The stamp was like a gemstone, glittering bright. I lifted the letter to my nose and sniffed it: paper glue and dust, but it was different from all other paper and dust, because it came from across the sea.

"I'll go back to work." My speech was still garbled due to the swelling.

"Not looking like that." Olina glanced at me. Her fingers were busy with the sewing in her lap.

"You won't," Mother agreed.

"The pain will go away." I shifted on the chair as if to prove it. Everything ached and burned.

Peder's gaze measured me. "Not for another few weeks yet."

"One week," I promised.

Ole finally sat down by the table and let Mother fetch him coffee. "He should be treated the same, he who did that." His voice was quivering, with anger perhaps.

"Wouldn't do much good." Mother sounded weary and wiped her brow with the back of her hand.

Peder was still measuring me. "Marit went to Rødde farm. Perhaps you could go there too."

"Is it far enough away?" Ole's cup shook when he brought it to his lips. "Won't they know?"

"Probably, but she wouldn't see *him* all the time." My brother's lips curled with distaste.

"They say I asked for it, don't they?" I could not help but say it aloud. Neither of my brothers answered, which was a good enough answer for me.

Peder sighed and stretched out his legs. "You should have been more careful. It never pays off taunting those who have more to their name."

"I should have gone to the priest. He would have set things right."

Peder shook his head. "Hansteen would rather believe a farmer's son than you."

"I would have had the child to prove it."

Mother sighed; Peder shifted. "Stories like that never end well. They would say you were hungry for gold."

"They already do, I reckon." I looked to my brother for an answer.

Another shrug. "Sure they do. It was a stupid and reckless thing you did."

"I didn't get with child on purpose."

"That doesn't matter if they think you did."

I clutched the letters in my hands so hard the ink was starting to smear. "Are they laughing?"

A pause. "Yes." Peder's gaze dropped away. "They're laughing."

They all bent their heads then: Olina over her sewing, Mother over the knitting, and my brothers over their cups. All bent their heads in shame but me. Mother sighed and bit her lip. Ole fidgeted. I ripped open the bejeweled envelope in my lap and tried to catch a whiff of that other place as I pulled the paper out. Nellie's scribbles filled two pages. *Dear Mother and Father* . . . it began. *You will be happy to hear that we are settling in nicely in our new apartment here in Chicago . . .*

"What is she saying?" Mother asked. She never learned to read well.

I skimmed the letter. "She is doing fine. She complains about the weather . . . She says the streets are filled with people, but nobody really knows one another." She wrote it as if it were a thing to mourn, not to envy.

"You must read it out to me tonight." Mother's shoulders slumped with relief. She always worried that there would bad news: sickness, fire, or death. "We must write her back too. I won't see her again in my lifetime, I reckon." She folded her hands in her lap and sighed. "But at least we have those letters."

"Maybe we all ought to go to America." Peder's gaze narrowed. "We can own land there, not break our backs plowing someone else's dirt."

"There's not a single acre left unclaimed around these parts." Ole nodded. "We'll be tenants till we die."

"It's crowded over there as well." Mother lifted her head. "It is dusty and vile: horses rotting in the streets, houses burning down around people's heads . . . you've heard what your sister writes."

"That's in the cities, Mother. It is different in the country. Black soil as far as the eye can see." Ole's voice had turned wistful.

Mother gave him a look. "Who have you been talking to?" She picked up her knitting from her lap; the needles clicked softly as her fingers worked the yarn into neat rows.

Ole did not speak more of it. He knew Mother did not like talk about America. She was foolish like that. Shortsighted. I looked down at the pages in my hand and a lump formed in my throat, making it hard to breathe. I hated my sister for having escaped, leaving me behind to rot.

That night, after writing down Mother's words, useless sentences about the goat, crops, and her terrible gout, I added some extra words to the letter: *Little Brynhild is not doing so well. She has problems*

finding her place in the valley. She was attacked for no reason, bleed-
ing badly from the stomach. It seems they have it in for her. Perhaps
the best thing would be if she could join you in America. If your hus-
band has any amount to spare that could help pay her fare, I am sure
she could be a great help to you in the house. I signed the letter, *Your*
Mother and Father.

3.

Nellie

Chicago, 1877

I folded the letter and pushed it back into the envelope. The stiff paper had turned soft, as I had already read it many times, once aloud to my husband, John. I lifted the little piece of home to my nose to see if I could catch a whiff of pine, wood smoke, and soft, damp moss. Størsetgjerdet felt so very far away; it seemed like a lifetime since I last crossed the threshold and entered, beheld the cramped quarters, the soot-stained walls and the rough-hewn chairs, the rickety spinning wheel in the corner. I had no use for such a tool in Chicago; I bought my yarn in skeins ready for the knitting needles. The scent of wet moss was replaced by that of burning coal and horse sweat, boiling food from a dozen kitchens. The sound of chirping birds no longer greeted me in the mornings; instead, I heard the racket of wagon wheels on the bricked street, children crying and mothers scolding, men scrambling down the stairs of our tenement building ready to go to work. I did not regret the change, but sometimes I longed for the quiet. It is in your blood, I suppose, if you grow up as I did, high up, yet still far below, stern faces of mountains flecked with snow.

You will always long for peace.

I could barely see my family's faces anymore; they remained blurred in my mind no matter how hard I tried. I could see their bodies, though: Mother with her bony hands in her lap, always working on something. Father with his unkempt beard sitting before the fire, and Little Brynhild, still twelve in my memory, with square shoulders and hooded eyes, fists always clenched at her sides, as if preparing for an oncoming fight.

My heart ached for her as I put the envelope away in the empty tea box where I kept my letters from my family. The box had a picture of a ship on the side, which I thought was appropriate, since there was such a long sea journey between us. The ship on the box had sails, though, while I had traveled on a steamer, and the scent of tea leaves lingered and erased whatever smell there was of woodland. It was a pretty box, the prettiest one that I owned, and so it felt right to use it to keep such treasured words—even if not all of them were pleasant but made me fret and worry.

"I know only too well how she feels," I told John when he rose to have his breakfast. "That sense that there is nothing for you but struggle and toil." I poured his coffee and placed a bowl of porridge before him on the well-scrubbed table. My two-year-old son, Rudolph, sat perched on his father's knee, clumsily spooning breakfast into his little mouth. His feet were restless, kicking out in the air and landing on John's shins. I should have scolded him for that, but just that morning I did not have it in me. "What will become of her now?" I asked my husband. "You know what it's like once people are set against you, even if for no good reason. Once they have their eyes on you, it's hard to escape wagging tongues."

"Seems to me that *tongues* are the least of her worries." John looked at me with his soft brown eyes brimming with compassion for my sister. It made my heart fill with warmth to see his brow crease with worry for a girl he had not even met. He was a good man, my John. I was lucky to have him. "If they have beaten her as badly as the letter says, she should worry for her life." He blew on the porridge in his spoon. "Won't your father do anything about it?"

"Hardly." I fetched some coffee for myself and slumped down in the chair opposite his. "He's a broken man, my father, with no will to do anything at all. Ailments and loss have taken what little spirit he had. Mother is different, but she cannot protect Little Brynhild. They are not well respected in the valley, and those with more means will always have a louder voice." I sighed and reached over the table to touch my little boy's dark hair. He lifted his gaze—as dark as his father's—and smiled at me with smears of porridge on his lips and chin. I wondered what I would do if someone hurt my child the way Little Brynhild had been hurt, and the mere thought of it made my chest contract and caused a sickening wave of anguish to spool out in the pit of my stomach. I certainly would not sit back and do nothing.

"I agree that she should leave Selbu." John spooned more porridge into his mouth and dried off his mustache with a pristine handkerchief.

"Yes, she should," I agreed. "She should leave and never return." My gaze fastened on my coffee, lingered on the brown, murky surface. My brow knitted with a fresh bout of worry. "I just wish the letter said more about what happened."

"It sounded like a terrible thing... bleeding from the stomach—"

"Hush," I scolded gently, and waved my hand in the air. "Not in front of the child."

"He is too small to understand," John reassured me in a calm voice. "You would prefer for her to come here, wouldn't you?"

"Of course I would. It would be safer for her, strange as that may sound."

"She could save up same as you," he suggested, not from any heartlessness but only because we did not have very much.

"Of course, but it took me a very long time." Years of toiling, milking, and cleaning. Sleepless cold nights in a maids' loft, and an ache in my back that I could not get rid of, and which only grew worse after Rudolph was born. I had paid for my crossing with pain as well as labor. "I worry that something more will happen to her before she has the money together or that the misery will eat at her and ruin her spirit before she arrives." In my mind's eye, I saw my mother's scrawny form—still with no face—and the sense of hope-lessness she emitted cut into my heart even across time and distance.

John's warm hand came to cover mine on the table. Our gazes locked and he smiled. "I shall see what I can do. Perhaps I can work some extra hours . . . I know how much you care for her."

I gave him a shivering smile in reply; I hated to burden him with more than he already had—we were hoping to have a house of our own—but it was true what he said, I cared about Little Brynhild. More than I did for any of my other siblings. Perhaps it was just be-cause she had such a hard time getting along; she was born with all these sharp angles and thorns and got in her own way more often than not. I was thirteen when she arrived in this world, almost a woman grown, and Mother was already fading by then; her smiles had become fewer and her laughter scarce, while I still had some to go around. Little Brynhild was mine in a way, before I left her behind.

Perhaps it was guilt I felt that made it so important to offer her my help.

"I would have had a miserable life if I'd stayed in Norway," I said, "but fortune has been good to me since I came to America. Perhaps the same will be true for her." I rose from the chair and crossed the creaking floor to John's chair, bent down, and pressed a kiss to his cheekbone. "I am grateful," I told him, and smiled when he squeezed my hand. "I know it will take time for her to get the money together even with our help, but whatever amount we can spare is certainly of more use to her than my tossing and turn-ing on the pillows at night."

"Worry is a poor bedfellow," said he.

"It certainly is," I agreed.

WHEN JOHN HAD left, I hoisted Rudolph onto my hip and grabbed the rolled-up rug with my free hand. Together we made the perilous journey down the steep, narrow stairs that descended the outside wall to the yard below. My son rested his cheek against my shoulder and looked up at the cloudy sky above.

"Birds." He pointed with his chubby hand. I could still see sticky flecks of porridge on his fingers even though I had dried them off. Small children are often a challenge like that, always filthy in some way, but my boy was worse than most. No matter how often I was at his face with my damp cloth, he always seemed to grow a mustache of grime above his upper lip. I thought that it might have to do with how we lived. It was not a clean house, dusty and infested with coal smoke. It did not matter how often I scrubbed the floors of our apartment when everything outside of it was filthy. I did not complain, though; it was better than what I came from—we even had a bedroom—but I could not help but dream of having a house of our own. A place where the dust stayed outside whenever I closed the door and I did not always smell the neighbors' potatoes boiling on the stove. I knew, though, that in order to get good things in life, one had to be patient and plan ahead. Take stock and save—be wise. Paying for Little Brynhild's crossing would certainly upset every plan I had laid, but then again, perhaps my son would not always be so grimy if I had a sister around to help me out. Perhaps my days would be better if I did not have to do all the work myself, and maybe—just maybe—I would not lose another child if I did not have to be so tired all the time.

We arrived at the bottom of the stairs and stepped out in the yard: a cramped, uneven space framed by fences of graying boards. On one side, outhouses and sheds stood huddled together like a flock of frozen sparrows. There was no pavement, only the trampled soil, and whenever it rained, puddles would form and the ground would turn muddy. Above our heads, laundry hung on taut lines that crisscrossed the space between our building and the one on the other side of the fence. The sheets and shirts moved with the wind like little sails. They made a rustling sound, like leaves, scraping against one another on the lines, stiff and hard but doubtlessly clean. A bright red skirt had bled excess dye down on the shirt that hung below.

I never much liked to hang my wash out like that for everyone to see. I always dried our own underthings in the apartment. It was different with wash I took in for money—I did not much care if my neighbors saw the mended pants and yellowing undershirts the unwed immigrant men brought in for me to scrub. My line was always full.

I put my son down in a patch of grass next to the outhouse, scanning the sparse greenery for hazards: rusted nails or pieces of glass, sharp edges of metal. I had performed the same survey the day before, but one never knew what people dropped. One day the summer before, I had found him squeezing a dead rat. Sometimes the older girls in the building looked after the little ones, but so early in the morning they would be busy helping their mamas or readying for school. I was on my own for another half hour at least before my friend Clara would come out with her small daughter, Lottie, having sent her posse of older children out the door. It was easier then, when there were more of us. I did not fret so much whenever I had to turn my back on my little one if there were other women about to keep an eye.

In that bleak early morning, though, I was all alone as I hoisted the rug onto the line that traveled all the way from the building to the fence and got the beater out from the shed. No one knew whom it first belonged to; we all used it to clean the few rugs that covered the worn floorboards in our apartments. My rug had been bought from a fellow Norwegian, woven from scraps of fabric, mostly blue and gray. I dreamed, of course, of thick rugs with oriental patterns; flowers snaking across vivid red and emerald green, but that was not something we could afford, and so I settled to take care of what we did have the best that I could.

Rudolph laughed as I started beating the rug before me; he always did like the sound. It scared him but thrilled him too. He all but clapped his little hands and the sound of his joy filled the chilly yard. I could not help but laugh a little too, just from the sound of that childish laughter. Soon I did not even feel the chill, as my vigorous beating had me sweating and huffing. Underneath the blue plaid headscarf my hair was drenched through, but I went at it a little longer than I had to, just to keep him laughing like that.

Little Brynhild had not been so easy to please as a child.

"Come," I said when I was done, then hoisted my son back onto my hip and brought him with me as I went to put the beater away. I carried him to the stairs and sat down on a step with Rudolph in my arms, cradling him tight while waiting for Clara. "Once there was a—" I started, but I was not in the mood to tell fairy tales. They reminded me of Little Brynhild too, and no matter how much I tried, I could not quash the worry that rose in me whenever I thought of that letter.

It was written in my sister's hand, that much I knew, but I did not know if they were her words, or if it was Mother who had asked her to write that plea for money. Not that it mattered—I had no reason to doubt the truth of the tale, and even if Little Brynhild had changed since I left, I could not imagine that she had lost that pride that always got her in trouble before. Whenever I thought of my little sister, that was what I remembered: how she always refused to bend her neck but held her head high and stubbornly clenched her jaws. When other children teased her, or a schoolteacher or neighbor scolded her, she never shed a tear but bit back the best that she could.

It would have cost her to ask for that money—the situation had to be dire.

The worry in the pit of my stomach moved again, made me feel a little sick. Without thinking, I tightened my grip on Rudolph, who wriggled and complained until I loosened my hold. "I am sorry, my sweet," I murmured into his soft, dark hair. "I did not mean to hurt you." I did not know if it was he I spoke to or the phantom child of my sister, who had seemed so close all day, as if she sat right there, in my lap, next to my son: a stubby little girl with a square jaw and eyes that cut, even when she was small.

I remembered one day when she was six or seven; it was late in summer and the sun burned like an ember, painting the sky in shades of gold. I was outside at Størsetgjerdet, coaxing our cows inside for the night. They were a couple of skinny things, even in summer; bad stock, my father said, but I loved them anyway.

"Come, then." I called them in from my spot a few steps from the barn door. "Come so, Dokka, come so, Staslin." The animals regarded me with large, dark eyes but did not heed me at all. Their heads just dipped back into the grass while their jaws worked slowly, tirelessly. Their udders, swollen with milk, swung back and forth below their bellies. I was growing impatient and was about to get the switch when I heard the barking of a dog, loud and insistent—angry sounding, and close. I stopped and shaded my eyes with my hand while scanning the steep hill for signs of the animal as the barking came ever closer. It was chasing from the sound of it, and I wondered what it was it had found; a fox perhaps, or a hare.

The ruckus came from behind the tree line and so it was hard to tell, but soon the barks were joined by other sounds, snapping twigs and rustling branches, and I figured it had to be something big and was prepared to see a moose calf come jolting out of the woods. Instead, I saw my sister come bursting into the open, running as fast as her little feet could muster, straight up that steep hill. Even from the distance, I could see the panic in her eyes, the terror drawn on her features. She did not run home, though, but ran straight by. She was blind with fear—too scared to think!

Soon I could see the dog as well: a slick-looking mongrel with bared teeth and a black coat, chasing her up the hill.

"Little Brynhild!" I called out. "Little Brynhild!" But she did not heed me. Soon another patch of wood swallowed her up, and the dog followed suit, crashing through the underbrush. I lifted my skirts as high as they would go and set out after them as fast I could. My heart was hammering all the while, and my lungs soon ached for breath.

"Little Brynhild!" I cried as I reached the dense growth of spruce and pine. "Where are you? Answer me!"

I did not get a reply, but I could hear the dog's angry barks before me and continued in the sound's direction. I saw all sorts of things in my mind as I ran: sharp teeth slicing through soft skin, blood beading on a plump leg. I heard the sound of bone crushed between jaws.

Finally, I could see them before me: the girl stood close to the waterfall, on top of the steep embankment. Behind her, the river ran red with iron, rushing past her with the sound of a storm. One wrong step and she would fall. Little Brynhild's face was flustered and she had lost her headscarf; her brown hair had escaped the braid I had made and hung about her face in slick tendrils. She was clutching a pine branch in her hand, longer than her arm, and was waving it aimlessly at the crouching dog, which was growling and showing its teeth, creeping ever nearer.

"Tsjuh!" I called out, and grabbed a lichen-covered rock from the mossy ground. My aim was off, but it did not matter; I was out to scare, not to harm. "Tsjuh! Go home!" I cried at the growling beast, and grabbed another rock from the ground. The dog startled when the rock hit close to where it crouched. Little Brynhild, having heard me, took up the words:

"Tsjuh!" she cried out. "Tsjuh!"

I threw more rocks and clapped my hands loudly as I moved in closer. The dog seemed confused then, and looked between us as if unsure of where to strike; but it was still angry, still showing those teeth. I knew that what you have to do is make the dog scared of *you*, so I bellowed from the top of my lungs as I rushed toward the animal, clapping my hands wildly. Finally, it rose and jumped away so as not to be trampled by the angry creature that came rushing forth. The dog paused between the trees, looking back, hoping perhaps that there was still hope for quarry, but I bent down and got a branch of my own, a rotten thing with moss hanging off it, and started hitting it against the ground, shouting all the while from the top of my lungs.

Finally, it slunk away and disappeared into the woods, finding me too much of a hassle to take on, perhaps. I turned to Little Brynhild and scooped her up in my arms. The girl shivered against me, but there were no tears.

"It wouldn't go away!" she cried.

"You must not let it see that you're afraid." I scolded her with a voice hoarse from shouting. "They can smell it, the dogs, and then they'll come for you."

"I wasn't afraid," she lied while her arms wound tight around me and she cleaved to me for protection.

"Why did it chase you, then?"

"Because it wanted to bite me."

"Is that so?" I had no time to lecture her just then. She was still shivering, was still stiff as board, and she was not a toddler anymore so I could already feel the strain in my arms, even if I was strong. "Maybe the dog is mad," I said. "Do you know who owns it?"

I could feel her nodding against my neck. "He only laughed when it chased me," she said. "He didn't even try to stop it."

My jaws tensed up with anger, but I found no words to give her.

I carried her all the way back home.

Receiving the letter reminded me of that day. It was the same sense of imminent danger—and the same instinct to lift my skirts and run to her aid, screaming.

That same night, as we lay in the loft, I had sworn that I would always protect her, and I felt called upon now by her words of distress to fulfill that very promise.

"The world is not kind to those who are different," I whispered into Rudolph's hair as we rocked gently back and forth on the step. "But then again," I continued, "she may not always be so kind to it either."

4.

Brynhild

Selbu, 1877

How old are you, Little Brynhild? Sixteen?" Gurine's blue eyes were kind. She had just been looking into my mouth to inspect the damage done to my teeth. We were perched on wooden chairs in the kitchen, next to the flour-strewn table. Outside the windows, the sky was gray, but the fields had turned green and the birch trees sprouted leaves. Summer had arrived and the barn was empty while the animals were grazing up in the mountains. Usually I spent this time of year up there, tending them on the summer farm. Not this year, though. Not while I was still so poor. Instead, I stayed behind with Gurine, cooking for the farmhands and the family, cleaning, scrubbing, and sweeping floors. Mother was distraught by this. She had been hoping I would go to the summer farm and not have to see much of Anders that summer. I did not care much at all.

"Seventeen," I murmured, and rubbed my jaw, still swollen even after all those weeks. I had seen my face for the first time since it happened in the mirror in the farmhouse. The bruising had started to fade, turning a ghastly yellow.

Gurine's face was concerned under the faded headscarf. "I wasn't surprised when you didn't come to work, but I worried when you weren't in church. You never miss church."

"Father wouldn't let me go," I was quick to explain. I would not let her think I was a coward. "I wanted to come, but he said I couldn't be seen like this, and I was—" Still bleeding, but I could not bring myself to say that aloud.

"You shouldn't be here, though." There was fear in her voice. "Why ever did you come back *here*?"

"Father said I couldn't be home anymore. I had to work." That was not what Gurine asked, though. She asked because of Anders.

The old woman gave me a look and lifted a lukewarm cup of coffee to her lips. "Did Paul say that because he was afraid people would think you are lazy, or because he wanted to punish you?"

"Punish me, I think."

"And the . . . ?" She raised her eyebrows, motioned to her stomach with her hand.

"Gone." I cradled my own cup of coffee in my lap.

"Well, that's a good thing, then." Gurine pursed her lips. "You should have that tooth pulled too, what's left of it."

"Have no money for that." I shrugged. "It was a poor tooth anyway. He did me a favor knocking it out."

"Hush." She looked stern. "Don't say such a thing. He has done you nothing but harm. You're not still pining for him, are you?"

"No, no—I'm not." I would rather see him buried, but I did not say that.

"That's something, then . . . And you're sure that it's gone?" Another motion to her belly.

"Yes." It did not bother me to say it. I had had many nights to teach myself how to answer that question. It was only a lump of flesh, after all—nothing to ache for. I handled flesh all the time; skinned and cut, bled and cooked. That tiny lump that slid out of me was no different from any other slick meat. No different from the pigs I cut with Gurine, the hares I skinned, or the kids' legs I cured with salt. Just flesh—nothing special at all. It might not even have lived through birth. Children die all the time.

"You shouldn't be *here*, though. I'm sure that if Paul knew for sure who it was, that he—"

"I don't mind. I can stay on. I don't see *him* much anyway, as long as I'm in here." I looked around at the large iron cookstove with the black pans resting on top; the bucket of potatoes in the corner, skin wrinkly and tough after winter storage; the blue chairs with peeling paint; the soot-stained ceiling and timbered walls; and let out a breath of relief. "Anders never comes to the kitchen." None of the men ever did.

"But why would you want to?" Gurine's blue eyes peered at me.

"It wouldn't be better anywhere else; everyone knows what happened. At least this way they'll know I'm not ashamed." I watched a gray kitten Gurine had let in stumble milk-drunk away from a bowl by the stove. I reached out a hand to let it sniff my fingers and felt the silken fur as it went by.

Gurine looked worried. "They might think you're still hoping—"

"Maybe, but I can live with that." The kitten had jumped onto the windowsill and tried to catch an orange butterfly on the other side of the glass. The cat's childish antics made me hurt inside.

Gurine shook her head again. "You should seek service elsewhere and leave Selbu behind."

I nodded; on this we agreed. "I hate this place."

"*Hate* is a very strong word that shouldn't be used lightly."

"Nevertheless, I do. I am tired of always being laughed at."

Gurine sighed, put her hand on mine, and squeezed. "Where do you want to go, then?"

"Big Brynhild says it is better in America. No one cares who your parents are. I think I could do well over there. Big Brynhild calls herself Nellie now."

"That's a fancy name." Behind her on the stove, water began to bubble in a pot. It was for the potatoes. We should have peeled them long ago.

"I could take another name as well."

"You know it's an expensive journey."

"Big Brynhild did it. She worked for years to do it." The kitten had all but given up on the butterfly and hit the floor with a thump. It went back to the bowl in search of more milk, its tiny tail straight in the air.

"If I were your age maybe I would go too." A longing came into Gurine's voice. "They say there's plenty of land, and big cities."

"Big Brynhild seems happy enough." I bit my tongue to curb the unbidden jealousy that flared to life when I said my sister's name.

"It's a good dream." Gurine rose and started for the stove, where the water was bubbling in the pot. I rose too and tightened the apron at the small of my back, where it still ached.

"In America," I told Gurine, "I could marry well. I'm sure of it."

SHE WATCHED ME, Gurine, with those blue eyes, when it was time to eat. Looked at me as I watched the men cross the yard through the window. They were working on the barn this summer while the cattle were away, tearing down walls and building new ones.

The salted herring and the cold potatoes were already on the table with stacks of flat bread; all that was missing was the porridge and the lump of butter. Anders and his father—another Anders— were the last ones to come inside, discussing something or other. The farmer's hand rested on his son's shoulder. Before they went in, they whipped the caps off their heads, as not to offend the Lord.

"Will you carry the porridge, Little Brynhild?" Gurine's voice was soft, her eyes sad.

"Of course." Gurine was too frail to carry much at all.

"Are you sure you want to do this?"

"I don't mind." I lifted the deep wooden serving tray, filled to the brim with gray, pasty porridge. It was heavy for sure, but my hands did not shake. I slipped out the door and heard Gurine behind me, following with the butter.

"Here." She got in front of me and opened the door to the next room, where half a dozen men were seated on benches by the table, nibbling on fat fish and breaking pieces of flat bread between grimy, callused fingers. It went quiet when I came in. They all looked at me, as I thought they would. Their eyes were wary, as if I were a dog that could not be trusted and they waited for me to bare my teeth. I approached with the tray and placed it on the table. A few of their spoons dipped into the porridge as soon as I let it go.

"Thank you, Brynhild." The farmer himself spoke. "It's good to see you back on your feet."

I nodded in his direction and did not look at Anders beside him. I could see his hands, though: strong and rough, marred by fading bruises. Bruises from hitting *me*. The men did not look at me after the farmer spoke. Their heads bent as they shuffled the food into their mouths. They thought that was it, then—that I was safe and would not bite. That I would take my lesson and learn from it, be humble and meek and know my place.

That was what they thought.

"IT'S GOOD TO see you regaining your strength," Mother said the next Sunday. I had gone home with my parents after church and would return to the farm in the morning. I sat outside on the stone slab that served as a step by the door, scrubbing out a black-scorched pot. Mother carried wash from the creek; the heavy weight made her wiry frame bend. "How is it down there at the farm?" She dropped her load in front of me.

"I'm still a little sick, but I can do my share of the work."

Mother sat down beside me, smelling faintly of fresh river water. "He always had a hungry eye, that boy down there. I've seen him in church, looking down the aisle as the girls arrive." I could see her scalp through her thin hair. She had lost most of her teeth in the lower jaw, none of them knocked out as far as I knew. She shook her head as she stared out on Størsetgjerdet: the timbered shed and the tiny barn, the small well house farther up, and the dark, dense woods that surrounded the place. Then her hand circled my wrist and squeezed so hard it hurt. When I turned my head in surprise, her gaze bore into mine. "Little Brynhild, now you'll listen to me! You nearly *died* from that beating; he nearly killed you, that boy, and he still could! You shouldn't be anywhere near him . . ."

I scoffed and tried to pull my hand away. The pot had fallen to the ground. "I *didn't* die."

"But you could have." Her gaze burned in the dusky light. "You lay in that bed for *weeks*. Not talking, not eating, bleeding down in the hay—"

"But I rose." I finally managed to free my hand and rubbed it where it hurt. "I got up, and it wasn't even a week before I ate—"

"Don't you think I know death when I see it? It was plain on your face! You could have died, believe me! You *have* to find service elsewhere." She sounded angry, but for once, she was not. It was fear for me I saw in her eyes, and it was a strange thing to witness. No one ever feared for me that way.

"I shouldn't have been so stupid," I murmured. "Shouldn't have—"

"Well, you did, and nothing to do for that now. Just don't let him get another chance to finish what he started."

"My jaw might be broken." I rubbed the tenderness.

"It will heal in time." She pulled her pipe out of the pocket of her apron, the little tin box she kept with it too, and set to stuff the pipe with tobacco. "Your womb, though, might not. There was a lot of blood."

"I know."

"Why would you even want to see him?"

"I don't hope for him anymore."

"Never should have, either . . . What were you *thinking*? Farmers' sons don't marry us, you know that. You never should have tried to force him—never should have messed with him at all."

"I was only thinking that—"

"Well, it's the thinking, Little Brynhild." She knocked her own head lightly with her fist. "It's that thinking that gets you into trouble. That teacher put ideas in you."

"He said I had a good head on my shoulders." I could not help that my voice bristled a little with pride.

"Well, what are you going to use it for? Have yourself killed? Beaten to death by some smug boy?" She lit her pipe; the sour smoke came wafting from the dark wood.

"I want to go to America."

She gave me a look sharp enough to cut timber. "Bad enough I lost one daughter over there."

"She is doing fine. Nellie is happy as can be." My voice grew thick with envy.

"*Nellie*." Mother snorted. "As if her Christian name wasn't good enough for her."

"They can't say *Brynhild* properly. She wrote that in the letter."

"Stupid girls." She stretched out her legs on the grass before her as she sucked on her pipe. "They always want something more than they have . . . Well, go to America or China for all I care, but don't go back to that boy. You have to seek service elsewhere."

"I won't go back to him"—he would not even want me to—"but I will stay on."

She looked at me then, through the pipe smoke, and shook her head with confusion. "But why, Little Brynhild? *Why?*"

"I have my reasons."

"And I bet they are poor."

"He won't lay a hand on me again." I lifted my chin and fixed her with my gaze.

"No?" She squinted back at me. "How do you know? Have you cooked up some fine plan in that clever head of yours?"

"It was just a lump of flesh." The words came unbidden, tumbled out of me, lay there between us like so much gristle.

"No." Her hair bun bobbed when she shook her head. "Don't even try to fool yourself. It was a child, not some lump."

"Nothing worse than a piglet. I cut pig's meat all the time—"

"It was *not* just a lump of flesh." Her pipe waved in the air.

"Yes, it was: a lump that no one wanted me to have, so now I'm better off anyway."

She sighed. "Things are certainly easier."

"Just flesh . . ." My brow was wet with perspiration; I had to wipe it with the hem of my apron. Mother looked away.

"I tried to get your clothes clean again." She touched the bundle of wet fabrics with the tip of her shoe. "I think the skirt is better, but the blouse with the lace is gone."

"Some stains won't wash away." I meant for it to be a comfort, but instead she started to cry. I did not know what to do with that, so I just sat there beside her while her shoulders shook and she wiped tears with the back of her hand.

"Promise me you will work somewhere else," she said when her tears had all dried up. "They won't let you forget about this, Little Brynhild. They will always find ways to remind you . . . That night will stick to you always."

"Oh, I'll go." I picked up the pot and the rag from the ground, resumed that eager scrubbing. "But I won't go just yet."

5

Anders had a shot of liquor every night before he went to bed. The last thing I did at the end of each day was to leave it for him on the narrow stairs so he could take it with him to his room. Before, he had wanted the whole bottle, but his father had put an end to that by the time I returned to work, so now he just got that one dram to see him to sleep at night. It was I who poured that drink for him from a bottle stored in the kitchen.

It was such a little thing—entrusting him to the maid. Let *her* make sure it was only that one drop, not enough to make him useless the next day. Maids also helped with other small things, like keeping the kitchen free from rodents when the lazy cats failed to do their jobs.

They never expected me to hold a grudge.

I waited for months to be certain they had forgotten. Waited, until the trees shed their leaves and the cattle came home and the men ceased calling to me whenever I crossed the yard, asking me if I wanted to take a stroll to the lake or hike up my skirts for some pebbles and a fist. If it was true that I bled like a pig. I waited, until Anders forgot to look away and clench his jaw when I entered the room. Until his gaze slid off me as if I were not even there.

Then I waited some more.

They thought it was the flu when he got sick. He brushed it off; it was nothing. He still had his liquor every night.

Then came the pain and the vomit. The house filled with bellows from his room. His mother took care of him herself: brought down pails of bile, brought up cold water and a cloth. Sometimes she had to rest, though, and I was to help him then, dry him off and give him water—which was fortunate for me, since he was no longer having that dram at night. I sat by his bed as he slept, pale and sweating, shivering from time to time. His hands did not bother me anymore; they had lost their power. I was paying him back, a grain for each hit.

Soon nobody but me would remember what happened by the lake.

THE FARM TOOK on a gloominess over the next few days, while Anders lay there shivering. The doctor came and went again. I held my breath while he was with Anders, but he suspected nothing. I could not believe how gullible they were, how sure that no one could touch them. They did not think it possible that someone would dare to raise a fist against them. Prideful. Stupid.

Gurine whispered that the doctor thought it was stomach cancer. Sad, she said, for such a young man.

"But not a good man," I reminded her, lying in the darkness in our shared bed, listening to the wind outside and the lowing from the barn.

"No, not a good man but a *young* man, with years to repent and become a little better than he is."

"That one will never become anything but what he is."

"No, I think he won't, seeing that he won't last another day."

"I wish I could say I was sorry for that."

"No." Her hand patted mine in the dark. "If anyone is allowed not to grieve, it's you."

When he *did* die the next day, it was as if I could breathe again, ever since that night. I walked through that house, through the sounds of his mother weeping; brimming with a delight so strong, I could barely contain it. I helped prepare for the wake and funeral, baked and fried, cooked meals for a hundred people. I saw them file in and respectfully shake the farmer's hand, dressed in their Sunday best. The farmer's wife was like a ghost beside him, her haughty face furrowed with grief. I could not help but smile. It was such a small thing, entrusting it to the maid.

Mother came to the kitchen to find me. She and Father had been inside to taste what the big farm had to offer on such a day. Father waited for her in the yard; I could see him through the window. Mother wore her black headscarf and I could smell fermented trout and strong liquor on her breath. Nothing was spared when the farmer buried his heir. Gurine was out with the other maids, carrying silken sour cream porridge and slices of roast for the funeral guests, so we were all alone. Mother sucked her finger and dipped it in a sugar bowl.

"Have your tears all dried up now, Little Brynhild?" She licked the sugar from her finger.

"I don't know if I had any to begin with."

"It's all very sad, him dying like that. Cancer in the stomach." She shook her head. "I wonder where that came from. Might have been something he ate." She did not look at me at all, but her eyes kept wandering around the room, to the boiling water on the stove, the sliced meat, the ham and the lefse laid out on the table. Her hand, quick as a rat, got hold of a lefse with sugar and stuffed the whole thing into her maw.

"I don't think you can get stomach cancer from eating." I found a piece of cloth in a drawer under the tabletop and placed some pieces of roast and a few sausages and cured meats on it, wrapped it up, and tied it off. I placed the package in Mother's waiting hand. No one would notice on a day like this.

"You never know." Mother shrugged, and the package disappeared under her shawl.

"He got what he deserved, that is what I know." I cleaned my hands on a rag.

"Yes." Mother was still chewing. "Strange that, how the Lord sees fit to punish sometimes, and other times not."

"Don't let the priest hear you talk like that." I gave her a dark look.

Mother laughed, but there was no joy in it. "What he doesn't know won't hurt him."

"We'll see, won't we, on reckoning day, if your sins are tallied or not."

"Yes." Mother gave me a thin smile. "Won't we just see, Little Brynhild?"

My father called from out in the yard. "Berit!" he bellowed. "Berit!" He was tired of waiting for her. People passed by him, somber-looking as befitting the day, but he did not heed them at all. He held his cap in his hands, stomped his foot, and kicked up dust from the ground. Angry, always angry.

"You better go before he makes a fool of himself." I passed my mother a final treat, a piece of mutton to chew on.

"Did you see him after he was dead?" she asked before popping it into her mouth.

I nodded. "When he was laid out on the dining room table."

"Good. That ought to give you some peace, then."

I shrugged. "It's of no concern to me if he is alive or dead."

Mother spat gristle into her palm. "Better dead is what I say."

"Never let the priest—"

"Oh shut your mouth. He was bad, that man. He'll go to hell for what he did." She licked the grease from her lips. I could smell the liquor on her breath from across the table. It made her tongue a slippery thing.

After she left, I watched her make her way across the yard to Father. He had lit his pipe while waiting and used his free hand to smack her head when she arrived; it bobbed on her shoulders from the impact. The farmhands smoking by the barn sniggered. I hoped my parents would leave before they started arguing for real. My mother could hold her ground well enough and delivered blows like a man twice her size. Sometimes it got ugly.

I went back to the work at hand, carving and cutting. Anders was in the ground; his eyes, which had seen me so broken, were gone. Soon worms and beetles would eat them all up, and there would be no witness to my shame.

God will not always punish; my mother was right about that. He might not even help those who strive to help themselves, but I could. For weeks after his death I barely slept; I lay awake beside Gurine at night staring into the darkness, riding that joy as a liquor. I kept imagining his sallow face twisted up in death throes; I touched my aching jaw with my fingers, remembering his blows. I chuckled to myself sometimes—could barely suppress the sounds, and bit into the pillow to contain them. Other times I had to rise, go to the window, and look out on the yard, because I worried that Gurine would wake up from the bed shaking, as peals of silent laughter coursed through me.

It was strong and pure, that joy; it made me feel powerful and happy. I had never felt anything as strong and pure as that. As if I could do anything. As if there were no limit.

I had paid him back.

I HAD THE night off on Christmas Eve to make the steep walk up to Størsetgjerdet and spend it with Mother and Father. There was enough snow on the ground that I had to use snowshoes, following a track between tall pines and naked birches; I was not the first one who had walked up there that day. I figured it was my brothers. They usually came up to wish their parents a happy Christmas and gift them some coffee beans and sugar.

Dusk was already bleeding into night when I arrived. Through the window, I could see a single candle burning on the table. Mother would be there but not sewing today. She would not work at all on Christmas Eve. A pale oval obscured the light: Olina was expecting me. It was not much of a life for her, stuck in that house with Mother and Father. Even *I* was a welcome respite, no matter that she did not like me much.

She swung the door open as I arrived and ushered me inside. The fireplace was well stacked, with proper logs, no less. Father was no woodsman, so the fuel often ran out. Someone must have taken pity and gifted them a load. Peder perhaps. He often grew sentimental around Christmas and wanted to honor his father and mother. Never mind the time Father struck the axe in Peder's calf rather than the log because he had annoyed him some way or the other. It was a nasty cut and bled badly—Peder lay in bed for days. He still had a scar to show for it, white and angry like melted tallow.

Father was deep in the bottle before I arrived; he sat by the fire and did not even look up when I came inside. The set of his shoulders was tense, and that worried me. He was mulling over something then, growing angrier as he sat there sipping, smoking, and tending the fire with a stick. Mother had had something to drink too; I could tell from the rosy glow in her cheeks. Even Olina had added something to her coffee; I could smell it on her breath.

I took off my shoes and left them to dry, hung my shawl on the line, and placed a painted wooden tin by the table. The snow melted like teardrops on the wool, dripped down on the floor. Soon the whole room would smell damp. I joined my mother and sister by the candle.

"Did Peder and Ole stop by?"

"For sure." Olina motioned to the coffee grinder on the table. "They brought coffee and tobacco for us."

"How are things down at the farm this Christmas?" Mother asked. "I saw his parents at church. They both looked worse for wear."

I shrugged and poured myself coffee. "They have other sons. They are hardly the first couple to lose a child." I did not like either one of them, and not only because of Anders. The farmer was a hard man who treated his cattle badly, and his wife was too haughty to clean. She did not have much when she married, yet she still saw fit to look down on us maids.

"It's different when the children are grown," Mother said. "You know them better then; you are used to them. When they are small, you always expect something to happen. Grown children are the worst to lose."

"How do you know?" She had never lost a grown one.

It was Mother's time to shrug. "I had sisters. Brothers. It took a toll on my mother." It was strange to see her just sitting there, leaning on her elbows. No mending in her fingers, no wool in her lap.

"Wish we had lost some," muttered Father. "Much good they do us. Nothing but trouble—"

"Oh shut your mouth," Mother snapped. "Let me have my Christmas Eve in peace." She pushed the worn Bible toward me. Paper like silk; the most precious thing she owned. "Read something for us, Little Brynhild. It's a holy night."

I opened the book and read from Luke. As I read about the cruel king and the birth of a savior, the snow started falling outside the window, making the night seem almost peaceful. I thought about the farm, where there had been butter, cheese, fish, sausages, and sour cream on the table that day. From the look of the empty pot, my family had eaten porridge with lard. I pushed the book away. What good could those words ever do? None of us could eat the gospel.

"Read on," Mother urged me.

"It won't do any good."

"You used to be so fond of the Bible and couldn't get fast enough to church."

"I changed."

"Yes"—her gaze was upon me—"ever since that night."

"What night?"

"You know which night. You changed since that. There's no laughter left in you—"

"It's true." Olina nodded, looking much like an old woman in that moment; hands folded, chin bobbing. Her hair, the same brown color as mine, was fastened at the nape of her neck with a knitting needle. "You never were much fun, Little Brynhild, but you weren't always this angry."

"She is ashamed," muttered Father. "She is ashamed for what happened, and she should be too."

Before I even knew what I did, the coffee grinder was no longer on the table but in my hand. I hurled it across the room but missed his stupid head by an inch or two. The precious machinery flew into the wall and gauged a deep wound in the wood. I stood by the table, heaving for breath while the red fog slowly subsided. "Watch your mouth, old man, or I'll be coming for you next!"

He looked at me with eyes like a snake. The pipe was still in his hand, but the stick he had tended the fire with had fallen to the floor. "Next, huh? Who did you come for first?"

"Stop it!" Mother's lips were thin, her nostrils flared. "I will not have any fighting at Christmas!"

"She is not right, that girl." He shook his head. "And that beating left her mad as a dog." He eyed me warily while picking up his stick. "She'll kill us in our sleep one night, mark my words."

"No madder than you, old fool." Mother went to pick up the grinder. I wished that it had struck him. I wished that he were dead. "Sit back down, Little Brynhild." Mother gave me a look. "Bad enough if you have ruined the grinder. Wherever will we get a new one?"

I slowly sat back down on the chair. My jaw throbbed with pain. "It's what he gets for talking like that."

"You know what he's like." Mother sat back down as well. The handle had come off the grinder and she tried to put it back on. "Pay him no mind."

"I won't have another word about that night."

Another look from Mother then. "Well, there isn't much more to say, is there? You are still here and the boy is dead."

"Strange, that," Father muttered while shoving the stick deep into the fire, "how he is dead and you are still here."

"It means there's still some justice in this world." Mother's hands forced the grinder apart and coffee grains littered the table.

"I'll seek service at Rødde in the new year." My voice was steady again. "I meant to tell you a while ago."

Mother looked up, surprised. "I thought you didn't want to go."

"I changed my mind." I rubbed my tender jaw.

"Are they still giving you a hard time, down at the farm?"

"Not at all, but it's become such a dreary place since he died."

"No reason for you to stay on, then, is it?" Father again. "Now that he's gone."

"Be quiet!" Mother barked across the room.

"I can speak in my own house!"

"This is barely a house!"

"What is in your tin, Little Brynhild?" Olina wanted to change the subject. She did not like them arguing and hoped that my surprise would cool their tempers.

"Lefse," I said, "from the farm, with regards."

"How nice of them." Mother's face twisted up with spite. "Nice to know they have enough to spare."

"Don't you start with that again." Father spat on the floor.

I opened the tin and set it on the table. Their fingers were like talons, sinking into the soft bread. Olina closed her eyes when she licked the sugar from her fingers. I ate a piece of my own and savored the sweetness of it. *To have this every day*, I thought, *and never want for anything* . . . I looked at my mother and thought her a fool for having settled for so little.

After we ate, I read new letters from my sisters aloud. Nellie wrote that she would be pleased to welcome me in Chicago, and was sorry to hear there had been trouble.

"How does she know?" asked Mother.

"People talk," I said.

When we set to answer, I added another few lines to Nellie. *Little Brynhild is still having a hard time*, I wrote. *Any little amount will help, so she can join you in America and leave this all behind.*

6.

The Atlantic Ocean, 1881

I did not enjoy the sea. My family caught fish in mountain lakes and creeks, and I was not used to salt water. My body did not agree with the dancing motions of the waves and revolted. I vomited into the sawdust on deck, and then I went back inside and ate the dry crackers and drank the poor tea they served to the passengers in steerage. I held my chin high despite the sickness. I knew it would not last. I knew there was nothing to do but endure— and that every hour that passed was an hour closer to freedom. Nevertheless, I was sick all the way from Trondhjem to Hull, and barely recovered on the train to Liverpool, where we boarded the steam liner to New York.

I had embarked on the *Tasso* in Trondhjem with Sigrid, another young woman traveling alone who wanted a companion for security and comfort. Her aunt knew Nellie in Chicago and the two of them had made the connection between us. I did not like her much. Sigrid was as pretty and cheerful as could be, could cook and clean but barely read. She helped me when I was sick, though: made sure my trunk was not lost in England and wiped my slick brow with a cloth.

The steam liner was a crowded, noisy place. I had never experienced anything like it: the roaring sound of the engine, the scent of oil, the sight of water foaming off the hull. The reek of so many people stacked in bunk beds along the walls. Water was scarce in steerage, and we did not get to wash much. People lived and slept in their clothes. We did not remove our shoes at night, as there was no trust between us. Some passengers had brought their own food supplies with them, scared by letters from relatives who had already made the journey and suffered. The Norwegian stretch of the compartment smelled strongly of salted herring and infants' filthy bottoms.

At night, the Scandinavians gathered around a table bolted to the floor. The women in worn headscarves knitted socks and dreamed aloud about acres of land and herds of cattle. They sent sideways glances to the neighboring tables where noisy Irish and Germans laughed and spoke in garbled tongues. Farther down the room, some men played cards from the sounds of it. Sometimes they played the fiddle too.

They danced some nights, in filthy sawdust on the deck. Young girls laughed, old men leered. Empty bottles were thrown in the sea. Sigrid danced too, encircled by the arms of some handsome Swede or Dane. I did not. I sat with the elderly women, hands folded in my lap. I did not want to be a part of the swirl of life around me. I did not want to make friends. Whatever could my fellow passengers offer but more stories of failure and hunger? I could see the desperation that had sent them running hiding behind their smiles. Their hardships were carved on their faces in deep furrows and lines. I knew enough about poverty and strife already—I was there to forget all about it. Still I woke up at night pressing my fists to the soft of my belly, just as I did as a child when falling asleep without food. Maybe it was the reek of them, all those bodies stacked in the beds. Maybe it reminded me of home, of dark winter nights with nothing in the pot. My mother's silent anger when she had to pull on her shawl and walk down to the valley to beg for scraps, again. My father's muttered curses, his endless complaints about this man or that who owed him something or offended him somehow. It took nothing then, to have that fury in him flare to life and leave bruises in its wake.

That ship reminded me of hunger.

Four years I worked hard to make it happen; saved everything I could and kept the money with me always. Nellie sent me money too: foreign bills enclosed in letters. When I rose before dawn at Rødde farm to milk and cook and clean, it was all that I could think of, how the drops of sweat on my brow would become coins and bills to help pay my way across the sea. Every spiteful word I took, every humiliation, was a part of the price I had to pay.

Sigrid had no such concerns. Her ticket had landed in her lap, prepaid. Her aunt had done well in America, it would seem.

"She has so many children," she told me one day while we were sitting on deck. She was mending a shawl while I was fighting another bout of sickness. "She needs someone to look after the younger ones."

"Her husband must be rich," I muttered, head bent, breath labored. We were so far out at sea by then there was not a bird in sight; the sea around us rippled like silver in the sunlight. I could not look at it much as it made me feel worse.

"Not really"—Sigrid's needle paused in midair—"but he might be one day, my aunt says."

"Is he a tailor too?" Many Norwegian men left their pitchforks for pretty seams in Chicago. Back home they would have been laughed at, but not so over there.

"No, he works at a brewery." The needle descended into the red cloth. I wished I could have a shawl like that, fine-spun and bold in color.

"Men can be all sorts of things in America, it seems."

"My brother left last year. He never wanted to farm, so it was a good thing for him."

"Not much land to farm, either, even if he had stayed."

Sigrid put her sewing down in her lap. "What about you, Bryn-hild? What will you do in Chicago? Help your sister out or seek service?"

"I am done with service." I spat bile down in the sawdust. "I want to have a household of my own."

She smiled. "You want to get married, then?"

"Don't we all?"

"I suppose." She went back to the sewing, her dark lashes fanned out on her creamy skin. "Do you want children, Brynhild?"

"If I can." I spoke before thinking. Had I not been so sick, I would have flushed from the slip. I put my hand to my jaw where he had hit me. It ached under my fingers.

"It's not so hard, I've heard." The silly goose giggled beside me. "You just have to make sure to get married first or else you'll be in a lot of trouble."

"That, at least, is the same everywhere."

She gave me a puzzled look then; she truly was not bright. She fumbled with her needle and went back to the mending at hand. "Where did you serve before leaving?" She bent her head so all I could see was the white-gray top of her headscarf.

"Rødde."

"Was it nice?"

"As good as any place, I suppose." It was hard work and little rest. Not far enough from Selbu that they had not heard. They were already whispering when I arrived, not just about the child and the lake, but about me too. They thought me strange and easy to anger, a little bit touched—veins laced with bad blood. That is what they said.

"Will you miss it?" Sigrid cut the thread with her teeth.

"Not at all." I had left it behind.

"Have you thought of a name yet?" Sigrid changed the subject. I had told her when we first boarded that I wanted to change my name, as my sister had done, and she had not let up asking since, hoping, perhaps, that she could have one I discarded. She did not have it in her to come up with anything on her own.

This time I nodded. "Bella," I said.

"Bella? Oh, that's pretty." She smiled.

"It is," I agreed. "Nellie said I had to pick one that could be said as easily in Norwegian as in English, and I decided on Bella even before we left Hull."

"Did you?" Her eyes went wide with wonder.

"I did. It's after the queen Isabella." I had learned about her in school.

"Who?" She did not know, of course.

"A Spanish queen," I told her patiently. "She conquered the new world alongside her husband."

"Is that what you will do too?" The silly smile was back on her face.

"I aim to," I said, as in jest.

IN THE BUNK bed next to me in steerage, Anna, a young Norwegian woman from Telemark, slept with her small daughter. The child, Mari, was quick and lithe and had a head full of golden curls. I sometimes played with her and made her balls of yarn.

"You will be a good mother one day," Anna said to me as I was sitting on my bed offering Mari a gray ball. Anna's face was red and flaking, her matted hair twisted in a bun. "I'm sure you will find a nice Norwegian man in Chicago. There are more men than women there now, so it'll be easy to find a good match." She picked up her headscarf from the mattress and tied it at the back of her neck.

"Leave her be, Anna," her sister, Martha, said. She shook out a pillow and smoothed the blanket on her bed. "Maybe the girl doesn't want to marry."

"Of course she does. Why else would she travel so far? She wants to settle better than she could back home. She is clever, you see; she won't be happy with some poor man."

"Even poor men are richer in America, I hear," I agreed. "They say you can make your own fortune there. That it doesn't matter if your father was a tenant or a lord."

Anna nodded vigorously. "You can be your own man—"

"You still have to know the tools of your trade," Martha cut in. "Hard work is necessary, even there."

"I'm not afraid of work," I told her, "and neither will my husband be. I have no patience with laziness."

"Then I'm sure you're going to prosper," said Anna. "America was made for people like you." She went on to tell me that they planned to settle and farm. They had humble dreams, shared by many, but I was not one of their lot.

"I'm going to my sister in Chicago." I tossed another ball of yarn to Mari on the floor; the girl laughed and tried to catch it. "She is much older than me and has been there for years. She lives with her husband in an apartment where she takes in wash and does some mending. I'll start there, helping her, but I won't stay for long."

"Just until you find a husband." Anna laughed and lifted Mari into her lap.

"Just that," I agreed, although I feared it would not be that easy. I was a plain woman, tall and broad. Suitable for a farmer who needed someone strong—but not for the sort of man that I wanted. A sudden thought of Anders then, his face slack in death. He would have married me in America, I was sure of it. Nothing would have stood between us then. Pity for him that did not happen. Pity for him he was dead.

"I'm not sorry to leave the old country," Anna said, "but I am sorry to leave Mother behind. She will be lonely now, with both her daughters gone."

"It's the way it has to be," Martha said behind her.

"Father too," Anna continued. "His eyes have been failing him of late. I wonder how they'll do without us."

"They'll manage." Martha again.

"What about you, Brynhild? Will you miss your mother and father?"

"Of course." I looked down in my lap, busied my fingers with pieces of yarn. "Mother cried when I left." That was true, but she would change her mind soon enough when my letters started to arrive, telling her of my good fortune. "Father gave me his Bible and wished me luck." This was a lie. "They only want us to be happy in the end. They know there's nothing for us back home."

"It's a shame." Anna shook her head and clutched her daughter to her chest.

Martha spoke up. "It's not true what they say, that you should bend your neck and make do with what the Lord has granted. The Lord provides opportunities too."

"Mother says America is an ungodly land." Anna smirked and her eyebrow rose in a telling manner. They had been quarreling with their parents too, then, about this trip across the sea.

"They had no means to escape when they were young. It makes sense that they would think like that." It was lazy of them, though, not to fight for something better.

"Anything to get them through the day." Anna sighed.

"They should welcome it, the chance we got." Martha shook her head.

"They don't believe that fortune can be a friend," I said. Little Mari smiled at me, clutching her new ball. "It's dangerous to believe in luck when you have none."

"And you, Brynhild, do you believe in luck?" Anna's eyes shone in the dim light.

"I believe that luck can be made."

AFTER TEN DAYS at sea we poured off the ship in New York as a river of rats with matted coats and quivering whiskers. Our lungs expanded, breathing in America; our bellies groaned with hunger, but not for food, no. We washed from the docks and into the city, haggard-faced and reeking of brine, tails whipping as we scurried down the streets, hauling our heavy trunks along. We would devour it all—yes, we would—have our share of fortune's blessings delivered on our plates.

PART TWO

Bella Sorensen

7.

Nellie

Chicago, 1881

The day before Little Brynhild arrived, my friend Clara, and Laura, who was new in the building, helped me with the laundry so I would not have to fret about it on my sister's first day in Chicago.

My small apartment was hot and steamy; several zinc tubs littered the floor between the table and the stove, intercepted by heaps of sorted laundry. We had heated water, filled the tubs, drizzled in soda crystals, and were at it on our knees, with plungers and scrubbers. Our skirts and aprons were soon soaked through, and all children banished to Clara's apartment, where her oldest daughter looked after them all.

It was filthy work, as most of those who left their laundry with me were unmarried Norwegian men who lived in cramped quarters. Some of them had landladies who offered to take in wash, but they found that their clothes were as grimy as before upon their return. Others lived in such squalor that no service was available, and so they brought it to me: shirts stained with tobacco and liquor, pants covered in dust and flecked with gravy, undershirts so ripe that the scent lingered in the air long after the garments were washed and hung, and underthings reeking of urine.

It was good money, though, and I could not afford to say no. We had sent many envelopes across the ocean since the first time we heard of Little Brynhild's distress, and though we did not feel it keenly, it had meant that I sometimes had to choose the poorer meat, and that the house of our own that we dreamed of for so long had to wait just a little while longer. I never thought of it as a kindness, however, but more of a thing that had to be done. Little Brynhild could not stay in Norway, it was as simple as that—and I had to do what I could to make sure that she escaped. The way Clara talked about it, though, you would think I were a saint.

"No one ever helped me," she said as her strong hands curved around the plunger and set to churn the water. "We are three sisters who made it across, and we all paid for our own fare." She blew a stray black curl away from her forehead. She had stopped wearing her headscarf when she moved to Chicago, which seemed to me highly impractical. I sometimes found long hairs in the food when she served me a slice of bread or a bowl of soup. It did not help that she pinned it up; the hairs got loose anyway.

"We got a little help," said Laura. She was a tall, fair woman from the north of Norway, so skinny that her pregnant belly seemed awkward on her lanky frame, like a sudden hill on a smooth plain. Nothing like mine: a curve resting upon my hips, gently rounded and snug. I loved that belly, and could not help but touch it as often as I was able. At night, when my husband and son were asleep, I would pull up my nightgown and let my hands follow the rise and dip while I closed my eyes and wondered what was inside. It had been such a long time since one of my pregnancies had lasted enough to show. They had too often ended in aches and blood. This time, though—this time it was different.

I was careful not to hope for too much, however. Twice I had carried to term, only to find that the child was weak and did not live. First, it was a girl, the year before Rudolph. Second, it had been a boy, the year that Rudolph was two. The same year I was first made aware of Little Brynhild's plight.

I remembered how the thought had taken root in me then, that if I only had a little help—even if just for a while—perhaps my body would be stronger, and the children that grew in me too. If I only had another pair of hands to help me out, I could rest more and the babies would thrive. There had been several disappointments since then, and I often forgot about this hope that had hatched after the first letter of distress—it was not *why* I wanted to bring my sister over, but as the day of her arrival drew nearer, that butterfly of hope came fluttering back again. Perhaps it would be easier this time, because I would not be alone with it all.

"Little Brynhild has paid her share," I said aloud, even if Clara already knew that. She only said such things because she felt it was wrong for John and me to spend so much on my sister's fare when we needed comforts of our own. "Who helped you?" I asked Laura, mostly to have her talking. She had just moved in on the ground floor with her husband and two daughters, and we did not know much about her yet.

"My brother," she replied from her kneeling position. Her hands, buried deep in the tub before her on the floor, stopped moving and the scrubber rose to the surface, drifting between oily sheets of grime. "Ulrik's sister helped too. Both of them have been here for years. Bertha, Ulrik's sister, keeps a store—can you believe it? She sells ribbons, buttons, and such to wealthy ladies, and that would certainly never have happened at home. She is the daughter of a tenant, same as us . . . Bertha has offered for us to stay with her as well, but I don't know." She lifted an arm to wipe it across her damp brow, leaving a streak of filth, which traveled from her skin and onto the graying headscarf. "She drinks tea from china now, while we just have the tin. My daughters aren't well-behaved enough in her eyes."

Clara nodded with a knowing expression, still working the plunger in another tub; her face had become flushed from the churning, but only a little. She was as used to hard work as I was.

"It happens sometimes over here, when a person comes to money. They quickly forget where they came from and put on all sorts of airs." She snorted her disapproval.

"Well, they *did* come here to escape all that was wrong before," I said as I stood by the stove, waiting for another batch of water to heat up enough to use. It was the last we had brought in, and soon we would have to brave the stairs again, up and down between the yard and the third floor, carrying heavy buckets from the pump. I was not looking forward to it, and figured Laura was not either; she was about as far along as me.

"That is no reason to look down at honest people," said Clara.

"Maybe they're afraid that if they are too friendly, people will ask them for money," I suggested. "That could certainly happen." I knew well how desperation could make people become unpleasant. I only had to look to my own kin back at Størsetgjerdet.

"I don't see why you would defend them." Clara rarely defended anyone at all but seemed to find flaws even among the righteous. "Shit will be shit," she said, "no matter how much you scrub it."

"So if you and Olaf come to money and move into a fine home, you would still be shit?" I could not help but tease her.

"Sure." She paused the churning and tossed her head. "I am not ashamed of where I come from; the smell of goat will stay with me till the day I die, even if I go to the grave dressed in silk."

"Maybe it would feel different if you *had* the silk," I said.

"Bertha has surely forgotten all about the goats," said Laura. "She has covered up the stench with real perfume, I reckon."

"It's a gamble, that's for sure," I mused while pouring the water into a tub for rinsing. "Some of us do better over here while others do not, and it seems as if luck strikes at random. Brothers can be kings and paupers alike. You are lucky," I said to Laura, "to have family who can help. It is easier then, if you have a place to start."

"Your sister is lucky too, then," said Laura. "She will have you to help her."

"As if Nellie hasn't done enough," Clara muttered with her eyes on the churning water before her.

"Little Brynhild has worked hard at Rødde for years, and with everyone whispering about her. Now is her time to cross the ocean, and she has certainly earned her fare."

"What are they whispering about?" Clara lifted her gaze to meet mine.

I shrugged again. "Who knows . . . I only know that it's *something*. My family isn't thought highly of, and words travel fast, even outside the valley."

"People can be cruel." Laura gave a sympathetic nod, as the scrubber dropped from her hand again—she was not a very fast worker.

"It has been years since that attack," said Clara; "maybe she would have been fine back home."

"Yes," I agreed, "but maybe not."

One more night, I thought. One more night and the worry that had lodged in the pit of my stomach would dissolve and be gone forever.

THE TRAIN STATION was crowded and loud. All sorts of people were milling about in the domed entrance hall, some of them carrying large trunks or cases. A woman in a coat lined with fox fur and a hat that carried an assortment of floral bounty brushed shoulders with a crooked old woman with a thousand lines in her face. The latter shuffled toward the tracks with her head bent, her hair hidden by a knitted headscarf and a tattered shawl draped across her shoulders. A man in an expensive-looking suit sat on a bench reading a newspaper, next to a dark-haired family in simple garb who spoke among them what I believed to be Russian. Conductors and other officials rushed past in dark uniforms adorned with shiny buttons, neatly trimmed mustaches, and expressions that stated they were busy with important things—running late, perhaps. Young men sat behind wooden counters, along the tall walls of pale, polished stone and served the winding lines of travelers, counting coins and dispersing tickets.

Above them all, a clock in brass casing mounted on the wall told the time with ornate black arms. The smallest one, spindly and delicate, shivered a little every time it moved, counting down another second.

I could not see my sister yet, and the crowd was much too dense for me. I clung to John's arm as he pulled me along through the throng. I did not used to be so unsettled by masses, but something had changed in me over the years. Perhaps it was married life that had made me such a sheltered thing. It protected me, yes, but hid me too, away from the noise and the churn of bodies that moved at all times on the city streets. After John had put a little gold on my finger, I no longer had to be a part of it all. I still worked as before but from the safety of my home. I rarely saw people outside our own little circle and barely met a soul that was not born in Norway such as myself. I found that it suited me, but it also made me weak. When faced with the train station's clamor, expressed in a myriad of tongues, my heart beat faster and my skin turned slick. My mouth suddenly felt too dry to speak.

"How are you feeling?" John asked me, knowing very well of my weakness. "You're not faint, are you?"

I shook my head, though I did feel a little dizzy. I did not want him to worry about me, though. "It is just the air," I said. "It's too hot, and the smell is bad."

John laughed in his quiet way. "Not everyone who travels takes a bath before they board."

I smiled a little too; it was true what he said. Of all the scents that mingled in the entrance hall, the one of sweaty, unwashed skin stood out, closely followed by a cloying reek of soot. When I looked down, I could tell that the slick, white floors were grimy with black and spattered with a mixture of tobacco and saliva. I took care to lift my skirt a little higher.

"I know where her train came in," John said, having scanned a board on a wall beside one of the ticket stalls. A woman stood beside it, selling small bouquets of flowers from a tub. Lilacs mostly, and large, lush roses, finished off with bright blue bows. I wondered for a second if I should get some for Little Brynhild, but then I thought better of it. I did not truly have money to spend. I worried that we would not find her at the track, that she had gone in search of us and gotten lost—or even worse: that she had not been able to find the station in New York. That she had been robbed or otherwise prevented from boarding the train. It was a harsh world, and she had seen so very little of it.

The worry increased, grasped and held my heart, as we moved farther down the platform, stepping over discarded tickets, cigar butts, and sugar-stained paper bags, and did not see Little Brynhild anywhere. We passed by several tall columns where people with travel-weary faces crowded with their trunks; there was also a newspaper seller and a stooped old man who sold sticks of caramel, but I could not see my sister.

A sudden fear struck me: What if she had changed so much that I would not know her? What if the child I knew was completely erased from her features?

Just then, I caught sight of them: two young women standing by one of the thick columns with two worn leather trunks between them. I knew her at once, of course I did, but it still took me a second to reconcile the girl she had been with the woman she was and make them one person in my mind. She was tall—taller than I was. Her dark brown hair was pulled back from her brow and into a knot at the back of her head. She wore no headscarf. Her nose had grown a little bony, like mine, and her cheekbones rode high, like our father's. She wore a dark blue coat, which I knew she had bought especially for the journey. She had written about it in her last letter. It was too expensive, but she could not resist treating herself to something new, have a little slice of what was to come: a new beginning—a fresh start, far away from ridicule and strife.

She had not seen us yet but was speaking to the woman before her; lithe and blond, it had to be Sigrid. The latter did not reply to whatever was being said but seemed to hang on to Little Brynhild's every word, her lips slightly parted as in wonderment.

I was not able to hold back anymore. "Little Brynhild!" I called for her and let go of my husband's arm to run toward her the best that I could. "Little Brynhild!" I was not worried about the crowd anymore but lifted my hand in a wave as I ran. My cheeks were already aching from smiling; the relief burst like a bubble in my chest, mingling with the joy of her arrival.

She looked up when she heard her name and scanned the crowd with a narrowed gaze, as if squinting against the sun. She looked a little tired, as everyone did after the journey, with dark shadows under her eyes and skin an unhealthy, grayish pallor. She smiled when she saw me; her lips split and lifted, but she did not come toward me. She just stood there with her hands clasped on her belly and watched me arrive.

"I am *so* happy you are here." I felt tears coming on when I threw my arms around her neck and felt her cool cheek press against my own. "Finally," I muttered. "Finally!"

She embraced me in turn and patted my back. She had to bend down a little, as she was so tall. "Yes," she said when she parted. "Here I am at last." She sounded calmer than expected, more composed. "I am so happy to be here," she said, as she took my hand and squeezed it gently with callused fingers. She did not *look* so happy, though; her dark blue eyes did not twinkle with delight but seemed almost cold when she looked at me.

She was probably just tired—who could blame her?

Then her gaze slid away, just as when she was a child. She could never look another in the eye for very long.

"Let's get you home," I whispered in a voice thick with feelings, just as John arrived and reached out his hand to greet his sister-in-law for the very first time. "Meet my little sister," I said to him with pride. "John, this is Little Brynhild."

"Bella," she corrected me. "My name is *Bella* now."

8.

Bella

I had expected Chicago to be different, and told Nellie so, sitting in her apartment mending rough-woven work clothes with tiny needles. "It reminds me of home." It should not have done so; there was nothing there that looked like Størsetgjerdet. The tenement building was three stories high, and the single window looked out on clotheslines, brick, and sky. Inside, it was cramped but far prettier than home, with a high ceiling and papered walls, and a proper stove for cooking. John and Nellie even had a bedroom, albeit a small one, with an additional window that looked out on the backyard, a cramped space crowded with outhouses and sheds where dirty children ran wild. The women in the building met on the landings of the stairs that climbed the outside of the wall, peeling vegetables, mending or folding clothes while they chatted and called out to their children down there: blond girls in tattered skirts and ungainly young boys in caps and suspenders wearing nothing at all on their feet. Still, it reminded me of home somehow—perhaps it was the stench of poverty itself.

"It's nothing like home." Nellie pursed her lips and squinted at her needle. "I am married now, I have a new child on the way, and we keep this apartment. It's more than I would've had at home, where no one wanted to marry a poor girl with far too many bruises.

This place has been good to me. I mend clothes now instead of shoveling muck—"

"But you don't even speak the language, Nellie. How do you manage?"

"I have no need for it. John does all the talking with strangers. I only see Norwegians and Danes around here anyway, and they understand me just fine."

"I would still like to learn, though."

She shrugged in the chair opposite mine, stretching out her legs on the floor. She had a rug there, woven in shades of gray and blue. She also had crocheted white curtains in the windows and fringed edgings on the open shelves that were crammed with colorful boxes and mismatched pieces of china. The room smelled of old food and smoke, but the table between us shone from vigorous polishing and an oil lamp in the ceiling glimmered with brass. I could see how she thought she had done well.

"You always did like to learn." Nellie gave me a thin smile. "You always had to know it all. Just don't get *too* clever. No one wants to marry you then."

"How come?" I asked, to tease her. I already knew why that was.

"No man wants to be challenged by his wife." Her gaze, so much like my own, met mine. It was almost the only similarity between us. Nellie was tall as well but scrawny like Mother; hardships had drawn lines in her face. She was thirteen years older than I was, and looked like it could have been more. She had married late and this child was her fourth, but only one had lived past the age of two and was now a lively boy of seven. "You already know what you ought to know." She pointed at me with the needle. "Cooking, mending, cleaning, farming—"

"I didn't come here to be a farmer's wife." I pursed my lips and threw out my arms. My fingers still clutched the needle, and the red thread went taut between my hand and the garment, humming in the air like a thin cut.

"I know that." Her voice became a little softer. "I just don't want you to hope for things you cannot have. Even here, a young woman can only achieve so much."

"I just don't want to settle for less than I can get."

She shook her head and sighed, looking much like our mother in that moment with the plaid headscarf hiding her hair from view. "Mother always said that teacher filled your head with nonsense."

"No need to blame *him*. My thoughts are all my own." I took the heavy scissors from the table and cut the spindly thread. Down on the floor, we had sheets soaking in tubs and later we would be at them with the plungers. Then we would carry more water upstairs and start preparing John's dinner. My hands were never idle in Chicago.

"I worry sometimes, Bella." Nellie used the name I had chosen, and the sound of it sent a soft tingle down my back. "You never seem to be satisfied. Not even when your belly is full and you have a bed all to yourself."

"I could have ten beds to myself, and a girl to cook my meals, if I had the money."

"Why would you want that? Isn't one bed enough?"

"What would I do if I lost that one bed? I wouldn't have a bed at all, then."

"One bed all to yourself is more than you had at home."

"But we're not there anymore, and this place is supposed to be different."

Nellie glanced up at me over her sewing. "When you meet a man it'll be fine, I'm sure. You can stomach more than you think with a husband by your side."

I shrugged and looked at her sore, red hands, "If I had a little more than just enough, I wouldn't have to worry at all."

"Keep your fingers crossed for a man of means, then."

"And in need of a wife to steer him right." I added a smile to my statement.

Nellie chuckled. "Poor man." She put the shirt down in her lap and stretched her arms.

"Why settle for less?" I murmured with my head bent over the work, hiding my face from her view.

"Just don't hope for too much."

Nellie had been foolish to marry John Larson. I thought she could have made a better choice. Nellie herself spoke of him as if he were a blessing, and I despised her a little for that. She was wrong about what she said, that he would not have had her in Norway. She could have married just as well back home, had she only been a little clever about it. There was no need to go to Chicago to have a man like John Larson. Then again, she said she cared for him, but I thought she could have cared for someone else just as well.

I would not spoil my chances, though, would not be foolish like her. Traveling to America had only been the first step; the next one would be to move out from the cramped apartment, leave the restless nights on the bench in the kitchen, the tiresome mending and the heavy wash behind.

When I had some time to myself, I liked to walk around the city and just look at the people, the shops, and the traffic. I had seen much poverty in my life but never such wealth as I did in Chicago, where gleaming horses pulled shiny carriages with ladies in hats that carried whole forests of feathers and flowers. I saw beautiful houses and gardens bursting with green behind wrought-iron gates, department stores glittering with lights and smelling of rose and magnolia. It was so close and yet so far from the Norwegian neighborhood by Milwaukee Avenue, where the children ran in streets filled with muck and poked at dead animals with sticks.

I knew where I would rather be.

I used whatever money I had to myself to buy sweets. I had never seen treats like the ones they had in Chicago: sticks of brown caramel and hard pieces of candy in all sorts of colors. I felt like the woman that I ought to be then, traipsing down the sidewalk, sucking on it. It was as if the sweetness seeped into the rest of my body and made me feel light and happy. Rich even, walking there in my worn headscarf and heavy shawl with the taste of luxury coating my tongue.

We never had much candy in Selbu.

I brought home newspapers and read them all through even if I did not know the language. That was the very purpose of it, to force myself to learn. I used an English Bible too, since I knew the meaning of those texts. It did not take me very long; I have always been a quick study. Soon I could speak and read English some, and a new world opened to me then. Why was my sister content to let her husband speak for her? I ignored her when she scoffed at me as I sat there, poring over my Bible. Marriage, I decided, had made her both lazy and slow.

She did talk a lot, though, in the language she *did* know. Every day she sat out on the stairs with a basket of mending, chattering with the others, sipping weak coffee and threading needles. How could they say so much about so little? They spoke of their husbands and children, the weather and the costs, and the peculiar German family downstairs. They spoke of who had arrived and who had gone, and giggled about the men at the boardinghouses: young and carefree, easy on the eyes. They spoke of who would marry and who would die—they spoke of a new Norway in America, only better than the land we left behind.

They were all so foolish.

9.

Nellie

I thought Bella would help you with the laundry. Where has she gone to this time?" Clara blocked my way on the stairs, coming from the yard with a water bucket of her own. Her green eyes sparkled with resentment.

I only shrugged, as I had no good answer to give her. Bella had pulled on her blue coat and slipped out the door shortly after breakfast. I was so surprised that I did not even think to ask just where she was going. This had happened several times in the weeks since she arrived, and no matter what I said to make her understand that I needed her at home, it simply did not help.

"Well, let me carry the water for you, then." Clara reached for the bucket in my hand. "It will not do to have you running up and down these stairs with that belly."

I knew she was right. My dress was straining under the apron and I often lost my breath when working hard. I was happy to feel all the kicks and tumbles within, though; it seemed like a healthy baby. Its antics often kept me awake at night, but I did not care one jot. I would rather have it spinning in my belly than feel it fall silent in there.

Clara put down her own bucket and started for the yard again. I followed her down the stairs, tugging at my apron as I often did when uncomfortable. "She only wants to see the city," I said to her back. She was wearing a blue-and-white-striped cotton dress under the stained apron; her dark curls were pinned to her head as usual. "She can read English now—did I tell you?"

"Yes, yes," Clara murmured. "I am sure she is bright as a button."

"She just doesn't understand how badly I need her help."

"She is a woman past twenty, Nellie, not a girl of ten."

"Still, though, she just doesn't understand—"

"Is she a little slow?" Clara glanced over her shoulders as she hurried down the steps.

"No," I said, suddenly offended. "I just told you she is bright. She reads—"

"Yes, yes, you said."

"She is helping with all the children—Lottie likes her a lot."

"My daughter is too young to know any better." Clara strode across the yard with the empty bucket dancing in her grasp. The set of her shoulders told me she was angry. "All these years saving up for her, and this is what you get? A sullen creature who only eats and sleeps and will not work? I'd say you have gotten yourself a poor bargain, Nellie."

Suddenly I felt a little angry too. Who was Clara to have such strong opinions of my sister? Who was she to judge?

When Clara spun around by the water pump in the corner of the yard, her forehead was creased with lines. "How about her showing you some gratitude? You sacrificed a lot to bring her here, and you are in dire need of help! Your births have never been easy—you ought to take it slow and not run about as you used to . . . With another woman in the house that should have been possible to achieve—but no! She is out taking in the sights! It is not right, Nellie!" The bucket clattered on the flagstones when she dropped it and set to work the heavy lever on the pump. "I know you care for her and that you want to help her, but what if she does not help you in turn? Is it even worth it if she cannot bring up your goddamn water?"

I wanted to say a dozen things: how she was always neat with her needlework, and how she made Rudolph hot chocolate the night before. I wanted to say how she did not mind lifting the heavy tubs for me or how the sight of her reminded me of home—but I knew it made no difference what I said; Clara was set in her opinion. I could not truly blame her either for looking out for me. I would probably have been angry as well, if I felt that Clara's kindness was being taken advantage of.

"I only think that she was badly hurt back home." I settled for the one thing I thought might calm her down. I felt much like a child, standing before her while my hands twisted at the hem of my apron. My mouth felt very dry.

"The attack, you mean?" Clara's eyes were on me as she pushed the lever. That was what I had meant, but I also meant in other ways. Tongues can be powerful daggers if wielded right.

"She bled from the stomach." Only saying those words aloud made me feel sick.

"But you still don't know what happened?"

"No, I—"

"Maybe there are other things you don't know about." The bucket by her feet had overflowed, but she did not seem to notice. "You do not truly know how she was in the years since you left."

"What do you mean?"

Clara shrugged and scooped up the bucket with water drizzling off the rim. "Maybe she is lazy—maybe she's always this way."

"Oh, I do not think so." I just could not see it. "She has been working since she was small." Yet an old worry stirred inside me, one I knew well from my youth. The fear that someone would notice that my sister was different, and not like other children. I tried to push the feeling aside, but once stirred, it was hard to subdue.

Clara did not reply to my words but set off across the yard again, aiming for the steps. "Maybe you don't know her as well as you think," she muttered, just loud enough for me to hear. The words left me feeling sick.

We were halfway up the stairs, on the landing where Clara's

own water bucket rested, when Bella suddenly appeared, coming
fast down the steps toward us. My whole body sagged with relief
from the sight. She seemed to be in a good mood; her cheeks were
pink from fresh air and her gaze was bright and alert. She had tied
on the apron and donned a headscarf, which brought my hopes up
further.

Surely there would be no more exploring today.

"Good morning to you, Clara," she said to my red-faced friend.
"Shall I take that?" She reached for the bucket, recognizing it as
mine. "We better start heating the water right away," she said to
me. "There is much to be done before nightfall, and some of those
shirts reek with filth."

"Where were you?" Clara asked as she handed her the water.
"We thought you had abandoned your poor sister."

"Oh, I just went out for some newspapers to read. I am practicing my English," Bella chirped. Her height made it so that she towered above Clara even on the landing.

"You should have said so." Clara stole the words out of my
mouth. "She cannot travel the stairs with her load; she is much too
fragile for that. Her back—"

"It's fine, Clara." I put a hand on her shoulder; her dress was
damp with perspiration. "She came back—I knew she would." I
said it mostly to convince myself. "Thank you so much for your
help," I added. "Bella can take it from here."

Bella smirked before turning on her heel and setting off again,
up the stairs this time.

"She is not so bad." I said it quietly so my sister would not hear
me. "She came back."

"This time," Clara muttered, just as quietly. "But what about all
the other times when she didn't."

"You should not be so hard on her; just give her some time."

"*You* should not be a fool." Her green gaze landed on me. "I don't
think that one has a care for anyone other than herself." She picked
up her bucket and stomped up the stairs.

Her words stayed with me for the rest of the day, even though I tried not to think of them. I told myself that Clara was wrong, but a stubborn sliver of doubt remained.

John did not have much comfort to offer me either. "She just doesn't seem to be of much use to you," he said that same night after I had told him what happened with Clara. His brow was furrowed with annoyance and concern as he sat in our bed, propped up against the pillows, with Rudolph sleeping soundly beside him. He spoke very quietly as the walls were thin, though I was quite certain that Bella was already asleep on the bench in the kitchen.

"She helps," I assured him as I crawled across them both to my spot closest to the papered wall. On our single bed stand, the candle flame quivered a little and made the shadows from the clothes hanging from pegs on the wall dance across the naked floor. "It is not easy coming here, you know that. She only needs a little time. I can hardly blame her for wanting to explore a little and get to know the city." But even as I said it, I knew that I was lying. Not only to John but to myself as well.

Little Brynhild—*Bella*—had never been easy.

"I was hoping," I started again, more truthful this time, "that time had changed her. That a few years at Rødde had softened her some, but that does not seem to be the case. She still does mostly as she pleases." If anything, she was worse. Her mood would dip and turn for no reason, and she did not seem to notice when someone did something nice for her. Her anger, like our father's, had always been like thunder: loud and sudden, blazing with heat, but now it seemed that it never quite dissolved but always moved and shifted under the surface, ready to erupt.

She was never calm—always restless.

"How does she get along with the other women, besides Clara?"

My heart sank in my chest, just from thinking of Laura's raised eyebrows behind Bella's back, and the latter's silent smile, as if she had no use for any of them. "Well enough," I said, though I could tell that my friends were not impressed with the new addition to our household, not even those who knew little about how things had unfolded since she arrived. It had always been hard to express just why it was that people did not take to Little Brynhild. Was it because of the way she never looked another in the eye, because she sometimes said things that made her seem mean, or because she never seemed to share in other people's joy? Did people even notice those things or was it just me, looking at her with love, wishing so desperately for her to find her place?

Perhaps they *did* notice without even knowing, the knowledge like a silent whisper in their minds. She could be as sweet as sugar when she wanted to, which she rarely did. It was as if she did not see or understand how a little effort could help her reach through to other people.

It was as if she did not care.

"I just want her to be happy," I said. "It's all I ever wanted."

"I know." He turned his head to place a kiss on my cheekbone. "I am sure she will be in time. I had been hoping she would take on some of your load, though. Help with the washing, at least."

"Oh, she does, and she has a way with Rudolph. It is just hard to rely on her help, as I never know when she will be here or not." Even as I said it, I felt guilty. The desire to protect her had always been strong—and over here, she had no one else to defend her. If *I* did not stand up for her, she would be all alone.

"It seems to me that you spend just as much time worrying about her now as before she arrived," John said. "I had been hoping we could put that worry to rest now."

"Well, I no longer worry that someone will attack her," I said, and adjusted my head on the pillow. "I know that she is safe, and that's something."

"But do you get more rest now that she is with us?" He patted the swell of my belly through the blanket.

"Oh, I—" It seemed foolish now, how I had been thinking that my sister would be the answer to my plight. How I had imagined

IN THE GARDEN OF SPITE

that she would care for me through the pregnancy, and thus in-
crease my odds. I carried almost as much water as before, while
she was out walking the streets, sucking on caramels. The bitterness swelled in me for a moment before I gently pushed it away.

It would serve no purpose.

10.

Bella

Every Saturday there were gatherings at the tenements with strong drink and fiddle players. Nellie was eager for me to go. "That's how you'll meet a nice husband. Dance a little, Bella, dance and drink and show yourself off!"

I did not mind the drinking so much, but I certainly was no dancer. I had never felt graceful spinning in someone's arms, only awkward and dizzy, longing for it to end. I did go, though, because Nellie insisted. And I *did* want to meet a man and move out from the bench in Nellie's kitchen, where the scent of cabbage and grease clung to everything, and the neighbors downstairs kept me up at night, yelling to each other in German. I just did not want to meet *those* men.

They were poor Norwegians like me, with no real prospects. Some of them came from the Norwegian countryside but many from the crowded cities too. They were workingmen with strong arms and very little wit. Some were hard drinkers, some quarrelsome and angry. They came to Chicago looking for work and settled in the boardinghouses, waiting for luck and a wife. The other unwed women thought them wonderful, spun in their arms like there was no tomorrow. They would be happy enough to marry of one of them and settle in some small apartment like Nellie's.

Not I.

I only had to look to Nellie to see how well that went, and no matter how handsome those young men were. If I really was to prosper, I could not give in.

I had, after all, nearly married a farmer's son back home, and was determined not to do any worse in America.

There was one man, though, a blond carpenter from Bergen. Three Saturday nights in a row, he plied me with drinks and wanted to hold my hand under the table. It was my own fault. I had grown tired of being considered strange; I figured it did me no service if I was to find a suitable husband, so I had taken it upon myself to learn how to flatter: be sweet, kind, and amiable. I watched the other young women at the gatherings and women out on the streets as well. Saw how they moved their lips and widened their eyes, how they gently touched and pretended to be coy. I had tried some of these tricks on Edvard, the carpenter, and to my utter surprise, it had worked. Before I knew it, I was tangled with him somehow, was expected to accept the drinks he poured me and hold his hand.

When he wanted to walk me home, I always said no.

Then one Saturday, the gathering was in Nellie's backyard. Both she and John were there. She was spinning on the ground with her big belly, between rows of makeshift benches where her neighbors sat with their bottles, singing and cheering the dancers on. It was a dark night, but they had brought out lanterns, and the gentle lights obscured the squalor we all lived in, the dreary backyard and the outhouse—but they could not mask the stench.

Edvard too was there, of course, handsome, drunk, and impatient. When I went to use the outhouse, he followed me into the dark. He caught hold of my shoulder and spun me around to plant a kiss on my mouth. I gently pushed him away, told him to go back, and said I would be there shortly. I knew it would not do to make a fuss. I had handled drunk men before and did not think more of it.

When I came back, he had fallen asleep on a bench, a board on top of two barrels, and I let out a breath of relief. I was tired of it all, the noise and the people, and so I went upstairs to Nellie's apartment to undress and make up my bed. The party was loud, even when I was inside, and I wondered how the children slept through it all.

Just when I had slipped under the woolen covers, the door to the apartment opened. At first I thought it was John; the only light in the kitchen came from the coals in the stove and the night around me was dark, but then I realized it could not be. The figure in the door, swaying on his feet, was far too tall for that.

"Bella." Edvard stumbled onto the floor, crossed it in just a few strides, and then he was upon me.

"No." I tried to push him off. He reeked of liquor and sweat.

He did not reply but tugged at my blanket; his forehead was creased, his breathing labored. I tried to laugh and pretend it was in jest, while I fought to pry his fingers off the covers. Then suddenly I could smell it again, the water of Selbu Lake lapping at the shore; I could feel the pebbles burrowing into my back and the pounding pain of a shattered tooth. "Stop," I muttered between clenched jaws. "Stop it!"

He did not even hear me but kept pulling at the blanket. His breathing became even heavier than before. I was wriggling by then, trying to toss him off, but he was far too heavy.

He managed to wring the blanket from my hands and peeled it off my body. His knee landed between my legs.

"No." I was firm. "No!"

"Why?" His weight was heavy upon me. "I can be sweet to you, Bella. You let me kiss you before."

I did not answer, did not move at all while he kissed my neck and squeezed my breasts through my shift. The fear in me subsided some and turned into a cold sort of rage: Who was this man to think he could best me? I would never be at a man's mercy again. My arm moved, dropped down to the floor where the basket of mending stood by the bench. My hand found the rim, felt its way through folds of fabric, rows of needles, spools of thread, and landed on the scissors at the bottom. I lifted them high in the air and he saw them gleam just as they came down, and he tried to escape by twisting around. The scissors went through the fabric of his pants and lodged in the backside of his thigh. They protruded there even after I let them go. He bellowed. I shouted. He got a hold of the scissors and pulled them out with a gush of blood. The door sprang open and John was there, Nellie too, and half the party. They led the wailing man outside with much fuss and looks in my direction. Not Nellie, though. She sat down on the lip of the bench, pulling up my covers. There was blood in my bed, on my hands. My poor jaw throbbed with ache, just as it did after the lake, though no blow had landed there this time.

"He tried to force me," I muttered, "so I stabbed him."

"Yes." Nellie sounded faint. "Yes, I believe you did."

"YOU DIDN'T HAVE to hurt him," they told me later, the chattering women on the stairs. "You shouldn't have led him on if you didn't want him to come." I never replied but lifted my chin and pressed my lips hard together. Underneath the shield of my apron, my hand curled into a fist.

"You will never get married this way," Nellie said too, with her head bent over the mending in her kitchen. "I worry for you, Bella, I do. What happened to you back home? I know there was an attack, but no one ever told me more than that."

I shrugged and bent my head over the torn pants in my lap; the needle went in, came out. "There's no use talking about that now— and don't you go asking Mother." It would not do if Nellie knew. I had left it all behind.

Edvard from Bergen never spoke to me again, knowing perhaps that I would gladly have followed those scissors with something worse. I thought about it often: what I would do to him if I could. Sometimes it was Anders I saw in my head: skin slashed and teeth crushed. It was seething, that anger, restless and aching.

I liked Edvard well enough before that night, and had I been anything like Nellie, he could have been a good fit for me. I would gladly have taken him into my bed and never known his true nature—and neither would he have known mine. I did not want that for myself, though, being a carpenter's wife. Did not want to be another woman on those stairs. I thought of that night by the lake while lying on the bench at night, and knew I was not done with the spite. I had survived—just to spite—and I would rise in spite as well. Even though he would never know it, I would marry even better than Anders, only to prove that I could.

It would have been easy to slip in those early days, falter and settle for less. Those scissors in the drunk man's thigh was the best thing that could have happened to me. None of the Norwegian men who danced and drank in the backyards would even look at me after that. I had to look elsewhere to find a husband, and I had ideas.

II.

Nellie

It was unfortunate what happened with those scissors, especially since Bella had still not made many friends at the tenements. There was talk on all the stairs and rowdy laughter, and whatever hope there had been of seeing her settled with a man from our circle was waning by the day as the word spread. Who would want a wife who had bodily attacked a suitor and lodged a sharp weapon in his flesh? Not only would he live in peril of suffering the same fate, but he would also have to endure a lifetime of ridicule from the other men.

It was just how it was, and there was nothing to do for it.

For the longest time I thought that bloody night on the bench was what had sent Bella running to church.

It turned out I was wrong.

John and I belonged to the Norwegian Lutheran Church, and Bella joined us there when she arrived, but we were not zealous Christians. Our days did not have the hours for it, and though we said grace and John did a little loud reading from the Bible on Sunday nights, our concerns were mundane ones. We were at peace with God and aimed to keep it that way, but he did not fill our every waking moment. I wished for a house of our own and healthy children, and had little time to worry about our souls.

Little Brynhild had been pious at various times as a child, but I had never thought it anything more than a way of getting by. She had an excellent mind—it was almost uncanny the way she could recite Bible verses from memory, or remember whole passages of text having read them only once. It served her well in school and in church too. For a child who did not always know how to behave in an endearing way, who was often teased and taunted, her ability was a strength, and it made her appear very serious about the Bible—as if she had read the whole book ten times over, when all she had done was glance at it once. The adults made a game of it, outside the church on Sundays, asking her questions and having her recite verses from memory. People like that sort of dedication in a child; they think it is sweet.

That was why it made sense to me that Bella would seek out the church to find solace after the whole scissors affair. Religion had helped her rise before when people had given her a hard time. A vast knowledge of verses and psalms could come in handy even as an adult. I knew she would not have a problem getting along with the very religious, black-clad matrons of the congregation; her sullenness could easily be read as a sort of piousness. It did not suit me, though, this sudden interest in the church.

My back was worse than ever after my daughter Olga's birth, and some days I had to lean on furniture just to move around in my apartment. Bella being out all the time to meet with her new friends doing all sorts of charitable work was inconvenient at best, and her occupying the bench meant that I could not ask someone else to stay with me either. I needed her at home, and told her so, just a few weeks after my bed rest ended.

"Maybe I need God right now," she said in reply. "Maybe I find it hard to be new in this country with no husband or children of my own. Maybe it is a comfort to me to hear God's words in my mother tongue." She was sitting on a chair by the table, sorting through my needles. She was wearing a dark brown cotton dress, and her hair was hidden under a graying headscarf. Behind her on the stove, the water in the pot slowly came to a boil.

"We hear them well enough on Sundays." I was in pain and my mood was dark. "I don't see why you have to be so *involved*. They can care for the orphans just fine without you. Those old women with no chicks in the nest have nothing better to do with their time." I was biting my lip against the ache. I had taken a powder, but it had yet to work. My hand was busy rocking the cradle, where little Olga blinked against the light.

"It's a charitable thing to do. Not everyone has a kind mother like little Olga here." Bella smiled and reached out to pat the worn cradle. "They need young bodies with strength and conviction. The older women can't do that much."

"My back hasn't been good since the birth. I sure could use your help too." I hated the sullen complaint in my own voice.

"If John earned a little more, you wouldn't have to work so much." Her eyebrows rose a little.

"He earns what he earns and works late hours to keep us all fed." It just was not fair to lay it on him.

"What would you have me do then, Nellie? Stay at home every day as your maid?" She did not wait for my reply but rose from the chair and went to fetch the boiling water. It would go into a dish-pan on the table and be used to clean our dirty cups.

"No." My temper suddenly flared; my pain was such that I could not help it. "I want you to do your share of the work, not spend all your time with the women from church! Better still, you could find yourself a husband! I'm sure they have forgotten about the scissors by now."

"He shouldn't have come to the bench." She lifted her chin in that stubborn way that I knew so well.

"Well, I don't see why not. You could have been married by now," I snapped, then regretted it in the next moment. Of course he should not have come to her like that, but perhaps the prospect of marriage should have stayed her hand? It bothered me how she could not see that such was a poor woman's plight. We had all had to suffer indignities to arrive at a place of safety. We were not ladies with perfumed handkerchiefs who could pick and choose among powdered suitors. We did not have the luxury of fainting when faced with men's baser nature but often had to suffer to achieve our goals in life. I had been lucky with John—and I knew it—but my life before him had been painful enough. A girl without means had little worth in the eyes of the world.

"I didn't *want* to marry him." Bella snapped right back in my face. She poured the water so abruptly that it splashed onto her fingers and would probably leave blisters.

"Well, *who* then, Bella? Who is good enough for you?"

"Not a carpenter from Bergen." She dropped the dishes into the dishpan so fast and hard that a china plate chipped. It broke my heart to see it—I loved my few pieces of china.

"He was a little hard on the bottle, but they all are." I sighed, struggling to make her understand.

"Not the men at church," she replied, and added a triumphant smirk.

Understanding dawned on me; my hand on the cradle stopped. "Is that what you're doing?" I could not believe it. "You want to marry some upstanding member of the congregation?"

"I would think my chances of finding someone suitable are better there." She said it so calmly, as if it were just a matter of fact.

"Do you think you'll find someone?" I could see those men in the front rows so clearly in my mind: clean shirts and waistcoats, hats free from dust.

"There are a few, widowers mostly. They will be looking for a woman to take care of the house." She poured cold water into the dishpan to dilute the scalding heat.

"But would that make you happy, Bella? To walk in a dead woman's shoes?" It was usually not what young women craved—though there was the matter of convenience, of course.

"If not, I could afford some caramels," she replied, with just the tiniest of smiles. She soaked her hands in the warm water and did not even flinch when it touched her fresh burns.

"Oh, John would be pleased, then, if you found yourself a man." I spoke without thinking—I should not have done so.

"He wants me gone, then?" She did not look at me but busied herself with the hard, red soap, diluting it in the water.

I could feel my cheeks turn red. "He thinks it's time—but not to worry, he would never put you out." He had not handled the affair with the scissors well and had been wary of Bella ever since. I had done my very best to reassure him, but I could tell that he did not trust her. He rarely spoke to her anymore and his mood had been dark, even after Olga was born—the daughter he had so longed for. It had bothered him in particular that Bella staying with us meant we could not have his sister come from Minnesota to visit after the birth. He felt, and rightly so, that she would have been a better help to me.

"Don't worry, Nellie." Bella still did not look at me. "I will be gone before you know it." She set to scrubbing a hardened crust of gruel off a plate. "And then I will never go hungry again."

"I'm glad you are so hopeful." I felt a little faint. "None of us bears you any ill will. We saved every cent we could to have you come here—"

"I know, and I will pay you back." I could tell that her jaw worked under the skin.

"No, Bella, just be happy," I said in a voice that seemed to have lost all power. "That is the best way to pay me back."

And yet, as I was looking at my sister, her skin glistening in the heat that rose from the basin, I could not help but wonder if happiness was something she was even able to achieve.

If she would even know it if she had it.

12.

Bella

Chicago, 1884–1886

My future husband's name was Mads Sorensen. He was a night guard at the Mandel Brothers department store and brought me there one day to browse the silk handkerchiefs, taffeta dresses, and pearl earrings on display. It was good work at a fine establishment, and I would not mind tying my name to such a place.

Better still, he had a three-bedroom house in a pleasant neighborhood, far away from the tenements and the things that were being said about me.

He was not, as Nellie feared, a widower who had spent all his love on his first bride. He was a hardworking man with trust in God and wise with money. I did not care much for his looks; he was a short, stocky man with an unflattering mustache and was already losing hair, but that did not deter me. There was too much to like about a man with savings and prospects, and he was meek and gentle enough that I felt sure he would never raise a hand to me.

Love, though, it was not.

I was flattered that he had seen me at all and asked to escort me home after church. As the weeks moved by, we went for walks, and he bought me tea at an expensive teahouse. After learning about my sweet tooth, he always made sure to have a paper bag ready with pieces of candy of all flavors. Soon we had an understanding, and I knew he expected us to marry.

He spoke of it first when he walked me home one night.

"It must be cramped up there with two children and only one bedroom." He was looking up at the windows of Nellie and John's building. The street around us was mostly deserted, but a filthy man was sleeping with his back against a set of stairs and a scrawny dog was sniffing at debris. The brick pavement, running in shades of salmon and cream, was littered with vegetable peels and cleaned bones, brown-stained saliva and empty bottles. I could not wait to leave it behind.

"It is." I answered his question. "It was all much better back home. It's new to us, living like this." I looked around at that loathsome street.

"I suppose you had room enough on your father's farm." There was a twinkle in his eyes that made me unsure if he knew I was lying about my origins.

I stood my ground. "Yes we did, on our father's farm." If I said it enough times, perhaps I would forget that it was only a lie.

"Well, I have a different problem. I have a house full of empty rooms." He smiled as he said it, as if apologizing for his good fortunes.

"But many offers to fill them, I'm sure." Men are so fond of flattery.

"Not one I have accepted yet. It takes a special kind of woman to fill a house with warmth: someone kind and caring with a strong Christian faith."

"Are such women hard to come by?" I smiled my best smile, averted my gaze, and acted coy. I pretended that I wore a thick coat of the finest fur, not a threadbare thing of simple wool. Instead of my headscarf, I imagined a hat, bold and bright with an impressive plume. I found it gave me courage to imagine things like that—to see my future clearly before me.

"Tell me, Bella, what would you do with a house like mine?" Mads's cheeks reddened and his eyes shone toward me.

I thought for a moment and then I drew a breath. "I would make sure it was always clean and tidy, keep chickens in the yard and a boar in a pen. I would hang sheets to dry in the breeze, make jams and marmalade and wholesome dinners. There would always be something sweet for dessert." My gaze snagged his. "The man in the house would never want for anything. His clothes would be neat, his belly full, and his home would be a cheerful place where God was given rightful due. In time there would be children—"

"Bella." His hands caught mine and his voice was thick when he spoke. "Say you will be my wife."

I looked away and bit the inside of my lip until my eyes watered. It seemed right to shed a tear in that moment. "Yes," I said when I could stand it no more, "I do want to be your wife."

And so it was settled between us, right there on that filthy street reeking of rot and misery, with only a stray dog as witness.

WE GOT MARRIED at the Evangelical Lutheran Bethania Church on Grand Avenue and Carpenter Street early in 1884. Mads gave me gloves to hide my red, callused hands. They were soft and supple, made of leather. He gave me a well-stocked pantry too, and dollars to spend—but he could not fill those empty rooms.

Could not fill my womb.

I thought little of it at first. I was far too busy settling into my new life on Elizabeth Street. It was a fine house on a quiet street: two stories, a coal cellar, and a backyard bursting with apple trees and lilacs. It was a sensible house rather than beautiful, and I had most of the furniture changed on my arrival. Mads had never given much thought to such things and had merely kept what was in there when he bought it. Now I brought in comfortable chairs with wine-colored seats, crowned with carved flowers and polished to a shine; bow-legged tables of oak and chestnut; feisty rugs with exotic patterns; a mantelpiece of marble; and a floor-standing clock that measured out our happy hours. I had the kitchen repainted in the softest shade of blue and bought a sturdy new table with six wooden chairs, as white and smooth as ivory. It was easy back then to have Mads open his purse. He thought me so soft and sweet, so lovely to touch at night.

"How is my beautiful wife today?" he asked every morning when arriving home from his shift. I would be in the spacious kitchen, offering fresh bread and yellow butter, coffee made from the finest beans.

"Never happier," I always replied. "It is such a joy to be married to a kind man like you."

Our marriage was new and dripping with honey, and I was content for a while. I enjoyed being a married woman and walking by his side with my gloved hand resting on his arm. I liked to sit next to him in church, liked the way people looked at me, as if I were important. Suddenly I had a voice that was heard because I spoke for him too—a man of some means. I had gotten my stamp of approval and no one could peg me as a poor girl anymore. A man had chosen me above all else and thought me fit to run his household, mend his shirts, and cook his meals. He had given me his name to carry. The girl by the lake, beaten and bleeding, seemed nothing but a dream by then.

I saw to it that the pantry was always well stocked. Now that I had my own money, I just could not seem to stop. I saw the delicious beef and I got it, the link of sausages and the blood pudding too. I could not leave the butcher without it. When I came home, I placed the parcels on the kitchen table and peeled the bloody paper from the ruby red meat. I could not get enough of the scent of it. I had eaten so much porridge in my life, so many scraps and boiled potatoes. The beads of blood were my reward, a prize for being clever, for making my way around it all, the obstacles and the pain. I baked cakes too, so sweet they could barely be eaten. I made waffles, puddings, and tarts for my husband, baked apples, biscuits, and soft, golden buns. As much pleasure as they gave me, though, those sweet little treats, they were nothing compared to the meat, glittering brightly in the kerosene light. Food like my mother never tasted.

Food fit for kings and queens. I would not be hungry again, I swore, and stocked my pantry full to the brim: smoked and cured, cut and whole. To me it was all about the meat.

I kept chickens in the backyard as I had promised. I had a pen made but never bought the pig. I told my husband I just could not bear it, to raise an animal and then have it killed. In truth, I had no patience for it then, to raise my own meat when I could buy it. It is hard work, butchering a pig. Mads found me sweet and endearing, patted my hand, and said of course, we did not need it; we had other meat to chew on, soft and supple and ruby red.

At first, it baffled me how easy it was to have things done my way. The men I knew back home were a hard and stubborn breed. They said no just for the pleasure of hearing the word said aloud and enforced their will with fists and harshness. They let you know your place one slap at a time. Mads was nothing like that. He was a simple man in pursuit of a simple life. He wanted a woman to look after him, to fluff his pillows and iron his shirts. I liked this as it made him easy, but I despised him for it too. I never much appreciated kindness. To me it spoke of weakness and I never could stomach that. It made me worry about the future, the kindness in that man. He would have to be ruled, I decided, or he might become our ruin.

"He doesn't *want* anything," I complained to my sister. "He wants nothing for himself but what we have."

WE HAD BEEN married barely a year when bad news arrived in an envelope with my brother Peder's handwriting on the front. I had diligently written home ever since I came to America, telling my parents of my good marriage and lovely house, and had received replies in Olina's sloppy scrawls. I had never written to my brother, though, and never received a letter from him, which was why I knew at once that something was amiss. I stood on the floor in my freshly scoured kitchen and tore open the envelope while preparing myself for the blow that was sure to follow. I quickly scanned the ink on the page: Mother was dead just after Christmas. She had suffered a chest pain that would not go away, and passed on quite suddenly in her bed. Father had not noticed until morning.

"He was drunk for sure," I told Nellie when she came to see me later that week. Her daughter, Olga, was playing with a deck of cards by the end of the scrubbed kitchen table. "He would have noticed if her heart gave out if he hadn't been drunk."

"Even if he had, what good would it have done? Father could never afford a doctor." Nellie dabbed at her eyes with a handkerchief. "I so wish I could have seen her to the grave, don't you?"

"I wouldn't go back even for that," I told her, truthfully enough, "but I hope he wasn't drunk at the grave site."

"Peder would have kept an eye on him." Nellie was still crying. I was not. I was angry.

"What good did he ever do her? She lived such a miserable life—"

"Don't you blame this on Father, Bella. He has his weaknesses, but Mother was old and had lived a hard life. It was just her time to go—"

"Did you know he didn't marry her before she'd lost our first sister—do you remember her talking about that child?"

"Yes, she still lived with her parents when she had her." Nellie lowered the handkerchief. "She and Father married a month after she died."

"Why would she do a thing like that?" I poured us more brandy. "She could have gotten away then, when the child was dead. Why would she marry him after that?"

"Oh, people would still talk. That child wasn't gone just because it was dead." Nellie sipped from her glass. "Perhaps she loved him once."

"Young and foolish." I snorted.

"We should be glad for it," Nellie saw fit to remind me. "We would not sit here if she hadn't married him."

"She settled for nothing at all."

"But she had us, her children, and that's something."

"It's certainly more than I have." Mother's death had left an ache in me: a twinge in my chest like an open wound. A hole in the soil, next to a root.

"You are still young and have years to try." Nellie bent forth in her chair and helped Olga gather the cards. The girl smiled up at her with Mother's eyes. I wanted to tell my sister then, about the damage done by the lake, but the words would not come; they slipped and escaped like tadpoles in a pond. Soon they were all gone.

"I can't stand it anymore," I said instead, "to see other women with their children. Even the thinnest, meanest woman at church has a brood of her own. People like her for it. They think her children are sweet and keep asking her about them." I had fretted over my lack of children before, but never had I felt it as keenly as I did after Mother passed away. I kept thinking about that grave in the woods, as if the fresh loss opened the door to the other, and I did not quite know which one I was mourning. Maybe I mourned them both.

I was angry for what had been taken from me.

"People do that," Nellie said, referring to the congregation. "It's easy to talk about children."

"Well, they don't ask me, because I don't have any little girls to show off." I emptied my glass in one swift motion.

IT BOTHERED ME to see mothers on the sidewalks, leading their young ones by the hand. It bothered me to hear wailing babies through open windows, and see a woman's hand adjust a young boy's collar in a carriage passing by. I hated how the little ones looked upon their mothers with love. I came to believe that was all that I wanted; for a child's eyes to look at me like that. I wanted that love the other women had, that innocent adoration. What had those women ever done to have it delivered to them so effortlessly? What had Nellie ever done to have her belly swell time and again? Why could I not have the same?

On late nights when Mads was at work, I sometimes worried if God saw me after all and was punishing me for that poisoned dram. Then I remembered all the blood after the lake, and the thought that I was broken inside. I did not worry about God then.

The house around me was quiet—so quiet. No child's sweet breath filled the night. Still, I sometimes thought I could hear the sounds of small feet crossing the floors, or a tinkling laughter in my ear. Ghosts of the children I could have had, if I had not lain down with the farmer's son. I thought of Anders often in those days, while drowning my sorrows in expensive brandy and rubbing my jaw, which had never truly healed. I wanted to kill him all over again for the damage he had caused me. I felt regret that he was no longer alive. I should have done it slower, prolonged his agony further—or I should have done it more quickly, using my bare hands to extinguish his life. I should have made it bloody and painful: extracting his teeth and molesting his gut, just as he had done to me. I had been too kind to merely slip him rat poison, when what he had done to me had left me forever barren. My hatred simmered but had nowhere to go—the man was already dead, and no power on this earth could undo the damage done.

I raised a glass to the devil in those nights, huddled in my shawl at the kitchen table. I prayed that Anders was with him, facing eternal torment.

Soon I grew tired of the cooking and the housekeeping. Grew tired of making cakes. I grew tired of the church as well—all that exhausting humility. The house, which had seemed such a treasure trove at first, seemed to have lost all luster. The blue-painted walls in the kitchen seemed grimy, as if covered by a fine layer of dust. The wine-colored upholstery of my new chairs seemed tarnished like beef left out too long. Even the lilacs in the backyard seemed to fade before me, drained of both color and scent. No matter how often I swept the floors, debris always found its way in. I was sick of the somber, dark dresses I wore, the plain cross around my neck. I looked for other things to wear in plum-colored satin and emerald wool. I bought myself hats with lush velvet roses and feathers from rare and colorful birds. Things like those I had dreamed of while crossing the sea to this land. Instead of scrubbing out the pantry, I walked around in the city and stopped for expensive hot chocolate and tea.

"You'll bring us into ruin." Mads shook his head. He had a folded newspaper in his hand. His white undershirt was clean and neat; the suspenders hung off his shoulders. I was at the table in the parlor, my parcels laid out on the polished wood. I did not answer but looked at him while my fingers worked with lengths of ribbons and folds of soft cotton. "What happened to the kind and simple woman I married?"

"What happened to *you*?" I looked him in the eyes. "Since when did you talk to your wife in that way? Have I not cooked for you, scrubbed your floors, and aired your slippers? Why would you deny me a few luxuries of my own?"

"Because you don't need all those dresses. They aren't even fit for church!" His bottom lip quivered a little under the mustache.

I filled a small glass with pear brandy; my hand barely shook, though the anger was already building inside me. "I need something nice to look at, being burdened with the sight of *you* every day. Why do you want so little in life, and why does it offend you that I want more?"

He shifted on the floor then, with his gaze cast down, the newspaper crumpled in his hand. "I'm sorry I'm such a disappointment to you."

"It's too late for regrets now." I lifted my glass and downed it. "You should change your aims, though. We ought to live somewhere nicer—bigger." I looked around at the cramped room, littered with my purchases.

"Why? We have empty rooms as it is." He looked utterly confused.

"Empty rooms are a sign we have done well in life. God looks after his own." It ached to say it, as I would rather have them filled with little girls and boys. I could not admit this to him, though.

Instead, I lifted my chin and narrowed my gaze, measured him across the short distance.

"Does He now?" Mads replied with something like mirth tugging at the sides of his mouth. "My wallet is nearly empty, Bella—my savings are nearly gone!" He hit the table with the newspaper in a rare display of anger, but I was my father's daughter and it did not impress me at all.

"You have to make more, then," I hissed across the table. "You always knew it would cost, having a wife." If I was to be trapped in this house with this man, at least I would live as I pleased.

He slumped down in a chair. "We are not rich people, Bella. We cannot afford all that." The newspaper motioned to my parcels. "We cannot have beef every day."

"What would you want us to eat, then? Salted herring and porridge?" My lips twisted up with disdain. His pitifulness made me furious.

"Something . . . *sensible.*" He threw out an arm.

"Do you think God would love us better then?" I filled my glass to the brim. "Do you think he'd bestow great riches upon us if we ate more cabbage and beets?" I all but snarled when I turned to face him, so abruptly that my skirts spun around my ankles and liquor spilled down on my hand.

"It's just slipping away, Bella. All my money, into puddings and vanity." He shook his head and rubbed his brow.

"You shouldn't have married, then, if it bothers you so much! Maybe you're just lazy—*too* lazy to work to keep a nice house!" My gaze searched the table for something to throw: a book, perhaps, or a cup. A pair of gleaming scissors.

"We're perhaps not where you want to be in life, but I wish you would wait to spend until we have the means—"

"You eat the beef and savor the cheese, same as I!" I drank fast to quench the fury—to erase it with another sort of fire. The liquor slipped down my throat, sweet and burning, but it did not smother the flames of my rage.

"I wish you would not drink so much." His voice was meek—it fanned the flames.

"I wish you weren't such a foolish man." I could barely whisper the words. I filled my glass again.

"How can you speak so cruelly to me?" His mouth hung open and his eyes went wide.

"I was thinking of buying new china," I told him. My voice was still hoarse, but it carried. "We can't be eating off chipped plates." I wanted to bait him, to see if he would turn into a bear before me: rage, scream, and throw things too. Maybe that would be better than this sad and miserable sheep before me.

"They are not chipped," he bleated.

"Not yet, but they will be. Cheap plates always break." I clutched my glass so hard that my fingers ached. My gaze was trained on his neck, on the fat vein pulsing there.

"Who cares what we eat from, Bella?"

No one cared, and that was the truth of it. No one cared what we ate from but me.

AS MADS'S SAVINGS shrunk, my mood darkened. I kept staring into the pantry, at the sausages and cheeses, the mutton and the beef, and it never seemed to be enough. I bought more all the time, filled that pantry to the brim, but still it seemed so empty to me. Even when I had to throw some out or cut green mold from the cheese, I bought more. Even when it reeked of rot, I kept pushing more food in there. I thought that if I could not fill the empty rooms, at least I could fill that pantry to the brim, but the house always worked against me. It was a bottomless pit for my wants and needs that would never give me satisfaction. All it did was take, and taunt with that empty space—with what I did not have. Soon I would not even have money to spend, and that thought scared me more than anything else.

I would not be poor again, take in wash or mending and feel my hands grow sore from scrubbing other people's sheets. Never again—no more. I would never feel the ache of hunger and fall asleep with my knuckles buried deep in my belly to stave off pangs of pain.

I would never be hungry again.

I broke into a cold sweat and hives, sitting by the kitchen table, ogling the door to the pantry. Instead of spending less money or cooking less lavishly, I found myself unable to do anything but the opposite. I brought home even more butter, sugar, and cream, even more meat to fill the pantry. I was preparing for winter like a bear, adding fat to my body. It was my shield, that girth of flesh. No harm could ever come to me behind folds of fat and expensive clothing. No one could take the food from me if I had already eaten it all. It was mine then for sure.

I deserved that food, those clothes, that china. This was America, land of opportunity and second chances. Who you were before did not matter. So why did those snapping jaws come back to haunt me? Why could I not escape the sensations of poverty and disgrace? It all seemed terribly unfair. I had done everything right: I had married and settled, I had my own house, I went to church and I wiped orphans' faces. I had made a new life for myself. Yet the husband was weak, the house was wicked, my womb was empty, and the pantry reeked of rot. All I had wanted turned to dust in my hands and it left me so very disappointed.

13.

Nellie

I am so sorry to bother you, Nellie. I was just—do you have a moment to spare?" Mads Sorensen stood outside my door. His shirt was pristine and his tie neat; his brown coat had gleaming buttons of brass. His face, though, was pale, and his eyes looked pained. A dark blue bruise traveled from the crook of his left eye and nearly to his jaw. I could not help but gasp when I saw it, as I had never thought Mads the sort of man to get into a brawl.

"Come in, please." I stepped aside and he strode past me, into the messy room where I had been sorting through the laundry when he rapped on the door. Olga was sitting among the heaps of filthy garments, toying with empty thread spools, building herself a castle. Her face lit up when she saw Mads come inside. She had stayed with her aunt and uncle for a few weeks the summer before, after another one of my pregnancies had come to an abrupt and painful end, and had become very fond of them both. The sentiment was in every way mutual, and Mads did not even sit down at the table before he pulled a small doll from the pocket of his coat, made from soft rags and yarn, and offered it to the girl.

"A woman sold them on the street," he said as Olga's small hands closed around the treasure, followed by a bright smile. "I simply could not resist."

My little girl thanked her uncle politely, and clutched the doll to her chest, old spools all forgotten. "You should not spoil her so," I scolded lightly, though in truth I was pleased that he had such heart for my children. They rarely had new toys to play with.

"It looks a little like her, don't you think? It has the same light hair and the blue eyes." He fumbled in his pocket again, and this time his hand held a small orange when it reappeared. "This is for Rudolph." He placed it on the table, next to the empty dishpan. "I am sorry I could not find something of equal value to the doll. I'll keep an eye out for something."

"You shouldn't," I said again but took the fruit and placed it on the shelf next to my tea box to give it to my son after dinner. Then I brought out a cup and poured some coffee for my brother-in-law. It was a bad day and I moved slowly, shuffling rather than walking across the floor. I was ashamed of the state of the apartment too, as I had not been able to clean it as I would have liked. In addition to the laundry, the bucket of slop smelled bad in the corner and tiny fingerprints marred the glass in my window. Not that I worried that Mads would wrinkle his nose at me; I had always known him to be generous.

"So, what happened to your face?" I asked when we had settled at the table. I was thinking something might have befallen him at his work as night guard; perhaps a thief had come upon him in the dark.

His face twisted up with pain before he spoke, though it did not seem to be of the bodily kind. He touched the marking gingerly with his fingertips, then drew his hand across his mustache. He gave a deep sigh. "I don't know what to do."

"No? What is it that's so hard?" I knew it even as I said those words—why else would he come to *me* with his plight?

"She is completely out of bounds—out of bounds," he muttered, not looking at me but at a spot on the papered wall where faded vines entwined with dusty roses. "She threw a bar of soap at me— can you believe it?" His gaze shifted to my face; there was no trace of the happiness from just a few moments ago. "She will not stop spending, and when I complain, she uses foul language and she *hits* me." He said it as if he could not believe it, even with the bruise to prove it.

"Oh no." I had a plummeting feeling inside, as if all my hopes for my sister came tumbling down all at once. "I had been hoping she would be content." It was all I could say; I found no other words. Disappointment and shame mingled in me. How could she do this—harm her own husband—who had been nothing but kind, to my knowledge? "Go play outside for a while, Olga," I said to my daughter, who was back on the floor with the doll. For once, she did not tarry but obeyed me. She never much liked a tense atmosphere. "Don't go far," I called out as the door closed behind her.

Mads sighed and wiped a sheen of sweat from his brow with a handkerchief, then his gaze settled back on me. "I will not fight, but I cannot overlook all her spending—she will bring us into ruin, Nellie, though she will not see it. What am I to do? Just sit there and let her have it all?" He sighed again and his lips tightened as he shook his head with an expression of anguish. "She seemed so sweet when we first married; such a soft and caring *Christian* woman. I cannot see that in her anymore . . ."

"Oh Mads." I reached out and covered his hand on the table with my own. "I wish I could tell you to be patient, that all will work out in the end, but I don't know that it will." It cost me to say those words, to give her up in such a manner, but the bruised and battered man at my table surely deserved some honesty. "She was always such an angry child, but I had hope that maturity and a home of her own would settle all that. I am sad to learn that it didn't."

"She keeps talking of a child"—Mads swallowed hard—"thinking that it would somehow save us both, but we have been married for a while now, and God has not blessed us like that. I cannot help but think that perhaps it is for the best. That the Lord in his wisdom withholds that from us because it would not be safe in our home."

"No, Mads." I shook my head and withdrew my hand. "Not that. Bella has always loved children—she likes them better than other adults, I believe. She would never hurt a child."

"Then why does her womb remain barren?"

"It can be complicated for a woman." The thought of my own struggles sent a shudder through my body. "We never had it easy in our family."

His brown gaze met mine across the table as his lips twisted in a sneer. "She lied to me when we first met. She said your father was a farmer with several acres. I used to think it was sweet how she was ashamed to tell me the truth, but now I can only think of how easily she lied. I should have known it then that she would make a poor wife."

Against my will, I bristled inside. I knew he was in pain and spoke without thinking, but whatever did he know about growing up in squalor? "She was merely ashamed—as was I when I first met John. I didn't lie, but I can see why she did it. We all want to seem a little better than we are in times of courtship. Perhaps she wanted to forget it all; ours was not a happy home."

"Many immigrants come from poverty," he scoffed.

"She was always very proud," I said. "I would not hold it against her. If anything, it means that she cares about your opinion."

He gave a short, bitter laugh on the other side of the table. His coffee was still untouched. "She certainly doesn't *seem* to care. Whenever I speak against her she goes into a *rage*—and I have never lifted a hand against her, I will tell you that as well. I am not a violent man. Maybe I should be, though. Maybe a fist is the only cure for her folly."

I sat quiet for a moment trying to sort through my feelings, but they were not laundry, easy to place in one pile or another, and soon they became tangled in my mind. "It cannot be all bad," I said.

"She keeps a lovely house and is a good cook; your clothes are always clean and neat. If you ever have children, I know she will make a wonderful mother—just look at how kind she is to *my* children."

"Ah, yes." He sighed again. "Perhaps a child truly is the answer," he said. "I have heard that women can go mad without one. Their organs start to wander."

"Just give it a little more time," I said, at a loss as to what else to advise him. "She has not always had it easy, but she has a good heart underneath it all. As you said yourself, she can be both soft and kind—"

"As long as you don't speak against her," he interrupted, and gave another brittle laugh, brimming with both bitterness and bile.

"I don't know what to tell you." I honestly did not. "I don't believe that she meant to misguide you, but perhaps your marriage wasn't all that she had hoped for either."

He touched his fingers to the bruise again. "That much is abundantly clear."

"Perhaps she'll be better in time," I said again, to convince us both.

"Yes." He sounded weary. "Maybe she will—or perhaps she'll be the death of me. Who knows?"

I WAS IN a dreadful state for the rest of the day; not only was my back hurting, but I could not help but think of what he had said. I went through the motions of doing the laundry and preparing a stew with my head in a very different place. I had been hoping so dearly that Bella would settle into marriage and find an ounce of satisfaction, but clearly that was not the case.

While washing potatoes and cutting carrots, I thought that perhaps I should have spoken to Mads sooner—before they even married—but what would I have said? That Bella sometimes got angry and did not like to be opposed, that our family's way was to lash out? He would not even have believed me then, as all he had seen was her gentle side, and I *had* wanted to see her married, to a man with a house no less. No, there was nothing I could have done—but what was she *thinking*? Why would she ruin it for herself in this way? What foolishness had gotten into her head?

"Mama, is something wrong?" Rudolph sat by the table, reading his father's newspapers. He had always been keen in that way, telling my mood with only a glance at my face.

"Nothing more than usual," I told him, gesturing to my back. "See if you can find your sister in the yard; I'll call you in when the stew is ready." It was better if they were not there while I had such dark thoughts swarming in my mind. Hitting her own husband—what a disgrace! Then, quite unbidden, just as the stew came to a boil, I recalled Mother and Father, how their fighting sometimes came to blows, and my cheeks reddened just by thinking of it. Maybe Little Brynhild did not know any better—but how could she *not*? She was brighter than the rest of us combined . . .

John came home while the children were away, and the words came spilling out of me before he had even had time to sit down.

"He cannot be very kind to her," I said with tears streaming down my face. "She would not act in such a way if he were."

John sighed and regarded me calmly. "You know that isn't true," he said as he bent down to untie the laces of his shoes. "You know how she can be, not always guided by reason. Besides," he added, "she is not one to suffer in silence. If Mads had been cruel to her, she would have said so."

I could not argue with that, as I knew he was right, but I so dearly wanted it to be different. "Perhaps I should have seen her more often—helped her out. It cannot be easy to suddenly have a whole house to care for."

John shook his head, looking about as weary as Mads had a few hours before. "You should talk to her," he said. "No one else will, and her husband reached out to you for help."

I slumped down in a chair, still holding the wooden spoon I used for stirring. "I just cannot see what good it would do. She was never one to listen to advice."

But I knew that he was right.

IT TOOK ME nearly three weeks to work up the courage to seek her out. Olga and I went while Rudolph was at school. My daughter held my hand as we made our way down streets lined with elms and lilacs. She skipped and danced beside me on the dirt road, having not a care in the world. Her neat braid bounced on her back.

"What is that, Mama?" She asked and pointed to some colorful flower or a strangely shaped pebble, as we passed between the white-painted houses with lace curtains draped across the windows.

Oh, what I would not give to have a house of my own someday— like Bella had, though she seemed to be doing her very best to ruin her good fortune.

We found my sister in the kitchen, where she was trimming the wicks of some twenty kerosene lamps set out on the table, filling them with fuel and cleaning the soot from the glass chimneys with a cloth. She seemed happy at first to see us, and had me seated by the table while she continued her work, and placed a lump of sugar in Olga's hand, along with a kiss on top of her head.

"You look well," I said, as she did. She wore a burgundy dress with small white dots embroidered onto the fabric, which clung to her in a way that spoke of a new and expensive corset. Her hair was piled high on her head and pinned with tiny pearls. Though she was working and wore an apron, a cameo of carnelian rode upon her collarbone. Though Mads had means, he was not wealthy, and I could see why he was concerned.

"How is your back?" she asked me while pouring coffee and offering me a slice of cake.

"Well enough." Now that I was there, I felt pained—unable to figure out how to broach the subject, but I let her tell me about the things she had bought: satin gloves and a velvet frock, cuts of veal and lamb.

"Not that it makes any difference to Mads," she sneered. "He doesn't know a pig from an ox. I could serve him rats from the gutter without him knowing the difference."

I leapt at this chance but found I could not look at her while I spoke, and stared down at my coffee instead, rich and black in the delicate china. "You're so hard on him." I sipped the coffee, even if it was scalding hot. "Not very kind at all."

To my surprise, she did not try to convince me differently. "He is useless," she huffed, still vigorously polishing glass with the cloth. "He won't look for another job, although the one he has can't keep us fed. He thinks I should settle for less."

I took a deep breath before I continued; my hand shook a little when I guided the china back onto the table. "He looked terrible the last time I saw him—his chin was all black! He said you threw a bar of soap at him."

"Only because he was cruel to me." She did not even flinch.

"I don't believe that, Bella; I think *you* were the one who was cruel. Mads would never lift a hand to hurt you." As I looked at her, standing there so carefree in that lovely, spacious kitchen, I knew in my heart that I was right. "You have to keep your temper in rein. It never brought you anything but misfortune."

Finally, something like pain crossed her features. She dropped the cloth onto the forest of lamps on the table and slumped down in a chair. Her gaze landed on Olga, who was playing with a set of whittled animals on the clean-swept floor. "It's just so hard not having one of your own. I would be better then, if I didn't have this hole in me."

I followed her gaze to my daughter, to the collection of barn animals before her; sloppily painted cows, pigs, and horses that Bella had bought especially for her. "Do you really think that a child is all it would take to make you happy?" I asked. Somehow, I was not convinced. I thought that if she had a little one, she would soon find some other dissatisfaction to occupy her mind.

"Everyone has them. It's hard being the one left out." She moved restlessly on the chair and bit her lower lip, as if about to cry.

"But look at what you *do* have"—I motioned to the room around us—"a nice home, fine clothes, and more food than you can eat. Who would have thought that a girl from Størsetgjerdet could have all that?" It annoyed me how she did not appreciate her stroke of luck but always complained about the things that were lacking.

She snorted in reply. "I won't have it for long, as he doesn't make nearly enough. If we had a child, though—he would be better then, accomplish more. We both would be better then."

"It could still happen." I motioned to my belly, wanting to remind her how hard it could be, how I had struggled to have mine.

"No, I don't believe that it will." Her gaze slid away from me, back to Olga.

"Just be patient," I said.

"You should let me have *her,*" she said, and it was as if a bolt of lightning struck my insides when the meaning of the words sank in. "You can always have another one," she went on, seemingly oblivious to my shock. "Those few weeks she spent with us . . . she seemed to like it well enough and my cooking added some fat to her bones."

"You would take my daughter from me?" I could barely make my voice carry. My whole body tensed up and my heart raced in my chest. Olga stopped playing and looked up at me with alarm.

"Not *take*, no." Bella waved her hand in the air. Her gaze was void of malice but void of compassion too. "I want you to *give* her to me, to make *me* happy and give *her* a better life as well. We have a house and, even now, we have more means than John will ever have. She would have a good life with us, better than the one she has with you."

"Olga belongs with us." I forced my voice to be calm, as not to further upset the child, who was still looking up at me, the cow in her hand all but forgotten.

"Sisters and brothers may come along, and she must share what little she has . . . It will be cramped in the apartment." Bella lowered her voice as well.

"We won't live there forever—"

"Her hands will be calloused from work before she's even seven. If she stayed with me, she would be well fed. Her clothes would be whole and neat—"

"No." The word cracked like a whip in the air. I sat ramrod straight, despite my back. "I won't give you that, Bella—not a child."

"Mama?" Olga asked in a shivering voice, but neither Bella nor I minded her just then. Our gazes were locked on each other.

"But why?" my sister asked. "Children grow up with their relatives all the time." Her expression held no comprehension.

"She is *my* girl." She did not know what she was asking—*could* not know what she was asking.

"You could still see her—"

"No!"

"Mama?" Olga asked again, seeking a confirmation that all was well. I gave her a brief smile, which was all I could muster just then.

Bella looked down in her lap, where her hands fretted at her apron string. Her lower lip pouted slightly. "It would be better for us if we had a child. Mads would do better then. He would find another job for sure, and I wouldn't be so sad all the time if I only had the love of a daughter—"

"No." I rose from the chair and reached out my hand to Olga, who dropped the wooden animal and came to latch her hand into mine. "Children are not cattle to be bought!"

Bella laughed then, loud and shrilling. "Tell that to the little ones at the orphanages, delivered in the night, given up by mothers who want nothing more than to rid themselves of that terrible burden—"

"So be it." I pulled Olga closer to my body and placed my free hand on the side of her head. "But *my* children are not for sale."

"Not now, perhaps, but think ahead. In a few years' time you will loathe them all—"

"I am not like you, Little Brynhild."

"You are exactly like me, Big Brynhild." She rose from the chair and stood before me with her hands resting on her voluminous hips. "We share the same cross, you and I!"

14.

Bella

I had not expected Nellie to give up her daughter, though I surely would have appreciated it if she did. The girl was uncommonly handsome with a soft, round face, and I would not have minded at all to call myself her mama. I knew Mads had wanted her too, and spoke of it often. To him it was all so easy: well-off relatives took on less fortunate children in the family all the time to raise them and give them better opportunities. He figured that Nellie and John would count themselves lucky if we offered to raise Olga as our own. He knew nothing of the toil my sister had gone through to have those mewling infants at her breast, how sometimes reason gave way to baser emotions and stronger ties. It was unfortunate, though, as I surely would have liked to have her. That void inside me was like a rotting tooth; I simply could not help but prod it with my tongue, even if it hurt.

My request stopped Nellie from asking more about Mads, though, so in that respect it served its purpose. She no longer cared about his bruises and complaints once I had suggested taking Olga away from her. My husband had chosen a poor ally who could so easily be diverted. I was furious that he had enlisted her as his confidant to begin with; I had been hoping that his pride would keep him from such foolishness. I added a little laxative to his fish that night, and spent the next hours listening from my spot by the kitchen table as he rushed between the outhouse and the bed. There would be words as well—I could not have him running to my sister for every little thing, but just that night, his pain was all that I wanted.

None of it truly mattered, though—it was inconvenient at best. This world was brimming with the poor and unwanted and I had just thought of another way to get what I most desired.

That summer, they held a children's picnic in the park, where the little ones from the Norwegian orphanage were to have a bit something of what they so rarely tasted: cake and lemonade, sunshine and laughter. The park was brand-new with a road running through it; there was a stream adorned with bridges, and a boathouse with rowboats to rent. At its center stood a horse drinking fountain, providing some comfort to the creatures in the heat.

By the picnic area where the children gathered, they had raised a wooden platform below the ash trees, and generous souls were urged to step onto it to offer a lucky child or two a place in their home. Both the children and their caretakers knew it was a gamble; sometimes such offers turned out to be nothing but a workplace— the generous souls were merely seeking an inexpensive worker— but for those who were lucky, it could mean a good life, and perhaps even a family to call their own.

I was jittery with excitement when the day arrived and I was to step onto that platform and ask if there was a child who wanted to come home with me. I had put on my finest hat, with cherries and leaves of wax crowding at the pull, and a black velvet coat that was much too warm. I could not discard it, though, as I was already slick with perspiration, and my dress soaked through. It would not do to stand there in front of a lawn filled with children and their caretakers with dark stains marring the green cotton of my dress. I wore jewelry too—maybe too much. I wanted to appear as a mother, not a whore, and busied myself with unclasping my necklace and pulling the cheap rings off my fingers while I waited.

I was not alone by the platform; there were other women there as well. They all wore their Sunday best and little cross pendants, putting on a performance just as I was, and succeeding better at it too, to my chagrin. They were all Scandinavians, just like me, like the little ones would be as well. Some children were not orphans at all but came with their struggling mothers who wanted nothing more than to see their children in the care of someone who could properly feed and clothe them. Mads was not there in the crowd, but he knew what I was up to. I had told him of my plans the week before.

"We should consider fostering a Norwegian orphan, maybe two," I said as he had his sausages one evening. I had placed the newspaper before him on the table and pointed to an advertisement for the children's picnic. "Maybe it does not have to be my sister's child. Maybe any little angel will do." He had been a little stumped by Nellie's refusal—which served me well. Perhaps he would not go to her the next time he ached.

"It would be nice with a child in the house." He seemed somewhat uncertain, taken by surprise, perhaps, wanting to have his dinner in peace.

"Wouldn't it just?" I heaped his plate with more food. "I truly think it would be good for me to have a child around. A woman can go a little mad with no one to care for but herself and her husband. I would be better, then, I think . . . I would be happier for sure."

"It *would* be good to see you happy again, like you used to be before."

"You know how fragile women can be. We are meant to care for children." I looked away to hide the smirk that suddenly curved my lips.

"You are right." He let out a deep breath. "That's what's been bothering you all along—I said so to your sister. Of course you need a child to care for."

"Ours would be the happiest house." I rambled on and poured

him a drink. "I would make all kinds of good stuff, meats and puddings. Our orphans would be the best-behaved, most well-fed children in church."

I only had to get one first.

It was quite the spectacle on the lawn before the platform, with all the children gathered around picnic blankets and wicker baskets filled with donated treats. The orphans all wore simple garb: light-colored shirts and dark pants for the boys and starched pinafores for the girls. Glass bottles of pale lemonade shone in the sunlight, and the children's hands were filled with bread and ham. Some of the girls braided flowers into ropes, while the boys played with sticks and leather balls; their chatter rose like a song in the air. Among them sat the women who worked at the orphanages, demurely clad in navy blue. Their eyes were on the platform, silently judging us brave souls who dared tread upon the pine boards. The air smelled of fresh greenery and baked treats, with just a hint of lemon.

A woman with a drab gray dress was speaking right before me. She described how it was her pleasure as a Christian to open her door to an unfortunate soul, and I made a note to mention God as well. They would like that, the matrons at the orphanages. A little piety went a long way with such people. I was annoyed with myself for not wearing my cross; I should have thought to dust off my old church attire.

Finally, it was my turn, and I stepped upon the platform just as the gray-clad woman stepped down. I could not help but smile at the sight before me, all the little ones milling about. "My name is Mrs. Sorensen," I said as loud as I could, and pressed my hands to my chest. "I am sad to say that I have no children of my own." I dropped my gaze and added a quiver to my bottom lip while the audience let my tragedy sink in. Then I took a deep breath and straightened my back before continuing. "What I *do* have is a kind husband and a large house with many empty rooms, and a kitchen brimming with all sorts of nice food." I cocked my head and added a smile. "I do not want a child only to be kind." I raised my hands a little. "I want one because I believe it is in a woman's nature to care for our little ones." I made another little pause. "I keep a Christian home. My husband and I are both Norwegians and would very much like to raise a Norwegian orphan as our own. We both read and write in Norwegian and English and would make sure that the child is educated as well as clean and healthy." I paused again and looked around on the lawn. "Is there any child in need who would like to come home with me?" I did not expect anyone to speak up right away. The offers would come later, after I had departed the platform. The woman who spoke before me was already surrounded by matrons and mothers with toddlers in tow. I felt I had done well, though, as I departed and left the platform to another. My voice had been loud and clear enough to cut through the children's chatter.

I had prepared a basket of sweets, caramels and suchlike, to be distributed among the children in the hopes that it would charm one of their little hearts so much that they would beg their caretaker's permission to go and stay with me. The basket was waiting by the platform's edge, but I had not even reached it before a tall, thin woman guiding a scrawny boy by the hand approached me. I could not understand what she was saying, though. She was speaking Polish or some other such language; her eyes were fierce with desperation. Then there was a woman about my age, carrying a girl. She spoke Norwegian just fine.

"Oh, please take her," she begged me. "We cannot go on like this."

Behind her back, I could see a woman dressed in the orphanage's attire stride toward me with two boys following behind her.

And then there was a man appearing by my side. He did not have any toddlers with him but smiled at me as if he were amused. Something about him snagged my attention, though I could not at once tell what it was. Perhaps it was his eyes: glittering and dark.

"Mrs. Sorensen," he said. "I have the right child for you."

"Really?" I asked over the Norwegian mother's head. "I cannot see a child there with you."

"Ah, no. I thought she was better off away from this ruckus. But she is a lovely child—of Norwegian stock, and in dire need of care."

I gave him another look. His brown cap was simple, his shirt gray with age, but his speech gave him away. This was no ordinary worker at the docks. I had no time for distractions, though; I was to make an important choice, yet despite myself, I was intrigued.

"Just a moment of your time," he begged. "Please, Mrs. Sorensen. I will make it worth your while."

I smiled and apologized, and smiled again at the mothers and matrons, knowing full well that they would soon be watching the next woman who climbed onto the platform and forget all about me. Then I pushed my way through the throng, following the strange man's shirt-clad back, my basket of treats all forgotten.

"So tell me about the child," I said when he finally stopped under an ash tree. "I do hope she is something spectacular, since I just left behind several little angels in need of my help." I felt suddenly ashamed about how it had happened, how I had forgone all propriety to follow this man for no good reason at all. The shame, in turn, became anger. "I have prepared for this day," I told him. "If I return home empty-handed, depriving a poor unfortunate of a better destiny, the blame will be all on you!"

The man did not seem to feel my anger but chuckled a little at my words. "I *do* have a child, Mrs. Sorensen, and I believe she is meant to be yours." He paused and leaned against the tree, still with that aggravating smile on his lips. "She is not mine but left in my care. Her mother is indisposed for a while."

"Is she now?" It was my turn to be amused. "Why would that be?"

"Oh, poor choices were made, but who can blame her? I could spin you some story, Mrs. Sorensen, say that she was recovering from some injury, but that would be an insult to your wit, wouldn't it? This new world promises so much but often gives but a little, and one must eat. Surely we agree on that, Mrs. Sorensen?" The curve of his lips deepened as he plucked a leaf from a hanging branch and set to shred it.

"She is in prison?" I could not believe what he was saying. "And you want me to take her child?" I was about to laugh from the absurdity of it, but my fury won out, and I remained standing before him with my hands on my hips and my chin lifted high. We were about the same height, he and I, but I figured I could still make him feel small. "You are wasting my time, Mr.—?"

"Lee, James Lee." He whipped his cap from his head and gave me a halfhearted bow.

"Mr. Lee, you're wasting my time." And yet I did not go but remained standing there like a fool, wishing to feel that sizzling gaze upon me for just a little while longer.

"She is a sweet toddler, Mrs. Sorensen, only just a year, and as I said, it will be worth your while." He took a slow step back, as if about to go, yet waiting to see if I would call him back.

"How is that?" I could not help but ask. I could not *afford* not to ask. The image of my pantry flashed through my head, and so did the thought of Mads's dwindling accounts.

"Well, there is a mother, indisposed, but a father also, who is not joined in wedlock to said mother. He would rather not see the child starve, even if he can't bring her into his own home. He is prepared to pay you for your trouble."

My heart started racing in my chest. Here was an offer of money landing before me as if it were nothing. Money just for doing what I had set out to do in the first place, namely nurturing a child. "How long will the mother be gone for?"

"Two years at least, maybe three. Perhaps she will not come back for her daughter." He shrugged as if to say that there was some hope that could happen. "If we agree on terms, I will come by every month with cash. It can be a sweet deal for you—for everyone involved."

"What did she do, the mother?" I held my breath while waiting for the answer. I barely heard the clamor from the picnic or felt the heat anymore. All my attention was on him. To see him every month—no, I could not afford to entertain foolish notions. Yet his glittering eyes kept distracting me; the sight of his hands, long-fingered and lean, drew my gaze over and over.

"It's better if you do not know." The amusement was back on his face. "I know they say wickedness travels in the blood, but the girl is much too young to show any such inclinations."

"I was not worried." Why would I be? "Just tell me, why me? Out of all the women speaking here tonight, why did you come to me?" I had worked so hard not to stand out, so why did he pick me for this unsavory mission?

"Mrs. Sorensen," he started, the amusement all but gone from his expression. He buried his hands in his pockets and his body was so relaxed that anyone passing by might have thought we were discussing the weather. He was clever, I figured, clever and bright. "It takes one to know one, as you well know, and I could not help but notice that you appreciate the finer things in life: pretty dresses and suchlike. Your words, though, the way you speak—you were not always well off, and people such as yourself who have just come to money often crave more. I dare suggest that you are not yet quite where you want to be in terms of wealth."

I could not help but laugh at that, my anger from before all forgotten. It was as if he saw straight through me and I found it both baffling and amusing—though had he been a less charming sort of man, the same insight would have left me speechless with fury.

He cocked his head, looking slightly surprised, "You have a beautiful smile, Mrs. Sorensen, if you do not mind me saying so."

I promptly fell quiet. It would not do to seem weak. "Did you ask anyone else to take the girl?" I motioned to the picnic. It somehow would not be the same if he had been hustling all day but not found someone willing to take the child.

"No." Another one of those amused, secretive smiles, as if he knew what I was thinking. "Only you, Mrs. Sorensen. I take care not to waste my time."

Satisfied on that account, I thought it through for a moment. "Bring the girl to me so I can see her," I finally said. "Then we can discuss terms, Mr. Lee."

"I knew you would see sense." He reached out a hand to seal the agreement, and I found myself hesitating before touching it, as if the hand itself were dangerous. When I finally did take it, I found it firm and warm, barely callused—this was no working man in any common sense, just as I had suspected.

I gave him my address before we parted ways.

As I moved back toward the picnic, I dared not look behind me to see if he was still watching me. My coat finally came off, as the day seemed to have grown even hotter around me.

For the rest of the day, whenever my mind happened to drift, I could still see his dark, daring eyes.

What happened next was inevitable.

15.

"You are an extraordinary woman, Mrs. Sorensen." James Lee sat by my kitchen table drinking my brandy. Having him there made the whole room seem new, infused with a sweet tension that was not there before. We were alone in the house except for the child. Mads was working all night.

I had been fretting about it all day. Would he come or would he not? Would he truly bring a child to me and settle my dissatisfaction, even if only for a while?

I had told Mads of what was to happen but also told him not to expect too much. "You never know with such people," I said. "Perhaps they will change their minds and not show."

I had not told him that Anne's mother was in prison; I said she had been ill. I did mention the money, however, as an explanation for my choice. Children from the orphanage did not come with cash. He huffed at that, of course, found it immoral that what he deemed greed had steered me in matters of compassion, but he knew as well as I did that we needed the income dearly, and he would surely enjoy the cheese and roast as well as me.

"You barely know me." I sat down opposite James Lee and poured myself a glass, fighting to keep a steady hand.

"No, but I do know the extraordinary when I see it." He smirked at me, and again I felt that blush staining my cheeks.

"What about you? Are you an extraordinary man, Mr. Lee?" Having him there under my roof made me feel uncomfortable and exhilarated all at once. I did not understand myself. I had to search to find the right words, though I never lacked wit before. The house around me did not seem dirty and empty, or filled with the echoes of things not to be, but young and invigorated by his presence.

James Lee laughed and raised his glass in a toast. "You tell me, Mrs. Sorensen."

Between us on the table was a wad of cash, the bills greasy and worn. The little girl, Anne, sleepy and compliant with laudanum upon her arrival, was already in bed. Oh, how sweet it had been to hold her in my arms and press her soft form to my chest. Such a pretty child too, with dark tresses and blue eyes, almost as lovely as Olga. I could not wait to meet her proper when she arose the next day. I had already prepared another bed for me in the room where she slept, so I could listen to her breathing all night.

"She seems to be a quiet girl. A little dark for a Norwegian," I mused.

"We come in all sorts of coloring, don't we?"

"Of course." And the money was good so I would not complain.

He looked around the room, at my pots and pans. "You have a lovely home. It seems to me a good place for an enterprise such as this. What you need, Mrs. Sorensen, is children who aren't abandoned but secrets someone wants to hide. Then you could charge for their upkeep monthly, and even adjust the price. You'd be surprised to learn how many children like that are born in this city every day. Pregnant mistresses and whores abound." He leaned back in the chair and grinned with his hand around the glass.

"I am doing this from the goodness of my heart. It's not some *enterprise*—"

"Oh, come, Mrs. Sorensen, we both know you would not mind if it were." His eyes glittered merrily across the table. He swept a drop of brandy from his lip with a darting red tongue.

I could not help but laugh a little. "If I am to make this a business, my earnings will be hard won. It's not easy keeping children." I lifted the ruffled collar at my neck a little away from the skin for air. I could not help but think how it would be if it were *this* man I lay next to in bed instead of my stocky husband. This man, with the devil in his eyes.

"It takes so long for them to grow up too." James called me back to the matter at hand. "Which is why it might suit you better to keep those who merely need shelter for a while."

"For a simple man from Norway you know quite a lot about this type of *enterprise*."

"I was born in America, in St. Louis. My parents came from Norway, but neither of them was simple."

"Did they take in children?" I could not help but tease him.

He laughed. "No, I picked up that knowledge elsewhere." Now that I knew he was born in America, I could hear the American accent hidden in his Norwegian.

"Is this to say, Mr. Lee, that you are prepared to offer me more children to keep in my house for cash?" I had to look away while I spoke; I found the sight of his lips most distracting.

"It is." His eyes were glittering again in that way that they did and I busied myself with counting the cash, although I had already done it once before.

"It would certainly make it less wholesome, less about the goodness of my heart and more about Mammon," I muttered with my hands full of bills.

"What do you think would bring you more pleasure? Satisfying your conscience or lining your purse with gold?" I wished that he would not speak of pleasure. His hand around the glass distracted me—oh, to think what those fingers would feel like traveling on my skin.

"Do you think me so simple that it's all about the gold?" I tried to mask my discomfort with words.

"Yes, Mrs. Sorensen, I do." His smile never wavered. Our gazes met briefly across the table.

"What would your part in this *enterprise* be?" I dropped my gaze to the bills.

"I would provide the children, of course."

"And your price?"

"None—not from you."

I snorted. "No one does something for nothing."

He threw his head back and laughed. "I'll take my share on the other end," he said, when the laughter had died out. "I'll charge to find the children a suitable home. As for you, I think it is enough to know that I have a friend who might help me out someday." The longevity implied in his statement was both disturbing and thrilling. I did not quite know what to do with this man, with the way that he made me feel.

"So you want this to be a home for the children of thieves and whores." It was a statement, not a question. It did not leave me shocked, as perhaps it ought to.

"The money would never run out if you choose to go into business with me." His eyes glittered merrily.

"That is certainly a tempting prospect." I licked my lips, tasted the liquor.

"Isn't it just?" He laughed again; it was a soft, purring sound. "I can be a good friend to a woman such as yourself, who has seen hardships and seeks some solace." He winked at me across the table. "I would never take you for a fool, Mrs. Sorensen, you can be sure of that."

"What makes you think I'd be a suitable business partner for a man like you?" My chest heaved a little from the exhilaration, straining against the tightness of the corset.

James Lee leaned toward me and caught my eyes. "I know hunger when I see it. I know what you want and how you may get it. If you think you can trust me, the two of us may go far."

"No farther than this kitchen table, I reckon." I huffed and looked away, then felt myself redden from my own words. It seemed no matter what I said to him, it was treacherous somehow, brought all sorts of images in its wake.

He smirked and downed his drink. "We'll see, Mrs. Sorensen . . . We'll see."

"SO THIS IS her." Mads looked at us with wonder as he rose the next day to find me in the kitchen, spooning milk-soaked bread into Anne's little mouth. "This is the little girl who will make us all better."

"This is her." I gave him a smile. "This is Anne, and she is of good Norwegian stock."

"She is a good girl." He gently trailed the girl's scalp with his fingers. "Maybe you won't be so angry all the time now that you have her."

I swallowed the annoyance that flared up in me. "No." I pressed my lips tightly together. "Now I will be happy for sure."

I enjoyed having the girl around. She kept my mind occupied. I enjoyed bathing and dressing her, and the rare smile that lit up her features. I enjoyed that she wanted only me, and reached for me when I entered the room. I longed for her to grow older, to talk with her and sing songs to her. I ogled toys I saw on display in shop windows and brought home tiny dolls, although she was far too young for that.

We had set up a small bed in the vacant room and it was the happiest I had been since the first days of our marriage when I sewed and embroidered little covers for her pillows and hung white muslin curtains in the window above her bed. I moved a lacquered armoire into the room and filled it with small dresses, and even bought a music box to help her go to sleep. Little Anne was my darling angel who could fill the emptiness of the house. If Mads thought my spending on the girl too lavish, he did not say a word.

I enjoyed the smiles that greeted me at church functions, as the congregation admired not only Anne but the size of my heart as well. Mostly, though, I enjoyed parading her among strangers who did not know she was not mine. I was her mother for real then, proudly showing off my daughter. I told everyone who wanted to hear: the girl behind the counter, the clerk at the bank, and couples we met in the park, about how sickly she had been at birth. How I nursed her back to health.

I immensely enjoyed the money too, and the man who delivered it to my door.

I HAD NEVER understood what other women spoke of when they described their longing and need for a certain man. I had longed for Anders and been flattered by his attention, but my infatuation had been much about what he could provide. With James, it was different. It was raw, this feeling, like a pull. I lay awake in bed every night, no matter how tired, thinking about his hands on my skin. Come morning, I would look at myself in the tarnished bedroom mirror and judge the thickness of my brown hair and the shade of my complexion.

Maybe it was the kinship I sensed that made him so enticing to me. Maybe it was the sense of danger. Some days I loathed him for the lust he inspired, as I felt it left me at a disadvantage—as if he had a sway over me. Other days it was what pulled me through hours of cooking and mending. Potato peeling had never been as sweet as when I had him to think of.

James always came at night when Mads was at work. I never knew exactly when but placed a kerosene lamp on the windowsill to let him know when the house was empty. Our friendship was one of shadows and moonlight, a heady drug to the senses. I was surprised that a man like him would take such a keen interest in me, a housewife with a spotless reputation, but I reveled in the fact that he did. He brought out the best in me, James Lee: he helped me see the possibilities.

"I bet you could be anyone," I told him one night when the bottle between us was half empty. "I bet you could shed your skin like a snake."

"I once was a merchant from Germany," he said, chuckling, "another time a salesman from Prague. I have been an envoy to a Turkish ambassador and a general in the Swedish army. Mostly, though, I am nobody—just a Norwegian immigrant working at the docks. I have found that can take me far."

"You are such a slick fish slipping through the net." My flattery was entirely sincere.

"No more than you, my dear. You know how to blend in like me. It's the mark of a true survivor—we adapt and we change whenever we have to." The light from the kerosene lamp painted his face in gold.

"You cannot change your nature, though." I straightened up a little. His fingers were splayed out on the glass of golden liquor. Splayed out as on skin.

"Would you even want to?" I could hear the smile in his voice.

"Sometimes . . ." I looked at the bottle and scratched at the label, peeled it a little from the glass.

"Would you truly be like the dull people around you, satisfied with what little they have? No, Bella, you are more than that. Those other people, they are like mice, scurrying on the ground, but you"—he paused and lifted the glass—"you are a cat."

"Rats," I corrected him and lifted my gaze to his face. "They are rats."

"And you eat rats. You eat them all up, bones and innards and long pink tails. You are nothing like them." His voice had dropped to a husky whisper.

"Do you enjoy it, James? Eating rats?" I filled our glasses anew.

The sweet liquor smelled warm and safe; the man, however, was not. When I put the bottle down again, my heart was beating wildly.

"I eat what I need to survive—and yes, if I have my claws in a particularly fat rat, I like it." He said it as if it were nothing at all; a pang of sweetness exploded in my belly.

"You never even feel sorry for the rat?" I leaned back in the chair and did not even try to hide my admiration when I looked at him. I wished I had taken more care with my hair, and that my dress had not been so drab and plain. For once, it did not make me uncomfortable looking into another's eyes; our locked gazes were like a bridge between us, dripping with lust and danger.

"Did *you*?" he asked, and made me startle enough that I looked away. "Did you feel sorry for the rat?" He cocked his head and smiled.

"What rat?" I ran my tongue over my lips, suddenly feeling hot all over.

"Oh, I'm sure you have one, or you wouldn't be so comfortable asking me about mine." He sent me a lazy wink and sipped his liquor. Droplets of whiskey caught in his mustache and glittered in the kerosene light.

"If you are right and there *is* a rat, why would I tell *you*—a stranger?" I lifted my chin just a little.

His hand landed on mine on the table; his skin was cool from cradling the glass. "Am I, though? A stranger?"

"I have never had many friends." I halfheartedly tried to pull my hand away, but he grasped and held on with his fingers.

"Well, you have one now. You intrigue me, Bella. There's *malice* in you." He lifted his head and measured me, as if seeing me anew. He did not smile anymore.

"How would you know?" I fought to withdraw my hand again, but he held on.

"The same way you know me, I suppose. We are the same, you and I." He said it as if it were the truth.

I let out my breath and finally relaxed my hand under his, savored the feel of his skin. "The rat had it coming." I could not quite believe that I did it—spilled my secret as if it were nothing. It lay between us on the table like a red, pulsing thing.

"Rats have it coming just for being rats." His hand on mine had grown warmer. "What was your father like?"

"I did not kill my father, Mr. Lee." I laughed a little, quiet and insincere.

"I was only guessing. It's so often the father who brings out the claws in a woman . . ."

"My father is a good-for-nothing drunk with hard fists, but he's still alive. Unlike my mother, whom he wears—wore—down." Thinking of her death made my throat thicken.

"Was he protective of you as a child?"

"Not at all." I felt my lips twist into something cold and ugly. "He thought that I had it coming, everything that happened to me. Even when this old man down at the farm stuck his hand up my skirt when I was eight, he thought I shouldn't complain. I shouldn't have been alone with him in the first place, he said . . . Tenants' daughters weren't worth much back home, not even to the tenants. He acted as if I should be proud someone bothered sniffing up my skirts at all."

"And yet you left him alive." James's voice was soft; he gave my fingers a little squeeze. Veins stretched like snakes under the skin on the back of his hand.

"Maybe I shouldn't have. Maybe I should have eaten him up." I smacked my lips as if tasting it.

"No one would hold it against you, I'm sure." Another little smile appeared. They were intriguing, those smiles, as if he knew a secret. As if he found amusement where others might not. It made me want to see it too, what he found so thrilling.

"No one but God," I said, from habit rather than conviction.

"God." James snorted and lifted his glass. "He has not bothered for a long, good while."

"The devil, then." I gave him a smile to let him know I was only speaking in jest.

"Oh, *he*—he is all around us." James laughed a little and lifted his hand away from mine to fill our glasses. I instantly missed his warmth. "To rats," he said, and lifted his share; the golden liquor spilled down on the table. "To rats and those who eat them."

When our glasses were back on the table, I said, "There was one rat. One I met here, while I lived with my sister. He tried to force himself on me, so I stabbed him."

His eyebrows rose. "You did?"

"With scissors." I could not help but smile at the memory. "He bled some, but he did not die. He recovered with just a scar. The other women thought I was wrong to do it, but I wasn't. He had it coming. He shouldn't have tried to force me." The smile turned into a grimace.

"It's a shame he survived." James swilled the contents of his glass, looking at it with a thoughtful expression. "But you would surely have hanged if he did, so in that way it was a blessing. One needs stealth to accomplish an act like that and walk away unscathed."

"I know, I do—I was stealthy before." I did not want him to think me a fool.

"It's hard to be stealthy when under attack." He gave me an understanding look. "It's a shame, though, that he walks around with nothing but a scar for what he tried to do."

"Yes, isn't it just?" I wished that James would take my hand again.

"Men like that should never touch a woman like you. It's like a baboon courting a tigress." He lifted his glass.

"At least I got him with those scissors." I lifted my glass in turn.

I WANTED JAMES to become my lover since the very first day we met, even if I sometimes wished it were not so. He stirred something in me that Mads never could. Looking at him, I sensed danger and blood; looking at Mads I saw lukewarm milk left too long in the pot. The marital bed had always been disappointing to me. Ironed nightshirts and soft skin never much excited me; I needed a devil's touch. I wanted it to be a battle on the sheets, a dangerous fight to survive. I did not want it to be nice; I wanted it to hurt. I was certain James could give me that.

On the night when it first happened, the two of us were out in the backyard. It was a nice, moonlit night; a frog sang in the distance and we were sharing a bottle out on the steps. I had two girls living in my house by then, Anne and another one called Lizzie. The latter had been scrawny when she arrived, but my cooking had already put some meat on her bones. She was not yet three, which suited me well. I liked them best as toddlers.

James retrieved something from his pocket, so small that it disappeared in his fist. "I brought you a present." He reached his hand toward me.

I held out my hand palm up and felt him drop something smooth and cold into it. When I held it up to catch the light from the lamp we had brought with us, I could tell it was a pewter button. Stamped onto its face was a flower with four broad petals. "What is this?"

"Oh, just a token of something I took care of for you."

"What do you mean?" I still inspected the button. It was a fine button, but it meant nothing to me.

"I think you'll find that your rat is no longer around."

"Oh, you didn't." I cocked my head and looked at him; my heart was suddenly racing. The flickering light from the lamp licked his face with warm tongues.

His lips split in a smile. "I did," he said with undisguised glee. "That thing you're holding is from his coat. I thought that you might want it."

"How did you even know who it was?" I squinted toward him in the dim lighting, searching for some sign of dishonesty on his face, proof that he spoke in jest, but found none.

"Words travel fast, and that story about the scissors was well known. It was nothing." He took a swig from the bottle. "From Bergen, was he? That little rat?"

I admired the button with a new appreciation. "He truly is dead, then?" I could not yet believe it, that James had done that for me.

"Yes, quite . . . I left him in an alley behind his boardinghouse." He sounded smug.

"Are you sure no one saw you?" It would not do to lose my friend to the law.

"Of course, and I didn't look like me when I did it. I'm clever in that way." His laughter was easy; he was pleased with himself.

"I'm sure." I laughed a little as well; I held the button up to the light to let the flame ignite its luster. It needed a bit of polishing for sure, but it was a pretty thing. A dozen butterflies swarmed in my stomach when I thought about Edvard's death; it was only right— what he deserved. This justice was long overdue. I glanced at James again, his proud face when he looked at me. If I had been in jeopardy of losing myself to him before, this little piece of pewter certainly sealed my fate. Never before had I met a man who would do what needed to be done for my satisfaction. He saw me so clearly—saw me as I was.

"The news will get out soon enough." He took another swig of the bottle. "It seemed too gentle to let him off with just a scar."

"Well, this certainly seals our friendship." I dropped the button into the pocket of my apron. I could not stop smiling, could not quench the sense of triumph that had my heart racing.

"Seals a little bit more than that, I hope." James rose to kneel before me on the step. He took my hand and kissed it, then leaned over me and kissed me on the lips. I had waited a long time for that kiss, and when I finally had it, it was even sweeter than imagined, leaving me tingling and heady with want. James pushed me down on the stairs. Not rough yet, but almost gentle. Then his arms locked around my waist and his teeth sank into the soft skin on my neck, biting down. I hissed from pain but from pleasure too. "Let's celebrate the death of a rat," he whispered.

Not before long, James's fingers were tugging at my skirts, hiking them up over my hips. His fingernails scratched my thighs as he fought to get between them. He fumbled with his suspenders and dropped them off his shoulders. I know I helped him pull down his pants and was satisfied to feel him firm in my hand. Then he was inside me, pushing hard and careless. He hid his face against my shoulder to muffle his ragged moaning, held on to me like a drowning man to quench the shivers that ran through him. Soon I was shivering too. The moon shone brightly on the velvet sky; the frog still sang in the distance.

Not once did I think about the lake.

When we were quite done, we had drinks in the kitchen. I fried sausages and onions in the pan. I could not remember ever feeling so starved as I did that night; it was as if I could not get enough. My back was bruised from lying on the stairs, but I barely felt it; I was too excited.

James came up behind me as I flipped the second serving. His hand grabbed between my legs through the fabric of my skirts. His mustache was wet with brandy; it stung the torn skin on my neck.

"Yes," he said into my ear, "we truly are the same, you and I."

The next day I found a chain for the pewter button and hung it around my neck. I carried it with me always, tucked away under my shirtwaist. When Mads asked, I said it had belonged to my father and reminded me of home.

It was as good as a wedding band to me, that button.

Meant more than the gold on my hand.

16.

Nellie

I was so relieved when Bella took in those girls. Her asking to raise Olga had driven a wedge between us that I had found it difficult to overcome, and so I had stayed away for a while. When she had other children to care for, it was easier.

John had not shared my strong feelings in the question's wake but had thought it all very reasonable—generous even. "They only want to help," he had said one night, propped up next to me in bed, "and help themselves besides. It is hard for them not to have children of their own."

"If we had seven of them I would have seen the point of it," I replied, "but we only have the two, and so it seems strange that they would offer such help."

"Soon there will be three." John patted my belly through the blanket, though I barely showed.

"If we are lucky." I harbored even more doubts than usual. Not only did my body ail, but I was growing old too. If I carried to term, the birth would be hard—*too* hard perhaps. Age was no one's friend in such matters, and a sunset child was rarely a joy, at least not for the battered mother. Little Brynhild had been such a child, born after Mother had thought she was too old.

"Mads knows very little of poverty." John tried to soothe me by stroking my cheeks with the back of his hand. "To him, we might seem poorer than we are, and in dire need of charity." He tried to laugh it off, but it did not reach his eyes. It hurt his pride, I could tell.

"But Bella, though. She ought to know better."

"Ah, you know how she is." He rolled over on his back. "She only sees her own needs, not others'."

"Do you really believe that?"

"I do." He said it in a thoughtful manner. "She would want Olga for herself, not because it was best for the girl."

"You do not know her as I do," I huffed, and rolled over as well. Through the open door, I could just make out the bench in the kitchen where both of my children lay sleeping. I closed my eyes and made to sleep as well but could not stop thinking of what he had said. "Why do you think her so selfish?" I asked in the darkness.

"Oh, it is only from the way she treated you when you were carrying Olga, and the way she behaves toward her husband. She only took him for the money, that much is clear. She only wants what she can use to feel a little better."

"You should not speak such harsh words about my sister." My voice had turned cold, yet my heart was racing in my chest.

"No? Then why is it that you will not forgive her for asking to raise your daughter?"

To my own great chagrin, I could not answer that—could not figure why it wounded me so, why it made me want to hold my little girl tight. I felt as I had that time on the riverbank, before the snarling dog, when I snatched Little Brynhild up from the ground to save her from the danger.

That was how I felt—as if Olga were not safe.

Perhaps it was the memories of Mads's colorful bruises and our father's large fists that made me feel uncertain. Perhaps she reminded me a little of the latter sometimes, the way she raged and lashed with her tongue, and how she carried old grudges like painful pearls around her neck. It was not her fault. None of us who grew up at Størsetgjerdet escaped that place unscathed; some of us turned out meek and better, but others were too deeply wounded for that, or carried too much of that tainted blood—the kind that made you mean.

She did try, though; I wanted to believe that she did. I wanted to think that it bothered her conscience and pained her soul whenever that wicked streak surfaced. I would not believe that she looked at the markings she had left on Mads's skin and did not feel a thing. Her temper was a challenge, but surely she fought it! She, too, had to remember those nights after a beating, when she lay in the loft at Størsetgjerdet and wept into the hay, overcome with anger and humiliation. So much anger that had nowhere to go but into that musty mattress.

She would never do that to another, would she? She would never want to see another person so bruised. Not if she could help it— which sometimes she could not—but surely it pained her when she failed!

Perhaps I feared what would happen if my daughter was there the next time that wickedness burst forth. Perhaps that was why her request to take Olga had touched me so deeply and wounded me so.

Her foster daughters changed that, though, and after my first visit after their arrival, I could not even think what foolishness had possessed me to think such dark thoughts about Bella.

It was a clear day in fall; the trees had just let loose a torrent of colorful leaves, but the sun was still hot enough to warm the air. We let the girls out to play in Bella's backyard while we did her mending on the steps. Anne stayed close to our skirts, wandering about on stubby legs and filling her hands with leaves, while Lizzie, a little older, ventured all the way to the lilac on the other side of the yard to pick the leaves directly from the tree.

"Do not eat it!" Bella called across the distance, though it was doubtful that the child paid any attention. "I have to keep my eyes on them at all times," she huffed, but her gaze was sparkling and her movements were light, as if she had become a girl again herself, just from being in their youthful presence. I could tell of her joy from their appearance as well: the neatly combed hair and the ironed dresses, the thick, blue coats that cocooned their round bodies.

"One light and one dark," I noted, looking at their heads. "Surely you must be pleased."

"Oh, they are such treasures." She smiled down at them. "I only wish that they were mine for real."

"You never know with such things—perhaps their mothers will never recover." I did not say this to be cruel but because it was the truth. I also said it because I dearly wanted it to be so, that Bella would be able to keep them.

"That's certainly something to wish for." Bella put the mending down in the basket between us and strode out in the yard. "Come closer, Lizzie! Come closer! I will not have you walking behind the shed!" She took the girl by the arm and guided her closer to the other. "Isn't it fun with all the leaves?" she cooed, then filled her hands with the yellow downfall and threw them up in the air. "Look," she called, "it's raining leaves!" She scooped more of them up from the ground and let them drizzle upon the girls' delighted faces. Soon she was spinning each of them around in turn, stood there in the backyard with her brown dress and her apron, lifting each girl high up in the air to twirl with them in her arms, looking much like a goddess of fall when her skirts sent the leaves spinning too.

After several of these twirls, she showed the girls how to drizzle the leaves upon each other, and soon Lizzie was at it with much vigor, showering the younger girl in fall's gold. Bella kissed their little heads before coming toward me; her cheeks were red and her eyes were sparkling.

"Are you wearing your husband's shoes now?" she asked me as she neared the stairs, raising her eyebrows a little. She had noticed the much-mended foot attire that peeked out under my skirt.

"Ah yes, my feet are so swollen." I added another two stitches to one of Mads's shirts. "I can barely walk in my own shoes. It is worse this time, far worse."

"I offered to take some of the burden off your hands." She saw fit to remind me of it, and a bit of a sting erupted in my chest; I would rather not speak of that. Would not feel that darkness again.

"It will be better as soon as it's born." I made an effort to keep my voice steady and calm. "Besides, you have filled your house just fine without my help."

"Yes, haven't I just." She laughed and paused to thread her needle. "They certainly keep my hands occupied—and I might even take on yet another."

I laughed too. "I admire your heart, Bella. Even if the mothers *do* recover and they leave, it is a good thing you do, taking care of them while their mothers are sick. They are such small girls too, and no help in the house. Not many women would do that."

"Well," she chuckled, "it certainly impresses the women at church, but that is not why I do it, of course. I just cannot think of them suffering at some orphanage."

"What is that?" I motioned to her neck with the needle; a large red bloom marred the side of it. "That is a nasty sore. What happened?"

She lifted her hand at once to press two fingers against the mark. "Oh, nothing—I was careless with the iron."

"You burned your neck?" That sounded most peculiar. Why would she lift an iron to her neck?

"I was sloppy and distracted." Her good humor had suddenly clouded over with annoyance. I hated when that happened, as I never knew whether I would be able to coax her good cheer back again.

"Indeed." I tried not to, but now that I had seen it, it was hard not to look at that mark. It looked almost like a love bite, and I briefly wondered if the girls' arrival had reignited something between her and Mads, but then I thought that was unlikely. Mads was not the sort of man to leave shameful bruising on his wife. "You have to be careful, you have children to look after now." And I did not mean only with the iron. I had never thought of Bella as the type to chase men, but one never knew, and things had certainly not been easy between her and her husband. I just did not want her to ruin it now that things were going so well, and she had the little ones to fill the empty space around her.

"Did you hear about Edvard?" she suddenly asked. She did not look at me but at the girls.

"Edvard who?" I did not remember at once.

"Edvard from Bergen, the one I stabbed in your kitchen. He is dead." Her voice was very calm.

"What?" My mouth felt dry.

"Yes, he was *killed*." Bella's voice rose a bit. "He was gutted like a fish, right behind his boardinghouse. It was in the newspaper and all." She finally turned her gaze on me, brimming with astonishment.

"Oh, that's terrible." And I wished she had not told me. Why ruin such a beautiful day with talk of past quarrels and dreadful murder? "Do they know who did it?" I asked, only because I felt like I had to, and not from any real curiosity.

"No . . . they say it was a robbery"—she lifted her chin—"but I cannot figure how any thief would be foolish enough to think he'd have anything worth stealing." A mocking sneer appeared on her lips and lingered for a moment before it went away, as if it had never been.

"No," I agreed, feeling faint. "There is that."

"Maybe it was some drunken quarrel," she mused.

"That certainly sounds likely," I agreed. "I cannot say I mourn him, but it's a sad way to go."

"Yes, isn't it just." Bella's lips twisted up again, as if she could barely withhold the glee.

It pained me to see it, so I looked away.

17.

Bella

Chicago 1887–1893

For the first few years of our acquaintance, James was a fever I could not shake. He would often come to my door just as Mads left for work, and rap at the wood with his clever fingers, and I did not tarry in letting him in.

If I suspected he would come, I gave the children a little laudanum in their milk so they would sleep while James and I made use of the bed in the empty room. Our trysts were never quiet, never calm, but they never brought me back to the lake. Perhaps because I gave as much as I got. Often I would find myself on top of him, pinning his arms to the bed while I rode him; other times I would find his hand around my throat. I would force his head between my legs; then he tied me to the bedposts. It was shameless what we did, but in the end, it was just a game without a victor. I never felt bested with James Lee; he never aimed to make me feel small, and I found that I enjoyed our fight on the sheets. It made me feel alive. James could make me feel more in a night than Mads could in a lifetime.

When James was not there and the house felt dark and empty, I would sometimes slip inside that room with its walnut bed, and curtains of green damask drawn before the windows, just to take in his scent and savor it. It was like a whiff of summer on a rainy day, a taste of sweet caramel when all you had to eat was unsalted gruel. I felt that I cheated the house of my misery by keeping that room for us two.

I could have tolerated the endless cooking, the washing and the ironing, the sweeping and the folding, if Mads could have only been quiet. I had no quarrel with wifely duties—I knew what was expected of me—but I could not stomach his constant complaints. The words he whined at me whenever he saw fit, to spend less when he never earned more, our pantry void of fresh meat. I had not married him to live like a poor woman, and I had told him so many times, yet he never as much tried for a better position. Never even reached for a grander life than he had. How could I be blamed for losing my temper?

The meekness I thought I wanted when I accepted his marriage proposal served me no good in the end. He was weak—that was what he was—but still he felt it in his right to judge me. The resentment grew in me like a boil. Had it not been for James and the relief he brought, it might have come to proper blows. As it was, I was sometimes moved to hurl something at him, or land a hard slap on his cheek.

I was still a respectable churchgoing woman, though, and did not want it any other way, even if Mads was a disappointment. I had worked so hard to leave my sorry past behind, to climb as far as I had come, and I was not about to abandon the fruits of my labor, even if I despised my husband with his crisp shirts and polished shoes, his relentless demands, his whining and sulking. I wanted the house, even as I loathed it, even the mold-infested pantry. I had sworn to be a woman to admire—just to spite—and that was what I would be.

James Lee did not understand it.

"You should elope with me," he said one day at my table. His eyes were mischievous, his voice honey sweet. "Just think of what we could accomplish."

I snorted. "The two of us could never build a wholesome life together."

"Is that what you want? A *wholesome* life?"

"Isn't that what everybody wants?"

He lit his cigar with a sputtering match and puffed on the body until the tip smoldered. "I don't understand you—never did." His face was obscured by blue smoke.

"Be as that might, the two of us together would never work." James could always excite me, but he belonged to the shadows in my life, slithered there as a hot, sweet secret, fiery and strong. He was my lover and my friend—not a husband.

"You are not one for sentiments, that's for sure. At times I have thought you liked me—*loved* me, even—giving me of your time and your mind. Other times I think you quite despise me." I could not read his expression just then.

"Can't I do both?" I was fanning myself with a newspaper, chasing away the heavy cigar smoke that wafted across the table.

"You *do* know how to please a man. Too bad it's all lost on your husband." His eyebrow rose a little.

"Men are easy." My gaze fell on the window, where a few flies were battling for freedom. "Give them good food and comfort, let them talk about themselves . . . I'm not much to look at, but I know how to flatter."

"You are quite lovely, I'd say." James laughed. "Did you ever consider widowhood?" His eyebrows rose teasingly. "It would be easy; you know that." He always made murder sound as simple as picking ripe fruit from a tree. It was tempting the way he said it, as if we were children about to do mischief.

"Sometimes." In truth, I thought of it often. Especially when I was lying awake next to my husband, listening to his wheezing snores, imagining what it would be like to have him convulsing on the sheets. I remembered how delicious it was when Anders died, and so longed for that same feeling. I was angry with Mads for not giving me what I needed, for talking to me as he did, for being nothing but a rat, shivering and helpless. For forcing me to live with him, day after day through our marriage bond, and yet—I always thought better of it.

"I need his income. What I get for the children isn't enough." My pantry would slowly empty without him; my clothes would fall into rags. I would have to take in filthy lodgers, and maybe even wash and mend. I did not worry about suspicion—husbands die all the time—but I did worry about money. "He is not much of a man, but I need him."

"I'm sure there are other ways."

"Of course, but I don't much care for them." James meant I should kill my husband and join in *his* enterprise, but the life of a thug did not compel me—where was the spite in that? I leaned back in the chair and folded my arms over my chest. "I tinker with his coffee sometimes. I add a few drops of the children's medicine, or a few grains of rat poison if he has been difficult. It serves him well to lie there with stomach pains—it leaves him weak for a time too; it gives me time to think." Being with James had emboldened me. I did not pick the fruit from the branch, but at least I dared to taste it. I could punish Mads, or silence him for a while, and that, at least, was something.

I wanted my husband gone, but I could not afford it.

James Lee could always distract me. "Come here," he said when my mind grew bitter, and when I arrived, he pulled me down in his lap. His kisses were hard and tasted of tobacco; his hand in my hair was not kind. "Show me the button," he whispered, just to have me remove my shirtwaist so he could lay his hands on my breasts through the corset. Soon enough I was on the table with my skirts pushed up around my waist, and he was in me, hard and ready. Just where I wanted him to be.

I never grew tired of James Lee.

ALL MY FOSTER children left in the end. Both Anne and Lizzie went back to their mothers. I told myself I had always known the girls were borrowed, but it did not prevent me from missing their happy chatter and their light steps on my floors. The rooms seemed so very empty without them. James brought me other children, but they never stayed for as long as I liked. Whenever he appeared with a bundle for me to take, I already knew that the child would not stay, and so the bliss of motherhood eluded me.

In dark nights, with my jaw aching, I would cradle my empty belly in my hands and will it to come alive. Just one seed, one blessed stickling, to whisk all my misery away. I often wished I could bring Anders back to life, so I could kill him again for taking it all away from me—but none of my wishing could fill my womb.

The one thing to bring me solace happened in late 1888, when Mads sat me down by the kitchen table, which was not as white as ivory anymore but had taken on a gray, dusty shade.

"Do you recall the girl I told you about? Ole Olson's daughter?" he asked me.

"Of course!" How could I not? Mads had often spoken of his friend's wife, who was unlikely to survive after a hard birth. She had lingered for some months, but her prospects were dire. The couple had asked us to take the child should the mother die but the daughter survive. I had thought of the girl every day since, and visited the vacant children's room where the little beds and the neatly folded clothes lay ready to welcome a new child.

"They want us to come, tonight. The poor woman is not expected to survive much longer." Mads's bottom lip quivered. He felt sad for his friend, who was losing a wife.

"How old is the girl now?" I could only think of her.

"Eight months." Mads's face was grave before me, respectful of the circumstances, but I could not be more joyous. Eight months was perfect. She would have no memory of her first mother as she grew older, and could easily be weaned of the milk.

"I'll go change my dress." I wanted to go at once, and that very same night I met Jennie for the first time. Fair of hair and blue of eyes, always so quiet and gentle.

Her mother was close to death when we arrived, but she found the strength to place the swaddled child in my arms. With her face pale and damp against the pillows, she made me swear to keep her as my own, which I readily did. I even had a smile for my husband that night, for facilitating this happy occasion through his friendship. He might not have given me much of what I wanted, but *this* he had managed at least.

I felt triumphant when I left that bedside, as if I finally had received some justice—payment for all I had suffered. It was nothing more than what I deserved.

Jennie was mine ever since.

18.

Chicago, 1893

The World's Columbian Exposition overtook Chicago with a glorious madness. Out of the swamp rose a city of gleaming white, with all the wonders of the world inside, from the thousands of singers in the Choral Hall to the hundreds of roses in the Horticultural Building. You could see a map of pickles, a bridge of sugar, a chocolate Columbus, and a castle of soap. There was even a Viking ship, rowed all the way from Norway.

Had Jennie been a little older, I might have seen more of it, but she was at five a delicate child whose feet easily tired, and so we mostly stayed away. I did not feel bereft, however; my days with Jennie brought me more joy than any of the magnificence to be seen. Finally, I had a child without a living mother, and though she did have a father, I never truly feared that he would come and take her away—fathers so rarely miss their children.

All through the world fair year, the Norwegians gathered in a beer garden on the Midway. The latter was not a part of the fair but had become one nevertheless, with sword dancers, snake charmers, and beautiful girls on display. I had been there before with Mads, but he did not care much for excessive drinking, and the cigar smoke made his eyes water. He had wanted me to settle for a cup of hot cocoa. I insisted on gin.

This night I was alone with no surly husband in tow, and I meant to make the most of it. I had hired a girl to mind my darling Jennie, who would be sleeping soundly in her bed by now, her fair head resting on lace-edged pillows. Surely she would not mind my absence for one night. My friends from church were not there, of course, but I reacquainted myself with some of Nellie's friends from Milwaukee Avenue. They were still a rowdy lot, still eager to drink and dance. We sat at long tables in a pavilion lit by electric lightbulbs. A dusky woman dressed in red played the violin; colorful pennants hung from the ceiling. We lifted our glasses to king and country and to our Viking ancestors. It was pleasant to hear my mother tongue all around me, the singsong tunes of the dialects.

"Did you see the Javanese orchestra yet?" Nellie's old neighbor, Clara, asked. She had a beer in her hand and her eyes were glassy with drink. She had not quite taken to me back when I lived with John and Nellie—none of my sister's friends had, truth be told—but the brew seemed to have made her forget that we were never the best of friends.

"No." I shook my head. "Not yet. Do you come here often?"

"As often as I can. I won't miss a moment of the fair if I can help it." She threw back her head and laughed, showing off gums with a few teeth missing. I ran my tongue over the sharp edge of my own broken tooth.

"Mads thinks it too expensive to go." I could not help but roll my eyes.

"That's why he isn't here, then?" She looked around as if he would suddenly appear in the crowd.

"He is working, poor soul, but he doesn't begrudge me a night of fun." I forced myself not to smile from the lie.

"Sounds like a kind man." Beer sloshed from her glass and ran down her fingers. "My husband wouldn't be so kind if I went here without him."

"He probably likes to have fun, then, your husband." I looked down the length of the table, at all the laughing, red-faced Norwegians. "There are so many visitors from outside the city. I guess they all want to see the fair."

"Some came up from Minnesota yesterday and my cousin came from Indiana last week. Who would want to miss out on it?"

"Have Nellie and John been down tonight?"

Clara shook her head. "No, I haven't seen them. I suppose Nellie is ill again. You know how it is with her back."

"Our mother was the same," I told her. "It's the child carrying that does it, I think."

Clara shrugged. "Such a shame, but it's what we do best, isn't it? Carrying that lot."

"Yes, I have a daughter of my own now, too." I did not bother to mention that she was not truly mine. I instantly regretted it, though. The Norwegian community was small and Clara might know Ole Olson, and even if she did not, my sister could have told her the truth.

Clara's gaze flickered a little—she was obviously well informed. "It's nice, though, isn't it, to have children?" Was that pity I heard in her voice?

"Nothing like it." I held my ground, though anger and anguish were instantly there, filling my mouth with the taste of bile. I was about to say more but was interrupted by a man's voice bellowing to be heard above the crowd:

"Hide the scissors, Bloody Bella is back!"

I turned my head in surprise and saw Arnold, one of the old gang from Milwaukee Avenue. He smelled as if this was his third day straight spending all his earnings at the beer garden. He came slumping down beside me on the bench, his red-brown beard streaked with filth. "What happened to that poor husband of yours? Did he get too close?"

"What do you mean by that?" I downed my beer and wished for another.

"Pay him no mind," said Clara.

"Maybe he got a little close so you stabbed him like the other one." The man laughed aloud, happy with his own poor jab.

"The 'other one' turned out all right." Clara's voice was calm. "His wound healed just fine. It's nothing more to talk about."

"Well, he died, didn't he?" Arnold blew cigar smoke in my face.

"Not by *her* hand," said Clara, and I felt the weight of the pewter button under my shirtwaist. Its pressure on my skin, like a kiss.

"He wasn't good enough for you, was he?" The man was still laughing at my expense. I wanted to smash my glass in his face and see the shards slide in through his skin. I wanted to have him broken at my feet. I wished I were a man like James, who would not think twice of waiting for him in an alley with his blade sharp and ready. Perhaps if he was drunk enough—or someone had slipped something into his glass—maybe I could best him then.

Maybe I could crush him.

Clara smacked Arnold's head across the table. "Of course he wasn't good enough! He was a brute! You all are!"

"Well, what do you call *her* then, bloody scissors and all—?"

"A woman putting a fool in his place—and you should mind your place too, before she teaches you otherwise."

"Oh, I would not dare touch Bloody Bella." He looked at me. "Maybe you'd snip my balls off with those scissors." Yes, I thought, maybe I would.

A kind look then from a stranger next to Clara, who had heard the whole exchange. He gave me a smile and lifted his glass. It calmed me, that smile, made me see reason.

"What balls?" I asked Arnold, and Clara laughed.

"I have them right here, would you like to see?" His speech was slurred as he moved his hands toward his crotch.

"That is enough of that." The stranger rose from the bench. He was taller than any other man at the table, broad-shouldered and narrow-hipped. "I think you have outstayed your welcome. Maybe it's time to go take a piss?"

"I'll piss in my own sweet time," Arnold answered, but the fire was all gone by then.

The stranger shrugged and sat back down. "Let the woman enjoy her glass in peace; she seems like no scissors-wielding fiend to me. If she did happen to stab a man, he probably deserved it."

"He did! He did!" Clara shrieked beside him.

My tormentor muttered to himself. His gaze was unfocused as he stared into his beer, and a moment later, he lumbered off.

"Thank you." I nodded to my savior.

"Don't mention it." He reached out his hand. "Peter Gunness."

"Bella Sorensen." I shook it. He was a handsome man, Peter Gunness, with blond hair and a neatly trimmed beard. His eyes were very blue. "You don't live in Chicago, do you?"

"No." He gave me a smile. Not a wicked one like James's, but a nice and wholesome smile. "I came down from Minneapolis to see the fair. I have some work in the area."

"Everyone suddenly does, it seems."

He smiled. "You have a lovely city here. Maybe I'll come for good someday." His gaze lingered on mine just a little too long.

"That depends on the eyes who see, I think." I gave him just a hint of a smile. I found I would not mind if he moved to Chicago.

"Is that an empty glass, Mrs. Sorensen? Do you want me to fill that up for you?" His eyebrow rose and his smile still lingered. He blew a little stray hair from his nose.

"If you like." Who was I to say no to a free glass? Served by a handsome man, no less.

He still smiled when he rose from the bench. I watched him as he moved into the crowd, towering so tall above everyone else.

"He is a butcher." Clara followed my gaze.

"Is that so?" I was intrigued.

"I believe his sausage is very good. Recently married, though. A shame."

"How would you know about his sausage?"

She laughed. "Oh, no one really knows. He is picky, it seems, when it comes to customers."

"Can never be too careful these days."

"I wouldn't mind standing in line for that one, though." She glanced in the direction he had gone.

I shrugged. "He is a married man and we are married women." But my heart raced a little in my chest, as if I were a hound who had just caught the scent of a fox.

"I heard his wife is sickly—could just be a rumor; no one knows for sure."

"He seems a kind man." I wetted my lips with the tip of my tongue.

Clara smiled sweetly and looked away when Peter Gunness came back. He handed me the glass and sat down next to me where the drunkard used to be, straddling the bench as if it were a horse.

"Well then, Mrs. Sorensen, I think it's time you tell me all about yourself—and especially about those scissors," he said.

"Of course." I laughed, making merry of it all. It had been such a long time since that night, after all. The air was warm, the beer was strong, and the man was utterly charming.

When I closed my eyes, I thought I could smell a faint scent of blood coming off him.

19.

Nellie

"I am telling you, Nellie, your sister could not take her eyes off him!" Clara sat by the table in my new kitchen and regaled me with tales of the Midway and the fair. I had not gone as my back had been hopeless and made me walk with a limp—much like Olina back at Størsetgjerdet. "Oh, you should have been there to see it," Clara lamented. "It was quite the spectacle. She did not make much of a secret of her feelings."

"Not so much *feelings*, I think," I said, and made another stitch in the shirt in my lap. I had to give up the washing, but I still took in some mending. "She doesn't know him at all, so it was maybe not the heart that spoke." I added a wry smile, and rejoiced when I heard Clara's laughter in reply. I still knew how to deliver a salty line.

"Ah, but these things happen." Clara drank coffee from a barely chipped cup. "After a few years of marriage one starts to yearn for something more exciting. I was just surprised because she was so religious before. She was always at church, do you remember?"

"Oh, I do." I did not hold back but rolled my eyes. This was Clara, after all, and I knew she would not judge me. "She is a little less concerned with it now; she teaches Sunday school but isn't otherwise involved. As long as she did not go with him, I cannot see what harm it does if she became a little weak in the knees." In my mind, an image of that love bite I had seen flashed before me. It was years ago, though, and had nothing to do with this Peter.

"No, of course not." Clara's lips twisted up in a secretive smile. "But I heard him invite her to see the Javanese orchestra play the next day. I wonder if she went." I looked over at my friend. The years had not been good to her, though not quite as cruel as they had been to me. Her curls had turned a steely gray and deep lines had lodged in her face. Her nose, which had always been prominent, seemed both longer and broader. She still had that same smile, though— that same way of telling a story. I had missed her every day since I moved away. She had been more of a sister to me over the years than the one I paid to have cross the ocean.

"If she did, she didn't tell me," I said, a little annoyed that Bella had not told me of this handsome man herself. "Then again, she is a married woman—and he a married man. They may not want to let anyone know if they visited the Midway together."

Clara leaned a little closer. Her finger drew invisible circles on the tabletop. Even if the room was new, the table was not, and she had drunk countless cups of coffee there before. Perhaps even drawn the same circle in that exact same spot. "Has she done it before?" She had lowered her voice. "Does she . . . find her 'entertainment' outside the marriage bed?"

Again, I saw that love bite with my inner eye. "Not that I know," I said, "but she doesn't tell me everything. Never did." I put down the mending in my lap and sighed. "Their marriage isn't good, I can tell you that much. The way she speaks to him sometimes, it is . . . *repulsive*. I can barely stand to listen as she taunts him and mocks him. It's not right for a woman to treat her husband like that."

Clara was not laughing anymore. She knew me well enough to tell that I was upset. "She has always been a little different, Nellie, that's nothing new. One must wonder what sort of man he is, though, to let her go on in that way."

"Ah, he doesn't understand her." I shook my head. "He doesn't understand what he does wrong, and so he cannot correct it either—or talk to her about it."

"He is not so bright?"

"He is . . . different from us; a little rigid perhaps. He thinks there is only one way to be in this world, and then, when people turn out to be different, he doesn't understand how that can be. He is simple in that way, I'll admit to that, but he *is* the man she married."

"She makes a fool of him?" Clara toyed with her cup, swilling the remains of her coffee around the bottom.

"That she does. He is no match for the likes of her. He rarely, if ever, puts up a fight."

"And a fight she must have." Clara nodded with a thoughtful expression. "That man, though, Peter Gunness, he seems a decent sort. Many a tired wife has tried to sway him since he arrived, but the word is that he will not. He is true to his wife."

"A rare kind of man indeed," I said, and then instantly regretted it. I knew of many men who were true, my husband among them. "I fear that his resistance will only make her more determined, though." I could not help but laugh again; it was all so wicked.

Clara rose to fetch the kettle and fill our cups. She was just as at ease in my new home as she had been in my old one, and it touched me to see it. "I must admit that *he* seemed a little smitten as well," she said, "or perhaps it was just compassion. Perhaps he thought that whole scissors affair intriguing. It's such a silly thing, you know, how something as ordinary as a pair of scissors can suddenly be used as a weapon. Perhaps he admired her for it."

"Oh, she would certainly like that." I picked up the mending again. "What is he doing in Chicago?"

Clara sat back down again; the fresh coffee steamed in our cups. "He is working at the stockyards—is a butcher by trade."

I could not help but chuckle again as I slid the needle through the fabric. "She has always been drawn to such skills," I admitted. "When she was a girl, she would always go as close as she could to the butchering; often so close that she was blood-splattered in the face when she came home. If she was allowed to, she would stay on until the creature was all taken apart."

"I can see how Mr. Gunness is alluring, then." Clara squinted as she threaded the needle. "Perhaps she has retained a glow for the bloody trade."

A cold shiver ran through me. "It's hard to grasp what moves her, but perhaps a man with a cleaver does just that. What about the wife? Why is she not here?"

"She is sickly, they say. He means to go back home to her when he is done with his work here."

"Oh, that's a good thing, then. At least whatever is between them will shortly come to an end."

"Indeed," Clara agreed. "It will not do to have domestic disturbance now that she has that girl to care for."

IT HAD TAKEN me a while to get used to our new apartment. I could not believe the sheer number of doors. Whenever I opened one, it seemed like another one appeared before me. I had a proper pantry and a sitting room as well, which was something I had never had before. I bought two chairs cheap, and added a little table, so that John and I had a place to sit at night when the dishes in the kitchen were clean and our son was about to go to sleep on the bench. He had turned into such a fine young man, and I could not have been prouder when he started working alongside his father and earned his own wages. Olga was not too far behind; a few years and she would be making it on her own. What would we do then, with only Nora, my youngest, for company?

I could relate to Bella when such thoughts came upon me, how she must have suffered through the years without children. It was different with Jennie, though; she would stay even as other foster children came and left. That little girl was a blessing.

I often looked after her while Bella ran errands, either at our apartment or at their house on Elizabeth Street. I felt that she was a little mine as well, since she called my sister Mama. She had a sunny disposition, and Nora enjoyed being with her as well, as they were almost the same age. The two of them would play for hours, making up their own little world. Though things were not good between Mads and Bella, the child seemed to be—so far—untouched by their discord.

Then, as the year moved toward its end, the situation took a sinister turn.

It was John who made me aware of it, one night when he came home from work. Though we had entered the dark season, the paleness of his face could not be attributed to winter's hardships alone. He barely had time to shed his coat and sit down at the table, where dinner waited in steaming pots, before he opened his mouth to speak.

"I fear that Mads is gravely ill."

"Whatever do you mean?" I was busy filling his plate, and it took a moment for the words to sink in.

"We met him on the street," Rudolph said. He had come in with his father, having come from the same place of work, and was brushing off both pairs of shoes before entering.

"He looks like a man on his deathbed," said my husband. "I almost did not recognize him at first. His cheeks are all hollow and his color like ash. When I asked, he said it was a stomach virus, but it didn't look like a virus to me. It looked as if life itself was seeping out of him."

"He did look poorly." My son nodded from his crouching position by the shoes. "It is as Father said; it didn't look like some little thing."

The girls had come out of hiding in their room at the sound of their father and brother's arrival and were happily filling the bench, both of them hungry no doubt. When they saw John's somber expression, they fell quiet.

"Bella has not said a word," I told him. "It must have been sudden, this illness. Did he mention seeing a doctor?"

John sighed. "He said your sister was set against it, that she thought it foolish to spend money on a doctor when it would probably just pass."

My cheeks reddened. "She has her hands full these days. She must not have seen how bad he looked."

"Well, she won't have a husband for long if this is to continue." John drew a tired hand through his salt-and-pepper hair.

"Aunt Bella must think it's a stomach virus." Rudolph took his place by the table.

"Well, for all we know it is. They can be pretty horrible," I muttered, "and none of us are doctors." I felt ashamed on her behalf, to let her husband go and suffer. "Maybe she is treating him with powders and suchlike."

"Isn't there a doctor lodging with them?"

"He hasn't moved in yet. His position starts in January." Bella and Mads had decided to let a room.

"Now that's bad luck," John mused.

"I think you should go there, Mama." Rudolph's bright brown eyes met mine. "Just to make sure that they're all right."

I nodded and gave a deep sigh. "I will go first thing tomorrow."

BELLA WAS BUSY sweeping the kitchen floor when I arrived. Little Jennie, fair and lithe, walked in her mother's footsteps with a broom of her own, sweeping up what little her mother missed. I had expected there to be some sign of illness in the house—bottles of tinctures or medicine fumes, at the very least a hush in the atmosphere—but there was none.

"Nellie." Bella straightened up and stretched with her knuckles pressed to the small of her back. "I was not expecting you."

"I know ... I know ... It was just—John told me that Mads was ill." I was still lingering by the door, unsure if I should go inside a house with such a mysterious illness. Both my sister and her daughter seemed fine, though.

"Oh no, that's nothing." Bella waved it away. "He will be his old self in no time at all."

"Well, where is he? Is he at home?" I stretched my neck to perhaps catch a glance inside the parlor.

"He is in bed." Bella placed the broom behind the door and slumped down in a chair. Jennie quickly followed her example and claimed a chair of her own. "Come inside, Nellie. Don't just stand there and gawk. I don't know what John told you, but it's nothing serious."

"No?" I took a few steps into the room and started to unbutton my coat. "John said he looked half dead!" I should perhaps not have used such strong words, but I was frightened and upset. "You should send him to see a doctor," I said as I sat down with the coat in my arms.

"We will have our own doctor soon," she replied. "That will be nice, won't it, Jennie?" she cooed at the girl, who awarded her with a bright smile. "Then we will never have to spend hard-earned cash on such luxuries."

"Well, he could be dead by that time." Sometimes Bella had to have it spelled out. "What if it is not a stomach virus? What if it is something more serious than that?"

She shook her head, rose again, and set to making coffee. "I have seen him sick with such viruses before and I know they make him seem very poorly, but he will clear right up again. It's not as bad as it looks."

"What are you giving him, then? Surely he must have some sort of medicine?" I felt a headache coming on; it was impossible to talk to her when she was in such a mood, determined to be happy and refusing to see reason.

"I give him a tincture the pharmacist recommended," she said with her back turned toward me. "Three times a day without fail. He is much better already."

"What is the name of it?" I knew I had to test her, because sometimes—*sometimes*—she lied.

"Oh, I cannot remember, I keep it upstairs on his bed stand, next to the Bible, which, as you know, is the only medicine he truly wants." Was there bitterness I heard in her voice, or scorn? It was hard to tell with her back turned.

Just then, the creaking door to the hallway announced Mads's arrival.

John had certainly *not* been wrong about his condition. I took one look at his face and then I knew that the man was in mortal peril.

"Good God, Mads." I rose at once and walked toward him. He stood leaning against the door frame, dressed in his pajamas. His hand, which held an empty cup, shook. "My God," I repeated. "Look at you! You must see a doctor at once!"

"Do you think so?" he asked in a voice that barely carried.

"It's not so bad," Bella said behind me.

"I cannot keep the food down," he said. "It keeps coming up again."

"Bella!" I turned to her; my frown was so deep that the headache bloomed. "He *must* see a doctor!" I used the same stern voice I had practiced so often when she was a child.

She sighed. "It's a waste of money." She put a cup down on the table, presumably for me, and filled it with scalding-hot coffee. Jennie pulled her knees up to her chin and followed our exchange with worried eyes.

"I will go and bring the doctor here myself." I fetched my coat. I did not trust that anything would be done if left up to my sister. Mads barely nodded, but I think he was grateful. Relieved that someone other than Bella took charge.

When he went to put on a proper shirt in anticipation of the doctor's visit, I could not help but scold her. "It is terrible what you do, keeping him from the doctor when he is clearly very ill! What has gotten into you, Bella? Have you no heart for him at all?"

She looked at me as if confused. "I *know* how to make him better, Nellie. I can have him up again in no time at all!"

"Then why is he still bedridden?" I could not believe my ears.

"You are making a terrible fuss over nothing." Her eyes flashed with anger.

"*That* did not seem like *nothing* to me!" I flung my arm in the direction he had gone.

"Well, just bring the doctor if you like—he won't find a thing!" She all but stomped her foot. Her face was flushed and her nostrils flared.

"You cannot know that." I pointed a finger at her chest.

"Oh, but I do," she hissed in reply. "I know better than he does what ails him." She lifted her chin in the way that she did, making her seem both stubborn and proud.

Just then, Mads reappeared in the doorway, properly dressed this time. I gave my sister another stern look before crossing the floor to the door.

Just as I passed through the gate to the street, I heard her call out behind me, "You should have left it well alone, Nellie! He would have been just fine on his own!"

TO MY DISMAY, Bella was right: the doctor could not tell just what ailed my brother-in-law. He did think it was grave, though—grave enough that Mads stayed in the hospital for a few weeks. When he came home, he was better, but it took months before he could work as he did before the illness, and he never quite recovered but remained ashen-faced and delicate.

Bella made a great fuss about her sickly husband, lamenting to all that would hear, but she never apologized or thanked me for bringing the doctor that day, even if it likely saved Mads's life.

I was not too surprised, and pushed it away. She never much liked to be wrong.

20.

Bella

Chicago, 1895–1896

Mads's brother, Oscar, came to visit in the spring of 1895, having been summoned by my husband's worrying letters. He would stay with us for a whole three weeks, and I was very displeased.

The man was rude and did not care for me. Still, I made a bed for him in the room James and I so often used, laid out soap and clean towels and even some wax for his mustache. In the kitchen, I made sausages and mashed sweet potatoes. I bought smoked salmon and had clams delivered, made bread and served it with soft butter—yet he did not like me.

He and Mads would withdraw once the food was devoured to smoke and drink watered-down wine in the parlor while I soaked their plates and scrubbed the pans. No matter how I strained my hearing, I could not make out what they said behind the closed door, and that angered me even more. I wanted Oscar gone but was forced to act a good wife and serve delicious food that none of them even deserved.

One day, as I was mending clothes by the kitchen table, Oscar came to me. He was as dull as his brother, stocky and balding. Despite my laid-out soap, he smelled as ripe as a farmhand.

"How can you let him go on like this, Bella?"

I made another stitch and then I looked up. "I cannot make Mads do or not do anything. If you're thinking about his poor color—"

"He can barely work, he cannot keep his food down, and he is always, always in pain. He ought to see a doctor every week!"

"If my husband thinks he needs a doctor, I expect him to say so, or make an appointment." I preferred if he did not, of course. I knew very well just what it was that made him ill. I had been careful since he was in the hospital, though; it just would not do if someone, like my meddling sister, realized what I had done. I had not set out to kill him that time, just punish him a little, but it had been so hard to stop. I had kept picturing what sort of life I could have had with another man—someone like Peter Gunness—and the rat poison had been right there on the shelf. He might have died then, and I would have been free, had it not been for Nellie. It annoyed me how she had come barging in and made a fuss, but I was a little grateful as well, as I still needed Mads's income. I had been good and fed him very little poison over the past year, just enough to keep him meek. One never knew with such things, though; one day my hand might slip, or his body might give in. "We had a young doctor staying with us last year," I said to Oscar. "Mads received much advice from him."

"Not nearly enough, from the looks of it! Are you aware of his chest pains?"

"Of course, but it's not uncommon to feel a twinge when living under strain. The heart doesn't like a heavy load. If he made a better living—"

"He is ill, Bella, and has been for some time. I will take him to see a specialist first thing in the morning."

"Of course," I said, and cut the thread with my teeth. I did not like this at all. The specialist might not think of poison, but then again, he might. I had not given Mads anything since Oscar arrived, and I was glad for it now, even if I felt that both of them deserved a generous sprinkle on their clams.

Not enough to kill—just to do a little harm.

Oscar made to leave, but then he paused by the door. His gaze when he looked at me was cold and hostile. "Don't think you can fool me, Bella. I don't think you care for my brother at all."

"Really?" This made me curious rather than annoyed. I always took great care to be seen as a loving wife to my husband when his brother was about. "What makes you say that?"

"Don't think he hasn't told me how you always complain about his income, the state of the house, and even the size of his life insurance. Nothing is ever good enough for you!"

"Those are private matters." The anger quickly flared up in me and licked my insides with swift tongues. I would get Mads for this when Oscar was gone. I would have him retching and aching.

"Had he fallen ill and died, I don't think you would have shed a tear." Oscar's fat bottom lip quivered.

"I don't want Mads dead," I lied.

"I don't think you would grieve him for long, though, if he did. You don't think twice about accusing him or even throwing a fist—"

"Does he say that?" I tried to sound amused, though it was hard to sound merry when angry. "He must be more tired than I thought. Maybe he truly *ought* to see a specialist."

"Do you deny it?"

"Of course I do." I slipped a new thread through the needle's eye. My hands did not quiver one bit, and I felt proud. I was getting apt at this, putting on a deception.

"I saw bruising just this morning, right here at his temple." Oscar pointed with his finger at a throbbing vein. "He said you threw a book—"

"He hit his head on the bedside table when rolling over to fetch his Bible."

Oscar's face had become quite red. "Why would he lie about that?"

I found a little frock in the pile of clothes and set to mending a tear. "To gain your sympathies, I suppose. Maybe he finds me cruel to complain about the lack of money—"

"It's hardly a woman's concern."

"To feed our child *is*."

"I don't see why you keep foster children at all! It does nothing to improve the poor man's health to fill his house with strangers' offspring—"

"We only have the one now," I reminded him. "It's been a longing in me always to have children to care for, and soon they might not be strangers." I gently placed a hand on my belly and gave him a tiny smile.

The red color increased. "Do you—does he—?"

"No, he doesn't know yet. I wanted to be sure."

"And now you are?" He looked as if I had just told him I was about to sprout another leg.

"Yes, I am." I made another few stitches. "So you see, not everything is wrong between us."

He went quiet then, lost for words. "Well then," he said at last, "I'll leave you to it."

Who could ever hate a woman carrying a longed-for child?

THOUGH I HAD only told Oscar I was pregnant to appease him, the thought would not leave me alone. I kept touching my belly, though I knew there was nothing inside, and I dreamed of it at night, a belly swelling with a daughter of mine. Sometimes the dreams turned darker, and it was the grave I saw: the hole in the ground, next to a root, and the wet thing I slipped inside. The earth on top, so smooth under my hands, concealing the dread underneath.

As if it never happened.

When I woke up, sweat-drenched and breathless, I would be angry again and think of Anders and the damage that he did to me that night by the lake.

I clutched the pewter button around my neck for courage in those nights. James could always give me that. He was the only one besides myself I trusted, and even if the fever of our first years had mellowed some, he could still make me feel just as weak at the knees as I had been on that first day in the park.

It was a rare treasure to have a friend like that.

In those nights of dissatisfaction, I often imagined myself in his stead: What would I have done to better my situation if I had been James Lee?

Sometimes, if sleep evaded me, I would go downstairs and pour the brandy. I would light a lamp to finish my letters or pore over the newspapers. The first often brought to mind another dissatisfaction: though our letters were many, Peter Gunness never expressed any interest in me besides friendship. His wife was very ill but never seemed to die—much like Mads, I noted. Mr. Gunness dreamed of a farm where he could raise his own pigs and sell the best sausage on the market. I enjoyed dreaming with him. I could understand ambition, though my own had sadly turned to nothing but a useless husband with an empty wallet, borrowed children, and a pantry brimming with old food. Jennie was a blessing, yes, but she was already growing up, and though I did my best not to think of it, I could not completely forget that she was not truly mine. Her father sometimes spoke to Mads about it, how he meant to bring her home one day. My youth was waning—the years ran by. Was this all I would ever become, or could I still do something to save my bold vision: strike out on my own again and *have* that life I had so vividly imagined on the ship to America?

I read about clever schemes in the newspapers all the time: how they were done—and how they failed. I thought of H. H. Holmes and his magnificent enterprise that had so heavily relied on insurance fraud, and thought that maybe I could do the same. Only better. More clever. In a way that made sure I was never found out.

I thought about the sick man up in his bed, and then I thought of the house I sat in—both could certainly go—but there had to be a better way: a way that would not harm me at all.

I figured I should go into retail. I could build a business, burn it to the ground, and walk away unscathed. If I was a mother of a small child when it happened, nothing could be better. I saw it all so clearly: how I would clutch the child to my chest as I went to speak with the insurance man with tears dripping from my eyes: *It all just went up in a blaze! Oh, I don't know what to do! How am I to feed my child?*

If I was lucky, there might be even be enough in a scheme like that to buy me a better house. A house without tarnish and emptiness inside. Enough that I did not need Mads's pay anymore.

I still wanted the same things as I had when I arrived in this country: the happy home, money, and toddlers playing at my feet. My own children, not some other woman's, or as close to that as I could come—and why should I be denied such a simple thing?

People are so foolish; they beg to be deceived.

I chuckled a little when I realized how this plan of mine was good news for Mads.

I could not have my children as a widow.

MY DAUGHTER CAROLINE was delivered in January. She was a tiny, mewling thing wrapped in a piece of bloodstained cotton. The night was dark and chilly, the sky spangled with stars.

"I swear she's of fine Norwegian breeding." James was at the back door. He had buttoned his coat all the way up.

"Not so fine, I think." I looked at the dirty swaddling. "Her natural mother must've fallen on hard times."

"It's a harsh world"—James offered me a smile—"but the girl seems healthy enough."

I smiled down at the mewling bundle. "She is so fresh I can smell the womb on her. I could take her to the doctor in the morning and claim I had her myself!"

"I wouldn't recommend it. Maybe he'd sense that something was wrong."

"Men never do, not when it comes to children and birth; they would rather not think of it at all. But I'll take your advice."

"Good—and make sure to draw up an insurance policy. One never knows how long such tiny things last." He put a finger on the swaddling to pull it down and have a look at the newborn's face.

"I have hopes for this one." I looked down at her at well, watched as her little mouth formed a soundless O and her little fist waved in the air.

I wanted to invite James inside but was unsure how deep Mads's sleep was, as I had not tinkered with his coffee. The fool had not asked about my protruding belly, fat with cushions. He accepted mentions of "the happy event" with a gracious nod whenever it was brought up at church but seemed pained when I spoke of it at home. He knew it was not real, of course but had decided to go along with it. Maybe he was curious too, to see what this scheme of padding would produce.

James asked, "How is the old man?"

"Suffering from a faulty heart, according to the doctor. He takes prescribed powders and eats at certain times. Yet he does not seem to get better." James and I shared a wicked smile over the baby's soft head.

"A pity," said he, who would rather see him dead.

"Not so much." I quite enjoyed seeing him in pain.

James looked at the bundle in my arms. "Won't people suspect it's not yours when it's taken so long? You have been married for how many years?"

"Too many, and no—they will just think it an act of God. I don't care what they think either way." I pressed the child to my chest and wrapped my shawl tight around us both. The girl made another mewling sound but did not cry. She was a good child, I decided. An easy, quiet child. A child meant for light, not a hole in the ground.

"And the store?" James leaned his shoulder on the door frame and crossed his arms over his chest.

"It's coming along. I'm expecting deliveries in the morning."

"A confectionery store." He shook his head. "How did that come about?"

"It was a natural choice; it was already there, just waiting for a new owner. And I'm hardly the first person in this city to be tempted to stake my fortunes on sugar and sweets." It was the only business

I could make Mads agree to; he had gotten it in his head that the future was made of flavored sugar. It had taken all we had—a second mortgage and my meager savings—to make it happen.

"You might be the first with such fiery intentions." James raised a hand and let his fingers trail along my hairline to brush away a few stray strands.

"Hush," I scolded him but smiled.

"Won't you find it hard to build something just to tear it down?" His dark gaze narrowed.

"No, I find I like the sweets and the planning," I told him. "I like to watch it grow around me. One day I might build a business for real." If I could make that work, I would never have to rely on a man's poor pay again. I glanced at the girl's tiny face once more. This child was different; she would carry my name. She was no borrowed child—she was mine through and through. "Did you pay and settle with the mother?"

"She doesn't even know where the girl went. She didn't want to know."

"Good. I better take her inside, then, and make sure she doesn't get cold."

James gave an amused chuckle. "It's good to see you so happy."

"I'll be happier still when all is said and done with the store." I bent forth to receive a light kiss on the lips.

He tipped his hat. "I'm at your service, as always."

"Know that I'm grateful for that."

I closed the door gently and brought Caroline inside.

21.

Nellie

Chicago 1896–1898

Bella's store was a marvel, filled to the brim with caramels, candy canes, and sugared nuts. It had newspapers, magazines, cigars, and tobacco as well, neatly lined up on polished shelves. The counter was large and held a golden thread weight. Behind and upon it, small and large glass jars displayed the goods to the customers. The sign on the storefront spelled out the business's purpose in black and golden letters: *Sweets & Tobacco*. Bella cleaned it every day, balancing on a ladder.

I often went there to help her in the beginning, and rejoiced in how her mood had improved. She was humming to herself while tying on the white apron in the morning, and cleaning the shelves with a feather duster. Part of that improvement was due to little Caroline, of course. It was a wonder how that girl came to be. Not only had Bella been barren before, but she was not so young either—and yet there was Caroline, a well-shaped child who made her demands known through great bellows of her lungs.

I sometimes wondered if Bella was like me and had suffered through miscarriages, yet never told a soul. The thought of it pained me, that she would have carried such a burden in silence, year after year, too proud to admit to her body's failings. No wonder her marriage had suffered so, and that she had often been so glum.

When I asked her, though, she said that she had never lost even one.

Mads, too, seemed much improved since Caroline's arrival. He rose from his bed shortly after the birth and showed the child off to every neighbor who happened to pass by. He regained even more of his glow after they opened the store. He said it was a fresh start for all of them, their great opportunity in life. Bella only huffed and said that he sure was more useful wiping down windows and placing orders than he had been for the last few years, lying on his back in the bed.

I used to bring Nora with me to the store, and she and Jennie would help fill the shelves, spelling out the names of the various flavors as they worked in tandem with their smooth brows creased with concentration: "Sugarplum, lemon drop, peppermint, cinnamon, wintergreen, lavender . . ." Baby Caroline slept in a cradle in the back, where the door could be closed if she cried.

It was a joyous time for all of us and I was thrilled to see Bella so happy. She was always marvelous company when pleased, and our days at the store were filled with laughter and sugared treats in equal measure. Whenever a customer came in, Bella's eyes lit up and she brought forth her sweetest smile as she went behind the counter to exchange caramels and cigars for shiny coins. I thought that she might have found her place in life at last.

"Perhaps you were never meant to stay at home," I told her one day as we sat by the little table in the back where the window showed a view of the backyard, crammed with wagons, wooden boards, and crates stacked against the outhouse walls. "Some women fare better if they work outside the kitchen."

"Yes, but it wouldn't be the same if I didn't own it." Her fingers dipped into a bowl of toffee, bringing a piece to her lips—she always had a sweet tooth. "I don't think I could work for another again, not after Rødde farm."

"Well, you always had a good head on your shoulders, and now you can put it to use."

"You should encourage Olga to come and work for me." Her eyes lit up with the idea. "It would be better for her to work for her aunt than in some other place with strangers. I would always be fair to her, and I could certainly use the help, with the children here all the time."

I quickly repressed the fear that flared in my chest. My daughter was fifteen and certainly not a child anymore. Bella could not take her from me even if she tried. "That's a good idea." I forced my lips to form the words. "It will be useful for her to learn how to manage a store."

"Won't it just." Bella fished out another piece of toffee. "I am sure she will like it here, with all these delicious goods to sample." The toffee disappeared in between her lips.

"Certainly," I agreed, and reminded myself again how much my sister's mood had improved since the store opened.

Olga would surely be safe.

I WAS AT the store less after Olga started her apprenticeship. I wanted to give my daughter space to find her place without her mama looking over her shoulder. She seemed excited by her new work, though, and often regaled me with stories when she came home. She spoke of the little boy who always came in for cigars, reeking of them though he said they were for his father, and the woman who bought peppermint candy to mix in with her gin. She told me of the lovesick young man who sought to impress his sweetheart by offering a new flavor of candy every day, and the baker's daughter who bought caramels to comfort herself whenever her father had been cruel.

She seemed taken with her small cousins and had decided to teach little Jennie how to knit a scarf. She also could not say enough good things about Caroline, the sweetness of her face and the way it would light up in a smile whenever Olga came in.

She told me that Mads was rarely there anymore, that he had

taken to his bed again, suffering as bad as before. This was indeed worrisome news, and I went to Elizabeth Street a few times to check on him myself. It was as my daughter had said; he was back in bed with an ashen pallor, suffering from vomiting and cramps. Bella had told me that his heart was poor, but I could not see how that would cause such an upset. He said he was seeing a doctor, though, Dr. Miller who had lodged with them before, and so there was very little I could do but offer him broth and cream puddings.

It worried me, though, the poor color of him.

Yet my daughter's latest news worried me even more.

She came home one night in her red-striped shop girl dress and apron, took off her coat, and slumped down in a chair by the table, where I was peeling potatoes for dinner.

"You are early," I remarked.

"Aunt Bella said that I could go," she said, chewing her lip a little, as she did when lost in thought.

"Did she close the store early?"

"No, I just—I don't think she wanted me there." Her gaze danced around the room, taking in everything but me.

"What is it?" I put down the knife. "What is it you're not telling me?"

"Ah, it's nothing." The girl seemed sullen. Her hair bun had come a little undone, and strands of blond hair danced around her face. "Is Nora still at school?"

"No, she is playing with the neighbor's girls—now tell me what is wrong."

"It is—" She paused to chew her lip a little more. "I just promised Aunt Bella not to tell."

"Really?" My heart instantly set up the pace. "Then I certainly think that you should." Though I was not entirely sure if I wanted to know what had left my daughter in such a state.

"Perhaps it is nothing," she said without conviction. "Perhaps I am making it out to be more than it is."

"I think you should tell me and let me be the judge of that." I had given up on the potatoes and wiped my hands on the apron in my lap.

"There is a man there sometimes." She chewed her lip again. "I don't think he is very kind."

"How so?" My heart was still racing.

"Oh, it's just the way he looks at you." She shrugged.

"What is he doing there? Is he buying candy?"

"No! He is visiting Aunt Bella. She seems to know him well, though she has never properly introduced him to me. She sends me out in the back when he's there, tells me to look after the children . . . I don't like it, the way she acts around him, whispering over the counter, and how she wants me not to tell . . ." My daughter looked utterly miserable, sitting there before me with her hands in her lap; her fingers were restless, rubbing against one another.

I put my hand on hers to stop their nervous movements. "Was he there today?"

"He was, and when I came out from the back to ask for more milk for the bottle, they were standing with their faces so very close. Oh, I wish you could have seen him, Mama; he is all dapper and fine-looking with fur on his coat, but he does not seem like an honest man to me. If he were, Aunt Bella would not send me out and ask me not to tell you about him."

"You are a clever girl." I squeezed her hand. "You did right in telling me. When does this man come about? Is there any special day?"

"No, but he is never there before noon."

"I will look in on the store more often," I promised. "Perhaps I'll catch a glimpse of him. What did your aunt say when she asked you not to tell?"

"That you would only worry, and it was better that you didn't know."

"That I didn't know what?"

She shrugged again. "That she did not say—but surely it must be wrong, her seeing him like that, with Uncle Mads being so ill and all."

"We'll figure it out." I gave her hands a squeeze. "Don't mention to your aunt that you told me."

IT TOOK A few tries before I came upon a stranger in Bella's store, and when I finally did, it was not who I expected.

In the weeks that had passed since Olga confided in me, I had had time to spin the most wondrous stories in my head, even thinking that Bella's barrenness perhaps had been Mads's fault, and that she had found herself another man to perform that particular service. What other reason would she have to nurture an illicit—perhaps even dangerous—relationship? If word got out, wagging tongues would rip her to shreds, and she knew that.

The man I found in the confectionery store, however, did not look like the one Olga had described, though he certainly looked comfortable, sitting behind the counter, eating sugared nuts from a tray. Strong fumes rose from the glass in his hand, and from the matching one held by my sister. The latter had taken great care with her appearance: she wore a frilly blue dress underneath the apron and had put up her hair with tortoiseshell combs. I could see Olga through the open door to the back, where she sat with Caroline in her lap. She sent me a worried glance through the gap.

"Nellie." Bella beamed as I came in, seemingly very much at ease with the situation, which puzzled me some. "How fortunate that you came in just now. This is Mr. Gunness." She motioned to the blond man at her side. "He will be lodging with us for a while, in Dr. Miller's old room."

"Is that so." I heard my own voice sounding brittle and unsure. The man rose to his feet, and I could tell that he was unusually tall.

"Mr. Gunness works at the stockyards," Bella prattled on. "He is a butcher by trade."

I remembered it all then, what Clara had told me about their meeting in the beer garden. "This is my sister," Bella said. "Olga's mother, of course."

"Of course." The man seemed polite enough and his beard was neatly trimmed. Now that I looked closer, I could see some silver among the blond strands. "Happy to make your acquaintance," he said.

"Likewise." I felt faint. "But what with—isn't Mads terribly ill?" This was hardly the time to bring a stranger into the house.

"Oh, but Mr. Gunness and I have known each other for a long time, and he knows all about Mads's condition. It's such a comfort to me to have another man in the house now that my husband is bedridden." She smiled sweetly but not to me.

"How long will you stay for, Mr. Gunness?" I made no secret of my distaste.

"Oh, another four weeks at least. Then I will go home. I have a sick wife and a young daughter." He said it as if to appease me. It was hard not to believe in his good intentions as he had such an honest look upon his face. His eyes were very bright and very blue.

"A butcher, huh?" I could not help but send my sister a look—even if the man was honest, it did not mean that *she* was.

"It's such an admirable trade, don't you think?" She did not even bat an eye. "We're having such lovely evenings together, playing cards in the parlor. Mads too," she added quickly, "when he is up to it."

"Mrs. Sorensen is a wonderful cook." He deftly returned the praise and sank back on the wooden chair. "I must have gained several pounds since I moved in."

"Oh, but you have not tried my waffles yet." Bella continued the shameless banter.

Through the gap in the door I saw Olga shake her head, though I did not at once grasp why that was. "I only came in to see Olga," I told the merry couple behind the counter.

"Go ahead." Bella motioned to the back. "Take some sweets home for Nora," she offered. "She is barely even here anymore."

When I had entered the back, Olga bent over the feeding infant and whispered into my ear, "That's not him. Mr. Gunness is just a lodger. You have to try again."

And so I did.

IT TOOK ME a while longer than intended, as my back took a bad turn and I could not walk about as much as I liked. It helped that Olga reported that her aunt had started sending her and the girls out with the pram to walk a bit in the park, most commonly on Fridays. Olga no longer saw the man so often in the store, and deduced from this that Bella must have noticed her reluctance toward him and started to plan ahead so that both her niece and her daughters would be out of her hair whenever the strange man appeared.

This made it easier to know when to go, which was a blessing, as my back did not much like those long trips on the streetcar.

Over the weeks, I had started thinking that there perhaps was a perfectly reasonable explanation for his presence there. Maybe he was a wholesaler or suchlike. That did not explain the secrecy, of course, but Olga might have gotten that part wrong.

When I arrived at the store, I was surprised to find that the door was locked. At first, I thought it was I who had not been firm enough when trying the handle, but no matter how many times I tried, the door remained firmly shut.

When I took a step back to assess the storefront, I could tell that the sign in the window read *Closed*.

This was both irregular and disturbing. There was no good reason why Bella would close the store on a busy afternoon. I stepped up to the door and looked inside at the familiar interior, the counter and the glass jars. I did not see my sister, though, but figured she might be in the back, so I lifted my hand and rapped on the glass.

At first, nothing stirred in there, and I lifted my hand and rapped once more. I called for her too. "Bella, are you in there?"

The store remained dark and quiet.

I was about to turn and go to the park in the hopes of finding Olga and the girls. Maybe my daughter would know if her aunt had stepped out, if something was amiss with Mads perhaps. Just then, something moved in the dimly lit store, and I moved a little closer to the glass to get a better view.

It was the door to the small storage room, usually locked, which slowly slid open in there, revealing my sister's ample figure. Without thinking, I lifted my hand, curled into a fist now, and hammered on the glass once more. The residue of fear and the lightness of relief dueled inside me as she moved toward the door. When she came closer, I could see that she was adjusting her clothes: straightening the lace collar of the shirtwaist and checking all the buttons, dusting off the gray skirt with her hand.

I felt cold and barely wanted to enter when she finally turned the key in the lock.

"Olga is not here," she said by way of greeting. Her face was flustered, but from embarrassment or anger, it was hard to tell. "I sent her to the park with the girls."

"Why was the door locked?" I knew she wanted me gone, but instead I took a few steps inside. If she wanted me to leave, there was obviously something to see.

"I just needed a moment's silence," she said as she retreated behind the counter. "I have such a terrible headache—"

"Oh, come." What sort of a fool did she think I was? "Why would you be in the storage room all by yourself? That never cured any headache." There was nothing but shelves in there; not even a chair to sit on.

"What do you mean?" She did not smile, but her eyes had lit up with mirth.

"Well, you were hardly alone in there, were you?"

"I have no idea what you mean, but I do think you should go. This headache—"

I moved as fast as I could with my poor back and ripped open the door to the storage room. There, with only a kerosene lamp as company, a man stood casually leaning against the candy shelf. He was dressed as Olga had described, in a long coat with fur trimmings; his mustache was thick yet neatly combed, and his slanted eyes glittered merrily in the warm light from the flame. He cocked his head when he saw me, and his full lips split in a smile. "I am merely inspecting the shelves," he said, and rapped his knuckles against one.

I stepped away at once—aghast at the sight and unsure what to say. The man followed me out of the cramped little room.

"Oh, come, we are all adults." He threw out an arm, as if to say it was all such a little thing, of no particular consequence.

To my astonishment, I could tell that Bella was smiling behind the counter. "Nellie, this is Mr. Lee," she said, with amusement written all over her features. "Mr. Lee, this is my sister, Mrs. Larson."

"A pleasure." He made a deep bow, in mockery no doubt.

"Mr. Lee was just leaving." She sent him a poignant look.

"Oh, I was," he replied at once; that mocking smile never once left his lips. "Have a wonderful day, Mrs. Larson." He hurried toward the door. Once there, he turned with his hand on the knob. "I will see you soon, Mrs. Sorensen." He tipped his hat, and then he was gone. The bell above the door jingled in his wake.

"Bella, what is this?" I hissed at my sister and moved up to the counter, standing opposite her, with only a few jars of striped candy between us. My heart was beating very fast—I had not liked the look of that man, his glib mockery and too-easy smile.

"It's nothing—I just . . ." She did not complete the sentence but started fussing with the brown paper bags stacked near the thread weight. She did not look at me but still had that half smile lingering on her lips.

"You cannot be doing this—not now, with Mads so ill, and your little girl—"

"Well, that is just it!" Her eyes flashed when she finally looked at me. "Mads is ill and I have my needs, which he is certainly not in any condition to—"

"Bella!" I slammed my hand down the countertop, "People will talk, don't you see? There is no such thing as a secret, and especially not when you meet him so publicly."

"It is *my* store," she said, looking for a moment like the girl I left behind, petulant and angry, and not the matronly woman she had become.

"And *your* marriage too—you make a mockery of your husband, who's lying there so very ill. Who even *is* he?" I slammed my hand down on the countertop again.

"Oh, just a friend." She shook her head as if it meant nothing.

"A friend, huh? That I have never seen before?" I rolled my eyes and made no secret of it.

"You don't know everything about me," she hissed, ripping the paper bag between her fingers.

"Clearly I do not!"

"What will you do then, Nellie? Will you tell Mads that I have a visitor at the store? That will *not* improve his condition." She lifted her chin at me. Her eyes were very cold.

My anger subsided some and turned into a tired sense of hopelessness. She was right to ask; whatever would I do? More than anything else, I wanted to cry. Why was there never any peace around her? "This is utterly irresponsible," I muttered. "What about Caroline?" I asked. "Is she even Mads's child?"

She looked at me for a moment, still with her chin raised high. "No—and he knows it."

My chest filled up with ache for him; the tears were closer than ever. "Is it *his* child then? Mr. Lee's?"

She shrugged. "I do not believe that she is."

"Mr. Gunness?" I could not think of any other.

She shook her head but did not reply. Whenever I tried to catch her eyes, her gaze just slid away.

"Whose is she, then?" I gave a deep sigh, feeling faint with exhaustion.

"She is mine," Bella said with triumph in her voice. "That girl is only mine." And that was the last she would say on the subject no matter how much I prodded and begged.

I found I had utterly failed in my mission: there was nothing I learned in the store that day that I could use to put Olga at ease. It cost me many sleepless nights, tossing and turning on the pillows. What was I to make of this? What was I to do? If word got out, Bella would be the harlot and poor Mads would be the fool. Yet when had she ever listened to me? She never took advice, thinking her own counsel always the best. What could I do but hope that it would pass? Telling Mads was not an option, not while he was so ill. It pained me to think that he knew he was not Caroline's father, and I wondered if he had *chosen* to go along with it for the sake of a child, and if it caused him misery. Still, just the thought of asking him made me blush, and I knew that I would never do such a thing. I could of course ask my sister how her husband felt—but sometimes she lied, so there was no use.

What bothered me the most, though, was the careless way in which Bella had spoken of her affair—as if she felt no remorse at all, as if she did not even care that it was wrong.

It made me trust her less, and I could not help but wonder what *other* secrets my sister kept.

What she did when no one saw.

22.

Bella

Six months in and my wondrous store was not a wonder anymore. The competition was too steep. Mads was not the only man to think the road to a better future was paved with hard candy; Chicago was booming with confectionery stores. The coins in the secondhand cash register were fewer than I would have liked, and the store was not paying the expenses for its upkeep. The customers were not clamoring at our door, and the little bell above it was slowly gathering a sheen of dust.

I found that I had much preferred opening the store to running it. The days behind the counter felt long and useless. I kept skimming the glass jars, stuffing myself with butterscotch candy. Jennie, too, grew soft around the edges, puffed up like a cloud from all the treats. I had to keep a bottle of brandy in the back to help me get through the days. Having Mads around became so exhausting that I sent him back to bed, suffering from another bout of vomiting. He only came out to go to kiss little Caroline or eat his meager meals. Since we started taking in lodgers, it had been harder to see James at night, and I had thought that the store would be a perfect place for us to meet, but my sister and niece made it hard. Their disapproval wafted like sour smoke around me, and I soon regretted offering Olga that position, even if she helped me with the children.

The only true respite I had was those weeks when Peter Gunness stayed with us. I relished having that man at my table, with his fine looks and strong hands. What he lacked in conversation skills he certainly made up for with practical help. My house almost felt as new when he left, with no creaking doors, jammed windows, or smoking ovens—he had taken care of all that. It took weeks before the filth came creeping back again.

I thought that I could care for a man like him.

He never behaved indecently toward me, though, which certainly was a disappointment. I had figured myself so clever, sending Mads to bed just when Peter arrived home, but it turned out that it made no difference. Mr. Gunness was determined to stay faithful to his wife, no matter how well we got along. He even took pity on Mads and brought him newspapers and good cigars. It was aggravating, the decency in that man—and certainly not what I had planned for.

I had wanted to keep the confectionery store going for a year, to last until the expenses were all paid, but I soon realized that it cost too much. The store bled money in a steady stream, adding to our debts every day. I ought to wait, though; to avoid suspicion, I ought to make it thrive before I set it ablaze. No one would suspect arson if the store did well and the finances were in order. Before the store opened, while I constructed my plan, it had not even occurred to me that *sales* would be a problem.

Then an unwanted solution arrived, as a godsend from a fiery place.

I had grown attached to Caroline. I loved being the mother of this beautiful child, the way she depended upon me and closed her little hand around my fingers. I certainly did not ignore it when her body grew hot and her cheeks turned red with fever. I gave her drops to keep her calm and relieve some of the discomfort. I washed her little body with cold cloths and dripped laudanum and brandy into her milk, but the girl's illness had deep roots, and she did not get any better. Perhaps she should have seen a doctor sooner, but I was too worried about his verdict. It was better to just tell myself that everything would be fine.

There was just so much in those days: the candy store and the finances, and everyone knows what it is like with sick infants; either the fever breaks or it does not.

When my sweet little Caroline died, I was beset with anger. I screamed and wailed so loudly that Dr. Miller had to prescribe me a powder. Mads's face was ashen; his eyes looked like pieces of coal, but he did not share the rage I felt so deep within my bones. How could it be that I wasn't allowed to keep this girl who had been all mine? I ached with longing and regret and my jaw hurt me all the time. I felt it was a punishment—an insult from above. I thought that my house was cursed, and that the rooms always strived to be empty. I kept Jennie in my bed at night to have her safely under my watchful eye, lest the void in that house would take her too.

"It happens," said the doctor, and he was right, of course. He signed the death certificate and listed the cause of death as congestion. Caroline was shrouded in white and placed in a casket, while Mads arranged for a plot at the cemetery. We sang Norwegian hymns at the funeral, standing by the open grave. All our friends from church were there, shedding tears for that innocent life and telling me how sad it was—but how blessed we were there was another on the way. The Lord giveth, the Lord taketh. His will is in everything, they said. We were blessed to have had her even for a time.

THE INSURANCE COMPANY paid out after Caroline died and that kept us going for a while longer, but I could not force those numbers. As the padding on my belly grew, the debts of our candy store followed suit. The storage filled up with uneaten candy, worthless when it was not on the shelves. Jennie had become quite obese, and so had I under the cushions. I grew worried that the longer I waited, the less profit I would make when the store burned down.

Finally, I decided I could not wait for the numbers to turn.

I bought coal oil and kerosene and placed it next to the rose and wintergreen candy in the storage room. Then I sent for James Lee. He arrived at the store at midday and served himself from the open jars of soft licorice and vanilla kisses. Jennie was playing out in the back, which made me feel a little nervous. I looked around the room, took in the colors in the jars, the scent of spice and molasses, knowing I would never see them again. Then I motioned for James to follow and showed him the fuel and the box of matches.

"I'll make it look like an accident." I spoke quietly so the child would not hear us. "I'll say that the lamp fell over in here, igniting some of the newspapers."

James was chewing on a piece of licorice; his breath was strong and sweet when he kissed me. He laughed when he felt my padded belly against him and gave the cushion a slap.

"Jennie is here," I warned him.

"To hell with the child." He still kissed me, and made me feel heady too. I hiked up my skirts and let him get to it, up against the storage room wall. I tried to be quiet so Jennie would not hear us, but he did not care at all. He lifted my leg up and held it while he burrowed in between my legs. Glass jars and tobacco tins rattled on the shelves. I came undone with his lips on mine, and a fine dust of sugar in my hair, but it did me good, yes, it did. I was no longer nervous when he lowered my leg and helped me brush off my dress. His kisses tasted of strawberry drops.

No matter how severe my hardships, James could always make me forget.

When I stepped outside, Jennie was still playing with her dolls in the back. She was humming to herself, quite oblivious. Little did she know that soon she and I would be running out in the street while tall flames ravaged the store behind us, leaving nothing but cracked jars, ashes, and glassy rivers of candy in its wake.

———

IT WAS A bad year for the Sorensen family. They lost the store and lost a child. Thank the Lord for Myrtle, then, who arrived in 1897. Always a plump and wholesome child, she was greedy on the milk but slept like an angel. It was a lovely spring, green and lush. I felt a peace with Myrtle that I had not sensed before, perhaps because she was so utterly content. Jennie treated her like a sister from the very first day and wheeled her around in the backyard. Myrtle was never sick and she never complained. How could I not love her?

The insurance money from the store was not as much as I had hoped for when all the debts were settled. I had been hoping we could finally shed that wicked house, but no—we did not have enough to do so.

I kept worrying about what we would do when the money ran out. How would I stock my pantry then? The house around me seemed filthier than ever, covered in grime I could not wash away. No matter how hard I scrubbed, everything seemed gray and greasy. I cleaned my hands, and cleaned them again, but I could still see soot clogging my pores. My whole kitchen reeked of mold, it seemed, and I inspected the cupboards daily, expecting to see black spots marring the painted wood. Just thinking of the day when the cash had shrunk to nothing made me heave for breath and grab for a rag to wipe cold sweat from my brow. I could see them so clearly in my mind's eye: Mother and Father at Størsetgjerdet, boiling thin porridge on water and rye. The taste of stale lard and rotting potatoes coated the back of my tongue and made my heart race in my chest.

The only thing that brought me some comfort were the smiles on my little girls' lips.

NOT TWO MONTHS later, I sat up one night in the children's room, waiting for the scent of smoke. When I could hear the crackle of flames from the parlor, I raised the alarm and got us out in the yard.

There I looked on while my husband in his pajamas uselessly battled the flames with buckets of water handed to him by neighbors. I held Myrtle in my arms and had Jennie by the hand. My belly was padded with a cushion.

James Lee was long gone by then, shirt singed and hands sooty.

I was rid of the house at last, and relished watching it burn to the ground.

23.

Bella

Chicago, 1900

Our new house on Alma Street was in every way better than the one that burned. The cast-iron range was twice as big as my old one and we could even afford an icebox with the insurance money after the fire.

Behind the white house grew cherry trees and currants, bursting with glossy fruits. It felt like living in a garden, that house, with flowers bursting from every surface, both inside and out, as the walls were papered with floral designs. On hot days, the air smelled green and sweet, not stale and moldy at all. The house had a proper porch as well, where I enjoyed spending my evenings reading letters, mending clothes, and polishing pairs of small shoes. Myrtle and Jennie each got a kitten upon our arrival to comfort them after the horrors of the flames. They turned out to be toms and were at each other's throats constantly, leaving festering wounds. They were at peace on the porch with me, though, keeping me company while I worked by kerosene light.

My new daughter, Lucy, was sleeping soundly in a cradle. If she stirred, I rocked it with my foot. She was a peaceful child, just as Myrtle had been.

I felt content in the new house and set my pride in making our home hospitable and nice. I made the beds every day, aired every mattress and every sheet, cleaned every pot with salt and lemons—took care that the pantry was always full but that nothing was left to rot.

My girls were immaculately dressed in the pretty frocks we bought after the fire. My chickens had a brand-new home out back and I even considered that pig again.

It made me feel close to Peter Gunness.

There was no doubt I had done right in torching our house on Elizabeth Street. The money we collected had given us the new beginning that I had so longed for. I did not miss my days in commerce but thrived on being a mother and a housewife whose biggest concerns were her daughter's painful teething and finding time to iron ribbons for the girls' perfect braids.

The only thing that did *not* work in those days of honey was Mads. What little trust he had had in me was gone, and he did his very best to make my days miserable. I suppose I should have expected it. He was a fool—but not *that* much of a fool. Even he would eventually notice how his sickness rose and fell with my moods, and the fires had done nothing to ease his suspicions. Not even the insurance money they brought in was enough to lighten his mood. He ought to have relished all the good food on our table, but instead he had become fearful of it, insisting on feeding himself from the pot or waiting to see if I ate what I brought before tasting it himself.

"What's in all those bottles you keep in the cupboard?" he asked me one day as we were enjoying a pleasant dinner of lamb chops.

I instantly went stiff with annoyance. He had no business in those cupboards. "They are tinctures and such that can come in handy." I lifted my chin a little.

"Arsenic and cyanide?" His mouth twisted up as if the lamb on his fork was distasteful. He clearly *knew* just what was in there.

"The first one is for rats and other pests. The cyanide is to clean jewelry." I wanted to smile at his foolishness but did not. The knife slid through the tender meat on my plate, met the fine china with a clicking sound.

"Is that so?" He rubbed the stubble on his cheeks. "Do we have many rats around?"

"We used to, but not anymore." Now I could not help but smile, though I certainly did try not to. He wanted to intimidate me, though he should have known better after all these years. I was not so easily rattled—and he could not prove a thing. Even Dr. Miller blamed his poor heart.

"The arsenic took care of that?" His voice was as dry as kindling.

"It did." I was still smiling as I chewed a piece of mutton.

"You and your potions." His lips twitched. "Do not for a minute think I don't know what's going on!" He hissed the words in my direction.

"What *is* going on?" Little Jennie looked between us with her innocent blue eyes, her pretty features marred by worry. She was twelve, and in charge of cutting Myrtle's meat at meals and helping the smaller girl spoon the food into her mouth. She had been so absorbed by this task, by completing it to my satisfaction, that she had not paid much attention to our words. The venom in my husband's voice had changed that.

"Look what you've done!" I hissed right back at him. "Worrying the children—have you no shame?" I grabbed my plate off the table and marched to the counter, where I finished my meal, standing. "I will not sit at the table with you when you act in such a foolish, unbecoming way," I told him.

He thought himself so clever, Mads, being cautious about the food—but I noted early on that if given a choice, he would most frequently choose the option in my right hand, or the one that I held back and not the one I reached out. I tried it out many times to be sure, offering coffee or a piece of pie, and eating the one he did not pick myself, just to put him at ease. After a while, I knew that I could surely work around his new, annoying habits and feed him whatever I liked just by using these tricks. Not that he needed my help to be miserable; though I rarely gave him anything at all, the man looked gray, just a shadow moving through *my* rooms.

Another night, as we sat out on the porch, he launched another feeble attack.

"I will have you know that I have written to Oscar and told him that if something happens to me, he should look to you for answers," he suddenly said.

I was sewing on a blue striped dress for Myrtle just then, squinting in the poor kerosene light, while rocking Lucy's cradle with my foot. When I heard what he said, I looked up.

"What could possibly—" I did not get to finish the sentence.

"If I end up dead in my bed, know that he will look into it and won't be satisfied before he knows the truth!"

I wetted my lips with the tip of my tongue; my vision swam for a moment. "You are sick and not yourself. Surely Oscar won't believe a word of your nonsense."

He sighed and sat back in his chair. "I've known you for too long, Bella. Long enough that your constant talk of the size of my life insurance bothers me."

"Well, that's for the children's sake. What would happen to them if something happened to us?" I lifted my chin when I looked at him.

"I know that you say that, but the fires got me thinking—"

"Some very bad thoughts, Mads. None of them worthy of a good man such as yourself." Inside, I was cold with fury.

"Well, how can I ever trust you after those fires?" His mouth fell open under the mustache and remained that way for quite some time.

"What exactly is it you're accusing me of?" I lifted my chin a little more.

"Well, arson and—murder!" he burst out. "You poison me with

your tinctures and powders! You are a vile woman, Bella—*vile*!" His jowls shook and his skin beaded with sweat.

I was so surprised that I stabbed my own finger and a fat drop of blood bloomed on my thumb. "How can you even say that to *me*, who cooks your meals and irons your shirts? I have never ever done anything but strive for a good life for us all."

"Sometimes I think you quite despise me!"

"Only when you talk like that . . . Look at what we have, Mads: a beautiful home and beautiful children. You just need a bit of rest. These last few years have been hard on us both."

He placed his palm over his heart and squeezed the fabric of his shirt. "I wish I could believe it's all in my head." Were those tears I saw in his eyes?

"Of course it is! Look at me! Do I look like a villain to you? I'm a woman past forty with small children and an unwell husband do- ing her best to make the most of things."

"Sometimes you're both hard and cruel—"

"Only because I'm tired. It's not easy taking care of everything. But all of that will be better now that we have this new home and money in the bank. I won't have to worry so much." I went back to the sewing, adding another stitch.

His hand relaxed on his chest. "Maybe you're right—I surely wish to think so."

"Of course I am, and you're sick and afraid. Write to your brother and tell him you were wrong. We shall speak no more of this."

The next day, Mads was in bed, retching into a bucket.

He stayed in that bed for days. Every time I thought of letting him heal, of not adding something to his food, my anger got the better of me. I sat by the bed, in a room reeking of vomit and piss, and spooned liquids into his mouth—into mine too, to put him at ease, but my health was robust so I was barely affected. I had not added much. He, on the other hand, was weak already, and the soup made him weaker still.

I wanted him dead; but then I wanted him alive, just so I could see him ache.

"When was the last time you felt sorry for someone?" he asked as we slowly went through a bowl of broth. "You always seem so cold to me. You cried at Caroline's funeral, that's true, but not after that, and never at home."

"I cried for a chicken just this morning," I lied. "Her leg was broken and I had to wring her neck. It was hard on me." I bit my lip as if battling tears.

"It just seems so wrong to me that you did not even seek my comfort—" He tried to sit up in the bed but failed, falling back onto the pillows propped up against the headboard. The pillow casings were stained with sour sweat.

"A wife ought to be strong for the family's sake and not give in to her own grief." What did he know of how I grieved my daughter? That sorrow was my own and not for someone else to see.

"Is that how it is?" I thought he smiled. Mocking me, perhaps.

"It is." I looked down into the broth and stirred it with the spoon, hoping—yet not hoping—that this would be the meal that did it. I had almost come to love my scorn for him. Living with hatred is like living with a being, an entity made of spikes and thorns. You get used to it—you embrace it and nurture it. Eventually it becomes a part of your soul.

I found I was reluctant to let it go.

Mads had been quiet for a moment, lying there with a thoughtful expression and broth on his stubbly chin. "I still think my illness is your doing."

I did not even hide my smile this time. "How can it be my doing when I eat and drink the same as you?" I lifted the spoon to my lips just to demonstrate.

"I don't know how you do it, but I know that you do. You have fed me wicked drops for years." His eyes narrowed and his nostrils flared.

"If you are so certain, why don't you go to the police with what you think you know?" I gave him another smile, one with hard edges.

"Oh, I have thought of it, but what can I do when the doctor blames my heart? And you are such a wonderful liar." His voice was quiet, void of emotion. He looked up at the ceiling, not at me, while blinking back tears. "I figure you could spin them right around."

"Leave me, then." I held out another spoonful of broth. My heart had sped up its pace, but only a little. My jaw, though, was pounding and aching.

He gave a bitter laugh that came out more like a rattle. "I would have left you a long time ago if it hadn't been for the children. I fear for them every waking minute—fear what their mother would do to them—" He broke off and went quiet again for a moment, resting against the pillows. "I do not take marriage lightly, Bella. God blessed our union, and I think he must have some plan with it all . . . Perhaps it is my task as your husband to *help*—to guide you onto a righteous path, away from all your devilry—"

"You're ill and don't know what you're saying." My jaw ached terribly; it was painful to speak. "This broth will make you better, just you see." I held out the spoon again; its silver handle was adorned with roses. My hand only shook a little.

"Still," he said after swallowing the broth. "I will not ask Oscar to discard my letter. Someone needs to know what's going on in this house." He grabbed a handkerchief off the bedside table and lifted it to his forehead to soak up the sweat. I could see a yellow tinge to the white in his eyes.

I knew in that moment that the time had come. My husband thought he had been so clever, telling his brother about his suspicions.

It did not suit me at all.

I had to let go of my scorn.

"HIS DEATH IS certainly long overdue." James Lee sat in my new kitchen and watched me grind meat for sausages.

"I needed him before. First for his measly pay, then to be a father to the children. Now he's become a threat."

"If you would only settle for a less *wholesome* life—"

"Well, I won't." I rolled my eyes. "I do know what I want, James."

"Oh, I don't doubt that." He lit a cigar; the smoke wafted across the table to curl around the heap of meat and a handful of purple hydrangeas that were slowly dying in a crystal vase.

"He's getting very suspicious—and it was foolish of him to tell me all he thinks he knows, what he has done. How can I let him live *now*?" I huffed a little and went at it with the grinding; the metal rattled inside the contraption.

"How could you let him live *before*, taking up your time?" James's eyes glittered toward me.

"I needed him, as I said. And it brings me no delight." That was the worst thing: how I did not even anticipate his oncoming demise.

"No?" James leaned on the table with curiosity in his gaze. Freshly ground meat spilled out from the grinder in pinkish-red swirls.

"Where is the satisfaction?" I asked. "Mads is no challenge to me—he is half dead already." I paused and wiped my hands on the apron.

"Would you rather he was a large brute with heavy fists?" James gave me one of his teasing smiles.

I shrugged before answering. "I want him dead, that's all I know. I want him dead and to be done with it."

"I would offer to help, but I believe you will find it more *delightful* than you think." He lifted his feet off the chair; his face had a thoughtful expression.

"Is that so?" I gave a wry smile in turn—I just could not see how any *delight* would come of this.

"Oh, there's nothing quite like scratching an old itch." He scratched his own mustache as to demonstrate.

"You only want me to kill again." I batted at his shoulder as I slumped down in a chair of my own: playful, like a kitten.

"Why would I want that?" He was playing along.

"So I would be more like you." We were still playing, but I meant it, too.

He pushed his empty glass toward me, asking for a refill. "You are already more like me than you think. I would, however, like to see you lose some of that *respectability* you carry around like a cloak—"

"Well, I'm killing him." I filled up his glass. "That's certainly not respectable."

"Where is he tonight?" James glanced at the door. "Is he up in his bed?"

"No, he's quite well again—or as well as he can be these days. I believe his stomach and heart are ruined. There was no reason to keep him up there, though, when he was soon to go anyway. He is back at work at the department store, making a little money, and that's something." I sighed and downed my own glass. The liquor was strong and heady.

James put out his cigar, then leaned so close that his face was just inches from mine. "What are you waiting for?" he asked. "You could have just let him die up there, quietly in his bed. Why are you putting it off?"

"Oh, but I'm not." I widened my eyes. "I'm merely waiting for the right day to arrive."

I closed the distance between us and gave him a kiss, tasting of meat, salt, and liquor.

ON JULY 30, Mads came home from work in the morning as usual. Before breakfast, he played with Jennie and Myrtle on the lawn. It was a lovely day with blazing sun; he never suspected that it was his last.

Later in the morning, I allowed Jennie to go to pick apples with a family on our street. It was a treat she was rarely given as I liked to keep her close, safely within my reach. I closed the door behind her and wiped sweat off my brow with my sleeve. If the perspiration was due to the sun or my nerves, I do not know.

This was new to me: killing a man in a day. He could find me out, or even survive if the dosage was not right. Neither of those prospects was appealing. I also had to make sure that the poison was properly laced with the food. If not, he might taste it and raise the alarm. I had spent hours in front of the cupboard pondering the bottles before I made my choice.

I crushed a pink tablet of cyanide and added the powder to the lemon filling in a piece of cake. Then I sliced another, equally sized piece, which I left alone. I strewed both slices with almonds, as it masks the bitter taste. Next, I poured our coffee, and then I carried it all on a tray to the parlor, where he waited in a black velvet chair. He was tired by then, ready to go to sleep, which was good, as it would make him even easier to fool. I held the poisoned cake in my right hand and held it back when I made him choose. I bit back a smile when his shivering hand reached for the one I had tampered with.

I sat down in the other chair and found my knitting. I was making little socks of the finest white wool for Lucy that day. I could see him while he ate, how the lemon spread dripped from the sponge; I watched as he devoured it all until there were only crumbs left.

"Would you like some more?" I asked.

"Another slice would be nice," said the oaf, "but you must taste it too, of course." He truly did not trust me anymore.

When I returned with more cake, he was already looking ill. His face was ashen and his movements seemed stiff.

"Are you not well?" I paused in the door.

"Just tired." Sweat beaded on his skin.

"Should I help you to bed and send for the doctor?"

"Just help me up." He staggered to his feet. "I'm not feeling well."

I took the arm he reached out to me and let him lean on my shoulders while we made our way to the bedroom. There, he slumped down on top of the bed. His eyes were dark and glassy with pain.

"I should send for the doctor." I pulled a sheet up his shivering body.

He nodded in agreement, I think. He could not speak at that point. From the sight of him then, I believed that the dosage had been right.

I left him and went back to the parlor, where I picked up my knitting. I could hear him make some noise in there, convulsing on the bed. I gave Lucy her meal and watched through the window as Myrtle chased the cat on the lawn.

When no sounds had emitted from the bedroom for some time, I carefully opened the door. One glance on the bed then, and I knew for sure.

OH, WHAT A ruckus I made after finding my husband dead. I ran out of the house and onto the street. I did not stop before I saw my neighbor, Cora, out on her porch.

"He is dead," I cried out to her. "He is dead!"

I threw myself down in the dirt, crushing pebbles and dust in my fists. I wailed down there, sobbed and thrashed and acted as if I did not feel the hands that came to rest on my shoulders, hear the gentle voices around me, or see their faces, white with shock.

I wept uncontrollably when they guided me onto Cora's porch, and waved away the cup of tea they tried to force into my hand.

"Go see if you can find her girls," Cora told her daughter, and the little girl ran down the street, braids whipping on her back.

A boy had already gone to fetch Dr. Miller, and the wait seemed to last forever as I sat there with my head bent, shivering and weeping. The neighborhood women fussed around me and brought me a shawl and a stiff drink. We could see Cora's daughter and my girls come up the street; she carried the one and held the other by the hand, just as a carriage arrived and stopped outside our house. Dr. Miller stepped down, brushing dust off his trousers.

"I cannot go back there," I whispered, "I cannot bear to see him like that."

"But, Mrs. Sorensen, you must. I will come with you, but you must." Cora squeezed my hand in hers.

We staggered down the street while Dr. Miller made his way toward the porch. Cora held me by the elbow and caught me when I seemed to falter.

"What happened, Mrs. Sorensen?" Dr. Miller paused and waited for us. "Where is Mr. Sorensen?"

"In his bed!" I wailed, and broke down again. I refused to go inside but sat down on the steps to the porch. "Oh, what am I to do now? A poor widow with three small children in my care—what will happen to us now?"

Cora sat down next to me and held my shoulders while I cried. I could hear Dr. Miller walk inside, his steps on the floorboards behind me.

The sun was blazing; the air was humid. Myrtle laughed on the neighbor's lawn. "Those poor children," I muttered.

"You better prepare for the funeral," said Cora. Women are nothing but practical. "You have to force yourself for their sake. Your girls."

Dr. Miller stepped back outside. He wiped his fingers with his handkerchief, adjusted his glasses, and put on his hat. "His poor heart got him in the end, it seems. I am sorry for your loss, Mrs. Sorensen." It was very convenient to have a family doctor who carried fond memories of my steaks, puddings, and stews.

"I told him not to work so hard." I sniffled, and dried the tears with my apron.

"She is falling apart, poor thing," Cora told the doctor. "She lay down on the street and wouldn't move."

"I'll prescribe a powder," the doctor said. "Something to settle her nerves."

"How can this be happening?" I wailed. "How can it be?" My hands were shaking.

"Did he eat anything out of the ordinary today? Did he take his medication?" Dr. Miller looked at me.

"Of course he did! I gave it to him myself. And then he had cake and coffee."

"Did he complain about anything? Chest pains?"

"He said he had a headache." I dried more tears. "He wanted to lie down."

"Well." Dr. Miller sighed. "I can see you are distraught, so I won't ask more questions today. He was a very sick man. Perhaps we should have expected it."

"At least he is at peace now," said Cora.

THAT NIGHT, AFTER Jennie's weeping had ceased and Myrtle's fussing had given way to sleep, I sat alone in the kitchen with Lucy in the cradle, rocking it gently with my foot. I had turned down the kerosene lamp and poured myself a brandy; the golden liquor sloshed around the glass as I lifted it to my lips. I closed my eyes and savored the taste, and then I prodded my insides. I was looking for that feeling, that same joy I remembered from Anders's demise. Surely it would be within my reach now that I had killed another man.

I recognized relief. I recognized hope and possibilities: the start of a brand-new day. I saw Peter Gunness there, his face flashing before me, and I saw myself content and at peace. I saw James too, sauntering through my mind in that feline way that he had. But I did not find that feeling, that red-hot flood of triumph I had felt after Anders died, and found I was dismayed by that fact.

Maybe Mads's death had been too easy to count.

I had been hoping for ecstasy, but as with everything with Mads, all I was given was disappointment.

24.

Nellie

The days following Mads's death were like a bad dream. One of those that does not make much sense but still lingers long after you wake up and leaves a sickening feeling.

I learned about the death early next morning, when Bella's neighbor, Cora, came to deliver the sad news and summon me to Alma Street.

"She is in no state to come and tell you herself, Mrs. Larson." Cora sat at my kitchen table, refreshing herself with some hot coffee. "Oh, she was so upset! Though we all knew that he was ill, so it shouldn't have come as such a surprise! She told me herself, out on the street. 'Cora, we'll be lucky to keep him till fall,' she said, but I guess it's still a shock when it happens. He seemed so hale too, in the last few weeks. My daughter saw him outside, playing with the girls that same morning. Perhaps he overtaxed his poor heart." She sipped the coffee.

"Yes." My vision was swimming a little, and I had to hold on to the countertop to keep myself steady. "My brother-in-law has been ill for some time."

"It will be hard for her now with three girls to care for, and two of them are still so young." Her face fell into concerned folds. "I advised her to get him in the ground as soon as possible, with this heat and all . . . She should not keep him at home any longer than necessary."

"Is he washed yet?" I crossed the short space to the table and sat down as well. I did not have any coffee, though; I felt a little sick, a little dizzy.

"Oh yes, she took care of that herself. Didn't even want any help. She is such a hard worker, your sister, and with such a robust constitution. She is certainly of the old country—nothing can slow her down." Clara served herself from the buttered bread I had put out on a tray; it was a little stale, but I had nothing else. The woman did not complain, though, but drizzled crumbs down on my clean table.

"What did the doctor say?" My voice barely carried when I asked. With my inner eye, I saw the bruise from the soap bar, and behind it all, I saw my father's swaying form, his fist poised to strike, his breath strong with liquor.

"That it was the heart, of course." Cora shook her head and tutted a little, then took another piece of bread from the tray. "I know Bella gave him all sorts of powders for it, prescribed by that doctor they know, but I suppose there's little to do once it's broken."

"Of course," I said. "He did have a broken heart." No blood then. No wounds or a nasty fall.

"And that vomiting too," Cora went on. "She told me all about it. It's a miracle that he did not die before."

"Yes, isn't it just." I saw that bruise again. "She wants my help, I reckon?"

"Oh yes, with the children, of course, but the flowers too. She gave me some coins for black-edged paper, so she can write to his relatives and such." Cora brushed crumbs off her hands. "You will go there at once?"

"Of course." I was already off the chair, looking for my shawl.

"I am happy for it. She is in such a terrible state and should not be alone." Cora rose too, leaving her cup on the table. "Jennie is an angel, of course." She tightened her own knitted shawl over her shoulders. "She helps as much as she can, but she shouldn't be alone with it, being as young as she is."

"Not to worry," I told Cora, "I will look after them all."

ALL THE WAY on the streetcar, I imagined what I would find when I arrived. I saw Bella sitting in darkness in the parlor, with all the curtains drawn, stiff and unmoving. I imagined the children filthy and starving. The baby crying from the cradle. I saw Jennie trying to comfort them all, bringing her mother and Myrtle treats from the pantry and dipping bread in milk for Lucy. She was only twelve—it would not do.

It was not what I found, though, when I arrived at the house on Alma Street.

As soon as I opened the door, I met a delicious smell of hot sugar and butter, and when I entered the kitchen, I found Bella busy with the rolling pin. Jennie and Myrtle were there as well, wearing little aprons. Jennie was in charge of the cookie cutter, while Myrtle's small fingers pushed one scalded almond on top of each perfect circle of dough. They had already baked one tray, and that was where the smell came from. It smelled even stronger in there, mingling with scents of woodsmoke and lemon. Bella wore black, that was true, but other than that she did not look much like a newly minted widow, with her hands covered in flour and her hair bun half undone.

"Oh Nellie!" She beamed when she saw me. "I was hoping you could help me with the flowers. We will take them from the garden, of course. There's no point in spending money on such vanity."

"What is this?" I took off my coat; it had already been too warm outside, and in that kitchen it was unbearable. "Cora said you were in mourning," I said, accusing her. "She made me think you couldn't be on your own."

"Well, I am—I can't." She grimaced and finally stopped her eager rolling. "But there's no one else here but me, so I have to go on the best that I can. Who will feed the children if I don't?" She wiped her hands on the apron; small puffs of flour rose in the air. Her eyes looked angry—she did not much like to be questioned. "All sorts of people will come to see him, and they will expect refreshments. It just won't do to have nothing to serve them."

"You could have waited for me." I scolded her lightly and went to kiss the girls. "Is Lucy asleep?" I glanced in the direction of the parlor, where the cradle mostly stood these days.

Bella nodded, suddenly solemn, as if she had just remembered how to grieve. "She is blessed, that child, to not know what has happened in this house. She does not have to endure grief as we do." She lifted a hand to her eyes, as if hiding a tear.

"Where is he? In his bed?"

"No, he is upon the dining room table. I had a casket brought in." Her lips quivered a little.

"I better go and see him then, before the neighbors descend."

"Suit yourself." She nodded in the direction of the door. "I won't look at him again until I have to. It's too hard for me." She looked down at the half-filled baking tray before her, bottom lip still quivering.

"You washed him, though?"

"Nothing but my duty. Just as it's my duty to write those cards that have to be sent." She shook her head so the loose tendrils of hair lifted. "As if *correspondence* is what I want to spend my time on just now." Her face twisted up with distaste.

"As you say, it's your duty. His family needs to be told."

"Well, they won't make it here before he's in the ground." She lifted her chin a little.

"So be it—they still have to know. Cora said she would stop by with the mourning paper as soon as she got back."

I stepped out of the sweltering kitchen and entered the dining room. I did not fear death—I had seen it many times before. I had washed my own children, and siblings too, but it still came as a surprise to see a body thus, so pale and smooth. Void of life.

Mads was almost unrecognizable in death. His brow was smoother than it had been for many years; all signs of strife and toil had left him. He lay there in his best suit, and a candle burned in the windowsill. She had combed his mustache, I noticed, taken better care of him in death, perhaps, than she had in the last few years of his life.

I put my fingers on the waxen hands folded on his chest. I wanted to think that his soul was at rest, wherever it was. It pained me to think of how he had struggled to maintain some sort of peace in his house while alive—that his time on earth had held so little happiness.

"Farewell," I whispered to his still face, the mask of him, cast in death. "I am sorry," I added. Something like guilt moved in me, twisted in my chest. *I hope it was not her fault,* I added, but silently, inside. Then my cheeks reddened with shame from even thinking such a thing.

The candle flickered when I opened the door and left, emitting a scent of hot wax and smoke.

Back in the kitchen, it seemed even stranger than before, how they were all at it with the sugar and the flour, with the dead man so close. Jennie's brow was creased with concentration as she pressed the cookie cutter down in the sheet of dough, pausing from time to time to keep Myrtle from eating the almonds by pushing her little hands away from the blue enamel bowl.

"It's all right," Bella said across the table. "She can have one, and you too." She was rolling out another batch of dough. They were baking for a whole army, it seemed. The grief from before was wiped from Bella's face; it looked like any other day. "Oh," she said when she noticed me. "Did you get a good look at him? I groomed him well, I think."

"Oh yes, he looked very fine." I felt faint again. The scent of melted wax lingered in my nostrils.

"It is a tragedy, of course." Her face rearranged again, displaying grief once more.

"Well, it wasn't entirely unexpected." I found a spare apron behind the door and set to tie it on. "Jennie will help me with the flowers later, won't you, Jennie?" I smiled at the girl.

"Sure, Aunt Nellie." She gave me a quick smile in return.

"It was sad about your father," I said, while setting to make more dough in the ceramic bowl.

"Uh-huh." She nodded, but I could not help but note the way her gaze went to Bella for approval, as if she was uncertain if this was the right way to respond.

"We are all crushed, of course," Bella said, and sat down on a chair, happy to leave the baking to me. "He seemed better too. He was going to work as normal."

"Sometimes it's sudden," I said, not to comfort but because it was the truth. "Did he have any savings? Anything to help you get by?"

"No"—Bella's lips tightened—"but he was insured, thank God, so that was lucky. We won't starve just yet."

"Good," I said, while whipping the eggs. I could not help but remember Mads's own words, spoken just after the fire when he had expressed similar sentiments. *Such magnificent luck*, he had said, in a voice dripping with bitterness.

I pushed the thought away.

I WAS THERE often over the next few weeks, long after Mads had been buried, to help with the girls and be of comfort. Sometimes I brought Olga or Nora, but most often I went by myself. I could not understand my sister—the nature of her grief. It blew as hot and cold as a Norwegian summer; sometimes it was as if nothing was amiss, while at other times she would cry her eyes out to strangers. When we were alone together, she did not want to speak of Mads at all.

I still came, though, for Jennie's sake if nothing else. Myrtle was too small to mourn, but it was different for the older girl. I noted that she had grown quieter since her father died. Only when her mother was around did she make an effort to seem lively. She did not shed her tears, even when her lips quivered and her eyes turned moist but made an effort to keep her grief inside herself. Bella thought her brave, but I thought it all very sad, and brought her out in the garden to pick flowers for Mads's grave. She seemed to enjoy that, to do something nice for him, even if he would never come back.

Then one day, as I was making a stew in the kitchen, there came a hard rapping on the front door. As I stood there stirring the pot, I could hear Bella rush from the parlor to answer.

At first, I paid little attention to the murmuring voices by the door. I glanced outside the window, though, to keep an eye on the older girls, who were out on the lawn, and caught sight of a stocky man on the porch. He seemed vaguely familiar. Then, suddenly, the murmur grew into proper words, shouted in an angry voice. I almost dropped the wooden spoon into the stew from the shock.

"You're an evil woman, *evil*!" the man out there cried. "He knew it would come to this! He always knew it would come to this!"

"You're grief-stricken." I heard Bella's voice, trying to appease the stranger. "Calm yourself, Oscar. We're all shocked by his sudden death, but he was ill—"

At this, I lifted the pot onto the cooler side of the stove, took off my apron, and stepped into the hall. I should have recognized him, of course, but I had not seen Mads's brother since their wedding. I lingered at the back of the hall, biding my time, ready to step closer if Bella needed me.

"He was not so ill that he couldn't unburden himself to me first." Oscar waved a piece of paper in the air, covered in thick scrawls. "I'm not surprised you didn't write to me at once, and saw fit to bury him before I had a chance to see him."

"The days are hot; it couldn't wait." She held up her hands as to ward him off.

"I will tell you this, though." The man hardly seemed to hear her. "I won't rest easy before I have proven your guilt. I have arranged to have him dug up." Oscar's lips twisted up in triumph, and a chill ran through my body, from my scalp and all the way to my toes.

"Whatever for?" Bella had placed a hand on the door frame, and I could see how her fingernails clawed at the wood.

"To look for evidence of foul play!" He pressed his lips tightly together.

"I would think his widow has a say in what happens to her husband's remains." My sister was not lost for words. Though I could not see it, I imagined how her chin had tilted up.

"I'm a brother and that counts for something," Oscar Sorensen sneered.

At that point, my silent watching ended. I could not let this go on. I quickly stepped up to the door. "Please," I said. "All this shouting! There are children here, and neighbors. Surely whatever is amiss can be discussed in a calm manner."

"Oscar thinks I did away with his brother." Bella's voice was filled with scorn.

"Please stay out of this, Mrs. Larson." Oscar pointed at me with his walking stick.

"I will *not*." I looked him up and down. Who was he to speak to me in such a way? "There has been a death in this house—"

"Oh, believe me, I am well aware!" He spoke with such anger that spittle flew from his lips and landed on my cheek.

"Then you should act appropriately!" I was so shocked at that point that my whole body shook when I pushed by him, wanting to reach the children, to get them away from the furious couple.

"They did an autopsy before he went in the ground," I heard Bella say behind me as I strode across the lawn. I was marching toward Jennie and Myrtle, who sat there in their mourning clothes, adorning the latter's new doll with flowers. Their hands had stopped midmotion, though, and their eyes had fastened on the spectacle on the porch.

"You ought to leave your brother to rest in peace!" Bella told her brother-in-law.

"Apparently the autopsy wasn't thorough enough—"

"His heart was enlarged! You know this!" She did not try to appease him any longer; her voice had colored with anger too.

"I have spoken to Mr. Jackson at the insurance company and informed him of my plans." His voice was nothing but triumphant.

"You're being a fool, Oscar. Whatever did you do that for?"

I turned back to see that Bella's brow had creased. Then I was with the girls and reached out my hands, waiting for them to latch on with their fingers.

"He said they have found that there was another policy as well, expiring on just that date," said Oscar—and despite the chaos that reigned in that moment, the words left me feeling cold.

"I have already spoken to Mr. Jackson—" she said.

"Fed him your *lies* for sure!" he cried.

"Dr. Miller said it was his heart and I have no reason to doubt that!"

From the open window to the parlor, I heard Lucy wailing in the cradle, wanting a change and some milk. I decided that I did not want to push by the screaming couple again, not with the two girls.

"Come," I told my charges. "We will go in through the back and leave your mama to speak to your uncle in peace."

"Why is he so mad?" Jennie's eyes were wide with concern.

"Oh, he is only upset that his brother is dead." I tried for a reassuring smile.

Just then, his dry, rasping laughter sounded from the porch. "You won't get away with this," he said. "I'll see to it that you don't!"

I rushed the girls along to the corner of the house, but even as we stepped onto the flagstones that led to the garden in the back, we could still hear their voices.

"Have you no shame, saying such things in front of his daughters? Attacking a defenseless widow—"

"*Rich* widow," he interrupted.

"Who is only trying to do what's best after an awful tragedy."
She would not be silenced so easily. "If I had wanted Mads dead,
why would I have waited all these years?"

"I don't know the workings of an evil mind—"

"Don't even *think* Mr. Jackson will help you in your folly. You
will have to pay for your insanity yourself!" There was real fury in
her voice now, and I found I feared for his safety. I silently begged
that she would not invite him inside, where she had all sorts of things
within reach.

"Oh, I'll pay if it comes to that." His voice was fainter now, as we
had arrived on the other side of the building. "I cannot leave my
brother to rot without justice!"

"It's all in vain, Oscar. The only culprit in his death was his weak
heart!"

"We'll see about that, *Mrs.* Sorensen!"

By the time we reached the kitchen, it was over. Bella came back
inside with a red face and foul mood that did not lessen all day.

I changed Lucy and brought the stew back to a boil. Jennie helped
me set the table while Myrtle trailed behind her, wanting to play
with her doll again. Bella sat in a chair, looking through the door to
the stove, left ajar for the airflow. She watched the crackling flames
without a word.

When Lucy fell asleep again and the other girls went outside to
bring in the wash on the line, I could no longer hold my tongue.

"What was that?" I turned to her with the wooden spoon in my
hand.

She came back to life slowly, as if surfacing from somewhere
deep in her mind. Her voice when she spoke was slow and quiet.
"Oh, it was just Oscar who—"

"No! Not that. The insurance policies—he said there were two."

"Well, it's just a silly coincidence." She did not look at me but at
the woven rug on the floor. "It happens that on the day Mads died,
our old insurance ended and the new policy began." She lifted her

gaze a little so it lingered on the spoon, which was steadily dripping stew down on the floor. "It turns out that both of them are valid, so I will get paid by both companies."

I was so calm in that moment, even if my heart raced. I dropped the spoon back in the stew and sat down on the other side of the table, folding my hands on the tabletop.

Bella continued to speak. "Now Oscar thinks all sorts of bad things about me—he claims that Mads sent him a letter, but I think he wrote it himself. He says that it's my fault that he's dead, that I did away with him on just that day so that I would get double pay."

My voice barely carried when I asked, "Did you?"

"Well, of course not!" She abruptly rose from the chair and started pacing the floor, her hands gesturing wildly in the air. "It just happened to be the right day, that's all! I did not even know that he had signed the new papers—I never took an interest in such things!"

"Was it the only day that they overlapped?" My voice was still calm—*I* was still calm—and I could not quite figure why that was. My heart pounded heavy and fast in my chest.

"Yes." Her eyes flashed when she looked at me, as if daring me to believe her. "Perhaps it was God's will." She threw out her arms. "Perhaps it was Mads who did it himself to leave us a little extra . . . he was in poor shape, as you know."

"But you didn't do a thing to hasten his departure?" My voice was weak, but still calm. My whole body felt as if taken with fever.

"No!" Another flash of her eyes. "And now he wants to dig the poor man up! Who treats his brother like that? Who will attack a defenseless widow—?"

"If you did nothing, you have nothing to fear," I reminded her.

"Of course I didn't"—she all but hissed the words—"but it's the indignity of it! The suspicion!"

"Are you getting very much money out of it?" I asked, though I would rather have not. I wanted the conversation to be over more than anything else, and yet I had to ask.

"Yes." Her gaze met mine, as briefly as the beat of a butterfly's wings. "I do get a lot of money."

"Then your troubles are far from over." I added a smile to mask my fear.

I wanted to believe her. I *would* believe her.

What else was there to do but believe?

She was my flesh and blood, after all.

25.

Bella

I thought the devil had forsaken me at last.

In front of me sat Mr. Jackson, the insurance man, with a bushy brown mustache and a silver pen in his hand. To his left sat his clerk, a man half my age. On his right-hand side was the insurance company's investigator, a thin, tall, sandy-haired man, Mr. Samuels. We were waiting for a representative from our former insurance company, a Mr. Wicker, but he seemed to be running late.

"What is astonishing to me, Mrs. Sorensen, is that you thought there would be no questions asked after your husband's death." Mr. Jackson leaned forth in his chair; his hands slid across the glossy surface of his desk. I myself was seated on a high-backed chair in front of him. The plain wood already grated at my backside.

"Not so untimely, I think," I said, clutching at a handkerchief. "My husband had a bad heart for years. It was only a matter of time—"

"Yet it happened on that *one* day out of the year that your two insurance policies overlapped . . ."

"I don't know anything about that." I lifted my teary gaze to meet his. "My husband took care of bills and suchlike. I know very little of such things."

"Did you even know there was a policy?"

"Well, we discussed it after our first daughter was born, to secure the children. I believe he made a habit out of it after that, just in case."

"Does it not surprise you that he died on that very day?" Mr. Samuels spoke.

"No—I didn't know it was a special day before you told me so."

"You didn't know there was an overlap?"

"No . . . I only learned it when I went through Mads's papers after he died, and even then I did not quite grasp—"

"Would you say your husband was depressed?" Mr. Samuels interrupted me. "Would he have any reason to end his life a little sooner than expected? He was sick, after all, and waited to die; perhaps he wanted to give you a boon . . . a little more than you would otherwise have?"

"Oh"—I shook my head and dabbed at my eyes with the handkerchief—"I really don't think he would. He was a very religious man, Mr. Samuels. Very concerned with his soul."

"Couldn't it be that he worried about his family, of what would befall you after he was gone?"

"Dr. Miller swore it was his heart," I answered, and added a few more tears. "I have no reason to believe that the good doctor was wrong, and Mads wouldn't leave me alone to fend for the children. He was a good man, he would never do anything wrong . . ."

Mr. Jackson spoke again, while the clerk scribbled in a book. "You see why we have to investigate this, Mrs. Sorenson. There are irregularities here, suspicious circumstances—"

"And the brother wrote," the clerk piped up, looking at Mr. Jackson, not at me.

"Yes, his brother wrote to us and advised us to take a closer look. That's how we discovered the duplicate."

"My husband's brother is a difficult man. He never much cared for me, nor for my children." I could not help that my lips twisted up with distaste. He had surely succeeded in making my life miserable.

"Why is that, Mrs. Sorenson?" Samuels asked. "Why did he not care for you?"

"Well, for a long time God didn't provide us with any children, and Oscar grew resentful of me then." I rubbed my aching jaw.

"Because you didn't have children?"

"Yes . . . I thought it got a little better after Caroline was born, but then she died and he resented me again. I have three healthy girls now, but he hasn't changed his mind. He maybe thinks I held back on purpose. That I *denied* his brother a child." I made it all up as I went along, one lie clasping hands with the other. Had not the circumstances been so dire, I would have quite enjoyed it. As it was, however, much was at stake, not least my neck.

"His death will leave you a very wealthy woman," Mr. Jackson said. "Have you given any thought to that?"

"No. I rather think I'm poorer for it, being left a widow. What good is money, then, if you have lost someone you held dear?" I sniffled a little and looked away.

"Are you yourself a religious woman, Mrs. Sorensen?"

"Yes, very much so." I cleared my throat.

"So you wouldn't lie about any of this?" Mr. Jackson asked.

"No . . . no, I would not dream of lying!" I lifted my hands as in shock.

"And you knew nothing about these policies?" His eyebrow lifted a little and the crook of his mouth too.

"No." I dabbed at my eyes again. "Maybe it's merely an act of God."

When I finally left that office, I was rattled to the core. I had clearly underestimated Oscar as an opponent. This was not good. I walked on perilous ground, and I knew it. How long would it be before they found out about the fires? Everything could unravel.

My greed had made me stupid.

I DID NOT like it at all, the scrutiny of the insurance companies, which kept pestering me and sending worrisome letters. Jennie cried in her bed at night because the children in school said her mother was a murderer. I could see the little rascals hiding in the garden sometimes; running off shrieking if they saw me. The aftermath of Mads's death had quite ruined the new house for me; the wallpaper seemed gray, all the flowers withered, and the paint appeared stained. Everything was filthy. The crystal drops in the chandelier seemed dull with dust, the icebox reeked, and my pantry filled up again with more food than we could eat. The preserves in the cellar grew a thick crust of mold. The venom people threw at me festered and spread through everything. I found no peace, I found no sleep—this was no way to live.

"I ought to burn it to the ground," I told James Lee one night when the children were asleep. I had traded my usual brandy for whiskey; I found some solace in the strong fumes in those days. Outside the window, the greenery was giving way to fall's wet decay. Everything smelled rotten, not sweet and green as before.

"It's not something I'd advise at this point." James was wearing a suit that night: crumpled and worn but a suit nonetheless. His bowler hat sat on the table, next to a bowl of half-peeled potatoes; the jacket was flung over a chair.

"There is a fire every day in this city."

"They are already looking too closely."

"They won't find a thing." I tightened my shawl around my shoulders. "Oscar doesn't have the means to have them do the whole autopsy, and the insurance companies won't pay for it."

"Still, they are watching you."

"They will never find me out. They never did before."

"You didn't kill a man then." He knocked back his whiskey and held out his glass for more. "Remember Mr. Holmes? He hanged." James had been deeply fascinated with Mr. Holmes in the years after the world fair, when the newspapers were rife with stories of his murder hotel. He had admired Mr. Holmes's cunning: how he had lured and killed his victims to sell the bodies to medical students and suchlike. James thought him clever to have constructed such a bold enterprise.

"They won't hang a widow and a mother," I claimed.

"Unless they do." I could not read his face. "One never knows with such things; if they are angry enough, they will. They might find you a disgrace to motherhood itself, and then all bets are off. People so often adore their mothers."

I smiled at that last part and tasted my whiskey. "If I can make the insurance companies pay what they owe me for Mads's death, and all suspicion goes away. I'll torch the house then, not before."

He shook his head, but he was smiling too. "You are a fearless creature, Mrs. Sorensen."

"They never found me out before," I repeated.

"One day they might." His brow creased with concern.

"But not today. I have some devil's luck in me yet." I had to believe that. I clung to that notion with all my might.

"And if they do pay—both companies—what will you do then?"

I looked down at the table, where the *Chicago Tribune* rested with grease-stained pages. "I haven't decided yet. Perhaps I'll buy a farm. I see advertisements for fine pieces of land all the time."

"Surely not a pig farm." James's face fell.

I shrugged. "Peter Gunness's wife is pregnant but very ill. They don't expect her to last."

"And now you want to take up with that butcher?"

"As I said, I haven't decided yet. First I have to manage not to hang." I closed the newspaper and pushed it away. What good were dreams if I could not achieve them?

James would not let the subject of Mr. Gunness go. "Is he your lover yet?"

I did not answer; what was it to James? None of his concern. "He is a fine and decent man. A good father too, I think." I lifted my chin a little when I looked at him.

"He will never satisfy you." The lips below the mustache tightened.

"How do you know? He has a bloody trade." Our gazes met across the table. He lifted his chin a little too, to match me.

"He will never be one of us." James's voice was full of contempt.

"Neither would I want him to be." I could not help but laugh. "I just need him to raise pigs and take care of us all." I looked away, to the stove, filthy with soot and food spills, and the bowl on the counter, brimming with rotting vegetables. These latest debacles had left me weak, sloppy, and blind to decay.

"You lust for him, that's it." James lit a cigar and blue smoke rose toward the ceiling.

"Would you judge me if I did?" My eyes were back on him. Our gazes dueled across the table; his was glittering and dark, with a sharp, sharp edge.

"Who am I to judge you?" James dropped his gaze, drank again, and left his glass to hover in midair. "I've always had the utmost respect for your lust." He added a lazy smile.

"I know you do." I smiled as well, and marveled at how his shifting eyes could still make my breath catch in my throat. "You have always been good to me in that way."

"I hope I always will be." He set his glass back down, leaned over the table, and caught my face in his hands. Then he kissed me. His breath was strong with drink, his lips as soft as ever. I only flinched a little when he bit me, and the taste of iron flooded my tongue. I reached with my hand for the peeling knife on the table and pressed it to his throat, not hard, but not too gently either. The knife was sharp enough, newly cleaned and whetted. I could tell from his breathing that he liked it, having the steel there where his vein throbbed. I knew he would be hard by now, aching for release.

"Come." My voice was a little bit husky when I spoke. I was not unmoved by him either. I lowered the knife but kept it with me as I led him by the hand through my night-quiet house, passing the open door to the children's room. I did not stop before we stood on the chilly floor in my bedroom, where the massive bed stood empty with no simpering fool in it. "I know you always wanted to play the husband."

He laughed, utterly delighted. "What a gift, Bella, my dear. Your marriage bed at last."

"Only for a visit," I said, but I laughed too. I whimpered when he pushed me up against the wall and fondled my breasts through the cloth of my dress and the stiff panes of my corset. His lips were at my throat, his favorite spot, and he chewed at the soft flesh there. I dropped the knife to the floor, dug my fingernails into his scalp, and spread my legs when he tugged at my skirts. By the time his hand reached its mark, I was slick around his fingers.

Over his shoulder, I saw the open closet where Mads's ironed shirts still hung.

"On the bed," I whispered, flushed with want, and pushed him roughly away, only to attack him when we tumbled onto the mattress, clothes and hair in disarray.

I pulled my dress over my head and he fished the knife from the floor to slice the strip of satin that held the hooks of the corset—too eager now to bother with them. Not once did I flinch when the cool metal moved close to my skin. My breasts lay large and heavy in his hands; he fondled them greedily and licked them with his tongue.

I pushed him over then so he lay on his back with me on top, and wrung the fabric of his shirt away from his chest. The peeling knife was back in my hand and I let it play ever so lightly over his nipples while straddling his hips, feeling his want for me strain against the fabric of his pants. He moaned and cursed me, sucked in a sharp breath as the knife drew blood. Not much; just a smear. The look of it on his pale skin excited me even more and I bent down to lick the little wound, earning me another outcry from James. His hand was in my hair, pulling hard to lift my head, and when I did, he kissed me again, breath hot and strained on my skin.

I was done playing. I sat back up and pulled his pants and underwear down his legs, far enough that I could get what I wanted. I climbed back on top of him and slipped him inside me. I always relished that moment, that delicious few seconds when he entered me fully and I could squeeze him hard with my insides. I still held the knife while I rode him, wild and carefree. My hair had come undone by then; my skin was slick with salt, and the pewter button danced on its chain. James convulsed beneath me when he came—and I did too, right there on Mads's bed. Just to spite.

James knew me well enough to know it. When we lay resting in each other's arms, he said, "You and your contempt for all and everything. You will torch the house again just to spite them, won't you? If you win the insurance claim."

"I'm good with spite," I told him. "And the devil hasn't let me down yet."

"No." James chuckled. "I suppose he is far too amused by your antics."

EVENTUALLY, THE INSURANCE companies had to give in. They had no evidence against me.

I went to their offices every day for a week, with all the girls, complaining about my misery. "How am I to feed these girls?" I asked Mr. Jackson with tears in my eyes. "How are they to live now that their father is dead and buried? It's certainly not *their* fault that he died on such a troublesome day."

Jennie sometimes cried at these meetings, from fear I suppose, as she disliked angry voices, but it certainly was effective. Lucy rode on my hip, dazzling the world with her large blue eyes. Myrtle clung to my skirts, as if I were the longed-for harbor in a terrible storm.

It was all so very perfect—and the insurance men in their fine suits could not wait to have us out the doors, promising a little too much, perhaps, in their eagerness to see us go.

No one wants a weeping widow standing on their marble floors, clutching a brood of little angels and lamenting the company's heartlessness to every passing soul. It does not speak well for their business.

Oscar had gone home at last. His silly experiment with the autopsy had been stranded when he ran out of money, and the new examination of the body had ended before they even got to the heart. They had not found anything to condemn me, and I always made a point of reminding Mr. Jackson and Mr. Wicker of that fact.

Oscar did me a favor in that way.

What he *had* done to cause me grief was telling every one of my neighbors and acquaintances of his suspicions. I saw it in the eyes of every wife on the street, and every deliveryman who came to my door, that they had all heard about the life insurance and Oscar's vile claims. No wonder my girl was being teased in school, when her uncle had been out spreading rumors about me.

But no one could prove a thing, and eventually I was paid.

Shortly after the insurance money arrived, I had James set a fire in the cellar in Alma Street, as I felt it would be better if we lived somewhere else. The children and I escaped out on the street, where kindly neighbors comforted us while the firemen battled the flames.

It did not burn down, which annoyed me some but pleased me too. Perhaps it would not be so bad to move back in if it was all re-done and furnished with new things. The dream of a farm kept haunting me, though. I could not cease longing for privacy and peace. Even when we lived temporarily on Sophia Street while our own house was being repaired, I felt I was being looked at every-where I went—that the taint of suspicion was with me always.

Jennie still cried every night.

I had money, though, and that was some comfort. Even if my nights were sleepless, I knew I could fill my pantry.

I had James set a fire on Sophia Street too, so I could get rid of the furniture from Alma Street, which smelled charred even after airing. It was better that the insurance company paid for the new things than I.

After both fires, they grumbled but could not prove a thing. At the last fire, I was not even in the house. "Maybe someone has it in for me," I suggested. "Maybe someone wants to see me stranded without a home. Someone, perhaps, with a grudge." I was thinking of Oscar, of course. It could not hurt to sow a tiny suspicion that perhaps he had agents with ill intent. I dearly wanted to get back at him for all the grief he had cost me, and he was a lucky man to live as far away as he did.

Should our paths ever cross again, I would surely repay him with interest.

The children and I went back to Alma Street after the renovation, but despite the new boards and paint, it still felt like a murky place, festering from within the walls.

I craved for a new life for us, my girls and me, far away from suspicions.

Surely I had earned as much, after all the trouble I had seen.

26.

Nellie

At first, when Bella asked me, I was adamant that I would not go. There was my back, for one, which prevented all comfortable travel, and then there was the rest of it: how Mads's death had left such a bad taste behind, and the fear that sometimes gripped me at night and woke me up with a sense of being choked, covered in cold sweats and beset with shivers.

I no longer felt at ease around my sister.

John knew it, and sometimes asked me after we had gone to bed for the night.

"What is it that bothers you so?" he would say with worry in his dark gaze. His hair had turned gray, and his skin was wrinkled, but his good sense and kindness had not changed.

"Nothing," I would say, but the lie would almost choke me, make my voice come out thick and muffled.

"Then why are you so rarely there anymore?" The way he looked at me then, as if daring me to voice what was truly the issue. He knew very well what was being said about Bella, but he seldom mentioned it at home, as he knew that it would upset me. My children knew as well. Olga would frown and sneer at it all, claiming the rumors to be nothing but lies. Rudolph took a more thoughtful approach, and remarked once, at one Sunday dinner, that their marriage had indeed been a powder keg. Little Nora, at thirteen, got in trouble at school for threatening to send her aunt after some boys who had teased her and called her names.

"Well, they *did* stop," she said when I confronted her. "No one wants to make Aunt Bella angry."

Nora was the only one of my children who still lived with us. Olga had taken a room above the hosiery store where she worked, and Rudolph shared a room with a friend. It felt empty and lonely without them, but they were growing up, and I had been much younger myself when I left home. The rooms around me seemed vast without them, though, and I missed the bustle in the mornings and the sounds they made at night. I truly should have spent more time with my nieces, helping Bella out—but I found it so hard to be there.

I believed her, I told myself. Of course I did believe her.

What else was there to do but believe?

And yet I woke up in a choke hold, covered in slick, salty sweat.

"That Oscar is long gone now," John said the night after she had asked me to go. "He did not find a thing. I think it's only because Bella and Mads fought like they did that people think such vile things now."

"I know," I mumbled into the pillow. "But it was that date he died..." This was the closest I had ever come to voicing my shameful doubt, and John took a hold of me and pulled me close to his chest.

"Hush," he whispered into my hair, to soothe me while I shivered in his arms. "Perhaps he did it himself, with all those powders the doctor described. Maybe he didn't want to be ill anymore."

"That's what *she* said," I whispered back. The scent of his nightshirt was a comfort; it smelled of him and clean cotton.

"If she had wanted to kill him, she would have done so a long time ago—she wouldn't have waited sixteen years to do so."

I let out my breath then; it was such a relief to hear him say it in his calm, composed voice. Of course she had not done it. Of course I believed her. Of course!

"I worry about the children, though," he whispered to me next. "She *does* have a temper, your sister, and without Mads there to take the brunt of it—"

"I know." Something tightened in my chest. "I do too," I admitted.

And that was why I agreed to go after all.

WE HAD A compartment to ourselves during the train ride: Bella, her girls, Nora, and I. The girls all found it such a treat to sit upon the green velvet upholstery and watch the spring landscape pass by outside the window. Jennie and Myrtle knelt together on one of the seats, the shorter girl in front of the other, and Nora took it upon herself to show little Lucy the view as well, lifting the girl up to the glass to watch the fields and the trees bursting with fall's vivid colors. Flat—it was all so flat out there. It gave me a headache to look at it. I never thought much of it in the city, with all the tall buildings everywhere, but once I left the crowded streets of Chicago, the flatness of the land was dizzying. It was as if my eyes still searched for steep hills and snow-capped mountains, ravines, clefts, and rushing waterfalls.

I felt like a stranger then.

The children's hands, sticky from the sugary treats Bella had brought, left marks on the windowpane. The scent of caramels and hard orange candy mingled with that of smoke and wood polish inside the first-class compartment.

Bella had money now.

"Look, there's a cow," Jennie told Myrtle. Her hand was looped around the little girl's waist to keep her steady as the train moved. "Can you see that, Myrtle? Oh, there's another one."

Nora hoisted Lucy higher in the air to make sure the little one did not miss out on the cows either, though she did not seem much interested. She held a grappling doll of leather in her hand and gnawed at it eagerly. Yet Nora insisted, "Can you see that, Lucy?

That's a cow. A C-O-W. You can ride one of them like a horse when you get older."

"No, she cannot," I corrected my daughter. "Cows are for milk, and beef, dear."

"Oh!" She puckered up her lips. It sometimes astounded me how witless she could be—*thoughtless*, more like it. At thirteen, she still had not found the patience required to learn things properly. Her mind was like a frog, leaping around in the grass. She had a boundless energy, though, and was almost never sullen. I was very happy to have brought her along as she could brighten any room with her presence.

"Mama says she will teach me how to ride a horse," Jennie spoke up, "when we have moved to the country."

I gave my sister a quizzical look, which she did not return.

"We have to find a good horse first," she said to Jennie. "An old and patient one that won't throw you off."

"Can Myrtle ride it too?" Jennie bent her head over her charge so her slick blond braid fell down and teased the younger girl's forehead.

"When she is old enough." Bella gave them both a smile.

"*I* want to ride a cow." Nora's laughter filled the compartment. I had aimed to gather her dark hair in a neat plait, but it was already unraveling down her back.

"Of course you do," I tutted at her. "You could join the circus as Nora, the cow-riding girl."

"Uh-huh, and then I could sell milk to the crowd at intermissions. You could go too, Jennie! We could perform together. You could have a horse!"

"A white one." Jennie joined in the dream. "Its name is Snowbell, or Winter Queen."

I looked up to see Bella smile to herself, clearly enjoying the girls' happy chatter. Bella's girls wore new blue dresses with neat white collars, but Nora's secondhand one was not so very bad either, with a little bit of lace adorning the red cotton. They were all lovely girls—happy girls. I thought I had been wrong to worry.

Bella and I had both brought our knitting and were spending the time making socks. Bella's were in the style that were much favored back home with eight-petaled roses, knitted black on white. I could tell by the size that they were for a man.

"Who are they for?" I nodded to her lap.

"Oh, I don't know yet." But I thought that she did because her cheeks reddened and a little bit of light had come into her eyes.

"A Norwegian, I'm sure," I teased her. "No one else will wear socks such as those."

"Oh, you never know who'll be in need of a pair." She huffed a little and started a new row. Above her on the shelf resided a magnificent black hat with a whole flower garden gathered at the pull. It much dwarfed my plain one of straw.

We had brought a deck of cards and books for the older girls to read, but mostly they wanted to explore, so we let them roam as they pleased on the train, though we warned them to behave. Myrtle and Lucy remained with us. The latter was soon sleeping, sprawled out on two empty seats and covered in a crocheted blanket. Myrtle sat quietly by her mother's side, watching the landscape flow by. She had always been such a docile child, and slow to walk and speak. She did not look like us at all but was darker and had softer features. She looked nothing like her sister either. Little Lucy was fair and always alert.

The day had been so good so far, and Bella's mood so nice, that I finally found the courage to ask what had been on my mind for some time.

"Do you think you will have more children?" I started, noting the ash in her hair as I did.

"Oh, I don't know." She briefly looked up from the knitting. "Why do you ask?"

"I just think it's strange that a woman your age has so many all of a sudden, when she couldn't have a single one before." I did not say it to be mean, only because I wondered.

"Luck perhaps—or the Lord." Her eyes were still kind when she looked at me. "Why is it your concern, Nellie?" She added a smile; it was all in good humor. "You have a brood of your own already; surely you don't envy me mine?"

"Of course not." I laughed a little. "I was just wondering if they truly were yours. I wouldn't hold it against you if you adopted them and passed them off as your own, I just—"

"Just what, Nellie?" Her voice whipped in the air. Little Myrtle startled, then promptly started to cry. I strongly regretted ever asking. "The girls are *mine*, through and through." There was a hard cast to Bella's jaw as she put down the knitting and set to comforting her daughter.

"Forgive me, Bella." I tried to smile. "I was just curious, that's all. I understand if you don't want to talk about it—"

"We can talk all day if you like." She straightened up with Myrtle in her arms, lifting her onto her lap. "I have nothing to hide."

"I didn't mean it like that." I felt hot and nervous—angry with myself too, for bringing it up. "You are very lucky, then." I bent my head over the knitting again, but the calm from before was gone.

Bella's mood was all ruined, though. "Oh, I can't wait to be away from the city for a while. They are hounding me, those people, saying all sorts of things to Jennie at school. It's only a matter of time before her real father hears about it." I wanted so dearly to go back to not having asked her about the children, but it was all too late, and she kept talking. Her jaws worked between the sentences, grinding her teeth together, and a deep scowl had appeared on her features. "How can they even say such things about a poor widow? Denying me my money—rightfully mine by law! As if I haven't suffered enough, living with a sick husband for all these years—and when Jennie burned herself in the Alma Street fire, barely anyone asked how she fared . . ."

"Yes." I felt faint. "It has been hard for you."

"And that Oscar." She did not appear to have heard me but rocked little Myrtle back and forth in her lap while she spoke; the girl was still mewling, but the tears had dried up. "He can forget about ever seeing his nieces after this. I won't have that vile man anywhere near them. How could he *do* such a thing? Have poor Mads dug up? And for nothing! I hope he chokes on that phony letter he brought—Mads would never have written such things. Lies and accusations, all of it!"

I nodded, suddenly too exhausted to answer.

"And it's surely not my fault that the houses caught fire—the city is rife with fires. It happens every day! I am so very sick of it, Nellie—all these lies that everyone is telling."

"Are you truly moving away, then?" I lifted my gaze a little, shameful of the wild hope that suddenly flared in me. "Is that why we are going to Janesville? Are you looking to buy land there?"

"No." Finally she stopped her angry rantings. "That is to see Sigrid, I told you."

"Yes, but—I didn't think you ever took to her." I had been surprised, to say the least, when she had announced her plan to see her old companion from the ship to America. Bella had nothing but complaints about the woman after arriving in Chicago.

"Oh, but it's different now." Bella sighed and lifted Myrtle down to sit beside her again. She fumbled in her purse for another treat for the girl. "It was a very long time since that ship, and we have both changed for sure."

I did not quite believe it and thought she must have some other reason to go there, but I was not about to upset things again, and so I did not ask her.

I remembered there was a time, not so long ago, when I would scold my little sister as if it were nothing, yell at her even—but I found that those days were gone. I no longer dared to raise my voice.

Mads's sudden death had seen to that.

SIGRID'S FARM WAS midsized but thriving, lying like an island in the midst of sprawling fields. The house was charming with two stories and a large cellar for storage. Hens littered the farmyard, and several horses traipsed behind a fence. Inside the red barn, there were both cows and pigs.

Sigrid herself had changed much. Gone was the slender girl from before; her hips had filled out and her bosom too, and her face showed the lines of someone who had worked much outdoors. Her hair, what could be seen of it under the headscarf, had become as white as chalk.

She was a lively woman, though, and brought us outside to look at every piece of equipment and every little space for storage, clearly proud of her home—of what her husband, Stefan, had accomplished. He was a Swede, which was an oddity. Norwegian girls usually married their own.

"I was so surprised to hear from you," Sigrid said to Bella as she showed us the vegetable patch, mostly empty now so late in the year. Nora, Jennie, and Sigrid's daughter, Louisa, were inside, practicing their poor skills on Sigrid's piano and looking after the younger children. "I never thought I would see you again, truth be told." Sigrid beamed. "I barely recall that journey; it was so very long ago. But I remember you were sick in Hull, and that you did not want to dance on the deck." She laughed good-naturedly.

"How many children did you have?" Bella deftly changed the subject. She still wore that very large hat; satin roses and velvet bows bobbed before me on the narrow path.

"Five that lived and two that we lost. The older boys have moved away now, so there's only Louisa and the twins left. What about you? Did you bring your whole brood?"

"Oh yes." Bella laughed again, though it sounded a little strained. "I only have the girls."

"And you, Mrs. Larson?" Sigrid's gaze turned on me as I came hobbling up behind them. Even if the sun was out, there was a chill in the air that did me no favors but settled in my back like a bite of sharp teeth. "Two besides Nora, but they are both grown and have moved away too."

"It's so hard to lose them to adulthood." Sigrid's face fell into sympathetic folds. "But they cannot stay at home forever. You are lucky like that." She looked at Bella. "Yours will not leave you for years to come."

"Never, if I have a say in it." Bella's voice was light, but I did not like the sound of it. She had picked up a stick from the ground and was poking the dirt. "I was thinking of buying a farm myself," she said. "City life does not much suit me since I became a widow, and I'd much like to leave Chicago. I was hoping to have a look at how you run things here."

"Of course—how exciting! Do you miss the farm life back home?" Sigrid's features lit up with excitement. "Stefan can show you all there is to know. Where did you think to settle? What do you want to grow?" The questions came pouring out of her. Had I not been so in pain, I might have appreciated it more, how eager she was to help my sister.

"I *do* miss it more often now." Bella started walking again and Sigrid fell in beside her. "I miss open fields and a clear view of the sky. In Chicago, there is smoke everywhere—and dust." She closed her eyes and lifted her face toward the sun as if to demonstrate how much better things were in the country. "I miss having animals the most," she continued. "I always had a good hand with cows, and I was thinking of pigs too."

As I wandered behind them, I wondered again just what it was we were doing here. Surely Bella could inspect farms much closer to the city than this—and she did not even like our hostess. I could tell by how her voice turned a little too sweet, while her eyes remained cold. How her lips twitched as if she fought to hide scorn.

"It's hard to do it as a widow, though," she said to Sigrid. "I was thinking I might have to marry again."

I all but stopped in my tracks in surprise. Why had she not shared these plans? Suddenly it *did* make sense, why we were out there. She wanted to find a man who did not know about her recent troubles. Someone who had not been tainted by suspicion. She really ought to have told me, though, as I would have been able to tell her that words travel faster than a bee hive to a meadow, and rumors of her plight might have reached Norwegians even here. I also found, as I passed by the empty vegetable beds, that the thought of her remarrying was worrying to me.

I should have seen it coming, though. Of course she would want to remarry. She had money now, that was true, and it would last her a good long while, but she would still want a man's help and companionship.

I remembered Mr. Lee, and wondered if she knew him still.

"If you invest in land, you won't have any trouble finding suitors," Sigrid said. "There's many gold diggers about, though, so you have to be careful."

"Oh, I'm no fool," said my sister. "I won't take in just anyone."

"You aim to build a whole new life for yourself." Sigrid laughed with delight.

"Yes." Bella chuckled too. "I think perhaps I do."

DINNER THAT NIGHT was lively. Sigrid's husband turned out to be an amusing fellow who took great care to make sure his wife was comfortable at all times, passing her salt and gravy before she even asked. Her twin boys were fifteen and regaled us with stories about rabbit hunting. Louisa, Jennie, and Nora had formed a triad in the way that girls that age often do, and were constantly whispering or sending each other meaningful looks, giggling a little even, though it was hardly polite. Myrtle was already in bed next to her baby sister, exhausted from the travel. Sigrid and I soon fell into reminiscences about the old country, while Bella and Stefan discussed the properties of barley and corn. She seemed to be serious about that farm, and a bit of hope that she would truly leave fluttered in my chest once more, quickly extinguished by a bout of guilt.

I told myself sternly that *of course* I did not want my sister to move away, and yet—somehow—I did.

"Would it be possible to borrow the buggy tomorrow? Sometime before noon?" she suddenly asked our hosts. "I have an acquaintance in the area that I would like to look in on."

"Who would that be?" Sigrid asked, voicing my own surprise.

"Oh, just a man who lodged with us some years ago. I thought I should see him, since I am here." She did not even blush but calmly dipped her spoon back in the pudding we had for dessert.

I looked at Bella with something like admiration. She truly was cunning sometimes, dragging us all out here just so she could meet this man.

"Who is it?" Sigrid asked; her spoonful of pudding hovered in the air.

"Peter Gunness," Bella replied. "A Norwegian in his fifties." She still did not blush or otherwise reveal any shame.

"Yes, I know who he is. Recently a widower." Sigrid's eyebrows rose in a telling manner, but she did not get a rise out of Bella.

"That is just why I want to see him," she replied. "I would like to give him my condolences."

"That is very nice of you. Of course you can have the buggy." Sigrid slipped the spoon between her lips. "Mr. Gunness will appreciate the kindness, I'm sure."

The next day, I stayed behind with the children while Bella went on her errand. Sigrid and I spent a lazy day in her kitchen with our knitting, while Lucy and Myrtle played on a blanket by our feet. The older girls were there as well, entertaining themselves with cutting silhouettes out of cardboard. They let Myrtle sit with them to watch, and Nora even made a silhouette especially for her, meant to look like a rabbit, but it seemed to me more like a bear. I did not tell her that, of course. Their happy chatter filled the air and soothed my sensitive nerves.

Whenever I thought of Bella's visit to the widower, I felt uneasy, though. I worried that the visit would not go as she hoped—and then I worried even more that it would. A rash new marriage was perhaps not the wisest of moves, seeing how poor her last marriage was.

I did not have to worry for long, though. Bella was hard-faced and curt on her return. "He was not there," she informed us as she pulled off her gloves. The massive hat sat crooked on her head; she must have been driving hard. "He will not be back for another few weeks. They said he had gone off to work."

"Oh, that's too bad." Sigrid looked up from her knitting. "He will appreciate that you called, though."

"For sure." Bella did not linger but went back outside to dry off the horse.

"She seemed a little disappointed," Sigrid remarked in a quiet voice, a half smile on her lips.

"She'll get over it," I replied in a voice thick with emotion. My insides flooded with relief.

Bella would not let the issue of marriage lie, however, and was at it again that same night when we gathered in Sigrid's sitting room. It was just us women then; Stefan had gone early to bed, and so had the girls, though we could still hear the three oldest in Louisa's room: eager chatter and stifled laughter. They would likely not sleep for some time yet.

We were knitting and sipping small glasses of brandy when Bella broached the subject again.

"You should let it be known that I'm looking for a husband," she said to Sigrid. Bella was still working on those socks—meant for a new spouse, no doubt. "You could just mention it if you meet someone you think is right, and have them write to me in Chicago. Tell them I'm looking to buy a farm." Her initial disappointment at not finding Mr. Gunness at home seemed to have dispersed. Now there was a tiny smile lingering on her lips, as if she were sucking on something sweet.

"Oh, you will be flooded in suitors in no time at all. So many would rather have the means to buy the land with houses and all, rather than build it themselves—and who can blame them."

"It has to be a Norwegian, though; I get tired if I have to speak English for very long, but that won't be a problem in these parts, I think."

"No, we have plenty of Norwegians here." Sigrid seemed excited by the prospect of acting the matchmaker; her face shone and her knitting sped up. "I can think of a few names already."

"Wonderful! I'm so pleased that you will help me." Bella briefly put a hand on Sigrid's knee. "I'm sure we will find the right one— and don't be shy about it either. I don't mind if people know that I'm looking. There's no shame in that. You can mention that I have money too. They'll like that."

"It's only been a few months—" I tried to say, but Bella cut me off.

"I need a man if I am to develop a farm. I cannot wait to look just for propriety's sake." She frowned at me. "I just cannot wait to leave Chicago," she added with a sigh. "Everything there reminds me of Mads." And then she started crying, lifting her hands to her eyes to hide her tears.

Sigrid was there at once with a handkerchief and comfort, hooking an arm around her shoulders and cooing into her ear.

I poured us all more brandy and waited for it pass.

Not before we were on the train back to Chicago and the older girls were out exploring did I ask Bella about her marriage plans.

"I thought it was Mr. Gunness you had your sights on." I was embroidering on the return, having finished several pairs of socks while with Sigrid. Flowers and leaves appeared on the cloth as I quickly moved the needle. "I admit that when I heard he lived nearby, I thought he was the reason we had come."

"It is—it was." She looked up from her knitting. "I think he would make me a fine husband." She shifted on the seat and gave a satisfied smile.

"Then why the charade? Why act as if you are open to any suitor that comes along?"

She shrugged in her seat. "I think he will be quicker in coming if he learns that I'm looking—and that someone may beat him to it." She fished a hard piece of caramel out of the brown paper bag by her side and popped it in her mouth. Then she sighed before starting a new row. "Men are not very complicated. Threaten to take something away from them, and they'll want it even more." Her face twisted up with something like disdain.

"Do you really think it will work?" I found her logic peculiar, but it sounded right as well. Maybe they really were that easy.

"Of course I think it will work. I had been hoping to find him at home, of course, but this is almost better. This way, he comes to me." An almost childlike smile followed the statement.

"Why didn't you tell me?" I could not help but ask. It bothered me that she had deceived me, even in such a small way.

"Oh, I thought you would not go if you knew the truth, and I much wanted your company. You're hardly ever at Alma Street anymore." The smile was replaced with a frown and a flash of cold eyes in my direction.

"I have a lot of pain," I said, feeling the lie burn on my tongue.

"So it would seem," she remarked but let the matter go.

I LOOKED IN on her a few weeks later, spurred on by guilt, perhaps, that I was so rarely there. I had brought waffles wrapped in cloth and hoped for a nice visit.

She was busy with letters when I arrived. Dozens of them littered the kitchen table.

"What is this?" I asked. "Surely these are not all suitors from Janesville?"

"No—no." She looked up with a wild expression in her eyes. "These are answers to my advertisement!"

"What advertisement?" I sat down before her.

"Oh, I'm offering a trade: this house for a farm, and I must say there are a lot of people who want to own property in Chicago." She rose to go to the stove for coffee. "Only today I had ten answers."

I picked up one of the letters and skimmed, but it was written in English and so I had to put it back down.

"You're really doing this, then?" I asked as she returned with coffee for us both. Her fingers, I noted, were black with ink.

"I am." She looked nothing but smug.

"And Peter Gunness? Did you hear from him?"

"I did." She grinned as she sat back down. "I have his letter right here." She tapped her fingers against a cream-colored envelope. "He comes to see me next week—I told you he would come running." She rolled her eyes but still smiled.

"That you did." I felt a little hopeful too. She seemed so happy then, planning her new life.

Perhaps she was right, I thought. Perhaps this was what she needed. Perhaps Peter Gunness was the right man for her, and a change of residence was good for her mind.

Perhaps things would be good from now on.

I *wanted* to believe that—so I did.

27.

Bella

James and I set out to look at Brookside, a promising property in LaPorte County, Indiana. I brought him along as an advisor, though he knew little of farming. Maybe I just craved the company.

"I have done a little digging," he told me in the buggy. "He probably didn't tell you, Mr. Williams, when he came looking at the house on Alma Street, that *his* house in La Porte used to belong to Mattie Altic."

"Who?" I was holding the reins just then; James was peeling an apple with his knife.

"A whore of some renown. She used to run the place as a first-class bordello." He seemed to take some pleasure in telling me this; his voice was smug and his eyes were daring.

"Is that so?" I accepted the piece of apple he pushed between my lips. It was very sweet, just the way I liked it.

"It used to be a lively house back in the day, with music, drinking, and whoring. The whole of McClung Road used to be a rowdy place; last stop before the prairie and all." Another piece of fruit pushed against my lips.

"And now?" I chewed and spat out a black seed.

"Decent farmers." He sucked on his own piece of apple. "Just the way you like it . . . I must warn you, though, the house has a reputation for suicides." He said it as if amused.

"Not for whoring?" I raised my eyebrows.

"That too, but untimely death seems to cling to the place. A couple of brothers who lived there died so suddenly that the coroner was called in to investigate, and the farmer who bought it next hanged himself in the barn. Some even say Mattie herself took her own life." He stretched out his legs and sighed with contentment; he always liked a sordid tale.

"Well, I'm not afraid of either suicide or harlots. I just want a place to raise my pigs." I looked back at him and added a smile. He had donned his thick coat that day, and so had I, as the weather was chilly.

His eyes blinked at me, lazy like a cat. "The place has certainly seen its share of pigs, and that's something if you mean to follow through with this plan—"

"Marrying Peter Gunness?" I could not keep the amusement out of my voice. It baffled me how much James was against it.

"Just that . . . Do you really think it's wise?" He nudged my calf with his foot.

"What else am I to do? Fend for myself as a widow?" I rolled my eyes in jest. We both knew that I would manage just fine.

"A new marriage would limit your possibilities." He straightened up beside me; his hand came to rest on my thigh.

I glanced at him. His dark hair had gained streaks of silver over the years; he was growing older, my friend, but it did not make him any less handsome. "What possibilities?" My gaze went back to the road.

"If you should ever dare another enterprise." His voice was honey sweet.

"I told you I wouldn't." I batted at his hand, which had crawled farther up my thigh.

"Things may change; perhaps you'll need my services again."

He gave my thigh a squeeze, and I wondered which of his services he referred to.

"I better make sure not to need your services then." I lifted my chin a little.

"Oh, but I think you will. Our kind don't change so easily, and it's hard to go back to that 'wholesome life' after doing what you did in Chicago." He let go of my thigh, but the warmth lingered.

"Still, I'm leaving it all behind." I nodded once to emphasize my words.

"To be a pig farmer?" The disbelief in his voice was priceless.

"Just that." I snapped the reins.

"And married to a butcher." He suddenly laughed; the sound was dark and velvet soft. "I can see the charm in *that*."

"You just don't like that I'm leaving Chicago." Another look at him and I could tell that he was looking at me too, with something almost like sadness. I could certainly sympathize. Of all the things I had to give up by leaving the city, the closeness to him was the only thing I would truly grieve. I took great pleasure in my friendship with Mr. Lee. "When I was a girl, I used to daydream of owning a farm," I told him. "Where I grew up, it was as good as a castle, and everyone listened to those who had one. I suppose I wanted people to treat me better . . . I decided that I would have countless cows and more maids than I needed, just because I could, but then, having worked on such farms myself, I was sick of it all for a good long while. It's different now, though; people repulse me after that whole ordeal with Mads, and it seems a good time to revive that old dream—to give myself what I wanted so much back then." I snapped the reins again.

"Dreams change for a reason," he noted.

"Maybe those reasons are poor." I fumbled for the bottle of brandy by my feet.

"I don't like letting you out of my sight." He helped me uncork the bottle. "You are bold but too careless on your own. I would rather be there to assist you, and make sure that your dealings go smoothly. It was a close call with Mads, and then the Alma Street fire."

"I'm quite capable, James," I muttered as I retrieved the bottle.

"Of course you are." His hand came back to rest on my thigh. "But if there's ever something I can do, never hesitate to ask."

THE PROPERTY WAS large, as expected. The orchard bristled with gnarled trees and bushes, while tall cedars would give plenty of shade around the house in summer. There was a sizable barn and a windmill, a small pond, a water pump, and several sheds for equipment and tools. The buildings needed work and the fields needed tending, but none of that came as a surprise. Mr. Williams's in-laws had lived there; they were elderly and could not care properly for the place.

The main house was square and made of red brick, with a wooden addition in the back. The building sported twelve rooms in all—Mrs. Altic's business would have had room to thrive. The double front doors led from the porch directly into a parlor with marble details; behind it was a beautiful dining room. Both rooms had exquisite, expensive flooring, though like everything on the property, it was run-down and old. Back in Mattie Altic's days, the house would have been made up to be as lovely and inviting as the girls themselves, but now it was only the expensive materials that spoke of a time when the liquor flowed and passions ran high within its walls. I wondered how it was that the former inhabitants chose to end their lives when living in a place so pleasing to the eye. How could one even be touched by sorrow and strife when living with such beauty? I felt giddy as a girl while flitting through the rooms, caressing the smooth paneling with my rough and callused hands. These walls would not tarnish, I felt sure of it. No invisible filth would ever coat the voluptuous roses that sprawled on the dining room walls, or diminish the iridescent green in the parlor that would work so well with my furniture.

The kitchen was located in the addition at the back of the house, below a room for hired help. It was large with a working table covered in oilcloth and dozens of cupboards lining the walls, along with a sizable flour bin. The cookstove was old, but that could be changed. The pantry was cool and perfect for meat. Behind the kitchen was a small hallway that led out back and housed the door to the cellar, where a large, heavy wringer was already in place. The cellar had a dirt floor and dozens of shelves that would be perfect for storage.

Two of the six bedrooms were located on the first floor, off the parlor and the dining room; the four remaining were upstairs. The rooms were not very large but fit for a bed and a washstand. As I inspected the rooms I could see it so clearly, how the walls would look with a coat of fresh paint or covered in lovely wallpapers. Beautiful rooms for my beautiful girls. I just could not wait to begin.

Mr. Williams was eager to sell me the farm. He pointed, gestured, and gave me numbers. It was all rather pointless, as I had already decided that I wanted it. Brookside was clearly worth more than my Chicago property, and Mr. Williams and I discussed it for some time before deciding on an acceptable deal.

"Is it a good place to raise pigs?" I asked Mr. Williams as we stood outside in the yard, where a few scrawny chickens flitted about under a large maple tree. There was a scent of hope in the air. Hope, manure, and fat, black soil. James was wrong, I decided. I would never need his help while living on this land.

"Oh yes," Mr. Williamson said. "There's already a hog pen."

"What about Mattie Altic? Did she keep pigs as well?" I could not help but tease him for the things he had failed to disclose.

The man reddened behind his beard. "I wouldn't know, Mrs. Sorensen. That was a very long time ago."

"No," I mused. "She probably didn't. She probably only kept girls."

I could hear James's laughter behind me; he was standing a little away from us, inspecting some bushes.

This was the place, I could feel it my bones—this was the place to flourish and thrive.

PART THREE

Belle Gunness

28.

Belle

LaPorte, 1901–1902

I had wanted to marry Peter Gunness ever since that first time I saw him at the fair. He seemed to me a decent man without any of Mads's limitations. A man like that, I thought, I could care for without hesitation.

Through the letters he wrote to me, I felt I knew him well. I saw a kind but firm man holding the pen. A man who could hold a child or butcher a hog with the same ease. Those months he stayed with us had done nothing to change my view. I felt I deserved a man like that for enduring Mads for so long. Peter was no young man either, past fifty when his wife finally died, but he was tall and straight as a rod; no gout or other ailment had diminished his physique. His blond hair had turned a pale silver since we met, but I did not mind those few changes; I had gone through a few myself. To me he was still that same man who had defended me at the beer garden.

I held no illusions of love. I knew Peter had been close to his wife and mourned her passing, but I thought such things would come in time. He liked me, that was plain enough to see, and we always had such good conversations. He was as eager as I was to start a new life after his loss. Though it had irked me before, how steadfast he had been in his loyalty to his wife, I could much appreciate such a character trait if it was *me* he was true to.

Our wedding was a small ceremony; all our daughters but his younger one were there. We celebrated our union with baked sweet potatoes and beer, ice cream and soft cakes for the children. I felt happy then. I did. My luck had finally changed and I was on my way to contentment—though I still carried James's pewter button around my neck.

The girls and I had moved to La Porte in the fall of 1900, while Peter and his two daughters joined us in March the following year. Shortly after the wedding, he set to repairing the buildings and preparing the barn for scores of hogs. I put up my chickens and did my best to make the house our own. I purchased new beds of walnut and brass and adorned every one of them with quilts. In every bedroom there was a marble-topped stand with a washbasin and a brand-new kerosene lamp. I wanted us all to be comfortable. I had my dark wooden furniture upholstered in green to go with the walls in the dining room, and I installed a new range in the kitchen. I did everything I could to make Peter feel welcome, even if the farm was mine. I brewed good, strong coffee and pampered him with treats while discussing barley and corn. I served him mutton and beef, waffles and puddings, and filled his glass with whiskey or beer, while planning curing, smoking, and salting. It was a relief to have a husband who did not mind if I had a drink from time to time. Living with Mads had been frugal and sparse, while Peter enjoyed the good things in life. He never took me for a fool, my new husband, or dismissed my advice. Though he would be the master of the farm, handling all the decisions outdoors, he still let me have my say, and agreed to keep some goats when I asked him. He valued me and I thrived for it. Never mind that his elder daughter was sullen and his younger one was not well; I still treated them as my own and saw to it that they were clean and neat and always had food in their bellies.

I was Bella Gunness now. Bella Sorensen was just as dead as poor, wretched Brynhild Størset.

———

THE FIRST TIME I saw Peter practice his skills, I knew I had done right in marrying him. He had taken a lamp and a bottle of whiskey to the barn when he went outside to butcher a hog. By the time I entered, the animal lay on the bench, its blood in a bucket, its hide scalded and ready for the knife. Peter had taken his shirt off; his white undershirt clung to his skin and sweat slicked his forehead. While I watched, he made incisions, quickly like a surgeon, using a steady hand. From time to time, he would pause to take another swig of the bottle he had left on the hay-strewn floor. The kerosene light painted him golden; the cleaver sank into the rough skin and made red ribbons in the flesh. I gathered the shawl around me and leaned against the wall, where I could hear the other pigs through the wood: soft squeals and shuffling, as well as the occasional grunt. That was our future in there.

"You don't have to be here, Bella. You can leave if you dislike the sight." Peter gave me a concerned look.

"I don't mind at all, I enjoy it . . . I helped with the butchering when I was a child; I told you so before."

He paused to smile at me. "I thought you said that to seem bolder than you are."

"I would think most women are accustomed to blood."

"Some of them don't like to see too much of it."

"How do they make blood pudding, then?"

He laughed and hacked with the cleaver. In his other hand was the knife. "Even if they handle the blood, they might not like to see the animal."

"False sentiments, I think, said only to make them seem fragile and weak." All women bleed and that is the truth of it. We slice, cut meat, and clean festering wounds. Sometimes we bleed out from childbirth or violence.

"You're not so fragile, though." Peter's lips twitched.

"No, husband. I'm not."

"Let me see then." He reached out and handed the knife to me, hilt first.

"Do you want me to cut?"

"If you think you can." Peter was still smiling. I stepped forth and took the knife from him. The scent of blood and muck was stronger in front of the animal. Behind me, I could feel Peter's heat coming off his body. I felt a shiver when I let the knife sink in to finish his stroke, unleashing a fresh wave of coppery scent.

Peter's arms embraced me from behind; his fingers closed over mine that held the knife. "I'll show you how it's best done." I let him guide my hand to slice and cut the pig apart into glistening flesh and tendons, hard muscles and firm fat. I realized then that I knew nothing at all. The butchering I had partaken in before had been poor handiwork at best. My new husband, though, he had the skills. He even let me use the cleaver. "If we are to make money from these pigs, it doesn't hurt if you can swing that too."

He was a very clever man, Peter Gunness.

When we were done with the butchering, sweaty and bloodied, we lay down in the hay like drunken youngsters. Our hands were everywhere, tugging at fabrics and grazing warm skin. I savored the feel of his hands on my flesh: callused from work and flecked with red. He tasted of salt and liquor, that man, and his passion was anything but gentle and kind. When he came undone inside me, he did so with a ragged moan. I loved that sound; it sent shivers down my spine and let me come undone myself.

"Next time I want to kill the animal." I plucked hay from my hair and brushed dust off my skirts.

He laughed, brushed his hand through his hair, and came away with a few wizened pieces of straw. "Not to worry, I will teach you all there is to know."

I wondered if the act of butchering excited him some, or if he had done it so many times, it meant nothing at all. If it was only me, his new wife, who made him so inclined to tumble in the hay. I did not mind much either way, but I thought it took some bloodlust to be as skilled a butcher as him.

As we closed the barn doors and went inside, where my Jennie was watching the baby, I thought of what a treasure this man was, who could teach me something useful and new.

I HAD ALL I wanted then: a man I had chosen for his kindness and skills, and five young girls who called me Mama. I had the house and the land, a barn filled with seeds, and plenty of healthy livestock. My pantry was bottomless, crammed with milk and butter, eggs, preservatives, and fine cured ham. Even the scrawny cat grew fat with cream.

I had done well for a poor girl from Norway.

All week long, we worked hard to get the farm running. We planned and hired men to work, and sought avenues for our produce. We went to church on Sundays and met with all our neighbors. They were humble people, farmers like us. Honest people, living off the land. It was just what I had wanted: a healthy, wholesome life.

I began gathering the children in my bed before they went to sleep, as a way of coming together after the busy days on the farm—much as my own mother had done when I was a child, out on the stone step at Størsetgjerdet. Sometimes I slipped the girls a treat, we played a game, or I told them stories. Sometimes we just rested together: Myrtle and Lucy with their heads on my shoulders, Jennie and Swanhild with their arms around the younger girls. By the foot of the bed lay Prince, the collie puppy we had bought as a guard dog who turned out to be more of a lap dog. Who was I to resist his pleading brown eyes and the girls' sweet begging? Prince, too, found room in the bed.

I thought to myself in those moments of bliss that this was all that counted: to have my girls happy and content, their sweet breaths against my neck. As far as Myrtle and Lucy were concerned, I was their natural mother, and they would never ever know otherwise. The two of them were mine through and through, and the love they felt for me was not tainted by questions or doubts. Jennie often thought of her natural mother, and Swanhild had only just lost hers, but the two I had raised from the day they were born carried no such scars. They were my angels, my all, and I swore in those moments of closeness on the pillows that I would always protect them from harm.

THE FARM HAD to earn; that was the only cloud on my otherwise bright horizon. It cost to set it up and it cost to have men working. If we could not make it pay, my money would be gone in no time at all. Despite all our efforts, I felt it moved too slowly. The money disappeared never to return, and I found myself sitting up at night in my new, elegant parlor, looking through the open door to the dining room, where straight-backed chairs with black velvet seats lined the polished table. I felt it then, deep in my heart, how dearly I wanted to keep it all: the husband, the house, and the land. This new me, Bella Gunness—Belle, as they called me in La Porte, because their tongues were lazy or they somehow misheard—was a woman of considerable means. She would never eat gruel or herring. I made a silent pact with the house in those nights, that beautiful old whorehouse with suicide in its walls, as damaged and bruised as myself. If it kept me, I would keep it, and we would be like sisters to each other. I would do what it took to protect her, always, and liked to think that she would do the same for me.

It put a strain on me, this pondering about money. I got angry with Peter when he spent needlessly, although I did not show it. This man was not like Mads; he would not be beaten or scolded and I had to curb my tongue. Instead, I sat alone at night, thinking and drinking his whiskey. I found that even if Peter treated me well, he did not respect my money.

Nothing to do for that, though, but hope that Brookside would spit the investments back in my lap. Still, it made me feel restless and angry to know that my cash dwindled in the bank. I found myself filling the pantry again with far more than we could eat. A rank scent of mold hit me whenever I opened the door. The situation made me careless too; maybe that was why it happened . . .

Baby Jennie, Peter's younger daughter, had been sickly from the start, and she never seemed to heal but neither to get any worse. Her skin was red with rashes that her sharp, thin fingernails scratched, leaving red swellings and bloody marks. No ointment or salve could cure her, and her belly was large with gas. She ought to have gone with her mother, I think. She was born with a foot in the grave. Peter did not see that but kept smiling down at the girl, shushing and stroking her trembling limbs while she screamed herself wet and red. He rocked her cradle while smoking his pipe and hummed to the suffering child.

I used laudanum drops sometimes, and Peter agreed to that. He too wanted to give the child some peace, a good night's sleep to conserve what little strength she had. It might have been too much—but I did not mean for it to be. The girl would have loved me as a mother had she lived, and I had no reason to harm her.

Whatever my intentions were, the girl died—and her father was not pleased.

29

Peter kept visiting the small coffin laid out in the parlor to cry over Baby Jennie's blue, waxen body. He dried his eyes with his handkerchief and dulled the sorrow with whiskey. I had not anticipated that; I had thought him a stronger man, accustomed as he was to death and grief. I did what I could to ease his loss and baked cookies and cakes, made roasts and nourishing soups. None of my cookery seemed to work, though, and my husband grew pale and thin before me. He went to the barn and did his work, but I could tell his heart was not in it. It puzzled me how broken he was, and one morning, after I had served him breakfast in the kitchen—ham and sausages, cheese and bread—I sat down before him and asked:

"Why is this so hard on you, dear husband? Children die, that's the way of things. She is not the first child you have lost, so why is it so hard this time?"

He did not answer at first, just stirred his coffee with a dainty little spoon that looked spindly and fragile in his large hand. "Tell me again of the morning she died."

"Well." I placed my hands in my lap, on top of the filthy apron. "She'd a bad night, you know that. She could not rest. She continued wailing all morning while you were away. Then she finally grew quiet, and I checked on her. To me, it looked as if she slept at that time. I'm certain that she did, because she made small noises in her sleep. I left her to it then, because I had covered her hands with those mittens I made, and was certain she wouldn't bloody herself. If she woke up I would hear it at once, as I never strayed far from the kitchen."

"Had you given her anything to quiet her down?" His voice was as hollow as a winter storm.

"Nothing more than usual. I think it was all God's work, Peter. I think it was he who called her home. Little Jennie was always too good for this world, such a little angel. Just as my Caroline was. I know what it's like to lose a child, my dear, but we will get through this, the two of us together."

Peter still looked ashen, but he nodded.

"She must be buried," I reminded him, and touched his knee gently. The coffin was still in the house, closed but unburied, surrounded by paper angels her sisters and I had made. He just could not seem to make up his mind. "Did you grieve like this for all your children?"

"It was some time since I lost one. I cannot recall how I felt then."

"Jennie was sick from the start. I was hoping but never certain she would live." I tried to put a hand on his shoulder, but he shrugged me off—I did not like that at all.

"She didn't seem that weak to me." He pressed his lips tightly together.

"You know how these things are; sometimes it happens fast. We ought to have her buried, though. She needs to be laid to rest." I shook my head with exasperation.

"Swanhild won't like to let her go. She's mourning for her little sister." Something stubborn had come into his expression, but I knew it was not so. The girl had recovered remarkably well and was outside this morning with Myrtle in tow, bothering the hired man, Smith, for sweets. It was Peter who could not let her go, and that angered me. This was our new beginning, our fresh and vibrant start. I did not want this inevitable death to tarnish all we had.

"Take her to Chicago." I rose from the chair and turned my back on him. I could not look at him just then. The weakness I saw in him reminded me of Mads and roused the same disdain. I did not want to feel that. Not for him, my new husband. "We already have a plot there. We'd better put it to use."

"You want to bury her with your late husband?" I could hear the revulsion in his voice.

"It's *my* land and I bury who I want on it. It seems a waste to arrange for a new plot here. She cannot stay in the house much longer. The coffin already smells."

"How can you speak of her like that?" I heard him rise from the chair behind me. "She is a dead child. A dead, innocent child—"

"Who nevertheless falls apart as all living things do when they die! You have to get her in the ground, that's all." The anger seeped from me then. What use was there in quarreling? The sooner I had this dealt with, the sooner I could have him back to his old self. I turned around and faced him. "I'm sorry, my dear, but it is hard for me to watch you grieve as you do. I wish you would take the child with you and arrange for a burial in the plot in Chicago. Your family needs your strength. I cannot take care of the farm on my own."

"Of course." His face was stiff and white. "Not to worry. I'll take care of it."

I THOUGHT THE whole thing over and done with once the coffin was out of the house, but I was wrong. My husband still looked sick; he was brooding and often drunk. He stumbled to bed in late hours, only to wake up with headaches that lasted all day long.

"This was not what we agreed on," I told him one night as he sat in the parlor drinking whiskey. "We agreed to run this place together as husband and wife. Now you leave me with all the work—"

"I am in mourning," he saw fit to remind me.

"What man can afford such sentiments? You have other children to feed, a farm to run, and a wife to keep happy."

"Have a drink with me, Bella."

"I won't! One of us has to keep a clear head." And I had already had my drink in the kitchen. "Those pigs won't raise themselves; they need to be looked after. You sitting here night after night feeling sorry for yourself will *not* produce the finest bacon on the market—"

"Feeling sorry for myself?" He laughed into the glass and sloshed the golden liquor around in there. "I just think I might have gotten a little more than I bargained for with you." He had not touched me in weeks, not since the girl died. I ought to be patient as he had just lost a child, but it made me feel resentful.

"What does that mean? You knew what was expected when we married—"

"Do you know what they say about you in Chicago?" He swayed when he leaned forth in the chair and placed his hands on his knees.

"Yes." I bit my lip hard to curb the anger. "I'm aware of what filthy things they say."

"My friends think me a fool for marrying you—even my own mother does. They think it might be dangerous."

I snorted loudly. "They say that of all women who come into more money than *they* can make in a lifetime."

"They say that of women who come into that money through fire and death."

"Life can be hard for any one of us."

"Are you truly so unfortunate, Bella?" He hid his face behind the glass and looked at me through the amber liquid.

"No more than any other, I think. Many struggle in life."

"Not as much as you, though, Bella. You've had poorer luck than anyone I know."

———

I TRIED TO ignore his moods. I took care of the house: washed and cooked, preserved and dried, cared for the animals and all four girls. Though Myrtle and Lucy were still young and at home, Swanhild and Jennie went to school several days a week. I thought it important that they were educated; the world was never kind to a woman lacking a keen mind. I often talked to Jennie about it. I wanted her to understand that a sweet face and a gentle husband was no one's ticket to happiness. I wanted her to have a profession, I told her. A profession, property, and money of her own. Only then would she be safe.

"Safe from what?" she asked me one day. She was fourteen then, and so carefully looked after that she knew little of what was out there, ready to prey on her innocence. That was the price for being guarded—it left you both defenseless and naïve.

"From men who would use you and take all you have." I was sitting before her at the kitchen table. The tabletop was heaped with vegetables, ready to be preserved.

"Why would they do that?" Her rosebud mouth hung open. She was picking the beans she was set to shell completely apart with her fingernails.

"To rob you or just be unkind. Some would even beat you and leave you for dead."

"Why?"

"They quite enjoy it. It brings out the juices in them."

"Oh." Her blue gaze dropped to the beans.

"The safest thing you can do is to fend for yourself. If I were young again, I would study law and become a lawyer. Not all girls have the minds for that, but I believe that *you* do, Jennie." I was peeling potatoes while we spoke; spirals of peel fell down on the floor. I looked at her across the table: the first child I properly raised. I knew Peter thought I was hard on her, strict and often angry. *Too* angry, he said. *Too* strict. But what did *he* know about being a young woman? What did *he* know about being prey? He was the butcher—always the winner. I envied that in him. Envied how he took it for granted.

Jennie was nothing like that; she was fragile and soft and needed to toughen, else she would perish when she stepped outside my doors.

"It was sad about the baby." She picked beans out of the leathery pod.

"Everything must die, and infants are so fragile. She was always sick."

"My sister lost a child, but it wasn't proper born yet." She had seen her sister in Chicago just the other month.

"She's young," I murmured. "She'll have another child."

"Why is Papa blaming you for Baby Jennie?"

I felt cold all over and ashamed too. Jennie heard more than she ought to, understood far more than she should. "He is mad with grief. He will soon come to his senses."

"I think it's a cruel thing. You were always so good to her."

"Yes." I put the knife away. "I treated her like my own, just as I do you. It truly is unfair, but that's what men do. They always blame and point fingers at others for everything that goes wrong."

The girl gave a sweet little sigh. "I hope no one else dies. It's hard to remember not to laugh, and my black dress is pretty, but it itches."

I could not help but smile then; she was still such a child. "I will buy you another black dress, then. One that is soft and doesn't scratch at all."

I often thought of James Lee in those days, and all the things he had warned me about that sadly had come to pass. I missed his easy company, the way he never condemned me, and thought myself quite the fool for choosing wholesomeness over him. Had it not been for my urge to spite, we could have been quite happy, he and I.

I had chosen differently, though, and now I was, yet again, burdened with a man who did not live up to my expectations but made my days both miserable and grim.

What happened the next day did not help one bit.

I WAS OUT in the stable drying off the horse. It had been a long day with haggling at the market, but I had returned to the farm with cash instead of vegetables and had a few fine deals in my pocket as well. I did not mind so much, then, that my day ended with horse sweat. Peter came in behind me, wearing just his undershirt, as was his habit. He carried a bottle and took a swig, but there was nothing tempting or lustful about him. He was merely a drunk husband who ought to know better.

"I see you've gotten things done while I was away." I could not help but being snide.

I heard the liquor slosh in the bottle as he lifted it to his lips. "I have been thinking, Bella." His voice was loud and clear enough; he had not been drinking as much as I feared. "We ought to send Swanhild to live with my uncles in Janesville."

I looked at him then. "Why have you been thinking that?"

"The two of you don't seem to get along very well, and she's still upset about the death of her mother."

It was true that the girl had not warmed to me as much as I would like, but then she had just lost her natural mother and moved to a new place. "How is moving in with strangers going to help?"

"I think it would easier if she didn't have to see me with another woman."

I pressed my lips tightly together and could feel my nostrils flare. "Haven't I been a good mother to her, cleaning the muck off her frocks? What kind of mother was your first wife, then? Cake for breakfast every morning? New dresses every month?" I could take much from this man, but he would not question my ability to take care of our little girls.

"It's just for the best, Bella. You do have a terrible temper, enough to make any child worry." The accusation hit me like a bucket of cold water. True, I could be angry; I was often tired from all the work, but my children knew me—they knew it would pass. It was only *he* who looked at me with worried eyes when a plate or a shoe hit the wall.

"I think it's you who worries. The poor girl never said such a thing."

He shrugged and drank again. "I cannot help but wonder if my Jennie would still be alive if I had been at home that morning."

"What do you mean by that?" My anger snapped like a hungry bird.

Peter did not answer but turned his back on me. "I've already written to my uncles. I'm sure they will take her in. It's for the best. Better with three than four little girls. It's easier for you to handle them then, if they're all yours."

With that, he left me alone.

WHEN I WAS back inside and had eaten some, I made the girls ready for bed. Then I counted the day's earnings and went in search of my husband. I found him in the barn, drinking and slicing through a rib.

"I didn't harm your daughter," I told his back, "but if I had, you should be glad of it, as the child was a nuisance every day of her life. It was a blessing to us all that she died." The hurt rose in me like poison, spilled out as anger and spite. My jaw ached and burned.

"I'm sending Swanhild away no matter what you say. She doesn't care for you, and you don't care for her." He chased the words with a swig of the bottle.

"Be as that might, she's your child and it's your decision. I won't say anything more against it." I nodded and placed my hands on my hips, thinking myself very reasonable.

"You can stop asking me about the life insurance as well. Swanhild is young and healthy and no one should profit from her death should she die." He looked back at me over his shoulder. His eyes were bloodshot and his brow slick with sweat.

"It was meant as a kindness. All *my* children are insured." I lifted my chin and clenched my jaws.

"It's just wrong." He glanced at me and went for the bottle again; the knife in his hand was filthy with gristle. "Even thinking of a child's death is asking for it. Writing it down like that is an invitation." His voice shivered with emotion.

"I never took you for a superstitious man, Peter Gunness." *My* voice was steady and calm.

"Well, I never took you for a harpy," he snapped, and looked back. His face had twisted up in an ugly grimace.

"Is that what I am to you now?" I could not believe what I heard!

Another glance at me then, before his face smoothed out and he put the bottle down. "What about *your* child who died? Were you alone with her as well when she passed? A regular angel of death, aren't you, passing the little ones those drops."

"That is one outrageous claim—and a terrible thing to say to a mother!" My voice was not so calm anymore. "All mothers give a few drops to keep the children calm! Your first wife did it too, I'm sure." I crossed my arms over my chest so he would not see how my hands shivered with fury. All of me felt hard and stiff; my jaw ached, ached and burned.

"Not as frequent and not so much." That ugly sneer was back on his face.

"Yet when her children died you didn't accuse *her*!" I heard my own teeth gnash together in my mouth; I had no control of it. My vision swam with black spots. It took all I had to restrain myself—but I had sworn it would not be as before.

I had told James that my enterprise was over.

Peter did not answer, just kept carving the meat.

"Small children are such fragile things; you never know what will break them." I forced my voice to be calm and even; it shivered only a little.

I would let him send Swanhild away, I thought, and when she was out of the house, he would forget all about it, every suspicion and every angry thought. All could be as it used to be before, happy and good between us.

I should have learned by then that what is broken rarely mends.

30.

The coroner, Dr. Bowell, and Mr. Oberreich sat before me in my dining room, with only the polished table between us. Oberreich was the stenographer and sat there with his little machine. Dr. Bowell asked the questions.

I sat in one of the straight-backed chairs, facing their stern expressions. They meant to have me feel like a child, but I was not new to any of this. I had sat in that same chair in other locations talking to other men like them. After Mads died, of course, and after the Alma Street fire as well. Insurance men and lawyers, coroners and priests—they all set out to make you feel small.

"What is your name?" Bowell asked.

"Bella Gunness." That question was easy. Oberreich's fingers clicked on the keys.

"How long have you lived here, Mrs. Gunness?"

"We moved here in November 1900."

"You lived here alone with the children at first, didn't you?"

"Yes, Peter came to join us at the end of March."

"And you married then?" Bowell did not look at me but kept his gaze glued to his notes.

"I married him on April first. He came down on Saturday night and we were married on Monday."

"How long did you know Peter Gunness?"

"I got to know him in Chicago the year of the world fair, and then later, when I kept a store in Chicago, he came back and stayed for some time. He worked there."

"Worked in your store?"

"No, he worked down at the stockyards." A sweat broke out on my forehead; my corset was too tight. I kept remembering all of James Lee's warnings and cursed my own poor temper. Nothing to do for it now, though, but to see the inquiry through. I knew our neighbors on McClung Road had said nothing but good things about me. I was a mother and a recent widow and surely these men would not take this any further.

"Was he a good man? Did you get along?" Dr. Bowell finally looked at me while he stuffed his pipe and lit a match.

"He was a very nice man." My voice mellowed. "I wouldn't have married him if he wasn't. I didn't just want a good man for myself but a nice father for my children as well. I never heard him say a wrong word to anyone."

"So . . . when did he die?" His eyes were back on the notes.

"What time in the night, you mean?"

"Yes, it was a Tuesday morning, wasn't it? Early in the morning, after midnight?"

"I can't tell you the exact time, I think I was too shocked to notice, and we never paid much attention to the time."

"All right." He made a note. "What were you doing Monday afternoon?"

"I was finishing up some work—"

"And what did he do?"

"He was working as well. He went into town to get supplies and when he came back he helped me out."

"What did you do on Monday night, then?"

"After I put the children to bed, Peter ground some meat for me. Then I made sausage while he was in the parlor writing letters. I was in the kitchen at the time. I washed up everything and finished up for the next day, and he was looking at some papers when I joined him. I think it was right after eleven. We were sitting there and I said to him that it probably was time to go to bed. He thought so too, and picked up his pipe and went into the kitchen. He always locked the doors before we went upstairs, and I heard him make some little noise out there. He always put his shoes at the back of the range to warm them, and I guess he must have tried to get hold of a pair, because he had only slippers on his feet. Suddenly, I heard a terrible noise. I dropped the papers and went to look . . .

"When I came out in the kitchen, he was rising from the floor with both hands pressed to his head, and I noticed there was water on the floorboards . . . I had a big bowl of brine on the back of the range, meant to go on some headcheese. The bowl was full and hot when I left it, and I saw that it had tumbled to the floor." I could see it all as I went along. See it so clearly in my mind, what just might have happened that night. "'Oh Bella,' he said, 'I burned myself so terribly.' I was so scared by then, I didn't know what to do. All his clothes were wet and I told him to take them off . . . I remember he said that his head burned, and I knew that baking soda and water is good for putting on burns, so I set to mix that up. I bathed a towel in it and put it on his neck."

"Was all the brine spilled?" Even though I was sniffling in my chair and dabbed at my eyes with my handkerchief, Bowell seemed deeply unmoved by my plight.

"Yes, I think the bowl was nearly empty. It was a common crockery bowl to put milk in."

"Was it boiling-hot?"

"It had stood for some time, so it wasn't that hot—but warm enough to burn for sure. I rubbed him with Vaseline and liniment after I had put on the baking soda. I was very distraught. I didn't know what to do to help him."

"When you were rubbing on that Vaseline, did you see the cut in his head?"

"Yes, I did."

"Was it bleeding?"

"Not very much. The bleeding seemed to have stopped."

"Did he have a nosebleed?"

"No. I didn't notice anything with the nose; I saw the cut on his head and asked him two or three times what happened." I could see the doctor's lips tighten. It was clearly a foolish thing of me to claim not to have seen the nose.

"What did he do next?"

"Well, we were just sitting there." What did Bowell want from me?

"He sat down, did he?" The doctor made a note while the stenographer clicked.

"Yes, we sat in the kitchen for a while. I was rubbing the Vaseline on and he said he was afraid he would lose hair because of the burn. I can't say exactly what time it was, but we sat there for a good, long while. Then he began to feel a little better, and I said I thought he should lie down. When he agreed, I told him he'd better not go upstairs but lie down on the sofa, as it was warmer in the parlor. He thought so too, and I went and fixed the sofa for him and took off his clothes, put on his nightshirt, and then I went to bed."

"So he took his shirt off?"

"No, I don't think he did." I quickly corrected myself. "He went to lie on the sofa and I told him to call me if he needed anything, and then I went to lie down with the girls." I spoke fast to cover up my slip. "I went up to sleep as I was tired. Then, suddenly, I heard him calling 'Bella' as loud as he could. The children woke up and were scared and I told them to stay put, and that I would go to Papa. I think I told them that Papa had burned himself. I put on my clothes for it was so cold, and then I went down the stairs and when I came down, Peter was walking around in the kitchen saying, 'Oh, Bella, my head! I don't know what's the matter with my head!'"

"I went upstairs and got Jennie up, and she went over to our neighbor, Nicholson, as I realized we needed help. When I came down again, I found him on the kitchen floor and he held his head and said, 'Oh Bella, I think I'm going to die.' I asked Peter where it hurt so badly, and got some water to clean up the wound, but he said not to touch his head. The next thing I knew, he drifted off and didn't answer when I spoke to him. When Nicholson finally arrived, he said that he thought Peter was gone. But I don't think he was before they came, I think he was only unconscious."

"When you first came down he was walking around?"

"He was walking around in the kitchen."

"Was he still doing so when you went upstairs to wake the girl?"

"Yes." Had he not been listening at all?

"How long were you up there?"

"I don't know."

"When you came back down, he was lying on the floor?"

"Yes, on his back, because I tried to turn him over."

"When Nicholson came, was he lying with his face on the floor or the back of his head on the floor?"

"Well, I don't know." Whyever did it matter? "I remember the last time I tried to give him a drink, he was lying with his face against the floor."

"Did you see that his nose was hurt at any time?"

"I never knew it was hurt before you told me about it." I never should have said that I had not seen his nose, but it was too late to take that back.

"About how long do you think it was from when he was hurt until he died?"

"Well, I guess he was hurt right after eleven, and I don't know exactly what time he died. Nicholson said he thought he was dead when he arrived, but I don't think he was gone then . . . I tried to feel for his pulse, but my hands were so cold they had lost all feeling."

"He was hurt at eleven o'clock, and Nicholson came about three?"

"That might be. I can't tell you the time exactly." I had already told them that, many times over.

"But you sat up with him for two hours after he was hurt?"

"Yes. I wasn't upstairs for long. I said good night and went upstairs, and was in bed just a short time before he called me down."

"But he seemed fine when you went up there, did he?"

"Well, the pain seemed to ease. He didn't lie down at first. He sat up or walked around until he went on the sofa. But he complained terribly of the pain in his head, and I thought of the pain that girl must have had, and she didn't complain as much as he—" I stopped myself. I had just read in the newspaper about a girl who had tipped some boiling brine over herself and barely lived. Her mother had told the journalist about the baking soda and the liniment, and the Vaseline for the blisters.

"How do you think he got that hurt on his head?" Bowell leaned forth in his chair, fixing his gaze on me.

"Oh, I don't know, Doctor. I had washed the meat grinder, wiped it off, and put it on the shelf above the range to dry. I found it on the floor after he was hit by the brine, and I think it must have tumbled down on him. That's what I think, but I didn't see it happen."

"Did he say anything about it?"

"He didn't say anything about it. I asked him what had happened, but he didn't tell me exactly."

"Was the door to the yard locked?"

"I don't know. Peter always locked the doors."

"Do you think it's possible that someone could have come inside without you hearing?"

"No. If anyone came in, I would have heard them."

"Had your husband ever had a quarrel with anybody around here?"

"I don't think he ever had a quarrel with anybody. He seemed to get along nicely with everyone."

"Have you ever suspected or been afraid that somebody might come inside and kill your husband? Hit him with that sausage grinder?"

"No, I have never been afraid of that."

"Did he tell you how the brine came to tip all over him?"

"He said he didn't know how when I asked him."

"Did he seem to talk out of his head after he got hurt?"

"Well, not at first, but after I went up and came down again, he seemed to be a little out of it. He asked me two or three times if I had sent for the doctor. I said I had sent Jennie to Nicholson's because it was too far to get to town. He was asking over and over again, so I suppose he was getting a little mixed up. He didn't say very much else but that his head was hurting."

"How did he break his nose?" There was that dratted nose again. I fastened my gaze on the chandelier above me, watched as a spider slowly crossed its net.

"I really can't say. I didn't know about the nose before you told me."

"When you were sitting on the floor after he got scalded, you would see it, wouldn't you, if his nose was cut?"

"I guess I could have seen it, but I didn't."

"Well." Bowell tapped his pipe on the table. "I guess that's all for today, Mrs. Gunness." He and Oberreich exchanged glances. I did not like it at all. The latter smoothed a piece of paper on the table.

"If you could be as good as to sign here . . ." I took the pen and scribbled my name, rushing to get them out of the house.

I WAS LIVID when they had left, so angry that my hands shook when I was peeling potatoes for dinner. Had they no regard for a grieving widow at all? Accidents happened all the time; just think of that girl with the brine. Kitchens are dangerous places.

He should not have hit me, though. Should not have tried, not with the cleaver so near at hand. He should not have blamed me for his wretched daughter's death.

"I'm glad to have Swanhild safely away." He swayed on his feet from the whiskey, and even spilled some on the kitchen floor. "I'm glad she is somewhere you cannot touch her. You are no mother, Bella . . . The only thing that comes from you is death."

Any woman would be angry then. "How can you even say that

to *me*, who cooks your meals and mends your shirts? *Me*, who have let you into *my* house on *my* land, to let you raise pigs in *my* barn!"

He shook his head and took another swig. "The price for my greed was too steep."

"Was it?" I was so mad that my teeth gnashed in my mouth, and my jaw felt like it was on fire. "I rather thought that ugly little child a bargain! She wasn't worth anything at all." I did not think of the child then; I was only thinking of him, of cutting deep where it hurt the most.

He lifted his hand then and lunged at me. I barely avoided the strike. Then I was there, back at the lake, with fists pummeling my face and feet kicking in my gut. The cleaver was clean on the table, ready for another day of chopping for the grinder. I took it and I struck him, and he did not see it coming. His nose exploded with blood as it cracked and he fell to the floor. I gave him another heavy whack then, buried the cleaver in the back of his head. That was the price for his insolence, I thought, as I sank back on the chair, breathing.

Suddenly it was upon me: waves upon waves of that delicious feeling I had so yearned for after Mads died. I was back in my bed behind the kitchen in Selbu, with Gurine resting beside me, sucking the sweet victory like a creamy caramel. I had bested him, that man on my floor. He had come at me but I whacked him down, and now he was nothing but so much meat, his blood seeping down between the floorboards, dripping into the bones of my house. My jaw throbbed with a dull ache, but it did nothing to calm the wild triumph that coursed through me. I was breathless with the excitement, and wished for him to come back to life so I could do the same thing all over again: hear the sound when his nose crushed, feel when the cleaver split his skull apart. Best him, once again.

That was what he got for coming at me with his fist raised. That was what he got for accusing me of his daughter's death.

He should not have done that.

When I regained my senses, I realized my mistake. I knelt down beside him feeling for a pulse, although I was sure he was gone. I had been careless—stupid even. How could I explain such a bloody death? I looked around me in the kitchen and tried to think of an explanation.

No sickness of the heart had ever looked like this.

I thought to blame an intruder at first but dismissed the idea at once. Peter was a strong man; no thief would be foolish enough to try him on. No one but me knew how weak the whiskey made him, how he would stagger and lose his balance, sway on his feet like a newborn foal.

I saw the brine on the range then, and the grinder on the shelf, took the scalding-hot brine and poured it on his head and shoulders. I took down the grinder next and put it on the floor.

It had just been an accident, all of it.

After I had taken a few drinks and thought out what to say, I woke Jennie up and sent her to Nicholson. Perhaps I should not have done that. It would have been better if I said he had left me. I had so much land now where one could hide a lump of flesh, even one as big as Peter Gunness.

Instead, I blamed it on the meat grinder.

31.

Nellie

John, the children, and I arrived at Brookside Farm shortly before the funeral service. We barely made it there at all, as it had all happened so fast. The message from Bella had been short and curt, and I could not help but think she wished we would rather stay at home.

Of course, we could not. Peter had been family, too, even if we hardly knew him.

I had been to the farm only once since they moved there; John had not been there at all. Bella had invited me back many times, but I always opted not to go.

I blamed my bad back or blamed the horrid weather. The long train ride or a lack of an escort. My English was not so good that I dared venture such a long trip on my own.

In truth, life had been good for me since Bella moved to La Porte. I no longer suffered from stomach pains and poor sleep. I no longer spent hours wondering and fretting, worrying about the state of my sister. I thought of my own children more often than I thought of hers, and the image of Mads had become but a specter in my mind, a memory softened by time. I no longer felt anxious when I thought of his death; the doubt could not unsettle me as it had before.

I had let it go.

This new death had brought it all back, of course, though I still felt composed as we sat on the train, heading for Indiana. I told myself that it was different this time. Peter had died from an accident, that was all—it happened often on farms—but before that, they had been happy together as far as I knew. It was unfortunate that it had ended so abruptly, though, and I thought that Bella had to be devastated—but then I recalled her eager baking after Mads's sudden demise, and figured that she might be all right.

Olga did not share my composure but wept silently into her handkerchief as the train rushed toward our destination. She was a grown woman now; her hair had darkened to golden wheat and she was almost as tall as her aunt was. She had begged a day off from the hosiery store to join us on this trip.

"Why are you crying?" Nora said beside her. "You did not even know him." At fifteen, she had yet to grasp the importance of decorum. She had put on her dark dress for mourning, but it did nothing to diminish her spirit. She was supposed to read a book on the journey, but instead she moved restlessly on the seat and watched the other passengers without any trace of shame. It made me sigh just to look at her, but I knew it would do no good to correct her. My youngest daughter had a strong will.

"I cry for Aunt Bella." Olga looked up from the handkerchief to lecture her sister. "Can you even imagine what it must be like to be widowed again so soon?"

"Husbands die all the time, Aunt Bella said that to me herself." Nora remained unconcerned and fished an apple out the paper bag propped up between them. It was wrinkled and old but sweeter for it.

"That was an incredibly foolish thing for her to say," I remarked, annoyed with my sister and daughter both. "When did she say that to you?"

"After Uncle Mads died." Nora bit into the apple and closed her eyes; when she was quite done chewing, she spoke again. "She said it when we went to the graveyard with flowers. Then she gave me a piece of candy to make me stop crying."

"She only said that so you would not feel so bad." Olga's nose was red from crying.

"She seemed to mean it." Nora shrugged.

Olga's tears had made my own heart catch up with me. "Those poor children," I lamented. "To lose another father so soon . . ." Now that we were on our way, I just could not wait to see them. I had brought some sweets from Chicago as a treat, though I doubted any sugar could make these days better. "So close to Christmas too," I mused. "It will be a sad celebration for them this year."

John had been very quiet ever since we got the note. He sat beside me, pale and stone faced, and barely said a word until Nora turned to him: "Maybe we should invite all them to Chicago, Papa?" she asked. "Maybe it would be good for them to get away from the farm."

In my stomach, the familiar churning came back, grinding acid and emitting pain.

"Let us see them first." John's voice was a little hoarse; his jaws were set in a grim expression. "We do not really know what happened yet." I could tell then that he was frightened. He worried about what we would find on Bella's farm in La Porte.

His worry made me worry too.

"She did not mention how the accident happened?" Rudolph put down the newspaper he was reading. He was sitting on Olga's other side, directly in front of me.

"No." I shook my head. "Only that it had been terrible."

"Most accidents are." He softened the words with a gentle smile under his brown mustache. He was engaged to be married, which baffled me some. To me, he would always be that sweet little boy who clung to my skirts. Now he was hoping for children of his own.

"Is your back all right, Mama?" he asked me.

I nodded. "Of course. It's as good as it will ever be."

"This weather won't help." John looked out the window. The landscape was frosty, but there was no snow. Only a bone-deep cold.

"Do you think Aunt Bella will have room for us all?" Olga looked over to me; tears still glistened in her eyelashes. We had been planning to stay the night, thinking that Bella might appreciate some help on the day her second husband went into the ground.

"Oh yes," I murmured. "She has room for even more. There's twelve rooms in all."

"It used to be a house of ill repute." Rudolph's smile was happy and bright.

"Hush." I slapped his knee and furrowed my brow, but his sisters were giggling with delight, all tears seemingly forgotten.

"Is it true, Mama?" Nora wanted to know. "Is it true?"

"Yes," I admitted at last, and could not help but smile a little too. Even John, in his morose state, curved his lips a smidge.

WHEN I HAD last visited the farm, it had been a beautiful day in spring. Everything had been green and the light crystalline. This time, when we arrived, the sky was bleak, and the fields around the houses black and hard with frost. The farmyard was littered with puddles of water covered in thin crusts of ice that broke to shards under our heels. The air was cold and damp as we scampered up the stairs and entered the farmhouse.

This time, the devastation was apparent in the household. The mirror that hung in the parlor was covered up, and candles burned on every surface; the candlesticks were adorned with black paper bows. The air was scented with woodsmoke, wax, and lemon from scrubbing.

Bella greeted us in a dress made from black silk, the double wedding band her only jewelry. Her hair was piled high up on her head, brown and silver in equal measure. Her face looked gaunt and her eyes troubled. I took her in my arms.

"Oh Bella," I murmured into her shoulder, taken aback by the tenderness that suddenly bloomed so fiercely in me. "That you should have to experience such misfortune . . . I am so very sorry for you."

"It was such a shock." She sniffled and embraced me back. "Such a terrible loss for all of us."

Jennie and Myrtle had followed in her trail like black little goslings; their stiff skirts rustled and the air was scented with hair oil from their glossy braids. Olga was with them at once, looping one arm around each girl and pulling them close to her body.

"Oh, you poor dears." She was sniffling again. "Oh, you poor, poor dears!"

Nora stood back, looking as if she wanted to be somewhere else. She lifted a foot to scratch her heel against her calf and looked around at the landscape paintings that hung on the papered walls. John and Rudolph had better manners and came toward Bella with their hands outstretched, about to offer their condolences.

"It's such a terrible tragedy," she muttered as she shook their hands. "He was such a wonderful husband, and so good to the girls!"

"Where is Swanhild?" I asked, looking around.

"Oh." Bella shook her head. "She was away when it happened, visiting Peter's uncles in Janesville. She won't make it back in time for the service."

"That's awful." Olga's eyes widened. "It must be such a shock for her as well, losing both of her parents in such a short time."

"Of course it is." Bella nodded with a grave expression. "But at least she didn't have to be here when it happened like the rest of us."

"What happened, exactly, Aunt Bella?" Rudolph asked. "If you do not mind me asking?"

Bella glanced at the girls before she answered in a quiet voice, "It was all so stupid—he was going for his shoes and then the meat grinder fell down and crushed his head."

I balked at the description; it sounded so very coarse.

"A *meat grinder*?" John sounded about as surprised as I felt.

"I know." Bella rolled her eyes. "One wouldn't think such a small thing could do such damage, but . . . that's what happened." She started walking, guiding us farther into her house of death. "I tried to clean him up, but water can only do so much. We had to close the casket. It was awful." At this she lifted a black handkerchief to her eyes and staggered a little so she had to use her free hand to steady herself against the wall.

Rudolph came to her aid.

"Here, Aunt Bella, you can lean on me." He offered her his arm, and she clung to it as we entered the dining room, where the pine casket rested on top of the table, surrounded by a few more candles.

"We will have to bring in more chairs, of course," Bella said as we passed by. "Every chair in this house, I reckon. I expect people to come from all over the place."

"No wonder," John murmured to me as we moved toward the kitchen. "It's not every day a man dies from a *meat grinder.*"

My stomach began to hurt again.

DURING THE SERVICE, I sat with Bella and her children in the front row of the ramshackle collection of chairs brought into the parlor. I was charged with keeping an eye on Lucy, who, at only two, found it hard to sit still on the chair. She kept looking back at the crowded room, wondering, perhaps, what all those people were doing in her home. I was happy for the arrangement, being so averse to crowds. Every seat in the room was filled, and there was even a gathering in the back of local farmers in their Sunday best. Peter Gunness had apparently made a good impression on his new neighbors in La Porte.

Jennie and Myrtle sat in their shiny black dresses, ramrod straight on each side of their mama. Jennie's braid was finished off with a black velvet bow, while Myrtle's dark hair sported a white one. Little Lucy beside me—and sometimes in my lap—wore a white cotton dress with a cascade of ruffles. Jennie was clutching a Bible in her slender hands. Myrtle held a rose of wax. She was anxiously looking up at the casket, while her front teeth gnawed at her plump lower lip. I wondered if the closeness to the dead scared the five-year-old, or if she remembered Mads's death two years before, or more recently the death of Baby Jennie.

Bella hid her face in her hands throughout the service and did not once look up. While the gray-bearded reverend spoke, her shoulders shook as in crying, and low moans and whimpers erupted from time to time. Olga leaned in from the row behind us, where she sat next to Peter Gunness's brother, to pat her aunt's shoulder and whisper words of encouragement. I was very proud of her then.

I felt it keenly during that service how very little I had known my new brother-in-law, and the feeling of guilt was strong and instant. I clutched Lucy tighter to my chest and thought myself heartless for abandoning them so.

I swore not to do it again.

When the service finally ended and the casket was to be borne out to the carriage, I rose with Lucy on my hip. Bella staggered to her feet, guided by my Rudolph's strong hand. She looked down while she walked, as if too broken to face the hardships ahead; her shoulders were slumped and she asked for her veil.

I knew why that was, though I would rather not have.

I had seen that her eyes were dry.

AFTER, THERE WAS coffee, and cakes lathered with whipped cream. Olga and I helped with the serving, while Nora had taken it upon herself to distract poor Jennie from the day's sad event. I could see them sitting on top of the stairs to the next floor whenever I passed through the dining room, as fast as I could with my bad back so the anxiety would not catch up with me. I let the girls be, as I did not think it any harm to offer my young niece some respite. She had certainly seen enough death in her short life.

I was alone in the kitchen, making more coffee, when Peter's brother, Gust, came in. The man looked haggard, but that was to be expected. He was tall and lanky like his brother, sporting a mane of graying hair, and a beard that was still fair. Wrinkles crowded his blue eyes, red-rimmed now, from mourning.

"Ah, Mrs. Larson, I just needed a moment's peace." He flung

himself down in a chair by the table, which was heaped with empty plates and remains of sweet cake. "Is it not strange how we celebrate our dead with lavishness?" He dipped his index finger into the cream on one abandoned piece and licked it off quite shamelessly.

"It's for comfort, I think"—I kept my voice even—"for those who are left behind."

"Yes, yes, of course it is. Forgive me. I am not quite myself today." He had the decency to look a little abashed.

"You are forgiven." I turned by the stove and gave him a smile. "I suppose I cannot interest you in a treat then, or more coffee?"

"No." He shook his head. "Just some peace. That is all I ask."

"I will be quiet then." I gave another smile and turned back, and for a while, it was just that: quiet.

Then Mr. Gunness spoke again. "Did your sister tell you about the inquest?"

"No." I glanced at him with the coffee measuring spoon in my hand. "What inquest would that be?"

He laughed a little, but it was not a kind sound. "I thought she might have kept that from you. She had to explain herself in front of the coroner."

I felt instantly cold; my hand shivered so that the precious coffee drizzled onto the floor. "What for?"

His lips pursed amid the beard. "They thought it all so strange, with the meat grinder falling down like that, on the back of his head, that the front was hurt too. I know it, as I saw him before we put the lid on." He did not look at me while he spoke.

"What does that have to do with Bella?" I tried to sound calm, but there was a pain in my chest, and it made it hard to breathe.

"They suspected her of foul play, though we are yet to see what comes of it."

"It's just some foolishness." I snorted. "Accidents happen." Yet the pain would not let go.

"All I know"—he leaned forward on the chair, resting his arms on his knees—"is that Peter sent Swanhild to live with our uncles because she did not get along with his wife."

"Is that so?" This was not what she had said—but that was maybe not so strange; who would want to admit to such a defeat? "It happens sometimes when a parent remarries. It is not so unusual."

"No, of course not." He straightened up again. "She was mightily upset about that inquest, though, mightily upset . . ." His gaze lingered on me a little longer than what was polite. "We know all about her, you know, about what they say in Chicago." He shifted again. His eyes had gone cold. "Our mother warned him against coming here, and I'm starting to think that she was right. The accident happened right here." He pointed to the floor in front of my feet. "The grinder fell from there." He pointed to the shelf above my head. "It's not so far that it would do much harm, or so I think, anyway."

The kitchen had suddenly taken on a sinister aura, and my chest hurt so bad that I thought it might implode. "I don't know anything about that," I whispered. "My sister is a good, honest woman."

He laughed again, just as humorless as the first time. "So good and honest that she's asked me to stay. To help out, she said, but I don't know—"

"You should not presume." My voice and hands shook, and a surge of something like anger took hold. "She is your brother's widow," I hissed. "*Of course* she would look to you for help."

I could not stay in there any longer and promptly abandoned the coffee. I rushed toward the back door as fast as I could, only pausing to fetch Bella's shawl off the hook behind the wall. Then I slipped outside, into the cold, and hobbled across the frozen ground, drifted among the farm buildings, aimless and upset in the bleak afternoon.

My thoughts were in turmoil, confused by his words—frightened too, from what he had implied. My heart was racing and the pain still lingered, and I wondered if it had burst—but then, I was still walking, so clearly it had not.

What he had said, it could not be—it *could* not.

This was Bella's second chance. Surely she could not have been as foolish as to—

No. She would not have done something so vile.

I looked back at the farmhouse, its windows brightly lit from all the candles inside, and I could not help but think of what had happened within its walls: the man bleeding out on the kitchen floor. Then I thought of Mads—and at last, I thought of *her*, the angry little girl who had clung to me when I carried her down from the riverbank, away from the snarling dog. I feared for her! For what she might have done, but for what it made her, too, *if* Gust Gunness was right. I thought she was not violent, but then I knew that she was. I thought she could not kill a man, but then I thought she *could*.

Her temper had always been a dangerous thing: ruthless, vicious, and boundless.

I drifted around on the farm for at least an hour, under black trees free of leaves, flitting between sheds and outhouse, the barn and the windmill, too upset to go inside, though the cold was taking its toll, and all the walking too, for a back that was not hale.

I knew I could not stay out there, but *he* was inside, Gust Gunness, and so was Bella, the grieving widow, and I did not know what to say to any of them. In truth, it was shameful for a woman past fifty to be so frightened of her own kin that she would rather brave the weather, but there was no honor in any of this. I could see people leave the farmhouse and go to their horses and carriages. Some of them walked along the driveway.

The house was emptying, and soon I would *have* to go inside. Someone was bound to notice my absence. In an attempt to escape the inevitable for a little while longer, I fled behind the barn, where there was nothing but rubbish heaps and bales of frozen hay, and was surprised to see that someone was already there: a small, black-clad girl sitting on a rock.

"Myrtle!" I hobbled toward her the best that I could on my frozen legs. "What are you doing out here? Where is your coat?"

She did not answer at first but just looked at me with a morose expression.

I sat down beside her on the rock, and she scooted over to give me space. "Does Mama know that you are out here?"

She shook her head and stared at her feet, dressed in leather shoes with straps. "She's busy inside."

"Did it get to be a little too much for you in there? Is the noise hurting your head?" I reached out and caressed her dark curls.

She shook her head again but did not speak. She seemed so very sad.

"Are you sad about Papa?" I tousled her hair a little.

She shook her head again; her gaze was still glued to the tips of her shoes.

"What is it, then, Myrtle? You know you can tell me. I am your aunt, after all." I put my arm around her and pulled her close on the rock.

"I saw something." Myrtle's large, brown eyes looked up at me.

"What did you see, Myrtle?" I pulled her even closer.

"Something that Mama did, when Papa died—"

"Hush, Myrtle!" I all but shouted. "Do not tell me!" My whole body froze and the chest pain was back. I let her go and abruptly rose to my feet, taking a few steps away from her. The girl was almost in tears, her eyes were big and frightened, and her bottom lip quivered.

"You can never tell a soul what you saw that night." My voice was shrill with fear, and I could do nothing to prevent it. "Not even your mama, Myrtle." I clutched at my chest while I spoke, at Bella's knitted shawl. "No one can know what you saw!"

Myrtle was crying by then, sobbing loudly and rubbing her nose with the back of her hand. My sanity slowly descended, called upon by the child's distress.

"I am so sorry." I fell to my knees in front of her, not even thinking that I knelt in my best dress. "I am sorry for shouting." I took the girl in my arms and sobbed along with her for a while. I let out a breath of relief when her soft arms came to embrace me in turn.

"Are you angry with me?" she asked in her sweet voice.

"No, Myrtle. No! It's just that we must never tell what we know about Mama." I spoke into her little ear. "It has to be our secret, do you understand?"

I could feel her nodding against my shoulder, her hot breath on my neck.

"We should go inside." I gently freed myself. "Not to worry." I gave her a smile, and her pale face lit up just a little. "As long as we don't tell, everything will be fine."

She kept my hand in hers all the way to the house.

THOUGH I HAD feared to see her, I found that I could be with my sister just fine as long as I did not think of what had transpired. As long as I pretended that all was good and well, I could stand beside her as we cleaned the china and swept the floors together. I could help her dispose of the remains of cake and pour cold coffee out the door. I could dress little Lucy for bed and take the glass of brandy she offered me as a thank-you. I could see the relief on her face when Gust retired to bed without even batting an eye.

I had not thought I could do those things, and felt strangely proud that I did.

Not even once did I think about confronting her about what I had heard. I wanted neither the lies nor the excuses, of which I was sure there were plenty, none of which would help. I no longer trusted her. I had not done so since the death of Mads.

I spent the night in agony. My back hurt, yes, but it was more than that. My soul was hurting, too. I lay on the mattress in Bella's house, next to John, who was sound asleep, and curled up on the mattress as well as I could, and bit into the pillow so as not to make a sound, and then I breathed out my pain. My tears that night were angry tears, but more than angry, I was frightened. The fear in me was cold and sharp, and made me feel so sick that I thought I might throw up.

Later, when we were back in Chicago, I thought I should not have done what I did that day. I should not have sworn Myrtle to silence but let the girl speak and taken the burden from her narrow shoulders, but I had been a coward. I had not wanted to know what she had seen—had not wanted the weight of that knowledge—and so I asked her to never tell a soul, and condemned myself by doing so.

It was shameful what I did then, refusing her like that.

That one act of cowardice would cost us all dearly.

32.

Belle

Jennie's sister, Mrs. Oleander, came to visit unannounced, shortly after Christmas. It was not convenient. The house was in quite a disarray. I had not found it in me to clean or even cook after Peter died. I kept worrying about the inquest, if something more would come of it. My heart jumped whenever a stranger entered the yard or if I saw Sheriff Smutzer in town. Though Smutzer was hardly a stellar sheriff but easy to dupe with a motherly smile, I felt frayed and hunted like a rabbit, and I did not like it at all.

I gathered the girls around me in bed at night and pulled the young ones so close I could smell the sweet scent of their skin. In those dark nights, my daughters brought me solace, for how could something truly bad happen to me when I kept these precious angels under my roof? The caress of a cherub's hand on my cheek or a kiss good night could make my eyes water. I could not truly be so bad when my daughters thought me the world.

"Are you sad, Mama?" Myrtle would ask. Her brown eyes were large with worry.

"A little," I would tell her. "I am sad that Papa died, but it will pass in time. All things that live must die. There's just nothing to do for it."

"We can pick flowers for his grave," the little angel said to comfort me. It was what we had done back in Chicago when tending Mads's final resting place. She had been very young then, but maybe she remembered.

"Yes, my dear, we can," I said, and then I burst out in tears again, not from grief, though, not at all. My tears were from anger and disappointment. I loathed Peter for using me, for being so unfair about the dead child, and for leading me to believe that he could be a good father to my children.

I had had such hopes for my new husband, and now it had come to nothing.

I was in quite a state then when Mrs. Oleander arrived, yet there she was, standing in my parlor, waiting for refreshments, no doubt. Jennie had already come in and spoken politely with her sister. I let the woman sit down and remove her hat. She was young and lovely to look at, though not as lovely as Jennie was. Her clothes were fine but not new. I poured her tea and found some old biscuits.

"This is not a very good time, I'm afraid. We have so much to do with the butchering, I have little time to be indoors and sweep floors."

"Oh, I just came to see Jennie." Mrs. Oleander lifted her teacup; her voice was a little high-pitched and she seemed far too happy. "I'm aware that farmers are busy people. This is a very new life for you, Jennie, isn't it?"

"It is very different from Chicago," the girl agreed.

"She's of great help," I told Mrs. Oleander. "She's in charge of the goats and the chickens, and goes to school too. She's very bright."

"How wonderful." Mrs. Oleander smiled and showed her teeth; her incisors were stained a pale brown. "What do you like best in school?" she asked Jennie.

"Algebra," said the girl.

"They are reading scripture too, and we go to church every Sunday. I wish we could be more involved in the good work of the church, but there simply isn't time. Jennie and I knit socks for the orphans in Chicago, though."

"I still play," said Jennie. "I practice the piano every day."

"You were always such a musical girl. Our mama was too, did you know that? She would be happy to know you are playing so much." Mrs. Oleander had a strain in her too-happy voice; something was not right.

"Maybe Mama knows that I play." Jennie slipped a spoonful of sugar into her tea. She always took her tea too sweet, but today I would not scold her. "They say that the angels can see everything we do, and Mama must surely be an angel now."

"Of course." Mrs. Oleander was touched; her voice had grown thick. "Mama is listening to your playing every time."

I could not help then but sigh and nearly rolled my eyes. I ate a biscuit to cover my impatience. "Why don't you play some now, Jennie?" That way we would not have to talk so much.

While Jennie made ready at the piano, Mrs. Oleander turned to me. "Isn't it so that your husband just died?" There it was, then, the reason she had come.

"Yes, it is so. Just before Christmas. How did you learn about that?" Jennie had not written her, to my knowledge.

"I read about it in the newspaper, the *Chicago Tribune.*"

"My, was it in the Chicago papers?" I had certainly not anticipated that. I really should have dug him down, not left him on display in the kitchen.

"It said it was a mysterious death, that a sausage grinder hit him." Her eyes were twinkling with that well-known light, that particular thrill of dread. People do like to see a spot of blood and have a nice soak in their neighbors' misery.

"Oh no, there was nothing mysterious about it. He went to La Porte in the morning to purchase a sausage grinder and saw one on the shelf that he wanted. He reached up to get it and it slipped and fell on his head and killed him. They brought him home dead." I sipped my tea.

"Oh! Well then!" She looked puzzled. Maybe the Chicago newspapers had given details.

"You cannot always trust the newspapers, they write what they like. No one ever came here to ask *me* what happened."

"Of course." She gave another smile, but the hand that lifted the teacup shivered. She ought to get herself some drops for her nerves.

Jennie was playing by then; her slender fingers danced on the keys.

It had been a very stupid thing to do, leaving him there on the floor, nose broken and skull crushed. I would never do such a foolish thing again.

THEN IT WAS the question of the insurance. Peter had drawn up policies for nearly thirty-five hundred dollars but with no named benefactors save for his next of kin. That, I figured, had to be me. That is, until Peter's uncles in Janesville put forth a claim on his living daughter's behalf. I had almost forgotten about that surly little girl. Now I had to deal with it all, her and his relatives both. Without writing first, I set out to travel all the way to Janesville. It was an arduous trip and I fumed all the way. For all the trouble I had had, at least I ought to receive whatever he left behind—even if it had to come through the girl.

When I arrived at the filthy old farm where she lived, I knocked on the door and introduced myself to the old man who opened it. At first, I was not sure if he would let me in at all. He kept standing there, staring at me through the crack. Finally, he relented and swung the door open.

"Come in, then," he said, and shuffled inside while another man, just as old as the first, emerged from the bowels of the building.

"I have come to take Swanhild home with me," I said when they served thin coffee at the stained kitchen table. "Peter would have wanted her to come home now, to her family. With her in the house, at least a part of him remains."

The two old men across from me exchanged looks. "Peter wanted her to stay here with us. He was very clear on that," said the one who had opened the door. I believed his name was Gunnar.

"Don't you think it's better for her to grow up with a mother and sisters who love her? You are not young, if I might say so, and raising a girl can be hard."

Another look then. "He seemed to think it best that we took her," said the other man, another Peter. His beard was so filthy and wild I could barely see his teeth when he spoke.

I gave them both a good, long stare. "And how long do you expect to live? You might just die on her around the next bend."

Gunnar opened his mouth again. "We are both healthy and sound in mind, Mrs. Gunness. No need to worry about that. There is also the question of her uncle, Gust, and what he would say if we let her leave—"

"What would he be complaining about? That you were foolish to let the girl go back home to a clean house and a caring family?"

"Gust has some strong opinions." Of course he did. Brothers always did. Brothers always came meddling. "He said that *he* would take her." The cards finally landed on the table. "He would see to it that she got her inheritance too."

"What inheritance?" I could not help but show my disdain. "Peter was no wealthy man. All he had was mine. It's *my* land and *my* farm, *my* livestock—"

"He is aware there was an insurance policy—two, in fact."

"Of which the girl will have all, I assure you—"

"Assurances don't mean much, Mrs. Gunness, not when there are no ties of blood. With Gust she would be with her true family." Gunnar still spoke for the both of them while Peter chewed his tobacco.

"Well, I don't care about that. Peter was *my* husband and so she is *my* daughter. I'm taking her home and that's the end of it." I was so angered by their insolence that my voice shook when I spoke.

The men before me looked away; the set of their jaws told me they were angry too.

"He won't stand for it." Peter spat tobacco on the floor. "Gust will not stand for this!"

I shrugged. "Let him try to take her. She is mine by right of law."

Gunnar gave me a dark stare. "There were questions after Peter died—"

"People always talk."

"Gust doesn't think she's safe with you—"

"Not safe with *me*, the mother who feeds and clothes her? Who can give her everything she needs, and then some . . ."

"Money isn't all, Mrs. Gunness," Peter said. His gaze was on the cup he cradled in his wizened hands.

"I assure you, hungry children beg to differ!"

There was nothing those old men could do to stop me, though. They would never manhandle a woman and a child, and even if they did, I was both younger and stronger. In the end, we simply walked out the door, Swanhild and I. The girl cried beside me in the buggy when we left that filthy farm behind. Not even caramels could cheer her.

"It will be better when we get home," I told her. "You'll see Jennie, Myrtle, and Lucy again, and go back to school—"

"My papa is dead!"

"Yes, he is; now dry your tears. Many children lose their papas. Nothing to do for it but straighten up and move on."

"I want to go back to my uncles," the girl howled.

"Well, you will never go back to them, so there's that. Now, dry your tears and be a good girl—have another caramel. I'm your mama and will look after you."

I have never been as exhausted by a journey as when I transported that little girl from Janesville to La Porte. When she did not cry she sulked, and she looked at me as if I were the devil himself. They had clearly been telling her stories, Peter's uncles.

I thought it was all settled then, when I had the girl back under my roof. Gust Gunness sent me letters, of course. He threatened me even—but what could he do? I was Peter's legal wife and as such the best choice as his daughter's guardian. I did not care that Gust threatened to go to the sheriff—the whole inquest had come to nothing. There were no witnesses, after all, and I suppose the lawmen in La Porte had better things to do than bothering a poor widow.

Swanhild settled back in, and after a few days she seemed much her old self: a not-too-bright but happy enough child who joined her sisters in play. I had bought the children a brown Shetland pony and a small cart to console them after Peter's death, and Swanhild was just as much in love with the little animal as the others. She often took turns in the stable feeding and caring for it. She even came crawling into my bed with the rest when it was time to calm down at night. It was a good bed, of brass tubes and knots, heaped with mattresses, quilts, and pillows. Above it hung a cross and some scripture I had embroidered onto cloth myself. It was spacious too, now that Peter was gone, though small bodies often occupied the vacant spot all through the night. Lucy, in particular, was quick to fill it, wanting to be close to her mama.

On the first night Swanhild came to join us, lingering a little on the edge of the bed before crawling up close to Myrtle's back, I told them about my childhood in Selbu. Myrtle always asked me about it. Selbu seemed such a strange land to her, a fairy-tale kingdom across the sea. I found it endearing and indulged her, although my childhood years had been anything but pleasant. It was different, though, to see it through my children's eyes; what had been sorry for me could become a gilded story for them. They knew nothing of hunger and strife; all they ever knew was butter and sweets—and I would not have it any other way.

"They used to call me Twist-twig-Paula," I told them, lying beneath a crocheted spread with a child in each arm. The girls all giggled around me.

"Why is that?" asked Lucy in her sweet, light voice.

"Because I was always out picking twigs for fuel. We used to twist them around each other like this." I freed my hands to demonstrate in the air. "And they called me Paula because my father's name was Paul."

"Why did you have to burn twigs?" Jennie asked.

"Because my father was too lazy to chop logs," I told her candidly.

"Was it the other children who called you that? In school?" Swanhild asked.

"It sure was." I chuckled at the memory. "Especially some boys called me that, and it was not to be nice." Everybody knew that my father loved his drink and did not properly care for his family. Everybody knew that we owned nothing more than the mended clothes we lived and slept in.

"What did you do?" Jennie asked breathlessly. She knew me too well to think I would just stand idly by.

"Oh, I packed some river stones into snowballs and threw them at their heads. I had very good aim in those days." That revenge had been long in planning, devised while I lay next to Olina in the loft at Størsetgjerdet, envisioning their pain and suffering at my hands.

"What happened?" Myrtle squirmed beside me; her dark curls tickled my nose.

"They bled some," I said, content. "One of them nearly lost an eye."

"Did they stop calling you Twist-twig-Paula?" Jennie had wound her arms around Lucy, who was already sleeping by then, her pink lips slightly parted.

"No . . . I guess that name had come to stay . . . but after that, they always called out from a distance. It's important to strike back in life," I told them. "No one else will do it for you—besides me, of course. I would strike back at anyone who harmed you."

"Were all the children in Selbu mean?" Swanhild wanted to know.

"Well, yes, but that's why I came here to America."

"Tell me about the goat!" Myrtle had had enough talk of mean children for one night.

"Oh yes, the goat . . . We had three sheep, two cows, and one goat at Størsetgjerdet when I was a child. The sheep were called Berit after my mother, and Hildur and Ullina after my sister and me. The cows were called Staslin and Dokka; the latter was old and gave very little milk, but we still kept her on since it was something. Then there was the goat; she was called Perla, because she was as white as a pearl."

"Was she pretty as a pearl too?" Myrtle asked.

"Oh yes. Perla was always my favorite. Olina and I spent hours outside with her, combing through her fur with our fingers. She had the loveliest little horns and her milk gave the best brown cheese you could imagine . . . Sometimes in winter, when Perla was in the barn, I used to go out there and press my head to her side while telling her everything that bothered me. If my father had been angry with me, or if someone had been cruel to me, Perla always knew all about it." I paused and looked around at the girls, at their wide eyes and parted lips, completely lost in the story.

"Sometimes I thought maybe Perla spoke to me as well," I continued, "and I made up a language between us: if she cocked her head to the right, it meant yes; to the left, it meant no. If she ate while I spoke, it meant it didn't matter as much as I thought. If she came with her head to be petted, she felt sorry for me."

"What happened to her?" Myrtle asked.

"She fell down a cliff and broke her legs. It was over for her then—my father came out with the knife."

Myrtle did not reply, but I could feel her shaking as she suppressed her tears. She was always softhearted, that one.

"We ate good meat for days after." I tried to cheer her up. "Perla was useful for a long while."

"I wish we could go there some day," said Myrtle, her tears all forgotten.

"Where?" I asked. "To Størsetgjerdet?"

"Yes," she whispered, and closed her small soft hand around mine.

"Oh, it's not the same anymore. My mother and father are gone now, and Olina—my sister with the bad foot—she lives there alone with her son. He doesn't have a father either." I looked around at my mostly fatherless brood. I did not mention that no one even knew who my nephew's father was. Olina did well enough at Størsetgjerdet, though, making herself useful as a midwife. I sometimes got a letter, filled with gossip and complaints about the weather. "So, you see, it's not only you who have lost a parent." I fixed my gaze on Swanhild and saw Peter's eyes look back. "It's not so unusual at all to be an orphan."

33.

One day Swanhild did not come home from school with Jennie. The latter came bursting through the back door and into the kitchen; she was panting with exertion and her eyes were wild. "They took her!" She stood in the middle of the floor. "They took Swanhild just up the road—!"

"Who did?" I nearly dropped the milk I was handling. Prince was disturbed by the sudden distress in the room and yapped around my legs.

"Some men! I swear I never saw them before."

"Did they go for only her, or did they try to take you too?" I held the dog in a firm grip to calm him.

"Only her—she seemed to know them. She wasn't afraid at all."

My surprise gave way to anger. "Did they say anything that you heard?"

"They said they were going to take her home, and apologized for taking so long."

"And then they drove off in a carriage?"

"Yes."

Fury is a seething thing; it writhes and it snaps but is mostly just there, boiling under your skin. Gust Gunness set it aflame. "I better see the sheriff, then."

"Who do you think it was?"

"I have no idea." But of course I did. I knew very well who it was. They were trying to defy me and cheat me of what was mine. I had Jennie finish dinner and drove into town.

SHERIFF SMUTZER'S OFFICE smelled of unwashed men and leather. His desk was surprisingly tidy, but I doubted he saw to that himself. He toyed with his mustache while talking to me and jotted down notes with a stub of a pencil.

"I *have* heard from Gust Gunness," he told me. "He has been sending several letters of late. He says that the circumstances of his brother's death make it unwise to leave the girl in your care."

"What *circumstances*?"

He shrugged. "The inquest for one, the uncertainty of what happened—Mrs. Gunness, if I may offer some advice, I would let them have the child. There's no need for your good name to be sullied further. I know she's like a daughter to you, but they are her family and will take good care of her." I could tell from his expression that he would prefer to have this dealt with quickly, that he found such domestic disputes tiresome at best. I could also tell that he did not fear me but thought of me as nothing more than a quarrelsome widow whom he nevertheless sought to charm, in the way that men who think highly of themselves are wont to do. He aimed to be popular, Sheriff Smutzer, especially among those of us with land and money to our names. He was also the sort of man who thought women incapable of bloody violence, something that had served me well after Peter died.

"The Gunness family is only after the money," I told him.

"Well"—he kept twisting his mustache—"that's what *they* say about *you*."

"How can they even think that?" I lifted my handkerchief to dab at my eyes.

"People can be cruel sometimes." He all but shrugged before me.

"But I was Peter's *wife*, and ought to take care of his daughter."
I shifted my gaze to the window.

"You could find a lawyer willing to pursue the matter, but as
things stand I would strongly advise against it. The circumstances
of your husband's death were—"

"Yes, I know." I put the handkerchief away. "But if I got her back?"

He shrugged. "It would be up to them, then."

Get her back, then, somehow. If Swanhild were in my home, lav-
ished with good food and nice clothes, and I got myself a lawyer
after that, no one could take the girl from me then.

I ASKED JAMES Lee to come and visit me at the farm. He arrived
on the train with his friend Joe. Joe was a simple man but could be
trusted as long as he was paid. He had helped James set the Alma
Street fire. I brought the men home and plied them with drink, fed
them roast and waffles. We had quite a feast that first night.

I had missed my friend James Lee.

Late at night, after Joe had fallen asleep from the whiskey, James
and I lay in my bed.

"I knew it wouldn't last." He sat up and rested his back against
the headboard. "As if you could ever have that 'wholesome life'
you talk about."

"I might have, if Peter had been a better man." I reached up and
trailed a finger down his face; I had dearly longed for the sight of
it through those awful days with Peter.

"He was not what you thought, then?" James's eyes twinkled
with mirth.

"No, he was a drunkard for one, and he blamed me for his daughter's death even if children are prone to all kinds of sickness, and
she was a very ill child." I rolled my eyes, just a little.

James lit a cigar and turned up the light on the bed stand. "You
couldn't appease him, then?"

"No, he kept bringing it up—"

"But the sausage grinder, Bella—"

"It wasn't really, it was the cleaver." I could not help but add a tiny smile.

He chuckled softly beside me. "It made for a damn fine story, though. All the newspapers wrote about it."

"I rather wish they hadn't." I sighed.

"Yes. It puts you in a sticky position." He puffed on the cigar.

"I can't pursue legal action, not under the circumstances. If I had Swanhild, though . . ." I turned over on my side and caressed his naked chest while he smoked. "I was careless, I know, and I'm paying the price."

"You just have to be more clever about it." His eyes narrowed to slits.

"I know." But how clever can you be when you have just beaten your husband to death with a cleaver? "I got away with it, though."

"Barely."

"No one hangs a grieving widow." I said it as if it were a fact.

"You keep taking comfort in that thought, but I'm not entirely convinced. Next time, you must have a hole ready out back. You should always have one ready and keep some quicklime around too, just in case." He put out his cigar and lay back down, rolling over so he faced me. "A wholesome life is not for the likes of us; we have crossed too many bridges for that."

"Had he only been—"

"Hush." He placed a finger on my lips. "It doesn't matter how he was or not; no husband could survive with you. You are far too lethal, Bella, my dear. It's running in your blood."

"I wasn't always." I took his hand and guided it away.

"No." He smiled. "But you have a talent, and it's important to hone one's talents."

"If I only get the girl—" I clenched my jaw.

"You will." He sounded reassuringly calm beside me.

"No one can come after me then. Not if she is spoiled and content." My hand curled into a fist upon the crocheted bedspread.

He laughed and rolled on top of me, burrowed in between my legs. "I think you should lay off the 'accidents' for a while." He closed his hands around my wrists when he pushed himself inside me. "I will always help you, you know that; but another dead man on your kitchen floor just might be too hard to explain."

JAMES AND I left Joe and Jennie to tend the farm and took rooms in Minneapolis while searching for Swanhild. We drove out to Gust Gunness's place every day, parked the buggy nearby, and watched Gust's daughters and sons playing on the porch. Swanhild was not with them, though. Only once did I think I glimpsed her: a pale face between the parted curtains in one of the windows upstairs.

"They are watching her every second," James muttered. He was sitting beside me, toying with the whip. "What kind of life is that for a little girl, being locked up like that?"

"They're expecting me." I spoke without taking my eyes off the house.

"You took her once before," he reminded me in a light voice.

"All within my right," I sneered.

"Is the money really that important to you, or is it a matter of principle?" He sounded curious beside me.

"They crossed me." I finally tore my gaze away, found the basket by our feet, and handed James a piece of ham. "I think they may have seen us here before. The children. The eldest girl keeps looking around, as if she expects someone."

"Maybe they've been told to be on guard," he mused.

"At least the weather is nice. It would be dreadful sitting out here in the rain." I smiled a little, as it was a ridiculous thought.

"They cannot keep her locked up forever," he assured me.

"Let's patrol the roads again. Maybe they have taken her out the back door. They have to air her sometimes." I rolled my eyes and took the whip from his grasp.

"Sooner or later, we'll find her," he said, but as it turned out, we did not. They treated that girl as if she were a princess, valuable beyond measure.

One day when we arrived, we could tell that something was different. The windows upstairs were wide open. The door to the porch stood open too, and the children ran in and out, chasing puppies.

"She's gone," said James. "They have moved her during the night."

I rested my elbows on my knees and hid my face in my hands. "Are you sure?"

"Well, yes, the house is wide open now. Anyone can get in."

"What do we do, then?" I looked up. James's face had turned cold and smooth as stone as he looked upon the house. He did not much like it when a hunt was cut short.

"We make a new plan." The stony expression was wiped from his features.

"Better do, and quickly. I have a farm to run. I don't have time to sit around here." I grabbed the reins and set us in motion. "So much trouble for one little girl," I huffed, and then, when we had been going for a while: "I need another child—a boy. About three months from now. Can you do that?"

James laughed beside me. It was a dry, throaty sound. "The new Gunness heir, is it?"

"That, my dear friend, it is." I smiled.

"I cannot guarantee Norwegian stock."

"To hell with that, as long as it's white." I felt hope again—*hope*—blooming in my chest.

"You'll be having a son, then?" His hand was on my back, warm and strong.

"Yes." I smacked the whip. "It's such a comfort to me in my time of grief that my husband left behind a living seed."

"And Swanhild?" His voice was terse.

"To hell with her too—I don't need her . . . Peter Gunness's son is so much better."

———

MY CONDITION SOON became clear for everyone to see, and I was happy I had not thrown away the cushions. About three months later, one late night in May, James came back to La Porte with the child, a healthy baby boy about a month old. There was a woman in the carriage too—the boy's mother, I presumed—there to keep him quiet and fed on the journey.

I took the child and gave James the money. "Tell her he will be well taken care of."

"I don't think she cares much. She's taken with drink, that one." He motioned to the carriage with his head.

"Nevertheless, I'm grateful to her." And I truly was.

"Give her a bottle of whiskey, then, and she will never regret the trade." His lips tilted up in a wicked smile, dripping with disdain.

I thought that all would be settled when I had Peter Gunness's son—surely the money would fall to me then—but Gust was a fierce advocate for his wan little niece. Our dispute ended up in court, where my lawyer fought well enough on my behalf, and in the end, I got most of the money for my little boy. I would rather have had it all, but most was certainly better than nothing, and the lawyer said there was little left to be done, and so I had to let the rest of the money—and Swanhild—go. The latter certainly bothered me the least.

It did not sit well with me, though. Did not sit well with me at all. I could not help but curse Gust Gunness as I sat up at night, drinking brandy next to the spot where his brother had died. He had cost me much chagrin and misery, that man, and I swore that if I ever crossed paths with him again, I would make sure to pay him back with interest.

What was it with brothers that they always came meddling and stuck their noses where they did not belong? Why was it that they always distrusted me so? I was sick of such men and their need to interfere. It made me think marriage was not worth it at all, if I always ended up with some brother on my doorstep, making problems and voicing concerns.

Perhaps I was better off on my own.

People in La Porte were touched by my plight, though, and the church was crowded when my son was christened. This little boy would have a good life, I thought, looking down on his small face under the lace cap.

This one would have a good life, if only for helping me fight back against that horrid man Gust Gunness.

34.

Nellie

Chicago, 1903

I had not been well since Peter Gunness's funeral. My sleep was uneasy and nothing seemed to bring me much joy. Not even after we finally could afford a house of our own did my mood brighten much, although it was what I had wished for always. Though my sister was far away, she seemed to be always on my mind—the children, too. Myrtle in particular. I wondered how she was after all that had transpired, if she had managed to forget whatever it was that she knew, or if she found the burden of knowledge unbearable.

Her dark gaze, wide with innocence, seemed to watch me whenever I closed my eyes.

For the first few weeks, after the story of the meat grinder had found its way to ink and paper, I waited for something to happen. I was always expecting a knock on the door, or a blazing headline with my sister's name in it. I waited for something to come tumbling down, and as we readied for the move, I was thinking of how to best arrange it if Bella's girls should suddenly end up in my care. I thought of where they would sleep and where to keep their clothes. I walked past the school they would go to, to make sure that the yard looked nice.

John noticed my dark mood with growing concern. He did what

he could to keep my mind occupied, speaking of wallpapers and upholstery—we would have a bigger sitting room now and were in need of more furniture—but I could not make myself come out of it.

He thought that it was the newspaper stories alone that bothered me, and he surely shared my concern about that. I suspected that he and Rudolph edited the articles when they translated them for me, but they could not shield me from people's talking.

"I think we should not go to La Porte again until they know what happened," John said one night after we had gone to bed; the candle was still burning on the bedside table. "There are too many strange occurrences happening around your sister."

"Do you think Bella had anything to do with Peter's death?" I asked with my heart in my throat.

"Of course not," he murmured, though I could tell that he did not mean it. He only said so because I had always defended her before, and he wanted to avoid an argument. He had no reason to think things had changed. "I just think about Mads, and that date . . ."

"You thought Mads could have done it to himself." I remembered our talk from that time.

"I still think so—but this meat grinder business is equally odd." He was on his back and had flung an arm over his eyes, so I could not see them. I thought that it maybe was on purpose.

My heart was racing, racing. "So what exactly are you saying, then?" I wanted him to voice it, the suspicion we shared.

"Nothing." He sounded very tired. "We do not *know* anything of what happened in that house, and we have to put our trust in the sheriff." He sighed and removed his arm; I could tell that his eyes looked tired, too. "I'm just glad that she lives in La Porte now."

I did not tell him about Myrtle then, although I knew I should.

If it all came tumbling down, then I would tell him.

If it all came tumbling down, I *had* to.

But the headline never came—no law enforcer ever came knocking to ask about my sister, and I was starting to think that perhaps Gust Gunness had been a little rash. Perhaps they held an inquest after all such farm accidents that ended in death. I knew little of the law and could not tell.

The worst thought of all to fly through my mind was the idea that I was wrong. What if I suspected my sister of such foul things for no good reason? What sort of woman would it make me to think of my sister in such a way if it had all been heresy and misunderstandings? Perhaps what Myrtle had seen had not been so bad. She was young and innocent; perhaps she had merely seen her parents in the throes of passion? That could certainly look both frightening and confusing to a young soul.

But then I thought that surely the newspapers would not have written about it if the death had not been peculiar, and then there was the memory of Mads's death that came drifting along whenever I was about to put the matter aside and ascribe it all to bad luck on my sister's part. Then again, I thought that surely the sheriff would have found it, if there was something be found, during the inquest.

As I packed all my things and brought them out again to rest on new shelves, my mind seemed to never tire of these thoughts, and even after it became apparent that nothing would come of the inquest, I was still startled by the smallest noise and dreaded to see the mailman on our street, fearing for what he came carrying. More than anything else, I worried that Bella would announce another wedding. When an envelope eventually *did* appear, however, it was a smaller sort of man it introduced, and I did my very best to rejoice in this new life, this nephew of mine, but his father's bloody death cast a shadow on it all that I simply could not be free of.

Yes, I did my best to stay away from Brookside Farm—not because I did not *want* to go there, to help those little children out, but because I could not bear it. Everything in me was repulsed by the thought, afraid of what I would find if I went there again. Afraid it was something I could not look away from, or silence as I had Myrtle. The farm had become a dangerous place in my mind, littered with traps and unwelcome surprises. I ran from all knowledge the best that I could; I did not *want* to know.

But only because I stayed away from Bella and her children, it did not mean that *they* did not come to *me*.

"ISN'T THAT YOUR niece?"

Clara and I were in my new kitchen, unpacking my cookware from crates on the floor. None us were young anymore, and Clara had become almost as slow as I was, but we managed well enough, lifting out pots and pans and dusting them off before putting them away. We both wore old dresses, frayed at the hem, and grimy aprons. There was no use wearing anything else, as all the pots were stained with soot and the crates they were moved in were covered in dust. A little bit of black was smeared on Clara's cheekbone.

I looked up and out the window, following Clara's gaze through my new front yard with its flowering bushes, and onto the street, where a slender girl with a long blond braid stood by the wooden gate and looked up at the house with a pensive expression.

"Sure." I was surprised by the power of the surge of love that suddenly erupted in my chest. I had not known that I missed her so much. "That's Jennie." I rose to my feet and rushed to the front door.

"Jennie!" I called when I had it open. I waved though she was just a few steps away.

"Aunt Nellie!" The girl was all sunshine when she unlatched the gate. "I did not know if it was the right house—they all look so similar, and I only knew that it was white." She chattered merrily as she came up the flagstone path. At fifteen, she was a young woman, and her face had shed much of its former roundness, taking on the sharper angles of an adult. Her dress was white and blue and reached her midcalf; a little straw hat sat perched upon her head. Her socks were very white and her black shoes neatly polished, though a little dust from the street had lodged onto the leather.

"Jennie." I opened the door wide in welcome. "What are you doing here?"

"Oh, I'm staying with my papa for a while," she said as she entered my new hall. "This is a very pretty house, Aunt Nellie." She looked around as in awe, though the hall was cramped and housed little but the stairs to the second floor. I knew very well what she was used to. "I am so happy that you could move here." She gave me a hug; her skin was smooth and chilled from the outside.

"Thank you so much, Jennie. It is not so very big, but more than enough for us, with only Nora living here." I swallowed hard as I said that last part, remembering how I had been wondering if I was about to take on all the girls from La Porte.

"I only came to see if Nora was home, and to see the new house, of course," Jennie said as she stepped into the kitchen. Her eyes were still wide, taking it all in. "Oh, hello, Clara," I heard her say in front of me. "How are you on this fine day?"

Another round of greeting ensued before Jennie finally settled on the bench, and I went to bring her a cup of milk.

"Nora isn't home, I'm afraid. She is working with Olga now, selling hosiery," I said as I served her. I noted how her face fell when she heard that her cousin was not there, and was charmed by how much she cherished my unruly daughter. "She will not be home before late this afternoon, but you're most welcome to stay for dinner if you like," I offered, to cheer her up.

Her lower lip came out in the tiniest of pouts. "I wish I could, Aunt Nellie, but Margret, my stepmother, would not approve of me being late."

"So your father has remarried?" I sat down in a chair opposite the girl.

Jennie nodded and clutched the enamel cup of milk between her hands. "They think I should come and live with them now, since Papa Mads died, and Peter."

"Oh, I'm sure that's not the reason why." Clara rose and went to the stove, for coffee, no doubt. "He probably thinks he can provide a better home for you now that there's a woman in the household."

"Maybe," Jennie answered politely, "but my sister said otherwise when she met me at the station. She said they had all been so worried, because of the writing in the newspapers and all."

"You should not listen to what people say," I huffed, while a surge of dread took root in my belly. It was one thing that I thought what I did, and quite another to hear that others might be thinking the same thing. People who did not know us. "Your mama cannot be very happy about this."

"No." Her gaze seemed to glaze over and she looked down into her milk. "She told Papa she would get a lawyer."

"Of course she did." I could not help but smile a little. My sister could never resist a fight.

"Will you be going to school here in Chicago, then, Jennie?" Clara carried cups of warm coffee to the table.

"Oh, I already am, only not today." Red spots bloomed on her cheeks—she was clearly supposed to be there and not with us, but I did not chastise her. I was much too happy to see her.

"It sounds like you are settling in nicely, then." Clara joined us at the table. She was as happy as I was, I reckoned, to have some respite from the crates.

"Sure." But the girl looked pained as she said it.

"Perhaps it's for the best," I suggested, finding that I did not much mind that Jennie was away from the farm. Likely, my own poor memories of it colored my view a little. "With the new baby," I added. "Mama must have her hands full."

"Yes, but he's such a handsome little boy." Her face lit up in a smile that made her blue eyes sparkle. "He is the sweetest thing you could ever imagine and he makes very little fuss."

It hurt my heart to see her longing. "Do you miss him very much?"

She nodded again. "And Myrtle and Lucy, too." Her expression suddenly darkened. "Papa says that he will not force me to stay, but I'm afraid he will be upset if I leave . . . but then Mama is *already* upset, and I don't know what to do."

"Where would you rather stay, then, Jennie?" Clara's voice was soft.

The girl on the bench shrugged. "Both places are nice."

"Perhaps you should try to stay in Chicago for a while." I offered my advice—which admittedly was different from what I would have said just a few years before. "You have to try out new places for a while before you know if you like them."

"You must too, then, with this new house." She looked around again.

"Just that." I laughed. "Though it would take at least ten wild horses and a leaky roof to drive me out of this place now that I have settled. We have saved up for years to buy it."

"Mama says the same thing about Brookside." Jennie chewed her lip. "She says it's where we *all* belong."

"And you always will too," I offered as comfort, "even if you stay here in Chicago."

IT DID NOT take many days before Bella arrived in much the same manner as Jennie had, only in a buggy. I sat by the kitchen window, giving my back a rest and admiring the flowers, when I saw her arrive. She parked out on the street and tied the horse to my fence, then walked toward the door. She wore a long, black coat that looked much too thick for the weather, the flowery hat, and a pair of men's shoes on her feet. When she moved, the trim of her coat dusted the flagstones around her. She did not wait for me to open but entered right after she knocked.

I had thought that I might find it uncomfortable to have Bella in my house after all the dark thoughts I had suffered, but the sight of her was so familiar to me, as if she belonged to my body, like a limb. As I watched her enter my kitchen, and she stood there on my floor in the flesh, it was as if I could not reconcile the real woman with the person in my head. She was just Bella—*Little Brynhild*—quarrelsome and difficult at times, but lively too, and generous.

Surely Gust Gunness had been wrong.

There was nothing lively about her this day, though, as she strode into my kitchen with hardly a greeting. "Did you know that Jennie is in Chicago?"

I nodded that I did and took her coat.

"That Ole Olson," she huffed as she sat down by the table. "He seems to think that he can just take her back!"

"Well, he has the right of blood," I murmured as I poured her coffee.

"Well, it is I who have had all the hardships involved in raising a child from infancy." Her brow furrowed and I could see her ample bosom's heavy rise and fall under the pearls that rested there. "Jennie had never been anything but happy with me, and she thinks of the younger girls as sisters."

I could not argue with that. "Jennie said you had threatened her father with a lawyer."

"Threatened? No, I have already spoken to a lawyer. He thinks I have every right to demand that she come home." She lifted her chin as if challenging the world.

"But she is no little girl anymore. Perhaps it would be nice for her to spend some time in Chicago?" I pushed the tray of rose-flavored cookies closer to her hand, knowing that some sugar would often brighten her mood.

Bella rolled her eyes—at Ole Olson or me I could not tell. "It's a matter of principle," she told me. "You cannot just give your child away and then expect to have her delivered back when she is all but grown."

This too sounded reasonable when put like that. "What will you do then?"

She picked up a cookie and measured it with her gaze. "Talk to Jennie, of course. When she first came here, it was supposed to be a visit, but when I came to bring her home, Mr. Olson informed me that he thought she could stay for a while, on account of him having a wife now." She rolled her eyes again, and this time I knew it was aimed at Mr. Olson. "He also did say, loud and clear, that he wouldn't stop her if she chose to go back to Brookside Farm. I only waited this long to give her time to miss us." She bit the cookie in half.

"She certainly seemed to do that when she was here," I said, truthfully enough. "She especially seemed to miss her new brother." Talk of her children was nearly as effective as sugared treats when it came to chasing the thunderclouds away.

"Oh yes." Her face softened at once, and a tender smile appeared on her lips. "He is an angel, that one, so happy and content. That I should receive such a gift from my late husband, it truly is a miracle." Her voice had grown thick as she gave her speech, and her gaze lingered halfway up my wall. I thought she might have given it before. "You must come and see him." Her gaze shifted to me. "He is your nephew, after all." She frowned a little as if to remind me that I had been a negligent sister.

"I will," I promised, "soon." Though just the thought of it made my belly ache.

"Oh," she suddenly lamented, as she sighed and stretched out her feet in front of her. Her shoes were very large and uncomely but doubtlessly comfortable. "I feel like I haven't done anything but chase little girls since Peter died."

"What do you mean? Have there been others?" I was genuinely surprised.

"Only Swanhild, Peter's daughter. I wanted her to come and stay with us after her father died—it would have been such a comfort." Her face took on a solemn expression and her lower lip quivered a little. "That Gust Gunness would not have it, though, and kidnapped the girl in plain daylight!" Her eyes narrowed to slits. "Then I discovered that I was with child and could not put more thought into it." She brushed crumbs off her fingers with her hands.

"But is she safe, though? Swanhild?" Kidnapping did not sound very pleasant—not that I readily believed what Bella said. I knew there could be another truth to it. I remembered Gust Gunness that day in her kitchen, how angry he had been, how ready to think her a murderess. What he had said about Swanhild: that Peter sent her away because she and Bella did not get along.

Bella shrugged. "I would think that she is. They would hardly go through such hardships only to mistreat her . . . However, the Gunness family isn't all that, truth be told. I went to fetch the girl at one of their farms, and the place was hardly fit for swine. Peter married up, I will tell you that." She lifted her chin again as she brought the cup to her lips. A flicker of anger appeared in her eyes, and suddenly I was frightened again. Suddenly she was there for a moment, that woman in my mind.

The one who could do whatever it took if only she was angry enough.

I wanted to reply but could not find the words. It had been such a little thing, just a shadow passing through her eyes, and yet it left me speechless.

It reminded me that nothing had changed. She was still the woman with the husbands who died in peculiar ways.

With my inner eye, I saw Myrtle again, sitting on that rock behind the barn.

"I thought I'd see Jennie at school." Bella put down the cup; her eyes were all normal. "It's easier, then, if she's away from her father."

"I'm sure." It was my turn to sigh. I had no doubt that she would win this fight and bring the girl back home. The Olson family were honest people, bound to lose against a foe like her. It saddened me, though, as I would certainly feel easier knowing that Jennie was safe in Chicago, even if the other three were still at Brookside Farm.

"It's not safe for a young girl in the city." Bella rubbed her jaw with fast, angry motions. "All sorts of things can happen to her here, where I cannot look out for her. All sorts of people will look to take advantage, and if they cannot get it with promises, they will get it with violence."

"That's a little grim, don't you think?" I was shocked at the sudden vehemence in her voice. "I raised two girls—"

"Oh Nellie, don't even try to convince me. I've been a young girl myself, and I certainly did not escape it unscathed." The furious rubbing had turned her jaw red. "She must be where she is protected—with me at all times."

"But children move away, Bella. Soon she will too, no matter where she lives now." I tried to catch her eyes, but they deftly slid away.

"Of course she will; I'm not stupid, Nellie, but when she does, it will be somewhere I know she's safe." She was still rubbing her jaw, and her face twisted up as if she were in pain.

"Are you all right?" I dared to whisper.

"Of course I am." The rubbing stopped. Her hand fell down in her lap. She breathed a little fast and lifted her other hand to wipe sweat from her brow. "I'm just worried, that's all."

I WAS CERTAINLY not surprised when the buggy appeared again later that day with Jennie next to Bella. I did not even want to think of what my sister might have said to convince the girl to come back to La Porte.

They would continue there the next morning but spent the night with us. John was not too thrilled about it, but what else could I do but offer hospitality? Jennie looked awfully tired and could certainly use the rest. She brightened a little when she saw Nora, though. The two of them quickly renewed their bond and spent the evening out in the garden.

Bella slept on the bench, as she had done every night when she first came to Chicago. She did not say much about what had transpired, but I could tell that she was pleased. She even made an effort to be pleasant to John, and the three of us played cards in the sitting room. Bella won all three games and offered us all brandy from a bottle she had brought in the buggy.

As before, I found that it was easy enough to let things be as they were before, if only I did not think about poor Myrtle, and

Bella's two dead husbands. It was almost shameful, how easy it was to pretend to forget, when everything seemed so pleasant and nice, and the brandy was rich and the game exciting.

One thing she had said that day stuck with me, though, so much so that that I brought out my paper and pen the very next day and wrote to our sister Olina, asking her, at last, what had happened back then, when Little Brynhild was attacked. Olina had been there at the time, and would surely know. It was the rubbing of the jaw and the tone of voice that did it, the fretting over young Jennie's safety. Suddenly it was as if I could have no peace unless I knew.

What I learned when I received her reply was what brought me back to Brookside Farm at last.

35.

Belle

The walls never did seem to tarnish at Brookside Farm. Maybe the place had seen so much misery that it was immune to the stains of sin. Baby Jennie died, Peter died, but my house was still the same: a silent sister that sheltered and comforted me as no place had ever done before.

I had no desire to burn it down. I wanted to keep it and nourish it, help it thrive and blossom—just as I thrived and blossomed within its brick walls.

Brookside was a beautiful place; the cedar and sycamore trees grew tall and green, and the barn gleamed, freshly painted. The chickens flocked around my skirts when I came out, and the hogs grew fat and happy. I had everything I needed right there on the farm: eggs, meat, and milk. The windmill spun, the orchard was bountiful, forty-eight acres of land, all my own.

I had gotten rid of most of the pigs when Peter died. I did not think raising them to sell sausages was my trade. After all the upheaval, I just wanted to be a regular farmer and a mother, taking care of us all the best that I could.

I no longer feared losing Jennie; she was at peace at home and only rarely spoke of Chicago with anything resembling longing.

She was my daughter through and through, or so I thought at the time.

My son, Philip, was a good boy who soon grew soft and content in my care. He did not miss his real mother at all. He was so small and trusting that he fell asleep on my chest that very first night. I had not wanted a son of my own—young men are often a menace—but now that I had one, I did not regret it. It could be wise to have a boy to stand up for his mother and take on the farm when his sisters were married. I planned for the future then.

I always planned for the future.

As much as I had, it still cost to run a farm, and it felt as if the money went out as soon as it came in. Although I had a comfortable amount of cash, the farm barely paid for itself and I could not help but worry. What if the crops failed, or the animals got sick? What would happen to us then, if our livelihood shrank to nothing? I would not eat poor man's fare again. I had crawled my way up from that deep, dark den. My pantry grew ever fuller as my worry increased, and I preserved as much of the produce as I could, lining the cellar walls with glass jars and filling the vegetable bins to the brim.

Now that I had what I wanted, my new aim was to keep it.

I hired Peter Colson in March. He was a good worker and a handsome man. I let him sleep in the room above the kitchen and found that I liked to have him around. He was easy to please, this new Peter. All I had to do was feed him and tell him what a great man he was and he would light up like the sun and work twice as hard just to keep me satisfied. After the demands of my husbands, it was easy to like Peter Colson. He laughed a lot and played with the children. At night, he joined me in games of cards, and later, after Philip's arrival, he joined me in bed as well. Though he was much younger than I was, we were not a poor match between the sheets. Colson had a fondness for rough play that suited me, and he never brought our secrets out of the bedroom. It did not take long before his gaze softened when he looked at me, and there was not a thing he would not do to please me.

I found myself thinking how easy it was to make a man happy. How easy to make him feel strong and wanted. I was certainly no courtesan—far past my prime and plain to look at—but even I could make a man like Peter Colson soft as clay. Most people, men and women alike, are foolish in that regard. They all yearn to be something special. There is much power in flattery and a hearty meal.

In the end, what all men want is a mother.

NELLIE CAME OUT to see me late in the summer, bringing Nora with her. My sister never learned to speak English well and needed an aide when traveling far from home. I was happy to see them, but the visit was not wholly pleasant. Nellie had grown very ill, for one, and walked slowly, blaming her bad back.

"Did you ever experience pain like this after you had yours?" she asked, sitting outside in the yard with a glass of lemonade, watching my girls and the dog chase the chickens inside the barn. The birds had been at the vegetables again and were now banished to their own enclosure.

"No," I answered. "I never had any problems after I had my children."

"Not even with the latest one? They say it's harder the older you get."

"No, I'm as spry as I ever was." I laced my hands and stretched out my arms to demonstrate.

She gave me a curious look. "So you seem," she agreed. "It's rare, though, having a child so late, and with his father dead and everything." Was it distrust that surfaced in her eyes?

"Yes, it's a shame." I fanned my face with my hand. It was a warm day. Far too warm for our heavy dresses. "The boy never knew him, though, so he won't grieve the loss."

"How do you like it, being a widow?" Another glance in my direction.

"Oh, I miss him terribly, of course. I had so many hopes pinned on Peter."

"And to die from the sausage grinder—" Nellie choked, and I gave her a curious look. Her face looked pinched and pained all of a sudden, and I moved uneasy in the wicker chair. My jaw tensed up a little.

"Indeed," I said. "It was a terrible affair, but such is life; you never know what's waiting."

"Your daughters must be distraught." Her voice was clipped and she looked at the chickens, not me.

"Well, they didn't know him very long, and I bought them a pony." The little animal, aptly named Chocolate, had become everyone's darling and was the envy of the children on McClung Road. I was very pleased with the purchase.

"Still, though." Nellie shifted on the white-painted wicker seat. "I got a letter from Olina." The pained expression intensified. "Little Bry—Bella, why didn't you tell me about that man in Selbu, the one who died?"

"Who?" I feigned ignorance, though my heart began to race.

"The heir at the farm, he who attacked you!" Her gaze shifted to me, brimming with tears.

My jaw ached. What was it to her? Bringing up that ugly story. "There was nothing to tell." My voice had grown harsh. I rubbed my throbbing jaw.

"Olina spoke of it as if everyone knew." She blinked rapidly to chase the tears away; her gaze was on the sky. "She said it was a shame that all your men keeled over and died."

I felt my cheeks go red—what sort of an ambush was this? "That's a terrible thing to say." I suddenly felt hot all over.

"Yes, isn't it just? But that's just like her, though; she never held anything back. She reminds me of Father in that way." Nellie lifted a hand to wipe at the tears.

"What else did she tell you?" I did not want to but had to ask. I was sweating profusely under my clothing.

"Oh, she said that the man who got you pregnant—*pregnant*, Bella?—died, but not before he had kicked the child out of you." I could not tell if that was anger in her voice. I had never heard her speak in such a tone, as if the words were traveling through rocks—through pebbles on a beach.

Having it spelled out in such a crude manner made me cringe. For a brief moment, I saw my hands curl around Nellie's neck to stop the foul words from coming out of her mouth. "Yes," I managed to say. "I worked at the farm still when he died; but what happened between us was an old story even then."

She went quiet for a moment. "It could make a person change, couldn't it? It could inflict wounds on one's soul." She was still wiping tears and I wished she would stop. "I heard of a man who lost his memory after a fall—"

"Life is a perilous journey," I cut in, "or was there something else on your mind?" My own mind was racing. Why did she speak of my soul?

Nellie took a deep breath. "Little Brynhild, it wouldn't be a person's own fault if they were . . . *different* after something so vile. Perhaps something in the head went wrong, like with that man after the fall—"

"Do you think there's something wrong with my head?" I felt an urge to laugh, but this was certainly not a laughing matter. I did not like where she was headed with this unfortunate train of thought. She had clearly not been sufficiently fooled by my grief.

"No." Nellie answered my question, but there was no true fire in the denial. "I just think that if one is in pain, there is help to be had—from a priest perhaps . . . Just because one has done something, it doesn't mean one has to do it *again*." She rubbed her forehead with her hands and her breathing became labored. Her scrawny frame quivered beside me.

"Calm yourself, Nellie." I held on to the armrests so hard that it

hurt, and it helped—I did not quite lose my temper. This was neither the time nor the place. "I am sure I don't know what you're
talking about." The words came tumbling through gritted teeth.

"Oh come, Bella, of course you do." It was her eyes, not mine,
that flashed with anger. "You should have told me! I should have
known! I wouldn't have let them go at you about the scissors, or
been so mad about your treatment of Mads had I known about that
man . . . though Edvard died too, of course . . ."

"They are gossiping about Peter's death in Chicago now, I reckon."
I was proud of how calm my voice sounded to my ears.

"Well, yes—it was so sudden, and they wrote about it, but—"

"That is not a very Christian thing to do, blaming a poor widow."
I lifted my chin and gazed at the sun, letting the bright light blind
me. My jaw was burning, throbbing and aching.

"You know how people are not always kind—and then when I
heard about that man in Selbu—"

"Perhaps it's the Lord's way of weeding out the bad seeds." I
made no secret of my scorn. The sun was searing in my eyes, distracting me from the fury inside. Why would she bring this up? She
was going at it like a thoughtless boy poking with a stick at something raw and fragile: a sea creature out of its shell, or a baby bird
tumbled from the nest.

Why would she hurt me so?

"What do you mean, Bella?" She sounded breathless.

"Only that a man who kicks a child out of its mother's belly perhaps deserves to die."

"Yes." Her voice was very quiet. "That's what Olina said too,
that he deserved it."

I suddenly felt more sympathetic toward my homebound sister.
"Olina would know, she saw me when I—"

"Yes, that's what she wrote."

"It's too late to mourn now, Nellie. I wanted America to be a
fresh start."

"Yes, but some things you can't run away from." She spoke so quietly that I had to strain my ears to make out the words.

"Clearly I could." I finally looked away from the sun; my eyes watered and my vision was impaired. I blinked away the red while I motioned to the yard with my hand, presenting the glistening green of cedars, the frilly-clad girls with the dog, and the fat hogs rolling in their pen. "I recovered just fine, I would say."

"Did you, though?" Her voice was still so quiet that it was hard to catch the words.

"I would not speak more of this if I were you." Though I almost admired her for being so plain with me. "Nothing good can come of it."

"But, Bella—"

"No!" Now it was I who shook. The anger in me boiled and lashed. "Leave it be, Nellie."

"Of course," she mumbled, and thankfully did not say another word on the matter before she left the next day.

I had no desire to harm my sister—where was the spite in that?—and hoped that she would take my advice. Surely she could look away if she wanted to—leave it well alone.

The sheriff had done so, and the insurance men in Chicago.

She had no proof, after all.

IT WAS LATER that year, when summer had given way to chilly nights, when I got word that a crate had arrived for me by train. I had not ordered anything, and felt a little bewildered.

"Is it very large?" I asked the boy who delivered the message.

"You better bring the carriage."

"Was there a note?"

The boy nodded. "It's at the station."

Nothing to do for it then but bring out the horses and go. I brought Colson with me as help while Jennie looked after the children.

At the station, I was presented with a large, square crate and a greasy envelope. I knew the writing at once, and my heart gave a twinge.

"Come," I said to Colson, "let's get it in the carriage."

"But what is it? Some new equipment?"

"No, just some jars I ordered. I completely forgot." I made my voice sound calm though I felt hot with both bewilderment and worry.

"Are they fragile, then?" he asked.

"Not so much," I guessed.

He hauled the crate onto the carriage. On the way back, I kept ogling the thing, certain that nothing good could come from it.

Back at the farm, I had Colson help me maneuver the crate down into the cellar through the outside trapdoor. He said nothing when I told him it was for storage. Since I already kept preservatives and produce down there, it was not an unlikely place to store jars. When the crate was safely deposited, I told Colson to go outside and dig a hole for rubbish. I told him to dig deep, as the garbage would likely smell. Then I opened the envelope and skimmed through the writing: *She told her mother she was to rest on a farm near La Porte. I trust it to you to see that she does.*

The time had come at last, then, to pay my dues to James Lee.

WHEN IT WAS night and all were asleep, I went down in the cellar with the crowbar. The crate was tightly sealed, but as soon as the top was pried loose, the smell flooded the room at once. Neither the oilcloth she was wrapped in nor the hay that was tightly packed around her could prevent the stench of decay.

The woman could have been about twenty-five years of age, with pretty clothes and nice, red hair. She did not look like a whore, and I wondered what kind of mess she had been in to end up in my cellar. Her purse lay with the body, but no name was inside. I hauled her up and placed her on a table I used for storing milk. She was a slight woman. I could easily carry her on my own.

I was both annoyed and amused by this crated surprise. Of course, James should not have done it—sending me a body by train! On the other hand, it was just like him to do something so bold to get a rise out of me, and that made me feel close to him. The crate would be untraceable, of course. He never much liked to put his head in the noose.

I went upstairs and looked in on both Colson and the girls to make sure they were sleeping soundly—they ought to be by then; I had given them all some laudanum. The oilcloth was a blessing, for the woman was messy. The train ride must have been hot. I wrapped her back inside it and brought her out through the trapdoor. Then I placed her in a wheelbarrow, found Colson's freshly dug hole, and tipped her in. I went to get the rubbish next, a heap that was ever growing behind the barn. I had meant to burn it, but now it was useful. I wheeled some loads to the hole and tipped them in as well, saw the woman disappear under broken glass and empty cans, bones and rotten hay. Then I filled in the hole with the shovel.

COLSON WAS IN the kitchen when I came back inside. "What are you doing up so early?" he asked while I heated water to clean my hands.

"I couldn't sleep."

"I slept like a rock. Must've been all the nice food you gave me."

"Just that." I sat down in his lap and hoped the dead woman's stench did not cling to me. "Why don't we make the most of it now, while the children are still asleep?"

"Oh, but you are such a kind woman, Mrs. Gunness." He was fumbling for my breasts through my dress, already eager as a pup.

"Just let me wash up first." I rose and went for the water. "I don't want to get you dirty. I just filled in the rubbish pit you dug."

"Now? So early?"

"Why not?" I dried off my hands. "The night was moonlit and I brought a lamp."

"Why, you are something. You never rest, do you? Working this hard, even at night . . ." He had come up behind me, his arms wound around my waist, his face burrowed into my neck. "There never was a woman as good as you."

"No." I smiled and tossed the towel on a chair. "I'm certainly not like the rest."

I let him have me then, leaning with my hands on the wooden washstand and my skirts pulled up around my waist. I rarely wore a corset on the farm, and my heavy breasts swung inside my blouse, tickled by the dancing pewter button.

It did not take me long to finish, excited as I was from the night's adventure. The young man behind me slapped my buttock as he finished, proud, no doubt, that he could take me to such heights. That he could make this old widow dance.

I closed my eyes and thought of James Lee.

Burying that woman stirred something in me. For three nights after, I could not sleep. I kept thinking about when Peter died; I saw it all in my mind. How the blows fell; how the blood sprayed, how his knees buckled.

I thought about the feelings I had that night: how strong I felt. How joyously alive. How utterly triumphant when he lay there— just a lump of flesh.

He could not hurt me again when he was dead.

I ached for that feeling—I yearned for it. It was as if my life were worth nothing if I could not have it again. I lay there at night with my hand pressed to my aching jaw and I longed—yes, I longed—to lift the cleaver again.

Sometimes, it was Colson I saw on the receiving end of my blade.

I WENT TO see James in Chicago and found him in his small apartment reeking of yesterday's liquor. His shirt was unbuttoned and his hair tousled. He had not shaved for some days. I never understood his desire to live in squalor despite his means. He said it kept him safe and out of sight, but to me it felt undignified.

Of course, I did not know all that he was hiding from.

He laughed when he saw me standing in his tiny kitchen. "I thought that present would get a rise out of you." He gave me a sloppy kiss on the mouth, then poured coffee into cracked china and sat down before me at his worn red table. "She's resting, then?"

"Yes, she's resting. I had my hired man dig a hole." My fingers closed around the scalding-hot cup.

"Didn't I tell you to always have one ready?" He raised an eyebrow at me.

"I never thought I would get lodgers by train." Even as I said it, the annoyance and amusement battled in me.

"I wanted to surprise you." He lit a cigar and extinguished the match with a flick of his wrist.

"Is this how it's going to be now? You send me bodies and I dig them down?" It was my turn to arch an eyebrow.

"You can handle it, I'm sure. Didn't you tell me you'd become quite the expert, butchering those pigs?" He was nothing but glittering eyes and smiles, and it was hard not to smile with him.

"How often am I to expect a delivery?" I bit my lip and looked down at the floor, not wanting to be drawn in by his charm just yet.

"My, you are more compliant than I thought." He sounded amused.

"I want them delivered to my door, though. You can't send bodies by train." And yet I could not stop the smile from forming on my lips.

He laughed and added something from a bottle to our coffee. "I promise I won't do that in the future. As for how often? That depends on my need. You certainly have the land to handle one from time to time. I won't give you too many, though. It must be neat and clean—no traces."

"I can do that." I finally looked at his face again, at the fullness of his lips.

"Don't you want to know who they are?" He blew out smoke, filling the small room with just one puff.

"No, that doesn't concern me. I just want to know what's expected of me." I shifted on the chair and took a deep breath, making ready to state my terms.

"I always knew you would be of use, Mrs. Gunness." He looked entirely smug.

"Yes, you always said there would be a time to pay." I sipped my coffee while holding his gaze.

"That's not why I like you, though. I hope you appreciate that." The smugness was replaced with a rare softness, one I did not know what to do with.

"I want you to do me a favor in return," I said instead.

"Of course you do." Another puff of his cigar.

"I was thinking I might marry again. A kind Norwegian man or such. A man of means, preferably." There was a plan in my head but it was incomplete, like jagged shadows playing on a silk screen.

A twitch of annoyance showed on James's face then, a wrinkle between his eyebrows. "You are fine on your own. A new husband might ruin it all—"

"I need help on the farm, and a farmhand is expensive." I said it fast and breathlessly, prepared for such objections.

"You know your husbands don't last, and then you'll make a ruckus trying to cover it up." The frown on his face deepened.

"Maybe it won't come to that." I leaned closer over the table; the hot steam from the cup warmed my chest.

"You know it will. You have no patience with those men." The frown turned into a sneer.

"Well, maybe I won't be marrying, then; maybe I just need a farmhand." The shadows on the screen danced and played.

"Don't you have one already?" A puzzled smile.

"He might not last." Quiet words that sounded like thunder. My breathing came faster. I felt hot all over.

James went quiet for a while; I could see his mind working. "What do you want me to do?"

"Find one for me and send him my way. Some young man with strong arms, fresh from the old country. A man of some means, of course. Say you are my brother, and that I'm looking for hired hands—or a husband, if that's preferable." I picked at the tight collar of my shirtwaist, trying to let in some air.

"What do you want them for?" His eyes were mere slits as he regarded me across the table.

"I haven't decided yet." I licked my lips and struggled for breath. How could I explain that the shadows were still dancing, that I just wanted someone to be there at hand—to have their bodies within my reach.

"Of course you have decided." James added more liquor to our china cups. "Now you've seen how easy it is to make them disappear on land such as yours."

"Maybe I just want the company." Maybe that was all. Maybe it would not come to carnage.

"Maybe you just want the cash." He gave me a wide grin.

"I can't have the one without the other." I smiled back across the table, but my heart beat hard in my chest.

"People disappear all the time in this country." He said it as if it were nothing.

"No one has roots here, and people move around . . . In the old country, families knew each other generations back, but here there's no kin so no one feels obliged to look out for one another." It was just the truth, what I said.

"No one keeps track of all the comings and goings." James happily played along.

"And the land is so vast. It's easy to get lost." I joined in his smile.

"Many bad men on the roads too." James winked.

"Will you do it, then? Will you send them to me?" I could barely breathe while waiting for the answer.

"Will you keep taking my crates?" His eyebrow rose again.

I nodded and stretched a hand across the table.

"We have a deal, then, Mrs. Gunness." His hand, so warm and deadly, met mine in a hard grip.

"That we have, Mr. Lee," I said, and the shadows danced and leapt on the screen. Joyous, I think, and free.

THE NEXT SHIPMENT from Chicago came a few weeks later. This time the crate held a man, foul looking. It came to my door by carriage, and the man at the reins looked as foul as his cargo, but he was burly and strong and helped me get the crate down in the cellar.

That night I gave the children laudanum drops. Colson was so tired on his feet that he did not need my help. I brought the cleaver and the saw with me downstairs. I had bought quicklime and even read up on anatomy, as I figured there would be some differences from a hog. I hauled the man onto the table and cut his clothes off with scissors. He felt just like another pig to me then, perhaps because I had not seen him alive. I felt no different, I think, than any undertaker filling his customers with embalming fluids. I made a mess of it, though. The oilcloth beneath him was slippery and the floor too, but at last I managed to sever his limbs. Then I placed the parts in gunnysacks and hauled them with me outside where the wheelbarrow waited. I tipped him into the hole I had had Colson dig for just another occasion like this, and covered him in quicklime and ash. Then I cleaned up the mess.

It was a good thing I had married Peter, I thought, cleaning my hands that night. He had taught me how to strike with the cleaver, and the easiest ways to separate limbs from a corpse.

I made some coffee and ate some bread, and then I went to find Colson.

———

IN THE MIDDLE of October, a man stood at my door, introducing himself as Lars Olsen from Montana. He came, he said, because my brother had told him I was looking for a carriage and some horses, which he had with him, right there. He wondered if I wanted to have a look.

They were fine horses and the carriage was sturdy, but I wondered why James had sent Olsen my way. He was not exactly what I asked for. He was elderly, for one, and I was not in any dire need of horses, although one could never have too many of those. Was that what James was sending me? A chance to gain some horses? If so, I thought it a poor trade for my hours spent carving in the cellar.

I invited the man inside. I thought he could be a suitor if encouraged, although that did not seem to be his intention. I said his horses looked fine and I would have a closer look come morning, and then I asked him to stay and rest a few days.

The farm and my cooking appropriately impressed Mr. Olsen. He was appropriately drunk too, come night. I had Jennie make up a bed for him, and when he had gone up, I went outside to think.

What was I to do with this stranger in my house? James must have had some purpose in sending him to me, and it had nothing to do with his horses. I thought about the night I had just spent in his company, and realized that Mr. Olsen had kept his coat on all through the meal. When he went upstairs to sleep, it was still buttoned.

He had something to hide, then.

When I came inside, I took a lamp and walked up the creaking stairs. I was very careful when I opened the door just a crack to look at him in bed. He was snoring loudly with the coat cradled in his arms. They were strong arms too, despite his age. Perhaps he would be a worthy opponent. When I went back downstairs, my pulse went racing, as I thought of how it would feel to tackle this beast to the ground. To have him at my feet with my hands flecked with his blood. To conquer and win another game, and even gain some cash as a prize. I could not stop thinking about it. I could not help but being excited.

What good was that man to anyone but himself? Better his treasure—whatever it was—was used to feed and clothe my children. That way he had some purpose in this world.

The next day, I told Mr. Olsen that I would buy his horses and pretended to go into town to get cash. Instead, I went to the pharmacist and purchased chloral, a more potent sedative than the laudanum drops, as I did not want to take any chances. I did not know this opponent as I had my husbands.

"I cannot sleep at all," I told the pharmacist, dressed in my widow's garb. "Perhaps this fine concoction will help."

I fed Mr. Olsen well that night, and laced his drinks before I served them. When the house was quiet, I went to his room. Mr. Olsen was snoring just as loudly as before; I knew he would be deep in his dreams from the chloral. Still, I was very quiet when I made my way across the floor. My heart pounded so hard it almost hurt and my hands felt clammy, but there was excitement as well. I was about to test my strength again and feel that wondrous feeling.

I pulled one of the pillows from under his head and was just about to cover his face, when he suddenly woke up and started thrashing. His legs flayed and his hands clawed at mine; it reminded me of wrestling with a young bull in the barn. I had to use what I had of strength to suppress his violent thrashing; still, I held the pillow firm until he went limp as a gutted fish. His hands fell away from mine, leaving angry scratches.

When I let go, my heart was pounding and my breath was shivering. My clothes were drenched in sweat. I picked up the coat from the bed and felt the heavy weight. I laid it out the floor and patted it down until I felt the rolls of cash sewn into the lining. There was my surprise, then, my gift from James Lee.

Lars Olsen lay as dead on the bed, but alas, he was not yet. I could see the pulse throbbing on his neck. I brought out a sheet and laid it out on the floor, and then I rolled the man down on top of it. He landed with a heavy thud. I wrapped him up good and hauled him with me across the floor, down the stairs, through the kitchen, and down all the steps to cellar. It was hard work, for the man was heavy, and though I was big and strong, I was just a woman. I managed, though, with much fuss. When we got down there, his head was bloody from the stairs, and I do not know if he was still alive. I gave him a few whacks with the cleaver to be sure.

It reminded me of Peter, dealing him those blows, and I gave him more than enough to see him good and dead. Then I hauled him onto the table and he was just meat after that. I bled him as well as I could and took the soft parts for the pigs. Then I sawed off his limbs, took his head off and brought him outside in gunnysacks to slip him in the ground. Ashes and quicklime. I covered him up.

Back inside, I moved his trunk to a room that was not in use and made up his bed neatly. Next, I cleaned the cleaver. Then I sat down in the kitchen with his coat. I cut the lining with my scissors and the rolls of money tumbled to the floor, almost a thousand in all.

It was well-deserved payment for a hard night's work, and I even got new horses and a carriage in the bargain. I threw the coat in his trunk then, and placed the money in a locked box I kept for that very purpose.

But I did not get that feeling. What I felt was barely triumphant at all; it was merely an echo of that joyous sense of power I remembered. I was satisfied with my work, yes, but the ecstasy evaded me— still as distant as a memory. Lars Olsen could fill my money box, but he could not sate my yearning. Killing him and taking him apart did nothing to bring me sweet bliss. I wondered if it was because of my nerves, or because I had expected too much. Perhaps that feeling could not be forced but had to erupt on its own. Perhaps it was like a snake: powerful but shy. All I could do was set the stage to try to coax it forth. Give it the proper bait and hope.

When Colson and the girls came down for breakfast the next day, I told them Mr. Olsen had left late the night before because he remembered he had to be in Chicago this morning.

I'd bought his horses, though, I said, and asked Colson to dig a new hole.

36.

Nellie

Bella did not invite us back to La Porte before Christmas, about which I felt relieved, but troubled, too. As much as I had wanted to stay away before—to turn a blind eye, as it was—I was now plagued by the notion that something terrible would happen if I were not there to keep watch.

I had taken up praying in earnest, for the first time in my adult life. I prayed for the children mostly, but for Bella too: that whatever was riding on her back would leave, and that her anger would mellow to peace. I prayed that her conscience would be vigilant and that her will would be strong. That she would not harm a fellow man again.

What else could I *do* but pray? It is the weapon of the powerless: a way to soothe an uneasy conscience when nothing else is left. For what *could* I do? Even if our conversation that summer, when I broached the subject of that man in Selbu, had been a terrible thing that chilled me to the bone, she still had not admitted to any wrong. I had not witnessed any evil deeds myself, besides Mads's bruises and the scissors many years ago. I could testify that she was eager to throw things when angry, and that she was no stranger to making a fist, but that was all. Aside from that incident in Selbu, I did not know anything that others did not know as well. Some of it had been in the newspapers; other things had traveled on people's lips for months. Heresy and speculations, yes—but, oh, I knew it to be true. Knew it deep in my marrow—knew it as I knew my own heart. She had as good as admitted it herself, too, by forbidding me to speak of it. Her face in that moment, out in the yard, sneering and cold toward me. I could barely see her in there, that little girl at Størsetgjerdet who clung to my skirts as I tended the goat. She had been swallowed up by something else, something dark with terrible jaws—like a wolf.

And even if I had my proof, what would I do? Go to the authorities and leave my little sister at their mercy? John would undoubtedly say yes, which was why I had not told him of our conversation that summer. I knew he would want me to go, even without any proof, to try to persuade the police to look into the deaths again, so I kept it to myself—my own terrible secret—and guarded it jealously against his prying.

I thought of the children too, of the pain it would cause them to lose their mama, and then I thought of Bella again, and the pain it would cause *her* to lose *them* . . . They were the one thing that brought her more joy than anything else combined. They were her angels and her stars at night.

No, I could not do it.

I thought that she had to be damaged somehow, from what had happened before, but what is damaged can often mend, I knew that as well. Be it a limb, a heart, or a soul. Surely Bella could heal herself and leave this all in the past. Her husbands were dead, and there was nothing to do for it but make sure it did not happen again. If she did not remarry, I figured, things would be safe and good. It seemed so clear to me then that it was the shackles of matrimony, the intimacy of bed and board, that brought out her terrible rage. If only she remained a widow, I thought, the wolf could be kept safely at bay—and that was why it pained me to stay away.

I wanted to make sure she did not marry.

————

SHE INVITED NORA and me back to attend the party she threw for the children at McClung Road the day after Christmas. She wanted our help, I think, just as much as she wanted to see us. She also wanted to show me, and all those who still wagged their tongues, that all was good at Brookside Farm. That she was a widow, not a fiend. That she brought joy to children, not death to men. It was easy to see, knowing what I did, and yet I forgave her for it. Perhaps I thought of it as her seeking a redemption. Perhaps I dearly hoped that it was so.

She met us at the station, dressed in a large bearskin coat, and with that flowery hat perched on top of her head. The horse that pulled the carriage wore sleigh bells around its neck. The snow was scarce in Indiana, though; it did not look much like Christmas at home, but she did not seem to mind.

"I want it to be a real Norwegian Christmas celebration for all the children," she said when we had climbed into the carriage. "A few of them are German, and some Swedish, but I don't mind. They will enjoy it just as much, I'm sure."

"Is Jennie at home? Is she excited?" Nora had come mostly for her cousin's company. It delighted me to see how their bond stood fast.

"Jennie has been setting the table and boiling rice porridge all day long. She's looking after the boy and watching the candles while I'm away."

"How is your son?" I asked.

"Healthy and plump as a piglet." She laughed. "His sisters spoil him. Even Lucy has taken to him, though I figured she might not since she has always been the darling before."

"She is a sweet child," I agreed. "And Myrtle?" My stomach ached a little when I said her name. I was still haunted by that day behind the barn—the way that I had silenced her.

"Healthy." Bella smacked the reins. The landscape around us

changed as we left the town behind and entered rural areas. Black fields topped with patches of snow surrounded us on both sides. Here and there, a horse was out, grazing behind weatherworn barns. "She is so sensitive, that child; her tears are never far away, but then they dry up quick as well." Bella continued to speak. "She was a little anxious about this gathering, to be honest. She couldn't sleep at all last night from fretting. She likes it better quiet, but I told her it was a nice thing to do. Not all of our neighbors can afford a proper Christmas celebration." A smug expression appeared on her face. "I stopped by some of the neighbors yesterday, since daughters in both households have been sick with fever, just to cheer them up with some sweets and toys, and I didn't see as much as a pine branch in a boot—nothing to celebrate Christmas at all. I thought it was the saddest thing."

I did not see fit to note how scarce our Christmases had been back when we were poor tenant's daughters. She was in such a jubilant mood that I let her have her joy in peace. It was better for us all when she was pleased.

The farmhouse at Brookside was lit from within by candles. A few pairs of children's skis were lined up against the outside wall, though I could not fathom how the children were able to ski with so little snow. Stepping inside, I could not help but think of the year before, almost to the day, when we were also gathered in that house to bury Peter Gunness. It had been lit by candles then, too, and the scent of wax was the same, but there were no black paper ribbons this time, and a lovely scent of boiling cream, evergreens, and spices mingled with that of the wax. In the fireplace, the flames danced upon dry logs.

A handful of children were already there, scattered on sofas and chairs; the boys wore their Sunday clothes and had freshly combed hair. Most of the girls were dressed in the somber colors of church as well, but Myrtle and Lucy wore white dresses adorned with frills and lace. The children chattered among themselves, in English for the most part, but some in Norwegian, too. They were so busy with one another that they barely noticed that we had arrived. On the table before them were bowls filled with nuts and caramels—no wonder the children's eyes shone with delight. Another couple of girls came in behind us, both of them wearing dresses that showed signs of wear under their equally poor winter coats. Their hair was neatly braided, though, falling down their backs in straight ropes.

"Are you well again, Gunnhild?" I heard Bella ask one of the newcomers.

"I am, Mrs. Gunness," the girl replied. "Thank you so much for the doll you gave me."

"Oh, that was nothing." But I could hear that she was pleased. "It would have been very sad if you had to lie in bed all through Christmas. I'm just glad to see you back on your feet."

"Mama said to say thank you from her as well. Those cough drops did wonders, she said."

"I knew they would." She chuckled a little and strode farther into the room, carrying the large coat over her arm.

A little hand slipped into mine. "Come and see our tree, Aunt Nellie." Lucy's eyes were sparkling with excitement and the smile was bright on her lips. If her older sister was hesitant about the Christmas party, the younger girl seemed to flower from the festive commotion.

"Of course." I bent down to steal a touch of her soft cheek against mine before letting myself be led across the Persian rug to the lavishly decorated pine tree that towered in the middle of the room.

It truly was magnificent. The green needle branches were hung with ropes of silver pearls, red and green apples, gold-painted walnuts, glistening angels glued to cardboard, paper lilies with stamens cut from gold foil, flags from the old country, and bits of glittering tinsel, and at the very top was a nest of twigs holding a golden bird. Half-burned candles sat on every branch, unlit now, to spare the wax.

"We made those," Lucy said with pride, and pointed to long ladders made from white paper, meant to remind of us of the climb to heaven.

"That you did!" I bent down to embrace her once more. "How very, very beautiful they are." I would have liked to lift the girl into my arms, but my back was such that I could not.

"I'm joining Jennie in the kitchen, Mama," Nora said over her shoulder. "Find yourself a nice chair and rest."

"Let us know when the porridge is ready," Bella called after her, before she turned her attention to her small guests. "Oh, how much fun we will have today!"

When all the children had arrived, counting over a dozen, ages ranging from four to twelve, Bella declared that no one was to touch the fragrant porridge that was bubbling in the kitchen before the Nisse in the barn had gotten his share. This made all the Norwegian children giggle and look at one another with fear-tinged excitement. They all knew this required the utmost care—no one wanted to upset the Nisse.

"What is that?" a girl with a pinched face and a tired brown dress asked in Swedish.

"Don't you know what a Nisse is?" Bella feigned shock and surprise. "He is a small man in a red cap who lives in the barn."

"Only he isn't a man." The girl who had been sick, Gunnhild, spoke up. "He is something else."

"Oh, you mean *tomten*." The Swedish girl's face lit up with understanding. "Mama says they don't live in America."

"Does she now?" Bella's eyebrows rose. "Well, I think they do, and that we have one right here on this farm. If treated right, he will help out with the animals and bring good luck, but if he's not, he'll cause all sorts of mischief!" At this, she pulled a grimace, and the children squealed with delight.

"We gave ours porridge on Christmas Eve." A red-haired boy in a too-big suit piped up from the floor.

"Yes." Bella nodded with a grave expression. "That's the most important day. If you forget him then, nothing will go right in the coming year. But we can give him porridge on other days as well." She was all good fun and sunshine, sitting there in her favorite chair with all those young gazes upon her. I knew she had been a popular teacher at the Sunday school in Chicago, and seeing her with these children, I could understand why that was. No one's attention wavered; she held them all firmly in her grasp.

As if summoned, Nora appeared in the door to the dining room, holding a large crockery bowl brimming with rice porridge. In the middle of the bowl swam a brightly yellow lump of butter, and the porridge was strewn with cinnamon and sugar. Food worthy of a prince, though now it would likely benefit Bella's mangy barn cat. Jennie came up behind Nora with little Philip riding on her hip. The boy was just as beset with ruffles as his sisters. The young women were smiling, clearly enjoying both the day and each other.

"Careful, it's warm," Nora warned as Bella took the bowl, but my sister was in such a bright mood that I did not think she would notice even if she burned herself, would not see the damage before it was done.

We set out. Bella, the children, and I. Only Jennie and Nora stayed behind to watch Philip and the candles. Dusk had begun to settle and Bella brought out a storm lantern, which one of the boys was bestowed with the proud task of carrying as we made our way across the farmyard and up toward the barn. I came last, of course, with my slow gait, herding all the children before me. Only Myrtle fell back and walked beside me, while Lucy was in front with the light bearer, her eager feet all but dancing on the ground, as she was allowed to guide all those children to *her* barn. Myrtle did not speak, but after a little while, her hand laced with mine. I thought she was perhaps afraid of the Nisse, and I could not blame her for that.

"How are things with you these days?" I conversed in what I hoped was a light tone.

"I am well, thank you." She presented me with a polite reply.

Her dark curls lifted in a sudden gust of wind that sent the dry snow drifting by our feet.

"Your mama said you couldn't sleep last night."

"I could after a while, but then Philip woke me up." This was said without any annoyance.

"Do you like your little brother, Myrtle?" I looked down at her and tightened my grip on her cold little hand. She had not brought her mittens out.

"I like him very much," she said, but despite the politeness and pleasantness of her tone, I could not help but worry. There didn't seem to be any joy behind the words, and I wondered if she was truly happy—if she had forgotten whatever it was she saw on the night her stepfather died.

The children before us had grown raucous in the dimly lit night and scared one another with sudden noises and ambushes from behind. It was all in good fun, though; they were all laughing, and I did not see a single child who did not seem to enjoy it, besides Myrtle.

When we arrived at the barn, Bella knocked on the door to the hayloft with a grave expression on her face. Then she swung the door open on creaking hinges and bid the boy with the lantern go in first. This he did with equal solemnity resting upon his round, childish features. When Bella too had stepped inside, the rest of us followed suit, pooling into the musty hayloft, treading on old boards that gave a little with every step, and made me wonder if they would hold all our weight. They did, of course, but I was resting uneasy when we gathered in a semicircle around Bella with the porridge. She placed the bowl in the hay with exaggerated gestures, making it seem a little too much like a pagan offering for my liking—the hayloft was dark enough. Then she abruptly turned toward the children with one finger pressed to her lips.

"Hush!" Her eyes were wide and wild in the darkness, illuminated only by the poor boy's light. "Can you hear the Nisse coming for his porridge?" All the children went quiet as mice; only their feet made sounds on the floor as they shifted their weight around. They were looking at one another and at her with a mixture of excitement and terror on their faces. "Can you hear his footfalls?" Bella asked, and the children fell even more quiet than before.

"Oh! He's coming!" Bella threw her arms in the air and started for the door. The children screamed with terrified delight and ran along with her. Even the boy with the lantern; the flame behind the glass quivered and shook. I pulled Myrtle close to my body as we exited last. The girl shivered a little against me, though from fear or cold I could not say. The other children were still running when we came out, fast toward the warmth and light of the farmhouse. Bella was waiting for us, though; her laughter rose strong and carefree toward the sky.

"The boy could have dropped the lantern," I chided her. "They'll have nightmares about that barn for weeks." But I was not truly angry. It almost felt like before between us, when I scolded her like that. As if those men had never died. The thought was enough to send tears to my eyes, mercifully hidden by the dusk.

"It was a true adventure, though, wasn't it?" Bella said, self-satisfied, as we slowly walked back toward the house. "They won't forget it anytime soon."

"Never, I think," I agreed, then squeezed Myrtle's hand and blinked away my tears.

37.

Belle

La Porte, 1904–1905

Colson grew cocky when the year turned, and thought himself my equal on the farm. He started seeking me out in my bed at night, not waiting for me to come to him, quickly closing the door again if one of the children was with me. At first, I thought little of it—he was a young man and could certainly keep me entertained between the sheets—but then our conversations turned worrisome, and I started thinking of the cleaver again.

"I think we should have new fences up by the road," he said, lying there beside me with his head on Peter's pillow.

"I think the fences are fine enough," I said.

"They're rotting," he said. "I think we should put up some new ones."

"I said we don't need it." I felt the first flickers of annoyance in the pit of my stomach.

"Well, I'll still do it."

"I think you better not." My mood was quickly changing.

"It's your farm, of course. But I think you're being foolish."

I lay awake long after he had fallen asleep, wondering how it was that he felt he could speak to me in that way. Did he think that he had some sway just because he kept me company at night?

Men can be stupid like that.

Another night, in his room above the kitchen, Colson said, "I think we should sell that old cow to the stockyard."

"She still gives milk—I'll decide when it's time to sell."

"She barely earns what she eats."

I had no quarrel with that cow; she had served me well for a long time. "She's in good health, there's no need—"

"I already made the arrangements. I can take her myself to-morrow."

"You shouldn't have done that." I was already seeing his night-shirt red with blood. Something in my voice must have warned him, though, because when he spoke again, his voice was meek. "I won't if you don't want me to, of course."

Then one night I saw him wearing a shirt from Peter's old chest. He clearly saw himself fit to wear my husband's clothing.

"You are stealing from me," I said when I confronted him.

"Sure I'm not, no one else uses it."

"Still, that belongs to *me*!"

"I just didn't think you would mind." The young man stood on the kitchen floor, looking pale. Did he think I was always butter and sunshine?

"Take that off!" I demanded, and found myself quite livid.

"I'm just borrowing—I can replace the shirts . . ." More than one, then—good to know.

"You aren't fit to use those shirts!" I threw the ricer I held to the floor; it bounced and spat potato grains.

"I'll put them back! I'll put them back!" He lifted his hands in the air in surrender. "Just please don't be angry with me. I didn't mean to upset you!"

"Take off my husband's clothes, then, and we will speak no more of it." No, he was not fit to wear that shirt. I could not think of *any-one* fit to wear that shirt, not even he who bought it.

"I feel terrible, Belle—"

"Mrs. Gunness to you."

"Mrs. Gunness, then. I feel terrible."

"As you ought to. Now peel that thing off and go to bed. You'll feel better in the morning. We both will." I was thinking that I ought to pay him a visit in the night. Perhaps that feeling I so longed for would be within my reach if I was already angry with my opponent. Colson was young and fit. Surely it would satisfy me to see him crumple at my feet. I had some chloroform in the cupboard and it was easy to administer in a simple glass jar—I did not dare to leave him lucid; the stakes were too high and too much could go wrong. I could not risk him waking the children. When I went up to see him, however, to make sure he was properly asleep, the bed in there was empty. Colson had flown the coop. Maybe he felt *something* then, much like a rat sensing a cat.

Whatever the reason, he was gone.

OLAF LINDBOE WAS not a man of great means, but he certainly had his charms and was not afraid to waste them on a well-to-do widow with forty-eight acres. No, he knew exactly what he did when he came to La Porte with his harmonica and his easy smiles. This young farmhand with only a few hundred dollars and a gold watch to his name was set on marrying me from the start. It was how he was to make his fortune, that boy: find an old widow like me.

For a time I played along; I let him think he had me all soft and tender, fed him nice food and cleaned his dirty shirts. I told him what a beautiful man he was, for he certainly appeared to be vain. Then I told him how my farm suffered from lack of a man, and how dreadfully lonely my nights were. He thought he had it all then, when I let him into my bed one night and fed him ham and eggs the next morning. I could see it in the way he moved, in the way he spoke to the neighbors. This foolish, handsome man acted as if he owned the farm already, dishing out his plans for this or that, as if I had no say at all.

Men like that never think that their charms can fail them, that the one they seek to fool can fool them in turn. They are far too vain for that. They think they can have the world.

I took great delight in seeing him lose consciousness after eating an orange infused with chloral, took even greater pleasure still in hauling him down to the cellar and giving him those final whacks. There was very little to gain from Olaf's death, but the pleasure was exquisite. I tipped him into a hole he had dug himself, and filled it up with rubbish. This time, after I had come inside and rested at the table, it came in a heady rush, that feeling. It came upon me in waves of the purest, most delicious sense of victory and spite. He thought he had me fooled, wrapped around his finger—well, look how that turned out! I bested him; I conquered him, and now he was rotting in the ground, because I was smarter than he was and could eat him up, tail, whiskers, and all. James Lee would have been proud.

I felt invincible that night—as if I had taken out an army all by myself. It was not as intense as when Peter died, but by God, it was *something*. It was a heady rush.

"He left when I wouldn't marry him," I told the neighbors when they asked, and took great delight in seeing them become all confused. Why would not an old widow like me marry a handsome man like him?

If I felt kind that day, I said he had gone back to Norway.

JAMES SENT ME William Mingay, a coachman from New York, next. He too came to La Porte in pursuit of a wealthy widow, wanting to trade city life for country life. I liked Will well enough; he was easy and comfortable to have around. He was no farmer, though, but brought a thousand dollars in cash with him. I had him installed in a room downstairs so I could visit him at night without disturbing the children. He had a tall, sinewy body that reminded me a little of the good things I had shared with Peter. Climbing on top of him and closing my eyes, I almost felt I was back in the first days after our wedding, when the sweetness was ripe and the juices never ceased to flow. When he held on to my hips and moaned beneath me, I could almost forgive the size of his savings.

That was, until the day I arrived in the kitchen to see his hand encircling Lucy's arm. He shook the crying girl and yelled at her. "How hard can it be to get me my shoes?"

As I was told by Myrtle later, the girls were playing in the parlor, bringing in shoes to use as hospital beds for their little dolls. They had been in all the rooms upstairs—except the one with the trunks, as that room was forbidden—and had taken down all the shoes they could find, including Mr. Mingay's. When the game had ended, they no longer remembered where the different shoes belonged—a fact that did not amuse Mr. Mingay.

It earned him an orange, that treatment of Lucy, a fat one laced with cyanide. No need for those whacks with the cleaver, then; the cyanide was all it took. As for Mr. Mingay, all I wanted was for him to die, and I did not even wait for that feeling of bliss. When it came to the protection of my children, I struck as hard and cruel as a viper.

There were others too, men who came to sell me their horses or work for me. All of them were so sure of themselves and treated me as if I were a fool. A sleazy smile and a pat on the rear, why would I not appreciate that? My nights had to be lonely; my days had to be bleak. A single woman would surely crave the comfort of a man, be happy and grateful to have their attention.

I gave them oranges.

I wrote to James and asked him to send more bachelors my way, but he dragged his feet. *You have an impressive enterprise at the farm, but I would advise you to slow down.* I sometimes thought he did not like it much that I filled my house with men who were not him.

He cared for me in his own way, though, and the crates from Chicago kept coming.

The children never noticed much of what was going on in the

house. They knew the cellar was forbidden to them and never attempted to go there. Jennie was more difficult than the rest, however. At sixteen she was not a child anymore. Sometimes I thought she looked at me with fear, or acted strangely around my house-guests. One day while we were sewing a rag doll for Lucy in the parlor, I asked her how she fared.

"Well." She looked up from the stitches. "I have nothing to complain about."

"You don't mind that I have guests, do you? It can be lonely for a widow living alone out here."

"Aren't you going to marry one of them? People think so, that you're looking for a husband." This time she did not look up but kept her gaze firmly on the doll.

I laughed. "Perhaps, but not before I find one that is just as good and capable as the one I lost."

"They leave so fast." A little frown appeared.

"What?" My needle hovered in the air.

"They are here one night and gone the next morning, and why do they leave their trunks behind?"

She was an observant little mouse, then. "They will send for their trunks in time. It's how the world is now. People travel all the time, looking for a place to settle down. They are just happy to find a safe place to store their goods."

"But why do they go in the night?" She sounded breathless.

"Why? Would you rather they stayed until dawn?" I made another stitch. I could feel a faint pounding in my jaw.

"I just think it's strange, that's all." The doll hung limp in her hands.

"You should not think so much. It's unseemly for a young woman." I could feel my lips tighten as I spoke.

"I thought you said it was no sin to be clever." Her eyes upon me were so large and blue.

"There is a thing as too clever, little bird. Take care not to be too clever." I opened my mouth to stretch the jaw.

"Yes, Mama." She bent her head; the blue thread from her needle wavered in the air.

"No one likes a nosy girl. When the men leave is no one's business but their own," I said firmly.

"All right, Mama." She dropped her gaze.

"And leave their trunks alone," I warned.

"I never touched them."

"Good . . . Now, do you think Lucy will like her new doll?" We had stitched it from cutoffs and used brown yarn as hair. I had even sewn a little cap for her head.

"Sure, Mama. She always loves a new doll." She gave the sweetest of smiles.

"You should think about that, then, how happy your sister will be, and not worry so much about those men."

"I will, Mama." Another flash of blue.

"Maybe Lucy will even let you name her." The ache in my jaw subsided some.

We finished our sewing in silence.

I GREW TIRED of waiting for James and decided to take the matter into my own hands. If he would not send bachelors to me, I would find them myself.

I placed an advertisement in the *Scandinavien*:

> **WANTED**—A woman who owns a beautifully located and valuable farm in first-class condition wants a good and reliable man as partner in the same. Some little cash is required, for which will be furnished first-class security. Address C. H. Scandinavien office.

Who does not love a single woman of means, someone to charm and gain from? There were plenty of answers to my little advertisement, one more blossoming than the other. Gold diggers all, from the looks of it—and like a gold miner I went through it all, sifted through dozens of letters and sorted out those I thought worth my while. Men with money, that was what I was after, and I told them that from the start.

Dear Sir,

Some time ago I received a letter from you in answer to my advertisement in the Scandinavien. *The reason why I waited to reply is that there have been other answers, as many as fifty, and it has been impossible to answer them all. I have chosen the most respectable, and I have decided that yours is such.*

First, I will let you know that I am Norwegian and have been in this country for twenty years. I live in Indiana, about fifty-nine miles from Chicago and one mile north of La Porte. I am the sole owner of a nice home at a pretty location. There are seventy-five acres of land, and also all kinds of crops, improved land, apples, plums, and currants. I am on a boulevard road and have a twelve-room house, practically new, a windmill and all modern improvements, situated in a beautiful suburb of Chicago, worth about $15,000. All this is almost all paid for. It is in my own name.

I am alone with three small children, the smallest one a little boy, the two others girls, all healthy and well. I also have an older foster child, another girl. I lost my husband by accident some years ago and have since tried to make do as well as I could with what help I could hire, but I am getting tired of this. My idea is to take a partner to whom I entrust everything, and as we have no previous acquaintance, I have decided that every applicant I have considered favorably must make a satisfactory deposit of cash or security.

I think that is the best way to keep away grifters who are always looking for such opportunities. Now, if you think that you are able to put up $1,000 in cash, we can talk the matter over personally. If you cannot, is it worthwhile to consider? I

would not care for you as a hired man, as I am tired of that and need a little rest in my home with my children. I will close for this time.
With friendly regards,

Bella P. S. Gunness

James came to visit with a crate. He laughed at my letter. "You make it sound like you're bestowing some honor upon them." He sat in my parlor drinking whiskey. The piles of letters from my suitors lay before him on the table. Petals kept dropping down on them from the flowers James had brought me.

"Well, I'm certainly worthy of some cash." I gave him a wide smile.

"Your farm seems to have grown some as well." He was referring to the number of acres I had given.

"Ah, but they will never know." They could barely count, some of them.

He sat on the sofa and I was in a chair. The open bottle was on the table between us. Above our heads, I could hear Jennie ushering the children to bed. Lucy was looking for her rag doll and Philip was in a foul mood. I itched to go to them, but I knew that Jennie could manage. I had given them red berry soup with laudanum drops for dinner, and they would all fall asleep fast enough.

"You *are* about to plant them in the yard, my dear," James pointed out in response to my statement. His eyes glittered merrily toward me.

"We don't know that for sure," I argued, though we both knew that I would. "I might marry again someday."

"But not any of these." He motioned to the letters. "I know you won't listen, but I still advise you to be cautious. You had a near miss with the butcher—"

"I'm not leaving them out on display," I cut in, a little dismayed. I was no fool, after all.

"I know it's hard to stop, Bella. Once the blood takes hold there's nothing quite like it. If we lived in the west when there was no law, or if we were soldiers in a war, your hunger for it would even be encouraged, but we're not." He shook his head with mock sadness. "We have to slip and squeeze around the law as best as we can. I have told you before to be clever about it—"

"It's just for the money. I will stop when I have enough." I lifted and downed my glass.

"No, no, no." He laughed and shook his head. "You're no more in this game for the gain than I am. Not anymore. There will never be enough money, my dear, because the money isn't the point."

"You think I like the act of murder." I briefly met his gaze.

"I *know* you like the act of murder." His eyes narrowed and hardened.

"I never used to feel such *need* before." I had done just fine after Mads, and after Anders in Selbu. For a time.

"It ages like fine whiskey, that lust; it grows and it blooms." He lifted his own glass and sniffed it before bringing it to his lips.

"I find that I'm angry." I clutched the glass so hard that my knuckles went white. "I never knew that I was so angry." My jaw started to ache.

"I always knew you were." His smile was close to pity. "I just never knew what for."

"I think it has to do with an old story that nearly killed me many years ago." My gaze drifted to the window, to the farmyard outside.

"I hope you will share it one day."

"I don't think I can." That story was embedded so deep within me it might never again see the light of day. Like a cancer, that story, gnawing at my bones. Bad enough that Nellie brought it up, peeling the scabs away from my wounds.

"Did you kill him, whoever it was?" The pity was gone, replaced with glee.

"Oh, I killed him." I turned my gaze back on him and matched his wicked smile. "He was the very first one."

"I'm glad you got him, then. It must be hard to have a pain like that if the one who caused it is still alive." The smile disappeared from his lips.

"It still hurts." I filled our glasses.

"Always will, I suppose." He sighed and leaned back on the sofa, his slanted eyes glittering again.

"If I just get enough money, that—"

"No, you're fooling yourself. There's no peace for the likes of us." He held my gaze for a long time.

"Lest we hang," I said.

"Yes, there's that." He lifted his glass high in the air. "May that unhappy day be far off yet."

I KNEW JAMES was right, of course. It had been a long time since it was about the money, though I kept telling myself that was all there was to the "enterprise." Perhaps it had been so when the fear of starvation was still chasing me through life, but now it was a different hunger that haunted me in the nights. It scared me, this rage I had just discovered. I wondered if it had been there all along, hidden beneath the hams and sausages, cheeses and spreads in my pantry. If it had disguised itself as my desire for riches, my *need* to always have more.

Maybe it had been my anger all along. Maybe I still survived out of spite, just as I swore to do after the lake. Maybe I got rich and fat just to spite—had my children out of spite—and killed my husbands too, out of that angry sense of *spite*.

Maybe I was still kicking at a dead man's corpse, daring him to come at me again.

I looked at myself in the mirror in my room and saw a stranger. A woman haunted and never free, plagued with an aching jaw. I felt ashamed that he still had such a hold over me. That all the things I did came back to *him*. I had killed him, after all, and it ought to be enough to keep him at bay, but no—he was still there, dwelling deep inside me. I wanted to kill him again and again, and that was what I did.

This is how curses are made: someone does something to another, and traps that person in a web with threads so fine they can hardly be seen. There is no escaping that web.

I could not escape that lake.

But even if I had found the name and shape of what haunted me, it did not make much difference. My days were too busy to dwell. I had children to care for, cows to milk, chickens to pluck and bread to bake. It was better that I felt strong, I thought, able to take down the biggest of men, than feeling like that ruined girl bleeding on the ground.

I tried not to think of her—and stayed busy.

The earth at Brookside was soft and hungry; it did not mind the dead at all. Just as the house embraced me and held me, the dirt kept my secrets safe in the dark. My neighbor, Mr. Christoffersen, told me that a doctor who used to live there kept his own graveyard, so the soil had eaten the dead before. It was miraculous to me, the way the dirt would swallow up the remains—just as the ground in Selbu had taken my little girl. When I flattened the topsoil with my shovel, the smooth surface gave nothing away. It was *my* house and *my* land and it would not betray me. It was a part of who I was.

If I had no ready grave or the ground was frozen, I sometimes rowed my suitors out on Fishtrap Lake. The water was a fine friend too, closing over the crates. It was hard work, though, as the makeshift coffins had to be weighted down—and dangerous too, as the lake was used by others. I had no control of the crates and their loads after they had slipped into the water. If they rotted and spat out their contents, there was no way I would know before the law was at my door.

I preferred the earth.

The area by the lake was fine for that purpose too, the soil around its edges soft and yielding. I could dig a proper hole myself;

it was not much trouble at all. Once a neighbor caught me, though, just as I finished up.

"My God," said he. "What is that smell?"

I leaned on the shovel and gave him my best smile. "Oh, a man passed by this morning. His dog had just died and he offered me five dollars to bury it on my land. It was a stinky thing so I brought it out here. I just didn't want it in my yard. I'm sure the smell will be gone soon."

He believed me, of course; why would he not? I was always sweet to those people. I lent them equipment and labor if I could, and pinched their children's rosy cheeks at church. No one cared if I had guests at the farm; if anything they found it endearing. All of La Porte knew it by then, that Belle Gunness was looking for a husband. I swear they made bets at the bar whenever a new suitor came with the train. They gossiped about it at kitchen tables over heaps of food and mending. Maybe they sighed and shook their heads when the newest suitor just up and left, often leaving me in a pinch. Such a horrid thing to do, they would say, leaving a woman to fend for herself in midseason to go with some horse trader or return to Norway.

Belle Gunness sure was in bad luck when it came to finding a man who could fill Peter's shoes.

It was a glorious enterprise, and they never saw me coming.

I always cared well for my guests, was ever attentive and listened to their woes. I offered my assurances that life would be better from now on. Now that they had found *me*. I wrote them long letters urging them to sell whatever they had and bring the money to invest in our future together. They like that, men: comfort and prospects. I offered them oranges too, juicy and sweet, to take their minds of all life's troubles.

Some men I liked more than others, those who were not lewd or fallen to drink. Those who could provide me with much-needed labor. I kept them with me longer. In the end, there was always *something*, though, a brazenness or a wrong word. None of them lasted very long, and certainly not to marriage.

Every time it was different. If I was in a quarrelsome mood, I gave them chloral. They did not die from that; they just slept. Sometimes the poison did not take as I wanted, and the men woke up and fought me before the cleaver showed them mercy. Sometimes it took a few strong whacks to have them die, as tendons and flesh can be thick and hard. Other times, I made a mess of things, leaving blood all over the floor.

If I did not feel like fighting, I gave them my trusted cyanide. They died on their own then—no bother at all. Just some sickness and convulsions, and they were gone. The taste and the smell were strong but could easily be masked with food. The orange was ever my favorite; so easy to tap into with a syringe.

When the men were good and dead, I hauled them down in the cellar.

I was a thriving enterprise and my money box filled up.

I felt safe then, safe in my castle, until Nellie came to call and everything went wrong.

38.

La Porte, 1906

My sister seemed nervous when she arrived; her hands fluttered between her chest and her lap, and she cleared her voice several times before speaking during our first conversation. She had come to borrow silverware for Olga's upcoming wedding, and she and Nora would stay with us for two nights.

Her nervousness made me uneasy in turn—I knew there was something bothering her, something she was not saying.

The visit started out pleasant enough. Nellie and I browsed the silver—of which I had plenty—while Nora and Jennie brought the girls out in the pony cart. Little Philip was nearly three by then, and played with his wooden horses around our feet as we sat side by side by the dining room table, looking at spoons and forks.

"I cannot believe she's getting married," I said in my sweetest voice, to make her feel more at ease. "She was a little girl only yesterday."

"Don't I know it." Nellie sighed. "And with a Catholic! Can you imagine that? Mother would have been aghast."

"Oh, she knew well enough that children will do as they please. She wasn't too thrilled about us coming here either." I lifted a long-tined fork and wiped off a tiny smear with my sleeve.

"She *is* old enough, it's not that, but it still feels like losing her somehow." Her voice was a little thick with emotion.

"I think all mothers feel that way. *I* sure will, when it's my turn." I handed her an ornate knife, one of my very finest. "This is a lovely pattern, don't you think? It's very modern, with the lilies."

Nellie inspected the silver in her hand, "Oh, she would like that. She wants everything to be elegant."

"How is it with money? You know you only have to ask if you need to borrow some for the wedding." It would suit me well, truth be told. Perhaps Nellie would let her suspicions slide if she were indebted to me. It never hurts to have a hold over another.

"We'll manage," she said, her lips pursed tightly together. I thought she was foolish. Surely they could use the help. True, they had more now than they did before, but a wedding was still a large obligation, and Nellie's new son-in-law had four older siblings with families of their own and several aunts and uncles in America. It would be a large party. I could not help but wonder if my sister saw through me—that it was *my* money she deemed tainted somehow. That she did not want to owe me. The thought sent my heart racing in my chest, and I quenched a wave of anger.

"Thank you, though," Nellie said. Her gaze darted from knife to fork to chandelier. She looked flustered; her cheeks had turned a crimson red. "I certainly appreciate the offer." She gave a wan smile.

"You need only say," I repeated, but Nellie did not reply. She was fingering the knife with a pained expression, and though I tried very hard to make things light and good between us, she never did seem to relax—which annoyed me and set me on edge in equal measure.

THE REAL TROUBLE started later that day. Nellie was in the kitchen with the children preparing vegetables for dinner while I was out caring for the horses. When I came back inside through the back door and set to unlacing my shoes, I could hear my sister speaking:

"You are very good at this, Myrtle. Look how pretty your potato peel spirals are, all long and even."

"I can make spirals too," peeped Lucy.

"You are a little too young, I think, to be handling such sharp knives. Next year, maybe."

"Mama lets me use the knife."

"She does not," Jennie said. "She does not, Aunt Nellie. It's just Lucy who wants to."

"Look," said Nellie. "You can fill this pot with carrot cubes..."

"Mr. Davidson cut them into shapes, like flowers."

"Who is Mr. Davidson, Lucy?" Nellie's voice sounded curious.

"He visited Mama."

"Did he now?"

"Lucy, I don't think you should—" Jennie started to say, but Nellie cut her off.

"Does he still come to see her?"

"No," said Lucy. "It's been a long time. He was only here once, like all the others."

"The others who?" Nora spoke, while I fought and struggled with the laces of my shoes, stiff with manure as they were. I had to get them off and get in there, or my children would right give me away.

"The other men who visit Mama."

"She has many visitors out here, has she?"

"Yes, and then they leave before breakfast."

"Lucy!" Jennie's voice cracked in the air. "I'm sorry, Aunt Nellie, she doesn't know any better." I could hear Nora chuckle in the background, finding it all so very amusing.

"But is it true, though?" said Nellie. "Myrtle, is it true that your mama has male visitors who stay only for one night, and then are gone in the morning?"

"Sometimes they stay a little longer," Myrtle said softly.

"But then they disappear?"

"It's no one's business but Mama's," said Jennie. She sounded afraid. I could hardly burst in there filthy and reeking without making Nellie even more suspicious, so I forced myself to stand still and listen while the horror unfolded in the kitchen. "She is just looking for a husband," Jennie told my sister. "I don't think she wants you to know."

"But why do they leave in the night?" Nellie asked.

"They remembered they had to be in Chicago," said Lucy.

"Oh, Lucy," said Jennie, "they have all kinds of reasons."

"Usually they remembered they had to be in Chicago." The girl stood her ground. I should perhaps have been a little more inventive with my excuses.

"Isn't it strange, though, that they all seem to figure this out during the night," Nellie noted.

"I don't know," said Lucy.

"We're not supposed to talk with them much," said Myrtle. "But if they stay on for a while, we have to. Sometimes they play with us, or do funny things, like with the carrot flowers."

"One of the men shook me," said Lucy, "but then Mama sent him away."

"And rightly she did," said Nellie. "No man should ever punish a child not his own." On that, at least, we agreed. My mind was swirling with what I had just heard, and I was thinking up ways to explain it to my sister. I could say I had become a moneylender, perhaps, or that I had opened my home to gentlemen traveling alone but had been too embarrassed to say so. Surely she would understand that, both the need for an extra income and the embarrassment. It was hardly proper for a widow to have strange men coming and coming.

Then, just as I thought the horror had mounted, a fresh wave hit in the kitchen:

"How are we with peas?" Nellie asked.

"We are almost all done," said Jennie. Clearly, the two eldest had been tasked with shelling.

"We could use some cabbage too with this," said Nellie. She was cooking up a soup with salt beef and greens. "You keep them in the cellar, yes?"

"Yes," said Jennie, "but—"

"We are not allowed to go down there," said Lucy.

"Oh, why is that?" Nellie asked.

"The stairs are rotten," Jennie answered. "Mama is afraid we'll hit our heads."

"She should have those stairs fixed, then," Nellie said. "How does she get down there herself?"

"There is a door out back," said Jennie.

"But sometimes she takes the stairs as well, if she is in a hurry because something is cooking on the stove," Lucy added.

"They can't be too rotten, then," Nellie said.

"I suppose not." Jennie sounded doubtful.

"Maybe she keeps something down there—like a secret," Nellie said.

"What's that?" Lucy asked.

"Well, we don't know if it's a secret," Nellie said. "Maybe she keeps jars of those sweets she used to sell in Chicago—or marzipan cakes and chocolate pudding." Lucy and Myrtle laughed. "Maybe you *should* go down there, just to see what's she's hiding," my sister suggested, and I could not for the life of me figure if she said it in jest or not.

"Oh, Mama would be mad then," Jennie said. "You better not do it," she told her sisters. I could hear Philip too then, making soft sounds. Jennie would likely have him in her lap while she did her work on the table.

"So what will we do about the cabbages, then, if none of you can go down there?" Nellie asked. "Maybe I have to go get them myself? If the stairs can carry your mama, I'm certain they can carry me as well." The sound of her voice increased as she moved, slow with her ruined back, toward the door to the hallway. I had my filthy shoes off by then, replaced by a pair of house shoes, and quickly moved to block the cellar door. When Nellie came out, the first thing she saw was me.

"Oh, Bella!" She startled and clutched at her throat. "I didn't know you had come in." Clearly she had not, or she would not have tempted my children to mischief. "I was just—"

"I'll get the cabbage," I said, turning toward the cellar door, "and some turnips too. These stairs really are dangerous. You have to know where to tread to be safe."

"Oh—oh, all right, then." She stepped back into the kitchen with wide and worried eyes.

I went down in the cellar, where the floor was still covered in stained and reeking oilcloth; my heart was working like a piston in my chest, and my hands were so slick that I could barely hold the cabbage I fished out of the bin. What was it my sister wanted? How much did she suspect?

39.

Nellie

I had said that I came to borrow silverware, but in truth, I was in La Porte to make sure there was no new wedding on the horizon for my sister. It had been like that for quite some time; if I had not been in La Porte in a while, I grew restless, suffered from stomachaches and shortness of breath. I was drawn there over and over again, just to keep an eye out. To make sure that all was safe and no new husband was afoot. It hounded me always, that worry and fear. I thought I could not bear it if it happened again, and I had stood by and done nothing.

It was always pleasant to see the children, and it lifted my spirits to see them thrive. I thought that I had done right then, in leaving what had happened in the past well alone. I never dared to ask my sister how she fared in that regard, but hoped the young ones' continued wellness and health meant that the beast had been thrown off her back. How could a woman who so patiently braided little girls' hair and polished small shoes to a shine be capable of such atrocities? It made so little sense to me.

Surely she had only been sick for a while.

If only she did not marry again, everything would be fine.

Then, having had that worrisome conversation with the children, and finding Bella hiding behind the door . . . I could not stop thinking about it: the expression on her face. The fury that blanched her skin and made her eyes look so dark. It did not help one bit that she was quite herself when she came back up from the cellar with a sizable cabbage. I could barely eat that soup after all; my appetite had fled and did not return.

I wondered how long she had stood there in the passageway, listening in on the children and me before I went out there. Wondered if her anger was directed solely at me, or if it encompassed the children as well. The thought of the latter made me feel ill, which in turn was what gave me the courage to sit up with her that night, alone, and to ask her, though I deeply feared the answer.

"The children say you are looking for a new husband." Our knitting needles' soft clicking filled the silence between us.

Bella made a clucking sound. "They would say that."

"But you don't?" I looked at her over the knitting in my hands. We had lit a fire, and the scent of wood smoke filled the air.

"As I said, I'm happy alone." She did not look at me, but counted the loops on her knitting needle, using a finger as aid. "I only crave some company from time to time. In an adult way." Now she *did* look at me, a long, telling gaze.

Oh, how I wanted to believe her. "So that is why they are gone before breakfast?"

"For sure . . . I don't care for them to get too comfortable here, or too friendly with the children." She took up the knitting again, her needles clicking calmly and rhythmically.

"But where do you meet these men?" I had completely ceased my own knitting.

She shrugged. "Some I know from Chicago, acquaintances passing through."

"I didn't know you were in the habit of socializing with men." I gave her a look over my newly acquired glasses. The half moons rested partway down my nose and still felt both unfamiliar and uncomfortable. They did help me see the knitting, though.

"I met many people while I had that store," Bella informed me, and pulled the knitting higher up in her lap. She was making a gray sweater for Myrtle and was working on the back. "I don't want to marry, but I don't want to be lonely either. Surely you can understand." Her chin lifted just a little.

"Just be careful," I said in a voice that did not carry as well as I hoped.

"Of course." She glanced at me. "I won't put anyone at risk."

"Lucy said that one of the men had—"

"That was a mistake." Her chin lifted just a little higher. "He won't come near her again."

Yet I could not help but fret. The anger on her face when I found her in the passageway had been so terrifying, and if there was nothing to find down there, why did she so jealously guard that cellar? I did not for one minute think that she kept stairs that could be unsafe for her children without doing anything to remedy that fact. Unable to sleep, I rose in the night and went down in the kitchen, hoping to find some of Bella's precious brandy to settle my nerves. A few laudanum drops as well, perhaps. To my surprise, I found Jennie there, crouched down in her nightgown and stirring the embers in the stove with a poker.

"Jennie," I said. "What are you doing up so late? Is Nora up too?"

"No," said the girl. "She fell asleep at once. It's only I who have problems sleeping sometimes and come down here for some milk."

"Well, I won't hold that against you." I smiled and sat down on a chair by the table. "I find it hard as well tonight."

"It upset you, didn't it?" She looked up at me from her crouched position. She had unbraided and combed her hair, and it hung around her face like a golden curtain.

"What did?" Again, that heart of mine acted on its own accord, setting up its speed. It took so very little since Peter Gunness's death to have it race in my chest like an untamed beast.

"That thing with Mama, about the men . . ." Jennie rose to her feet and dropped a few logs into the red inferno. Then she came and sat with me. "I knew it would upset you; that's why I didn't say anything."

"I understand that, Jennie." I smiled and took her hand in mine on the scarred tabletop. "I do wonder about that cellar, though."

"Oh don't." Jennie abruptly withdrew her hand. "Nothing good can come from poking around in Mama's business. What she does down there is up to her." The fear on her face was plain to see in the soft light.

"What do you mean by that? Is she *doing* something down there?"

"No—I mean, she is there sometimes, for a long while, and I have to watch the children." She was clearly uncomfortable; her shoulders were hunched and she was looking around as if she were a rabbit caught in a trap, eager to find a way out.

"And you don't know what it is?"

"No . . ."

"But, Jennie." I used my most reasonable voice—the girl was eighteen; she could take what I was about to say. "What if she does something dangerous down there—dangerous for her, I mean. Don't you think we should help her, even if she doesn't want us to?" I gently took her hand again. "Sometimes it's hard to see it yourself if you're in need of help from those who love you."

Jennie did not answer at once, but I could hear her swallow hard. "There is a room upstairs." Her voice was hoarse and very quiet. "She mostly keeps it locked now, but I know what's inside."

"What is that, Jennie?" I could hear the dread in my own, whispering voice.

"Travel cases, trunks, things like that. Coats, too, and hats." There was something wild in her gaze when she looked at me, and she clutched my hand so hard in her grasp that I could feel her fingernails cut into my skin. "She says she is keeping it for them. That they will come back for their belongings in time."

I let go of her hand and sank back against the chair. It felt as if

IN THE GARDEN OF SPITE

all the air had left my lungs at once. "I have to go down there and see." My whisper was brittle and weak.

"No, Aunt Nellie." She shook her head with vigor. "Nothing good can come of that."

"Oh, I'm not so sure about that, Jennie." I staggered to my feet. I would not look away this time. I would not! "Hand me that candle and the matches, if you please." With my inner eye, I saw Myrtle again, that day behind the barn. Oh, how I hoped she had forgotten it, whatever it was she had seen. I should have taken the burden from her then, but I had not. I would not make the same mistake again.

Jennie cried when she handed me the half-burned candle from the windowsill and the box of matches. Small whimpering sounds escaped from her throat. I had expected her to leave me then, to go back to the safety of her bed, but she stayed with me, and followed me into the passageway, too, when I moved so very slow with my poor back, across the creaking floorboards. The cellar door was to our right, a dark shape in the wall. I put my hand on the door handle and pushed.

Nothing happened. The door remained firmly shut.

I used more strength and put my weight against it, but the door stood firm.

"It's locked," I whispered back to Jennie.

"Are you sure?" Her eyes were wide in the light from the candle.

I nodded. "Do you know where the key might be?"

She mouthed *no* and shook her head.

We made our way back to the kitchen about as quietly as we had exited it before. Jennie was relieved, I could tell. Her whole face seemed to have smoothed out and her shoulders had slumped as well. I put the candle back on the windowsill and extinguished it. A string of acrid smoke curled from the wick through the air.

"Maybe it's nothing, Aunt Nellie. Perhaps she is doing nothing down there."

"Perhaps." I turned to her and took her hands in mine. "But she wouldn't suddenly lock the door then, would she? If there were nothing she was trying to hide."

Jennie did not answer but looked a little pained again. I hated to put such a burden on her but did not know what else to do. "Be careful, Jennie," I whispered. "Be very, very careful, but if you can, please try to find out what she's doing down there."

It had to be more than counting potatoes, or dusting off her jars of spread.

40.

Belle

How long would it take before Nellie added together the deaths of my husbands and the mysterious men who were gone before dawn? This was not good. Not good at all.

I had done everything in my power to appease my sister. I had given her good food and invited her for Christmas, done what I could to ease her worry, and yet she looked at me with suspicion and questioned my every move. Thought herself clever for sure.

I just wanted her to forget those things she thought she knew. It would be better for all if she did. What did it matter to her if my husbands died? It did no harm to anyone but the men in question, and the children and I were better off for it. My money box, too, was better off for it. Should she not rejoice that we thrived? Should she not be happy that I was my own woman, without a need for a good-for-nothing husband? Why did she only see what was wrong, and not all the good that came of it? The world was certainly no lesser place from my husbands' being dead.

Yet Nellie looked at me with fear and concern, and a little bit of pity, too, which bothered me even more. She thought she had it all worked out after she heard from Olina. Thought she could see both the wound and the knife that had cut me. She thought me damaged rather than strong—and no cheerful Christmas party seemed to be able to remedy that.

I did not know what to do.

If only she had stayed well away from the topic of my guests, and the cellar, but no. She had even tried to raise my own daughters against me, tempting them to do mischief. Although I had never seen a need to do so before, as my children were well-behaved and obedient, I had turned the slender key in the cellar door lock that very same day, and it had remained that way ever since—just in case.

Just in case my sister's words had taken hold.

I would never forgive her for tempting them so, and for allowing them to gossip about their mother. That was the problem with the little ones; as they grew up, their tongues became slippery and they spoke without thinking things through. Nellie should have known better, though, than to encourage such idle talk. The damage was already done, however. Nellie knew I had men coming to see me at Brookside Farm, and I was not at all convinced that I had managed to derail her with talk of a widow's needs—that all her suspicion was gone.

In dark nights by the kitchen table, I kept wondering if there was a way to silence my sister—and then I felt aghast that I could even think that way.

Was this who I had become? A woman who would raise her hand against her own to protect her tawdry secrets?

The answer to that came in the most horrible of ways.

A FEW WEEKS after Nellie had been to visit, I was in the kitchen pouring milk when I heard Lucy and Myrtle whispering in the passageway behind me. Jennie sat by the table with some mending, and the two of us exchanged glances at the sounds. I could tell there was fear in her gaze when it darted toward the door, which certainly did nothing to dispel my own sense of unease.

I thought it best to check on them and stepped out there, where the sight of the open cellar door hit me like a fist. I went cold, then hot. I barely noticed the stool they had brought in and stood on in order to get to the key above the door. All I saw was that open door and the darkness behind it like a maw. I heard the girls' feet as they scampered down the steps, not remembering at all that I had told them it was dangerous. I even heard them giggle, quiet and suppressed, as they slipped farther down in the darkness.

They were halfway down the stairs before I caught them. It would have been very bad for them to go down there that day. I had not cleaned up from the last crate yet; the oilcloth was still on the table with my tools scattered on top of it, and what little light filtered down the stairs would have revealed it all sufficiently to be hard to explain away. The victim's bloody clothes lay in rags on the floor.

I hauled the girls back up by their arms; they were both squalling by then, from fear or shame I could not say. Myrtle's face was red and teary; Lucy's was twisted up and pale. I proceeded to give them both a hard beating in the kitchen. I had never beaten them like that before, had barely smacked them at all. The force of my anger surprised even me, but the enterprise depended on their obedience.

If they did not do as I said, everything would be lost.

"We just wanted the marzipan cake!" Lucy cried. "Aunt Nellie said you keep sweets down there!"

"Well, I don't, so there's that," I told them; my hand was aching from the punishment. "You could have broken your necks on those stairs."

Myrtle's eyes were puffy and red from crying. She stood with her hands pressed to her cheeks and looked at me with horror in her eyes. It made me want to cry as well, but how else was I to teach them to never, ever go down there again?

When the air had gone all out of me and their tears had all dried up, the girls went to their room with burning cheeks. It was a harsh lesson, but at least I felt sure they would never do something so foolish again. Marzipan cake! Nellie and her fancies! How could she do this to me? I almost regretted letting her live!

Jennie had been sitting quietly through it all, squinting and flinching whenever my hand landed another smack. The mending in her lap was all forgotten as she endured her sisters' punishment.

Good, I thought then. *When she sees what happens to them, she will never venture down there herself.*

Then came the night when Lee Porter died.

The man was already married, as it turned out, so he sure had what I gave him coming. I had him down on the cellar floor; the oilcloth beneath us was slick with red and the cleaver in my hand smeared with the same. My hands were very red that night, as Mr. Porter was a heavy bleeder.

Then, all of a sudden—a sound—a quiet creaking on top of the stairs. I barely even noticed at all, being so intent on my work, but I knew that sound so well that it sliced through the haze and made me slow down the butchering. It was the sound of the door swinging open, but slowly, as if someone did not want me to hear.

A movement caught my vision then, and I looked up to see a flickering on the wall above the stairs. Someone was standing on top of the steps holding a lamp or a candle.

I paused to catch my breath and quiet my hammering heart. I looked at the mess on the table—at my hands so red in the light from the kerosene lamp—and quickly assessed my options: Should I step forth and show myself, bloody and reeking, to the person up there, and risk that they slipped away before I learned who it was, or could I be more clever about it?

I chose the latter option.

I unhooked the lamp from the ceiling and went to the door that led out into the yard. Then I extinguished the flame just as I slammed the door once, giving the illusion that I had gone outside. Next, I crouched in the darkness by the door, as quiet as I could, not even moving an inch, cursing myself all the while for not having had the wits to lock the cellar door from the inside—I suppose I was not in the habit, since it had never been a problem before.

The flickering on the wall was stronger then, when my own light was out, and so I was sure that someone was still there, someone with an uneasy hand, as the light lifted and fell on the bricks. I also thought I could hear a rustling, and the sound of uneven breathing.

I waited there a good long while, wondering if the person would come down or leave. I swear I was hoping for the latter, but I *had* brought the cleaver with me, and was clutching it hard in my hand as I sat there, waiting for that light to either grow brighter or disappear. My back started to ache after a while, and the muscles in the legs protested the strain, but I still sat there, breathing as quietly as I could, just waiting for that person to make up their mind.

I was fully expecting it to be one of the Greening brothers, the farmhands I had just hired, poking their noses where they did not belong. Wondering, perhaps, what the widow was doing in the cellar all alone, late at night, but when the person finally came down the steps, candle held high in a shivering hand, that was not who it was. There was Jennie, looking much like a wraith in her nightdress on the stairs, her hair hanging loose to frame her heart-shaped face.

I did not know what to do right then, if I should rush at her or stay quietly by the door. Perhaps she would turn and go back, I thought—and then I wondered if she had come there to look for me because one of the younger children was ill. When she had come halfway down, she lifted the candle, to better see the room before her: bloody table, limbs and all. Even from the distance, I could see how her eyes widened, and how the hot wax spilled down from the candle and onto her hand, shivering in her grasp. Yet she moved the candle around in a half-circle motion, let the light spill onto sacks of flour and heaps of potatoes, rows of jars and barrels of apples, until it found me, crouching by the door.

She startled when she saw me, turned and ran back up the stairs— her stealth suddenly vanished. I dropped the cleaver and was at her heels at once, chasing her disappearing light. As I paused in the kitchen to unhook the lamp above the table, I could hear her move on to the upper floor, and found her extinguished candle in a corner on the landing when I continued the chase, rushing after the sound of her footfalls until I heard the door to her bedroom slam shut. Then I slowed down the pace.

I opened the door and made no secret of it. *I* surely did not come in secrecy. Jennie lay on her stomach on top of the bed, shivering all over. Her face was burrowed into the pillow, where she made strange sounds: half crying, half whining. I sat down on the lip of the bed and she flinched. My red hand placed the lamp on the floor and turned up the wick. The air in there smelled of fresh linen and urine.

"Why did you have to do that, Jennie? What am I going to do with you now?" I placed my stained hand on the back of her head; strands of hair plastered to my fingers. "You knew the cellar was forbidden, so what did you go down there for?"

The girl did not answer but kept on shivering, making those ugly sounds. "You saw what happened to Myrtle and Lucy, only for taking a peek. What do you think will happen to you, now that you have seen the whole thing?" I sighed deeply and removed my hand. "I'd rather not have to let you go, but what you know now, it's dangerous."

She mumbled something deep in the pillow. I leaned closer to hear what she said. "I promise, I promise, I won't say a word . . ."

"I hope you speak the truth, Jennie. My friend James Lee in Chicago is very fond of me, you know. He wouldn't look kindly on you if something happened to me. If you ever tell a soul, you'll be dead one way or another." It brought me no pleasure to threaten her, but what was I to do? I had to make her understand the gravity of the situation.

"I will not . . . will not . . ." she whispered.

"Good, Jennie." I patted the back of her head again and pulled the quilt up around her shivering form. We had made that blanket together, she and I, cut scraps and hemmed the pieces into glorious patterns. "Go to sleep now. We won't ever speak of this again."

I took my lamp and walked out of the room, found the key on top of the door frame and locked her in to be sure she would not run off in the night. She was rattled and scared for sure. I would have to watch her closely until she regained her senses.

I stomped down the cellar stairs to finish my work on Mr. Porter, but my enthusiasm for the task was diminished.

Why would she do something so foolish?

I could send her away, I thought, while loosening Mr. Porter's arms from their sockets, but if she was far away from me, her tongue could easily loosen.

I could marry her off, I thought next, sawing off Mr. Porter's legs two inches above the knees. But then the intimacy of the marriage bed might tempt her to share.

I could send her back to her father, but that might be the greatest mistake of all.

She had made herself a problem and that was the truth of it, I figured, while gathering up the slops in the pigs' bucket.

No matter how I looked at the problem, what solutions I tried to come up with, the answer remained the same.

Of course it did. It always did.

She should not have gone down in the cellar.

THE NEXT MORNING, Jennie pretended that nothing was amiss, though she looked paler than usual and her blue gaze wavered.

"Did you sleep well?" I shoved some sausages onto her plate.

"Very much so, yes." Her voice sounded breathless.

"Mr. Porter had to leave us early this morning to go to Chicago and trade some horses."

"Oh," she whispered.

"He will be back, though, for his trunk."

Lucy and Philip were playing at the table, although they knew I frowned upon it. Myrtle picked at her sausage with a fork. Outside in the sunny yard, the Greening boys were digging in the chicken coop. There was a vault under there and I had told them I wanted to see it. Maybe I could store something there through the months while the ground was frozen. I liked the boys well enough, but the younger one had a soft spot for Jennie, and a blossoming of hearts might not be for the best. I knew there was talk in La Porte of how I always kept my Jennie close at hand—too close, some said, but what did they know of the dangers of this world, what horrors could befall a young woman?

"I've been thinking, Jennie." I joined them at the table. "Maybe it's time we thought about your education. You could go to California and study law as we talked about." I had always dreamed of something more for Jennie. Women lawyers were rare, but I thought it fitting for a daughter of mine. Not to mention how practical it would be to have her handle all my legal woes.

The girl did not answer, though, just bit her lip and looked down at the table.

"I could look at the advertisements and see if there is a good school for you. I so want you to have a profession, a proper career for a proper young lady."

"Yes, I know. Thank you, Mama." But she did not seem pleased at all.

"Maybe we should go into town, you and me, and get some of that red fabric you have wished for. You could use a new dress, I agree on that."

"Thank you," she whispered again.

"We could buy some sweets as well. You can choose what kind."

"Thank you," she said, but her heart was not in it. She had not even touched her food.

I placed my hand on hers on the table. "It'll be fine, just you see."

"Of course," she repeated, and her eyes met mine.

But we both knew it would not.

41.

Belle

Answering letters took up much of my time. Some days I had as many as four or five delivered. They were from my acquaintances in Chicago, from men who had seen my advertisements, and sometimes they were inquiries asking for a loved one's whereabouts. The latter was always a challenge. I had to be crafty so as not to have relatives knocking on my door. I could always say the men had moved on, but if the man in question had been close with his family, they did not always accept that. It annoyed me because I always urged my suitors to be discreet and keep our arrangement a secret. Still, some of them just could not keep their mouths shut, and told God and everyone they were off to see a widow in La Porte. Some even left a forwarding address for letters and suchlike. It caused me a world of trouble, fending off the relatives. Sometimes I said the men had gone to Montana or California, chasing an even brighter future there. I said they had learned of some fine opportunity to buy some land or invest. It took some cunning to have them look elsewhere. It took some cunning to make sure the suitors did not meet each other too. At times, I had to usher a departure when I learned the next one was on his way.

This day in November, I sat in the parlor and wrote to a man I did not expect to arrive for some time, but for whom I had great hopes. Mr. Helgelien was a Norwegian and good for some thousands in cash. Upon his arrival in America, he had run into some problems with the law and spent a little time in prison before settling down on his farm, which I now urged him to sell.

November 12, 1906
Mr. Andrew K. Helgelien

Dear Friend,

Today I received your long and interesting letter. Thank you so much. I have never before received such dear, true words.

It feels good to be honest and sincere, and then find a friend who is the same. If a woman is ever so honest and faithful, what good does it do when she is unfortunate enough to come into contact with falseness and deceit?

No, it would be better to be dead. It is a shame that you have had the same experiences as I have. There are so many false people in this world, so many who are low enough to lie and spread falsehoods, especially when they see someone who is a little more fortunate and can afford to live a little better than they do. They cannot do enough harm to us.

I have worked alone for four years now, and have done pretty well for myself. As you know, it is hard for a single woman, but I would rather live alone than have anything to do with false, mean, and drunken men.

There are so many Swedes here, and I do not like them either. Nearly all of them have been jealous because they see I can manage on my own and I suppose they will be worse when you arrive. Some of them have been good to me and helped me out at times, but there are many who would rather see me not make it.

Now, dear friend, I hope the worst is over for the both of us. It seems that I have known you for a long time even if we have never met, and I will live for the future and you, my good friend, from the first day you arrive and as long as I can. I really think we will live together always, because a true friend, who has the same disposition and heart as I, will surely get along with me, and then I will get my good nature back, because I will think that life is worth living and will do the best I can for us both. We will always have good Norwegian coffee and waffles, and I will always make you a nice cream pudding and many other good things.

My very best friend, it is just as you say, if you are going to take a few horses, you might as well bring a whole carload of stock with you here. Hurry and come before winter sets, and take with you all you can get in a carload, and do not stop anywhere longer than necessary. Do not leave anything up there because you cannot leave me later to go and get it. Rather sell your things a little cheaper for cash, for then you know what you have and will not have anything outstanding. I am sure you will find things here that are just as nice and useful as those you have now.

Do not even let the banks have anything to do with your money, not even to send it to you, because you do not know what will happen nowadays. One bank closes right after the other and the cashiers steal. Follow the advice I gave you in a former letter and sew the money into your clothes. You are the first one I have told this secret to, but it is practical, and I know you will do it.

I am very happy to have a friend in whom I can have confidence. However, do not let anyone know anything about our understanding. Let us keep it to ourselves for now.

Oh, please hurry and come before it gets too cold, and let me know in your next letter when you think you will be ready.

Live well until we meet.

Loving regards from your friend,

Bella Gunness

I enclosed a dried four-leaf clover I had been saving since summer.

I did not lie when I wrote. It was as if a spell came over me then, and the words on the paper rang true to me, even though I knew what would happen. For those few moments, though, while ink spilled on the paper, I was that woman—that lonely, struggling woman—who wanted nothing more than a good and capable husband, a wholesome life and arms to hold her. I could see it all so clearly before me: him and me together, his horses in the stable, and all the children healthy and fed. I pictured Philip a little older, helping him in the barn, and Myrtle and Lucy playing games with him: Red Riding Hood and the Fox. It was as if the boneyard outside were not mine just then but belonged to a different woman altogether.

The next letter I wrote was for James, and the bones were suddenly mine again. Jennie had been a festering wound that never dried up ever since she saw me in the cellar. She never said anything, or did anything, but something had wedged between us. She was not as sweet as before, not as compliant and trusting. She would flinch when I entered a room and look at me with scared blue eyes. I hated the sight of those eyes. I tried to soften her with promises and gifts, but nothing seemed to please her. I kept talking about California, but the silly girl looked at Emil Greening with longing in her eyes, and he would look at her in turn. When they spoke to each other out in the yard, my heart ran cold with worry. Surely she would tell him.

Emil was not the only hound sniffing around her skirts either. Mr. John Weidner, who worked at the coach house, was frequently around, wanting to call on Jennie. I let him into the parlor and had Jennie play some at the piano but was terrified of letting the two of them be alone together. I had always been protective of Jennie, but now I became a hawk. I did not want a single word passing through her lips without me there to hear it.

I knew I was putting off the unavoidable.

ONE AFTERNOON, ABOUT a week before Christmas, James arrived in a coach. With him was a professor from the Norwegian
seminary in California and his lovely wife. I had told Jennie they
would be coming, and that she was expected to return with them
to begin her studies.

"You are lucky," I reminded her. "Not many girls get such an opportunity."

"I am grateful, of course." The girl would not look at me. We
were in the kitchen and could hear the professor and his wife in the
parlor through the half-open doors, James too, chattering nonsense
about the weather. It was for our benefit, all of it. The professor was
a hired man, the woman a Chicago brothel owner catering to the
tastes of very rich men. Innocent and well-bred girls like Jennie
were always in high demand. The two of them did not know that I
knew who they truly were, however. With them was a satchel of
money that James Lee would get when they left with the girl the
next day—if she was to the madam's liking. We aimed to strike
twice, James and I, rid me of a problem and gain some in the process.

I ushered the girl inside to our guests, and she stood before
them shy as a kitten in her new blue dress, with red spots riding
high on her cheeks.

"My, aren't you a lovely girl." The woman introduced herself as
Cecily, although I knew her name was Laura Burns.

The professor, who called himself Smith, rose and bowed to
Jennie, shook her hand, and invited her to sit. He asked her what
she had studied before, and pretended to listen while she listed the
books she had read in school. I went out for more coffee and checked
on the roast.

"I'm sure you will love California," chirped Mrs. Smith—Laura
Burns—when I returned. "We have the best school for bright girls
such as yourself, eager to better themselves."

She did not sound like some posh professor's wife, but Jennie would not know that. She became eager, even excited, when shown so much attention. She told them about her fondness for numbers, and I asked her to play some on the piano.

"Endearing," said Mrs. Smith.

"Just the kind of talented girl we want at the seminary." Professor Smith had just a gleam of malice in his eyes. He knew where the girl was to go, and what talents she was to hone.

"You will get along fine with the other girls," Mrs. Smith told her. "They're all just as pretty and well behaved as yourself."

I paraded my children in there too, so they could tell our neighbors about the professor: detail his thick gray beard and the lovely red color of his wife's fancy dress. They each got to choose a cookie from the tray as a reward after reciting their names. They curtsied and bowed, wearing their Sunday best. Philip looked much like a little man in his long breeches and vest, and I felt a sudden burst of pride even if it was just a charade. Myrtle wore her dark hair in ringlets, and Lucy's fair hair was gathered in a braid. The three of them were so rosy cheeked and well behaved that I caught myself wishing the professor were real. No one in their right mind could ever resist my children's charm and good manners.

The dinner was roast and mashed potatoes. The peas were buttery, the gravy cooked with wine. I wanted Jennie's last meal at my table to be special. Mrs. Smith told us about her three children and their big house with servants in California. The professor told us about his studies at Harvard and Yale. I served ice cream, Jennie's favorite, and then I excused myself to put the children to bed. The party was already sluggish from the drops in their desserts by then.

When I came back down, my guests were in the parlor with Jennie, having coffee and thimble-sized glasses of sherry. I brought out a bottle of champagne from the pantry, and a celebratory cake lavish with whipped cream. I laid out five plates and cut the cake, then added a special filling to three of the slices, pushing my syringe in through layers of sponge and cherries. Two pieces were left plain on the table when I went to serve the first three. It certainly would not do to mix them up.

I steeled my heart then, when I served the cake, and told myself it was not done yet and I could still change my mind. It was just chloral in there, it would not hurt one bit. Would only make her sleep like a babe, dream of California perhaps. Dream of all the good things in store.

We ate the cake and drank the champagne. Jennie seemed a little wary; she lifted a forkful of cake to her nose as if to sniff it. Her lack of trust annoyed me, even if I knew she had reason to be suspicious this time. When I caught her gaze across the table, she gave me a quick, quivering smile and shoved the cake in between her lips.

"A little too much champagne, perhaps?" I asked when Mrs. Smith's head drooped down on her chest. The professor was already sleeping, his mouth open as he leaned back on the sofa.

"You used a hefty dose," said James. Jennie slept on the chair with the glass in her hand and champagne spilling down her blue dress.

"She cannot know what's coming."

"I will do it, Bella, don't you worry about that."

We carried the professor down first, as he was the biggest and most likely to wake up. He lay there on the oilcloth, gaping like a fish when I cut his throat with my doctor's knife, swift and easy like that.

James killed Miss Burns by strangling her in her sleep. He did not even bring her down to the cellar but did it there on the sofa. Her face turned red and then blue, her tongue protruding from her painted lips. Then he carried her downstairs.

Lastly, there was Jennie, the girl I had kept for eighteen years. She was light as a feather when we brought her down the steps, to the room she had so wanted to see.

"Off to California, then?" James leaned against the table, toying with the knife.

"Make it swift," I said, and he did.

She was just a lump of meat after that, just gristle and bones and tendons. I worked swiftly, taking them apart. One gunnysack for each of them: torso, arms, legs, head. Six pieces in all. Around me, the walls were lined with preserves Jennie had helped me make; the jars with her favorite kind of spread glistened like red jewels in the kerosene light. She always had such nimble fingers; her fruit was peeled and cut so fine you could barely see the knife's track.

"Such a waste," James mused, watching me work. "Here you've fed and raised the girl, and now it has come to naught."

"The world is hardly just." I sawed through Miss Burns's left leg. "She should not have been so nosy."

"No, she most surely should not."

"It is a shame, though. I know you cared for the girl."

"And look where that brought me." I placed the leg in the sack. "What will I do if it happens again? I cannot send all my children away."

He did not answer; he had brought a bottle of whiskey downstairs and offered me a drink. "Well, at least she never saw it coming."

"She died thinking it would be all right."

"Not everyone gets that: a happy death."

I finished packing up Miss Burns. The cellar had never been so bloody; gristle and fluids were everywhere.

We carried the sacks outside and wheelbarrowed them to the pit I had made ready. I wondered if I would miss Jennie at all, or if she would slip from me without a trace.

Down in the ground, as if nothing had happened.

James shoveled in dirt. "There were fifteen hundred dollars in that satchel, just as we agreed on."

"As if I would send my daughter to work as a whore." I grabbed another shovel and helped him out.

"Laura was very excited when I told her about the innocent girl living in the country. Old, rich men are partial to them."

"Well, no old men will touch her now."

"And she won't say a word about your enterprise."

"She shouldn't have looked in the cellar."

"Curiosity can kill even the finest of cats." He paused to take a swig of the bottle.

"Nothing to do for it now. It's done."

THE NEXT MORNING, when the children came down, the professor and his wife, Jennie, and James were gone. I gave them eggs and told them just how lucky she was to go to California to study.

I put an advertisement in the local newspaper, too, to share the good news that Jennie Olson had gone to California to attend the Norwegian seminary. I told people about it so many times—how good the professor and his wife were to her, what nice accommodations she had there—that I sometimes forgot that it was not so, that Jennie was rotting in the ground with the rest.

When I thought of Jennie, it was in California I saw her. She was a thriving young woman managing on her own, learning and gaining a profession.

42.

Nellie

Chicago and La Porte, 1907

I was puzzled by the letter from Bella telling me that Jennie had gone off to school in Los Angeles. What puzzled me more than anything else was that the girl had not written to me herself. Surely she would have been excited—and perhaps a little anxious—to travel so far away from home. It was not like her not to send a few words and ask for some reassurance. Bella was not always the best to give sage advice and calm a worried heart when excitement took hold of her. She only saw the possibilities in her schemes and could sometimes get annoyed if someone dared to question their magnificence, so I was surprised when no letter from Jennie arrived.

I was even more surprised when Nora did not hear from her either, though she anxiously awaited word, even more so than I did.

"Nothing today either," she would say every night as she helped with the dishes after dinner. "When will she write?"

"It's probably very exciting for her, coming to a new place with lots of new people. I'm sure she'll write in time, when she has settled in." I tried to make my voice sound calm and reasonable, and not reveal the feeling of unease that grew in me too.

"She has to know that I'm waiting," Nora still fretted. "And it happened so suddenly, too. She never said anything before she left."

"As Bella explained it, it was an opportunity that came out of nowhere, with this professor passing through." As I repeated my sister's words, I could sense the disharmony in them. The unlikeliness of such a thing happening was too great not to notice. "I will write to Jennie at the Norwegian seminary," I told my daughter. "Surely she will reply."

Bella had asked me to send all letters to Jennie to her in La Porte, for her to pass along, but I saw no sense in that, and asked her for the address in Los Angeles. It was when this request went unanswered that I started to worry in earnest. I did not name these worries, though; I only felt them there as something sticky and dark clinging to my mind, infusing every thought of the child with heaviness and shadows.

I knew that something was not right.

I asked a neighbor who had a friend with a niece who had gone to the seminary for the address, and after a while, she came across the street and delivered it to my door. I then wrote a letter to Jennie and enclosed a note in the envelope, asking the staff at the seminary to give the letter to Jennie Olson. I did not tell a soul.

Nora, meanwhile, had gone to see Jennie's sister, Mrs. Oleander, to ask her if she had heard from Jennie since she left. The answer she had gotten was disheartening.

"She only heard from Aunt Bella," she told me, sitting by the kitchen table, biting her bottom lip raw. "It did not seem to bother her, though. She seemed happy that Jennie could go to school, and praised Aunt Bella's generosity."

"And why wouldn't she?" My voice was still calm, still reasonable. "Not many girls get an opportunity like that." It was what Bella had said in her letter. "We should all be happy for Jennie."

"Yes, of course, but—why doesn't she write?" Nora stretched out her legs. "I sent my letters to Aunt Bella over a month ago!"

"Sometimes the mail is slow," I told her. "Perhaps she is busy at school—perhaps she had many letters to answer, and yours is next in line, just waiting."

"No." Nora sounded sure. "Jennie would have answered mine first."

When a letter finally *did* arrive from Los Angeles, I let out a breath of relief—it was short-lived, however, as the contents were not what I had wished for. My own letter to Jennie was in there, still in its envelope, and there was a note too, informing me that Jennie was not a student at that establishment. I immediately sank down on a chair with the letter in my hand, and sat there for a good long while, just staring down at the floor before my feet. I remembered Jennie the last time I had seen her, that night in Bella's kitchen, the worry and fear in her pretty blue eyes—and then I started to cry.

I went through several possibilities in my mind. I wondered if Bella herself had gotten the name of the school wrong, or if she had been tricked by that professor she said came to see them. Perhaps he was not a professor at all but a man with ill intent. But why would my sister not say so, if she suspected that the girl had been taken by fiends? Surely she would have looked for her then—visited every bordello in Chicago! And even if Jennie was not in Los Angeles but at another school somewhere else, she still would have written, if not to me, then at least to Nora . . .

I could not find a way out of the maze.

I waited for the usual eruption in my chest, the tightness and the rush of blood, the sense of my heart shattering—but this time it did not come. Instead, I was overtaken with a hopeless sort of sadness, a sense that all was lost. When I closed my eyes, it was not Jennie I saw, but Little Brynhild running across the moors, her square little shape coming toward me, wrapped in a woolen shawl, and with her brown hair hidden beneath a headscarf. Her shoulders were hunched against the wind, and her large eyes looked straight at me, reflecting the cold light from the sky, before her lips split in a joyous smile, beautiful and wild.

I remembered what I had promised myself, every night in the loft at Størsetgjerdet: that I would always protect her, even when God could not.

I knew I might be about to break that that promise.

I ENLISTED THE help of Rudolph, who had every other Tuesday off from work. I told him we were going to La Porte but did not tell him why, only that I had to speak to his aunt. His wife, Maria, was heavily pregnant, so at first he was reluctant to go that far, and asked if I could take Nora instead, but even if that had been possible and she could beg a day off work, I did not want to. I found I wanted to take my son not only for the aid and company but for protection too. This worried me even more than the task itself—though it was bound to be unpleasant.

I knew my family worried about my lack of sleep and my melancholy mood, but we all blamed my bad back for the changes. After Jennie went away, it had become harder to pretend, though, as my tears were never far away and I had problems following a conversation. John often asked, though he had been experiencing some poor health himself, and was often tired and craving rest. He was grateful, I think, when I told him it was nothing, and to take his powder and go to sleep. It suited me fine; I could not share my dark thoughts with anyone. It was as if the words were locked up in a vault deep inside, and speaking them aloud would cause all sorts of bad things to happen. It was *my* pain and mine alone, until I knew just what to do with it. I scolded myself countless times for silencing Myrtle, for encouraging Jennie—and then I sternly reminded myself that I did not *know* for sure.

But I *had* to know, I did.

Which was why I went to La Porte, with a shivering heart and a tormented soul, bringing along my reluctant son, who would rather stay at home.

"Has this to do with Jennie?" he asked as we sat opposite each other on the train, the newspaper resting on his knee. "I know that Nora worries about her."

I shook my head but did not reply.

"I hope Aunt Bella keeps a blanket in the carriage—it's terribly cold." He looked out at the bleak landscape. "Your back does not much like it when the temperature drops."

"She won't be there with the carriage." My voice was very hoarse. "She doesn't know that we're coming." I ignored his puzzled look. "We'll rent a buggy when we get there—and Rudolph, you will wait outside in the farmyard while I speak to her. I don't want you inside while I do."

"Mama?" The puzzlement on his handsome face increased. "What is this about? Did you have a falling-out?"

I just shook my head again—I could not tell him what it was.

I FOUND BELLA alone in the kitchen; she was at the table, cutting up a side of pork, deftly swinging the cleaver. The blood on her hands did nothing to lessen my unease as I stepped inside through the door to the dining room, without even bothering to knock.

The cleaver sang in the air, cut through the meat, and met the sturdy table with a bang.

"Bella," I said as I paused inside the door, and looked at her broad back before me, the curve of her neck and the mass of hair haphazardly pinned to her head. The cleaver sang and hit the table once more, and then she turned to me with a smile on her lips.

"Nellie!" She wiped her hands on her apron, leaving thick, red smears on the worn cotton. "What are you doing here? Are you alone?" She arched her head to look behind me, through the half-open door. Her face fell a little. "Did something happen?"

I shook my head. I had not found my words yet.

She cocked her head and lifted her chin, just a little. Something cold stirred in her eyes. "What is it, then? Why are you here?" Her lips were no longer smiling.

"Where is Jennie?" My voice was like something out of a cave— a vast, dark place built of dread.

She turned and set to bustle with the kettle on the range. "What do you mean? You know where she is! She went to the sem—"

"No! She did not!" I would not have any lies. Her back tensed up before me, whether from anger or fear I did not know. "What did you do, Little Brynhild?"

She turned to me then, her eyes black with anger. She held the kettle in her hand as if she were about to swing it. Her lips were pressed tightly together in a pale, hard line. "I have done nothing but to send her off to one of the best schools there is! She will study law—become something!" But her rage did not support her claim.

"Well, she's not there, so that didn't happen!" I found some spark in myself at last. "Your husbands I can look away from, as I think you may have been burned—but not *this*, Little Brynhild! I cannot look away from the destruction of *a child*!" I stomped my foot and closed my fists; the tears burned in my eyes.

"I have done no such thing," she hissed, but the kettle swung back and forth in her arm. "I would be very careful of throwing accusations of which you have no proof!"

"The proof is right here!" I screamed at her. "The girl is not to be found! How long do you think it will take before her family starts to worry? Mine already does—you *cannot* walk away from this!"

"The last time I saw Jennie, she was fit as a fiddle, and on her way to Los Angeles," she hissed. "And I have heard from her many times since."

"Show me the letters." My voice was shrill. "Show me Jennie's letters, and I will believe you!"

She shook her head, and something like a spasm twisted her features for a moment. "I did not keep them—the children took them and lost them in the barn."

"Oh, you're a liar," I accused her through gritted teeth. "You did away with her! What happened, Little Brynhild? Did she find out what you do in the cellar?" She came at me then, just a step, but it was enough that I stepped back as well. "She wondered about that, and the locked room filled with trunks upstairs. She worried that those men never left!" I could no longer keep silent—the words came rushing like a landslide. I no longer cared what happened to me next; the words wanted out, and I let them.

"You don't know what you're talking about." Her voice was disturbingly calm. "Coming in here, setting my children up against me! Encouraging them to disobey! Marzipan cake! What right do you have, Nellie? What right?" She swung her arm with the kettle out in a wide arc so that it hit the counter with a loud bang; the sound of splintering wood forced its way through the haze of my rage. On the table, the bloody cleaver was smiling, sharp and shiny, like a mirror.

"Rudolph is outside in the buggy." I had no tools to intimidate her but hoped that the words would be enough. "He'll go for help if you hurt me. I only need to call out!"

"That was a foolish thing to come here with your accusations—what do you think will happen next?" But my words had made an impact, I could tell; her gaze kept darting to the door, and the power with which she swung the kettle was not quite as forceful as before.

"You would not hurt me, Little Brynhild—not *me*!" I clung to that conviction with all my might. "I cared for you as a child, I held you when you were sick, and washed every scrape and bloody wound—"

"And then you left!" Her voice bellowed with such force that I staggered another step back. "Left me with that good-for-nothing man and his foolish, foolish wife! What sort of a good deed was that? Leaving me with that lot!"

"You know I had no choice?" The accusation had hit me as well as that kettle would have; it left a bruise just as black. "I did what I could, Little Brynhild—you know that."

"As do I." Her chin was tilted almost all the way up; her nostrils flared when she breathed. "I do what I must to get by—nothing more!"

"You know that isn't right." I shook my head and wiped my tears with hands that shivered and shook. "People are not cattle for you to slaughter for gain! Children are not for you to bury!"

"And yet I do." Her shoulders slumped as she lowered her head. The kettle fell quiet by her side.

"It has to stop." I was speaking from that cave again. "It has to stop, or they'll hang you, Little Brynhild! I'll see to it myself, if only for that beautiful child—" My voice cracked as another bout of tears came bursting out of me. "You will not harm another human being as long as you live, or I'll make sure that your neck ends up in the noose!" I lifted a hand and pointed to her chest.

"You would not," she said but sounded uncertain. There was no more fire to her words.

"Oh, I would." It was my turn to lift my chin and steel my gaze. "I'm cut from the same cloth as you, Little Brynhild. If anyone can, it's me."

Her lips twisted up in a smirk, but her eyes were dark with worry. "No one would believe you," she muttered as she staggered to the table and slumped down on a chair. The cleaver no longer scared me.

"They *would*." I spoke with more conviction than I felt, but surely if someone were to look into it, they had to find *something*. There had to be a trace. "You will still your hand and never lift it again—or I will see that you hang."

I scrambled for the door, dizzy and sick. We shared no parting words. I felt as if I had drunk a whole bottle of her pear brandy all by myself as I staggered out of there on shivering legs. I barely saw the rooms around me as I passed through the dining room and then the parlor. The scent of raw meat would not leave me but followed me out the front door, where the fresh, cold air hit me like a fist.

Rudolph watched me come out from the buggy, his eyes widened in alert as I paused on the steps and drank in the air. Myrtle and Lucy were out there as well with the pony and the cart, having just come back from an outing. I could see a farmhand in the distance with a wheelbarrow full of hay. The girls gave me curious looks as I made my way down the steps.

"Do you need any help, Aunt Nellie?" Myrtle called out.

"No, no." I hobbled toward them.

"Are you sick, Aunt Nellie?" Lucy asked.

"No, I'm not sick." Though I sure did not feel hale. I put a hand on their cart to steady myself. "Have you been to school?"

The girls nodded. Their worried gazes lingered on my face.

"Lucy." I cleared my throat and did not look at any of them. "Why don't you go and look in on the chickens? Your mama mentioned that two of them had gone astray, but I think there's something off with her counting." I forced a smile to reassure her. It was not fair to trick the girl, but nothing had been right with this day. Nothing had been right for a very long time.

Lucy still looked puzzled, but nodded and set off toward the chicken coop, leaving me alone with Myrtle. The older girl looked at me with something wary in her eyes, sensing, perhaps, that this would not be any ordinary conversation.

"Myrtle," I started, and I spoke fast as I did not have much time. Sooner or later, Bella would come bursting out the door, and I did not have it in me to speak to her again that day. "Do you remember after Peter died? When we spoke behind the barn?"

She hesitated only a little before slowly nodding.

"Do you remember that you told me you had seen something—and that I told you not to tell?" I forced another smile, though it felt more like a grimace.

Myrtle nodded again, even slower than the first time. Her hand was on the pony's dark coat, absorbing its heat through the mitten.

"Myrtle." My voice gave a little. "I have to know what that was." I adjusted my hold of the cart's wooden board and struggled to keep my tears at bay. They would do the girl little good.

"I can't—" she started to say, looking so unhappy that my heart broke a little. The edges of her mouth drooped and her gaze flickered from side to side.

"Oh please, Myrtle. If you remember, you *must* tell me!" I all but fell to my knees to plead. "It was wrong of me not to listen to you then—please forgive me and tell it to me now."

Her face scrunched up with fear and worry. Now it was *her* eyes that filled up with tears. "I cannot." She sounded utterly miserable.

"I will not tell Mama," I whispered, and held her gaze with mine, willing it not to slip away.

She chewed her lips for a moment, then stepped a little closer, rose up to her toes, and whispered quickly in my ear, "She hit Papa with the cleaver—Mama did."

Then she quickly stepped away, as if I were made of smoldering coal.

"Thank you, Myrtle," I breathed, and let the tears come at last. "Thank you so much for telling me that."

"Mama, are you all right?" Rudolph finally called from the buggy. His nose had become red from the cold, and the horse stamped its legs.

"Sure," I said, though I did not know if the faint sound of my voice would carry all the way to him. "I'm coming now." I hobbled toward him. "I'm coming, and then we can go home."

We had barely come off the driveway when we had to stop again, and my son had to hold my shivering form as I was sick by the side of the road. I felt raw on the inside, ravaged and torn. I knew I ought to turn her in—she had killed an innocent *child*—but God help me, I could not see her hang! Not her, not Little Brynhild, broken though she might be.

No law could ever make this right, but I prayed that my words would stay her hand, that the threat I had delivered would be enough to make her stop.

43.

Belle

I sat in the kitchen for hours after Nellie had left, staring at the meat on the table, and then at the cleaver beside it. The scent of it teased my nostrils; I lost myself in the rinds of fat and the ruby-red beads of blood scattered on the flesh. I did not even look up when the girls came inside, or when Philip woke up from his nap, calling out for his mama. I could not move away from that table.

"Mama?" Lucy's voice tried to reach me. "Mama, should we help with the food?"

When there was no answer to be had, the girls brought Philip with them into the parlor. I could hear them in there, whispering. I knew I should feed them—and yet . . .

I could not move away from that table.

My thoughts were spinning, yet I said nothing at all. Nellie would not leave me alone. Her words—her *threats*—came back to me over and over: *I will see that you hang!*

Would she, though? Would she really do that to me—or was there a way I could make this problem disappear? Ensure her silence in the best way I could? Nellie was in poor health, that was no secret. She had been struggling with her back for years and was not so young anymore. Maybe it would not be so strange if she suddenly died, following a dose of her medicine perhaps. There was not much spite in such an act, but at least it would keep me safe.

Keep us *all* safe.

But then she would hardly let me close to her cupboard *now*— after having me figured out. Might not even let me into her home. I found a strange sense of loss in that, to be barred from a place where I had always been welcome and never even thought twice about the fact. I did not like the way she looked at me either, that horror and despair etched on her face. It took me a while to recognize that what I felt was shame, as if I were a little girl caught stealing. I was ruined in my sister's eyes; she would never again admire me. I grieved that fact, and yet—

If she were not there, she could not hurt me.

Then there was another part of me that whispered of a different solution. I could simply do as she wished and stop. Many of my troubles would be gone if I did, and not only Nellie's threats. I was tired, for one; it took its toll, all this secrecy and planning—and then there was Jennie . . . The first few weeks after she left had been hard on us all. I caught myself about to call for her many times a day to help me with this or that, especially in regard to the children. I had not truly known before she was gone just how much I had relied on her. Philip fussed about the way I carved his meat, claiming that Jennie was the only one who did it right. Lucy cried every day for seven days while perched on the marble windowsill in the parlor, watching the yard outside in the hopes that her foster sister would come back. Myrtle kept her thoughts to herself, as was her habit, but she did not seem very happy either.

This annoyed me at the time. They should be *glad* that their foster sister got such an opportunity. Glad that she did not spend her life rotting away on a farm in La Porte but was able to see the world. There was nothing to grieve—only to celebrate—but my children did not understand that.

I tried to keep them occupied—keep us *all* occupied. I set out to teach them horseback riding, and we spent hours in the yard with Chocolate while their small fingers learned how to hold the reins. I tried to teach Myrtle some of the skills that Jennie had, like wringing laundry and cooking a roast, but she was only ten years old and unused to heavy lifting. She tended the goats in Jennie's stead, though, and helped me with the younger children. Both she and Lucy were some help in the kitchen, but they were not as fast and experienced as Jennie.

I told myself they would learn—that all of this would pass in time. Soon it would be as if Jennie had never stayed with us at all, yet the sense of bereavement persisted. Not even the thought of California could make it all go away. Not even storing her clothes and belongings in the trunk room could stop me from wanting to call for her whenever I needed help. The house suffered from her absence too; nothing seemed as clean as before, even if I scoured with lemon. I often cursed the day she went down in the cellar—now she had left us all in a pinch.

My *anger* had left us all in a pinch.

Then there was the trouble with Ole Budsberg. The man himself was nothing at all: a farmer from Wisconsin with money to spare who had sold off his farm to come join me. For a man his age, he was still spry, with a thick and lustrous red mustache. He was not poor company, but neither did he inspire me to keep him very long.

He had sons, though, with their sticky fingers all over his business. They kept sending letters addressed to him, and I kept putting them away, until the size of the pile urged me to act before one of them came to look for their papa. I gathered up the letters and sent them back to Wisconsin, addressed to the late Mr. Budsberg. With the letters, I attached a note of my own where I wrote that I hoped he was not offended that I did not want to marry him, and that I certainly had not led him on. I wished him luck in finding a new homestead in the West. That ought to stop their prying, I thought, but alas, it did not, and one windy day a man stood on my porch. I recognized him at once as Mr. Buck from the bank in La Porte.

"Good morning, Mrs. Gunness." He shuffled his feet and clutched his hat. Prince kept snapping at the hem of his coat.

I was very busy that morning, plucking poultry out back and boiling stock. My apron was dirty and feathers clung to my hands. I was not pleased to be disturbed.

"I'm looking for the whereabouts of a Mr. Ole Budsberg."

"What for?" I plucked feathers from my fingers.

"It seems he has borrowed some money from the Farmer's National Bank in Iola, and the payment is due. Since he withdrew some money here a while back, the bank in Iola has asked for our assistance in locating him."

"Well, he is not here."

"He did stay here with you, though, didn't he? I remember you escorting him when he cashed his draft—"

"He left a short while after that."

"When was that?"

"Oh, I don't know. I don't keep track of dates. He left to catch the two o'clock train; he was going to Oregon to buy some land."

"And you don't know when this was?"

"I don't keep track of dates." It was better that he thought me simple; it might prevent him from asking too many questions.

Mr. Buck left shortly after. It was an unfortunate thing, though, that Mr. Budsberg, despite all my warnings, would go and have unfinished business with that bank. I had told him to bring all he had in cash sewn into his clothes. He had not mentioned a loan.

Before long, another letter arrived, from the Farmer's National Bank in Iola, addressed not to him but to *me*, asking for Mr. Budsberg's whereabouts. The wording was strong and I worried that another stern man might soon arrive on my porch. I wrote to them then and said that Mr. Budsberg had been robbed of most of his money and clothes in Chicago, and that he was so embarrassed by it all, he had fled west to try to make up for it before his relatives learned of his shame. I think they believed me—they did not ask for him again—but the experience had been unpleasant. I did not care for such things at all. Other men came and went, but the trouble with Budsberg kept haunting me. What secrets did they keep from me, these men? Did they have loans and obligations too? Would more stern officials come to call? I kept staring out the windows, watching the road for signs of strangers.

I could not trust my suitors at all, and wondered as I sat there by the kitchen table, contemplating my sister's possible demise, if the enterprise was truly worth all the hassle. Whenever I remembered the cause of my anger, I felt ashamed. I was no puppet on a stage, I thought, moved around by strings. I was not that girl by the lake, begging for her life. My money box would never be full, and so I could stop at any time, and that feeling I chased—that *feeling*—it was there sometimes and other times not, and it was never as delicious as it was after Anders. It still came washing over me, though, especially if the man had been brutal or very large of stature. If he had offended me, or reminded me somehow of my husbands. But the feeling never lasted, and there I was again: preparing for a new dance with the cleaver.

I had known all along it could not last; sooner or later it would all fall apart—and what would I do then? Trust in my devil's luck, and hope that my tears would protect me? What would happen to my children if their mama hanged by the neck? They could never wash that stain away—it would haunt them always.

Unless I stopped. There was that.

I could do as my sister wished and stop. Nellie might never let me close to her again, even if I did, but at least she would not have me hanged.

And I would never lose a child again.

I MET RAY LAMPHERE in August, after a hard, troublesome year. I had not been myself since Christmas and Jennie, and the old restlessness was back, tugging at my bones. No matter what I did, I could not seem to find any satisfaction. My jaw ached so badly, I had to treat it with a ripe-smelling poultice, which did nothing to better my mood.

I hired Lamphere to do some work on the farm that was long overdue. All my troubles kept distracting me from repairs and other necessary work. I should have renewed my stocks and plan for the harvest ahead, but my heart was just not in it. It was hard to find capable hands as well; they up and left or I rid myself of them, deciding they were more useful for cash than as farmhands. I never felt sorry for that. I butchered pigs for meat and men for money—I took what I needed to live and thrive, but it kept landing me in a rough spot when it came to capable workers. Which was why I took on Lamphere, despite my better judgment and his horrid reputation.

Had I known then what was to come, I certainly would have let it be. Every deck of cards has at least one grinning fool, useless and annoying, that turns up only to ruin the game. Lamphere was just like that: a fool with jingling bells.

It was sweet enough at first. I was weary and happy to have a man in the house to do the heavy lifting. Even if he was a drunk and a vagrant, always unkempt and unwashed, he was eager to please and strived to shine. After his first day at work, laying new floorboards in the parlor, I knew he could never defy me; he was as soft and moldable as clay. His gratitude for the job made him act like a dog. I found I liked that. I had seen enough of those loud brutes with strong opinions and a desire to rule. That wrecked and foolish man came as a bit of a relief to me then. I did not have to feed him sweets or compliment his rude behavior. I did not have to coax and charm—he was as simple as they come.

I heard him hammering above me that first night, while I was working in the basement, butchering two young men James had sent me. I was not worried that he would find me out; Ray would never go where he was not wanted—or that was what I thought at the time.

I washed up outside by the pump, and then I wrung the neck of a chicken to bring back inside, and cut it some too, to explain my stained apron. It was late at night, but I felt certain that Mr. Lamphere would not even know to ask why I was out catching chickens so late.

My appetites were great that night, as they often were after butchering, and Ray was there, on his knees, pounding those nails in place.

"You better quiet down." I stood in the door to the parlor, still holding the poor chicken by its neck. "You may disturb the children."

He stopped at once and looked up at me with those drooping eyes of his. "Of course, Mrs. Gunness. I'm sorry, Mrs. Gunness."

I awarded him a smile. "Don't be. I like a hardworking man. It's so hard to find one these days who doesn't shy away from labor."

"Oh, I don't mind some hard work," he said, bristling. "I can work all night if that is what it takes."

"Well, you better leave it for now or the children might get anxious." But probably not, as I had given them drops. "Why don't you come into the kitchen with me to have some nice food and a drink?"

The latter made him light up. "Much obliged, Mrs. Gunness." He rose to his feet; sawdust drifted off his clothes.

"Call me Belle, please." I led the way into the kitchen, where the embers still smoldered hot in the range. I had some leftover soup in the pantry and placed it on the range to heat. Ray stoked the fire and added fresh logs. I poured him some whiskey, placed it on the table, and saw him perk up as a dog with a scent. He truly was under the sway.

"You have worked many places around here, haven't you, Ray?"

"Sure." He sipped his liquor. "All have given good references," he lied. He was wont to go missing for days and show up drunk in the mornings.

"At least you're doing good work for me. My floors have never looked so good."

"I'm good with the hammer," he said.

"I'm sure."

"The nails too."

"Of course."

I gave him a bowl of soup and some bread, and took some for myself as well. I wished I had something sweet but I had lost my taste for cooking. Not even sugar could mellow my recent discontent. Whiskey could, though, for a little while, and Ray Lamphere was the perfect man to share that vice with me. We kept sharing that bottle long after the soup was gone. Ray told me tall stories about his glorious youth, as all men do. They want you to know about the time when they were strong and reckless, filled with dreams and hopes, not used up and broken as they usually were when they washed up at the widow in La Porte.

Ray Lamphere had nothing to his name but a poor reputation and a taste for liquor, yet I did not hesitate when he said, "Just say if there is something else I can do for you, ma'am."

I took him to bed then, that very first night, and for a drunkard he did rather well. He was well hung and eager to please, and I felt sure he would not cause me any trouble. Ray Lamphere was as easy as a child, I thought then. I could keep him around in any way that I wanted. He would never expect me to be sweet or even kind but would depend upon me for every scrap he got: food and shelter, liquor and tobacco.

It suited me well at the time.

AS THE YEAR progressed, Lamphere was a lamb, eating out of the palm of my hand. There was not a thing he would not do for a generous serving of whiskey. He never went missing for more than a night after I cried when he did. He was always by my side, carrying, digging, and shuffling muck. He had a hand with the horses too but was clumsy when it came to butchering.

One night, as we lay in bed in the room he kept upstairs, I turned to him and said, "Mr. Lamphere, what if we got married?"

He looked at me in the darkness. "Why would you want to marry a man such as me?"

"I have more than you, that is true, but I'm a lonely woman fending for myself out here, and you have proven yourself many times as being a man of your word." If I was to end my enterprise, I might just as well do it with a man I knew how to control. It would not do to be a widow forever—having a husband would tether me, I hoped. Loose connections would always pose a temptation, especially if the man in question came carrying cash. No, it was better if I took a fool and kept to him. One of whom I expected nothing and who expected nothing in return.

Ray gave an amused sound. "Not all would say that I'm a man of my word."

"Well, *I* do. You never let me down, and you're a hard worker, just as I am."

"It must be hard," he agreed, "being a woman alone with all this." He could see it then, could see his glorious future before him, with acres of oats and golden corn, roasts and steaks and cakes.

"I need a husband," I said, urging him on, "one who can take care of all this. I'm tired of fending for myself all alone. I need someone who can manage the farm so I can spend more time indoors, doing what a woman ought to."

"I can be your man." He grinned in the darkness. I could feel his hand on my chest, playing with the pewter button.

"I'm sure you can, Ray, because we get along so well." I smiled and brushed his hair away from his forehead. "There would have to be some insurance, though. I will not marry you unless you're insured." Though I did not plan on killing him, I still wanted to know there was something to gain should he fall into a ditch and freeze to death one cold winter's day. "I know well enough how hard it is to suddenly be left a widow. It's a dangerous world out there and one cannot be certain of anything. Poor Peter was struck by the sausage grinder . . ."

"You've had it hard, poor Belle."

"So if you will ease my heart and purchase an insurance policy,

I will gladly be married to you and let you share in my good fortunes."

"They *are* good fortunes," he marveled.

"We will be so happy, I'm sure of it. Just let me know that you care as much about my future as I care for yours, and give me that little token of affection." I closed my hand over his.

"It doesn't have to be so expensive, perhaps," said the fool by my side.

"You want it to be worth *some*, or it doesn't mean much, your love for me." I did not think to earn then; I was simply being offended.

"I'd be a poor man to deny you that, as you are bringing both land and livestock to the table," he mumbled after a while.

"Yes, Ray, you would, and I know you're not a poor man. You're a good man, Ray Lamphere, and you'll make me a fine husband as soon as the insurance is purchased."

As the days went by, however, it became clear that the marriage was not even worth it to consider. I asked him about the insurance, and he said yes, he would look into it, but nothing of the sort happened. I asked him again, and he said he had been busy, but that he would get to it shortly.

He never did, though. He never gave me that measly insurance, so I sent him back to sleep in the barn. He swore and cursed and drank himself silly. He begged on his knees to be let back inside, but I had lost my faith in him.

Ray and I were over.

I kept him on the farm to do work, but that was it. He was no longer sharing either bed or board with me. I was angry with him for sure. How could a man like that not do what he could to be married to a woman like me? I had offered him a future and he had turned it down. He had made a fool of me too, for asking him in the first place. I did not let him go, though, no—I did not know what he would say to others if I did. Maybe he would tell them about my shameless proposal, and maybe someone would believe him too.

There was another reason as well. For all his faults, he appeared deaf and blind, never to take notice of what happened on the farm, like the crates that went in the basement. I was planning on ending that part of my enterprise too, but I was reluctant to tell James. He always had a way with words, could infuse them with such sweetness that it made it hard to resist his proposals. If I told him I was ending it all, he would see it as a challenge and work to find a way to bring me back to his wicked ways. He quite enjoyed seeing me thrive as a villainess. Sometimes I thought he saw himself as the artist and me as his work of art. I indulged this, but knew it to be wrong, of course. If anything, I fed from him, lapped at his wellspring and gorged on his guile—but I was quite my own.

Yet I was reluctant to tell him.

Then, at last, when fall turned to winter, Andrew Helgelien announced his arrival, like temptation himself come knocking at my door.

44

It was such a nice gesture." Andrew sat on the sofa in my parlor drinking coffee and eating warm waffles with raspberry jam. He had been with us a few days already and made himself quite comfortable in my home. "That little four-leaf clover touched me, Belle. I knew it right away, then, that I had to come and see you." He was a tall, broad man with a square jaw, and not too old. His hair was light and his eyes were blue. I did not tell him there had been other four-leaf clovers, mailed to other men.

He had caught me by surprise—he had promised to come so many times I had quite given up on him. I was winding down my enterprise and had no need for a man, but he was handsome and spry, and he had means. If I squinted, he looked like Peter, and that made me anticipate his end at my hands. The feeling was sure to come then. I would ride that sweet wave one last time. It was not as if I had set out to find another man to butcher; these wheels had been set in motion a long time ago. I could not truly be blamed if the fruit I had tended fell down in my lap a little belated.

What harm could it do to take on just one more?

"I thought you might need it, some luck to get you safely here," I told him. "It's a long journey and many things can happen." I poured him more coffee.

"It's a nice piece of land, just as you promised." His gaze drifted out the window. "It's a gamble, trusting people. You never know what you find when you arrive. You, though, Belle, I had faith in you at once."

"I have never lied to you, and I never will either. The world is too crowded with deceitful people as it is. We both know that too well."

"I truly can see it." His hand found mine on the armrest of my chair and squeezed it gently. "The two of us together, building something good for ourselves."

"So can I." I smiled at him. "Your letters gave me many reasons to trust you. I wouldn't open my home to just anyone, but I don't hesitate at all opening it to you."

"Even if—"

"Oh, I don't care about that old story. You were young and foolish and did your time. If God can forgive, so can I. What kind of woman would I be if I didn't recognize that men can repent their sins? I believe you're much changed since then."

"I am." He sounded sincere and gave my hand another soft squeeze. "I want to find a good woman and settle down. I want to have a real home and a future, and I truly hope that will be with you."

I smiled at him. "I've been waiting to find one like you for so long. I've been so tired of doing everything myself." I let a tear slide from one of my eyes. I could feel it so keenly in that moment, the loneliness and toil, the weight of it all.

"Oh, don't you cry, Belle, it will all be better now. I'm here, and we can proceed as planned." Only we could not, because he had not taken his money in cash as I had asked him to. Instead of sewing it into his clothes, he had entrusted the bank with it, causing much delay and trouble. He had agreed to pay off my mortgage, and thus become a partner in the farm, but his money had not arrived yet. We had already been to the bank to inquire.

I could hear Lamphere out in the kitchen, snooping around. He had made big eyes the first morning when he came in to tend the fire and found Andrew in the house. He did not like it at all, Mr.

Lamphere. He had been like a sullen child ever since. He could not keep away but kept circling my guest, looking at him with a hooded gaze. I had already told him many times to stay away and not bother Mr. Helgelien, but I was not sure if my warnings had any effect.

"Your man is loud today," Andrew remarked when Lamphere in the kitchen let slip a curse.

"At least he doesn't curse in front of the children." I sighed.

"You may not need him when I have settled in."

"That would be a relief; hired hands are expensive."

"I can work for two." Andrew laughed, folded the heart-shaped waffle in his hand, and shoved the whole thing in his mouth. "Waffles means yes," he said when he was quite done chewing. "Where I come from, if a man likes a woman and she serves him waffles, it means yes. If a man likes a woman but she says no, she serves him gruel instead."

"Of course it's a yes, my dear. It always was a yes." I patted his hand with my fingers. "As soon as we get our affairs in order, we will be happy as can be."

"Oh, I already am." He smiled at me with berry pits wedged between his teeth.

"I'm sorry I got so angry in the bank. I just don't want anything to stand in the way of our happiness."

"Not to worry, I know you want some assurance—"

"I've been so strict with myself and told myself I will not marry before our affairs are in order. But then I'm so eager to get on with it, I sometimes lose my temper."

"Your caution is very understandable, and no one regrets this delay more than me."

"I *do* trust you, and wish that I just could give in to my heart, but I swore to heed my mind this time."

"I'm just glad I can rouse such passion in you."

Lamphere in the kitchen had gone quiet; he was listening in, no doubt. "You rouse all sorts of passion in me." I gave another smile. "I'm sure everything will work itself out."

"It will." He fished another waffle from the tray. "And then we will be happy as can be."

A FEW DAYS later, Sheriff Smutzer was in my yard. I had not expected him and got a little anxious. Andrew had gone into town for supplies. The girls were in school and Philip was playing out back.

"Sheriff." I wrapped a shawl around my shoulders and stepped outside. My mind reeled off plausible causes for the interruption. I wondered if someone had asked questions about any of my former houseguests.

Smutzer looked immaculate with a clean shirt and shiny boots; he had arrived in his brand-new Ford, red and glossy like an apple. "Good morning, Mrs. Gunness, I hope you're all doing fine."

"Of course." I wished he would get to the point. I was already spinning explanations, stories about horse theft and fraud.

"I'm sorry to intrude on you like this. I just wanted to let you know that your man, Lamphere, has been telling stories."

"Oh? What kind of stories?" My heart started hammering in my chest.

The sheriff looked away and squinted against the sun. "About your friend Mr. Andrew Helgelien . . . Ray came in the other week and told me you harbored a fugitive. He said that Mr. Helgelien was wanted in South Dakota." His face turned hostile when he mentioned Ray.

"No?" I was taken aback for once; I had not seen that coming. "Well, is he?"

"No." Smutzer gave me a tiny smile. "It turned out to be a lie. Mr. Helgelien isn't wanted for anything."

"That's what I thought. He seems a decent man."

"Do you know why Ray would accuse him of something like that?"

I shrugged. "I have no idea, but I will certainly ask him about it. Ray hasn't been himself of late. He thinks a little too much of himself, perhaps, and doesn't like my new friend staying at the farm."

"So it would appear." The sheriff gave another tiny smile. To him, Ray was nothing but a troublemaker, someone who made his job needlessly hard. Which was likely why he thought it worth his while to drive out and report the transgression to me, the hand that currently fed him. "Well, now you know." Smutzer turned and made to leave.

"Thank you," I told his back.

"My pleasure, Mrs. Gunness." He turned his motor vehicle around and disappeared down the driveway.

When I confronted Lamphere with it, he denied the whole thing. He said he had never gone to see Smutzer about Andrew.

"The sheriff has it in for me. He wants you to turn me out." He was sitting on his cot in the barn, looking as miserable as ever.

"Why would he want that?"

"He doesn't like me." Ray shrugged.

"Well, be as that might, you can't go telling stories about Andrew. I can't have the sheriff showing up in my yard."

"Why?" Something sly had come into his eyes. "Does Mrs. Gunness have something to hide?"

"Whatever would that be?" I snorted. "Nothing unseemly happens here."

"Oh, I don't know about that." Lamphere started to roll a cigarette. "You probably heard us talk about him being in prison, but that was many years ago—"

"How would I know when it was?"

"You shouldn't tell the sheriff either way. You work for me and I expect you to keep quiet no matter what you hear or see."

"You want me to keep quiet about us too, then? Not to tell anyone what a minx you are."

I could not help but laugh. "That's right, Ray, not a word about that."

"Or how we almost married?"

"Especially that, Ray. Keep quiet about that." My mood instantly plummeted.

"I don't like him." He spat on the floor. "He wants to take my place on the farm."

"You shouldn't be jealous of Andrew, Ray. You're far luckier than him."

"How come?"

"Just trust me on that and let it be . . . and no more talking to the sheriff."

ANDREW'S MONEY CAME through at last, and we celebrated appropriately. I made a large, glazed roast and served Andrew a plate of sugared oranges in the parlor.

"Don't you want any?" he asked me.

"I love oranges, but they give me a rash."

"Too bad. They are sweet and nice, just as you are, Belle."

"You deserve everything sweet and nice." I leaned over and patted his hand.

I did not have to wait long before he clutched his stomach and croaked from the sofa, "I don't feel so good, Belle. Maybe some water—"

"Sure." I rose and stepped out. I listened through a crack in the door as he fell to the floor, heaving for breath. I had decided to make it swift and clean, let him die in his own time and then drag him down the stairs. I was in no mood for slaying that night.

He took his time dying, however. I checked on him twice, armed with a hatchet, just in case. The first time he was still conscious, and not as close to gone as I had hoped. When I bent over him, he lunged at me suddenly, tangled his hands in my hair and pulled. We had a bit of a fight then. The table turned over, and a chair went down too, but I managed to bring the hatchet high up in the air and struck his head hard twice. Still he held on, and the pain made me angry. I planted the hatchet in his neck, cursing him silently for making such a mess. The sofa was sprayed with blood and my carpet too was stained. His hands fell away and he went limp on the floor. His gaze was aghast when he looked up at me, dark blood pumping from his neck.

Why? he mouthed.

"We do as we must."

Why? His lips formed the word again; his teeth were all stained red.

"We all find our way in life."

The second time I checked on him, he was barely breathing and his eyes were closed. I placed rags around his neck to soak up the blood.

The third time there was no breath.

His carcass was messy so I rolled him onto a sheet of oilcloth and secured the package with rope. I took a hold of it and pulled him with me across the floor, heading for the door to the cellar. My scalp hurt and I was scratched and bleeding. I hated it when things got out of hand, and there was so much to clean before morning. I opened the door and started the descent; I had come a few steps down so his body rested on the threshold, when a pair of feet appeared at the top.

I had sent Lamphere on a fool's errand to buy a horse that did not exist. I had told him to spend the night, but lo and behold, there he was! Reeking of alcohol, his eyes wild.

"I knew there was something about that cellar."

"Be quiet, Ray, or you'll wake the children."

"I knew you were up to something." His voice was strangely calm, but fear hummed beneath it like a tightly wound fiddle string.

"Keep quiet," I hissed. "Come on, grab his legs." Nothing else to do for it. The damage was done, he was already there.

"Oh no." The silly man shook his head. "I won't go down in that cellar with you. You'll be planting the axe in *my* head next."

"Don't be silly, Ray. Whatever would I gain from that?"

"I wouldn't tell on you, that's something."

"We have been friends for some time now, Ray. If I had wanted you dead, you would be dead."

Still he stood there wringing his hands. "I won't go down there with you."

"Suit yourself, then. There's whiskey in the kitchen and good money to be earned if you help me get him in the ground after."

"After what?"

"After I take him apart."

"Right . . . Why would you do that?"

"He'll take up less space in the ground, and the pigs will want the soft parts."

He was quiet for a moment, and then he said, "They dug up some bones, the pigs, the other day. I was going to tell you about that."

"What kind of bones?"

"Shinbones, I think, and maybe something like a jaw."

"You should have told me."

"I didn't know for sure then."

"Well, now you do. Will you help me or not?"

He shifted on the floor and looked uncomfortable before me. "Sure I'll help you, for a price."

"Of course." There was always, always a price. "You can start by cleaning the parlor, then roll up the carpet and scrub the boards. After that, you'll help me dig."

He nodded and went away. I wiped the sweat of my forehead and kept moving. Andrew was heavy but I was strong. The faint light was a curse, though. The lamp I had placed in the cellar barely illuminated the stairs, and I had no way of knowing if Andrew left a trail. If he did, Lamphere would have to wipe up that blood too.

When I came back up, Lamphere was in the kitchen drinking. He had cleaned the floors and thrown out the water. He looked pale and his hands were shaking. He did not look at me while I cleaned my hands. I ought to be ashamed to be seen like that, bloodied and hot, my hair come undone, but no matter my state, Lamphere would always be worse. *My* hands were not shaking. I did not fear him as he feared me.

"You will not speak a word of this to anyone. If you do, I have friends who'll find you."

"That slick man from Chicago—?"

"Mr. Lee? He is one."

"You would still fry, though, if I told."

"Be smart about it, Ray. What you know has some value. You can make a fine profit if you keep your mouth shut and help me out from time to time."

"Digging graves?"

"Just that. I'm a wealthy woman and can pay well for your services."

"Maybe you'll just kill me either way."

"Why would I do that? It's hard work digging those pits. I could certainly use help."

He shuddered visibly by the table. "You're a dangerous woman, Belle Gunness."

"I certainly am no saint."

"I thought you were going to marry him."

"So did *he*." I toweled off my hands. "But be quick now, Ray; the body is out in the wheelbarrow and we have to get him in the ground before dawn."

Out we went then, lanterns held high, to slip Andrew Helgelien into the ground. It had not brought him much luck, that four-leaf clover. It almost never brought luck. We had a spot at Størsetgjerdet where those small, mishap clovers grew in droves, but they never brought anyone there much luck either. They lied, those clovers—their promises were hollow.

Lamphere worked in silence, filling in the hole. I held the light for him and was glad not to have to do the digging myself for a change. My hands were too rough and callused as it was. All the blood I had touched became brown stains, embedded deep within the skin. It would not come off, no matter how much I scrubbed.

After the ordeal, when the earth was black and smooth again, I poured Lamphere more whiskey in the kitchen. "Just be quiet now, Ray, and all will be well."

"I won't say a word," he swore.

I gave him some cash and promised more, but only—*only*—if he was good.

"It's in your best interest to do as I say."

"Always was. Nothing much has changed there."

"I can be a good friend to you if you like."

"Or you could kill me dead."

"That too."

"Not to worry, Mrs. Gunness." He folded the bills and put the cash in his pocket. "You can trust old Ray."

I could not, of course, and should have known that too, but misery always made me reckless—foolish enough to entrust a fool with the means of my own undoing.

45.

Nellie

Chicago, 1908

It had felt like such a brave thing to do, walking into Bella's kitchen to make my demands. When the sickness had passed after our encounter, I had been humming with it for weeks, that sense of power it gave me. Finally, she had given in and crumbled a bit before me; finally, I could make her *behave*. There would be no more dead children. There would be no more dead men. *I* had seen to that.

Oh, I knew she ought to hang. No one had grieved sweet Jennie more than me, but then I grieved for that other girl as well: Little Brynhild, with her large eyes and difficult disposition, the aim of our father's lashings more often than not. That little girl so at odds with the world—I grieved for her as well. All I had ever wanted was for her not to ruin things for herself. Ever since she was little that was all I had wanted, and so I could not bring myself to give her up. If I did, I betrayed that girl, as dear to me as if she were my own.

I thought that my words would be enough—I *chose* to believe that my words would be enough, and I told myself that it would not bring Jennie back, even if Bella hanged. All it would do was make us all more miserable, and with three little orphans to care for . . .

There is the law of men, but there is another kind of law as well: the law of blood and kinship. I had not even known before how sacred the latter was to me, and how little I trusted the first. I figured it was better if we could solve this all between ourselves and never tell a living soul. If only Bella stayed her hand, we would be fine. There would be a reckoning on judgment day after all, and she would have to answer for her crimes to a far greater power than the sheriff in La Porte—and all I ever wanted was peace.

There was only one flaw in that brave act of mine: I had not thought of how I was to ensure that she did as I said. For all my blustering words, I could not bring myself to go back there and pretend that nothing was amiss, so I had no way of knowing what she did or not, because I could not be there to watch her. All I could do was trust that she behaved, though I had no reason to nurture such a trust, as she had always been an accomplished liar. She had lied to my face many a time, not least about Jennie and her whereabouts.

I lied, too, in turn, because I did not want my daughter to worry; I told Nora that I had *seen* the letters from Jennie, and that the girl was fine but terribly busy. I did not realize before it was too late how Bella's lies had trapped me, too. Because how could I give up my sister then, without admitting that I had known the truth for some time? How could I explain to my husband that I had known that our niece was dead, and never even said a word? I felt much like a villain myself, laboring under the weight of those lies. Perhaps that was why I did not go back to La Porte, even if I knew that I should, for the children's sake if for nothing else; I did not like who it made me—how Bella's secret changed me, and so I chose to stay away.

Pretended that nothing was amiss—again.

I worried, though—oh, how I worried, and how I wished that my words were enough to keep her walking a straight and narrow line. Yet when a whole year turned, and I still had not gone back, I was starting to question if I ever would.

I often wondered if there ever was a time where I could have prevented what happened later. If I missed a crucial moment to intercept fate. Then I thought of what had happened in the wake of that dog—the one that chased Little Brynhild up the hill.

It was about a week later that a farmer called Gustav Olavsen knocked on our door at Størsetgjerdet. He was a poor sort of man—lying and cheating, but he had some land of his own and so no one spoke too loudly about it. His wife was a waif of a woman, often bruised and losing teeth, but no one spoke much of that either. His knocking on the door was hard and rapid—angry sounding. It was only me, Mother, and Little Brynhild at home, and so I went to answer.

The man was red in his face and had not even bothered to take his hat off as he stood before the stone step. His dark beard was unkempt and uncut, reaching halfway down his barrel chest. I did not like his eyes at all; they were hard as pebbles as he squinted at me.

"Is your father home?" he asked me.

I shook my head, unwilling to speak with such an angry man. At first, I thought it was *Father* who had done something wrong, stolen some liquor or failed to pay for this or that.

"Where is he, then? When can I speak to him?"

I shrugged and made to close the door, but then he moved, quick as a cat, and caught it before I could.

"Let go." I tried to wrestle the door from the man's firm grasp, but of course, he was too strong.

"What is this about?" Mother came to my aid, though she could not truly help with the door. She stepped beside me and I gave up, letting the man swing it open. Mother and I stood beside each other in the doorway, as was our habit, hiding the state of our home from strangers' view. It was no one's business but our own, said Mother, although I knew it was because she felt ashamed.

"What has he done to have you in such a huff?" Mother crossed her arms over her chest.

"Oh, it's not about him this time, but that girl of yours," Olavsen spat. His face was even redder than before. The fists at his sides were clenched.

"Which one?" Mother asked as calm as ever. "We have several, as you might know."

"The little one." His nostrils flared as he spoke. "I found her bothering my dog yesterday—throwing rocks. The creature was bound to a post."

I felt my own cheeks burn hotly when I realized that the man had to be the owner—the one who had laughed when Little Brynhild fled up the hill. My hands made fists of their own.

Mother did not think twice. "Nah," she said. "Little Brynhild would not do something like that; she cares for all living creatures."

"Well, that's what I saw," he said.

"Perhaps your sight is failing, then."

"What do you want Father for? Would you have her punished?" I asked.

"As she rightly deserves," he admitted.

"In *front* of you, maybe?" I crossed my arms over my chest as well. "I know you like to see little girls suffer."

"What is that supposed to mean?" His hard gaze eyes met mine.

"She told me how you laughed when your dog chased her. I think the priest would like to hear about that."

He huffed and spat phlegm down on our doorstep. "Good luck with that," he said, implying that he did not think the priest would ever side against him—and maybe he was right. It cooled his anger, though, that threat. He did not want a rumor like that to spread.

"Was the dog hurt?" Mother asked.

The man shook his head. "But only because her aim was poor."

"No harm done, then." Mother's lips twisted up with scorn. "I'll talk to her," she said, mostly to make him leave, I think, as she never did anything of the sort. She never told Father what had happened either.

When Olavsen was gone, I found Little Brynhild up in the loft.

She was sitting by the small window, on top of her mattress, clutching her woolen blanket. She had likely climbed up there the very moment she heard who was outside the door. The pale light that filtered in gave her round face a cold pallor. Her mouth was turned down at the edges and her gaze brimmed with defiant anger. When I settled down beside her on the mattress, she pursed her lips and her gaze drifted down in her lap.

I fussed a little with her shawl, pulled it further onto her shoulders. "It's not the dog's fault," I told her. "It's the master that rules the dog, not the other way around. It won't help punishing the animal."

She did not answer, but I could see her jaw working, grinding away in the dim light.

"Now, I'm not saying that you should throw rocks at Gustav Olavsen, but I think he deserves it more than—"

"I missed," she muttered, still not looking up. "I didn't hit the dog."

"I know."

"I was angry with it for scaring me."

"It's a dog, Little Brynhild. You cannot blame it for being what it is."

"Why not?"

I shrugged. "It is just how it is. A dog has its own nature. It cannot think like us."

She did not reply at first, and neither did she look up again. She just sat there staring down in her lap. "I could throw rocks at them both, then."

"No." I sighed. "Not at any of them."

"Why?"

"Because it will only make it worse for you. People like us will always get punished, even if what we do is just." I reached out and let my hand rest on her arm. "Let it go, Little Brynhild. That is all you can do. It won't do you any good to struggle."

She did not speak to argue, but I could feel her muscles tense up under the cotton, and a week later, Olavsen was back, claiming that

46.

Belle

La Porte, 1908

Choosing an ally like Lamphere was stupid. A drunkard is no one's friend—not even his own. I so dearly wanted to kill him, and no one would have batted an eye if he died. Men like Lamphere are expected to go to an early grave—but I had said I would not kill again, and so I stayed my hand.

It was the hardest thing I ever did.

We had barely entered the month of February when the next troublesome news reached me. My neighbor, Mr. Nicholson, came by one bleak cold morning. He stood in my kitchen, clearly uncomfortable, refusing to sit down.

"What is it?" I asked. "Why are you so strange this morning?" I was ashamed of the state of my house then; the table was crammed with dirty pots and pans, the floors were dusty, and I worried that he could smell the reek from the pantry. I could smell myself too: the unwashed skin. My shirtwaist was stained under the apron. Only the children were clean in those days, neatly combed and braided. We brought out the tub every Saturday, and they all had their turn in the water.

"I won't stay long." Nicholson toyed with the cap in his hands. "I just wanted to inform you that your man Lamphere is perhaps not your friend."

"That Lamphere, he is mad." I slumped down in a chair. "He has been gone now for three whole days; I cannot trust him at all. What has he been saying?" I felt cold with dread, but I do not think it showed.

"He is sitting at the bar with Elizabeth Smith, bragging that he has some sway over you, that he can make you bend your knee and give him whatever he wants. His words, ma'am, not mine."

"And what is it he thinks he knows?"

The old man shrugged. "He didn't say specifically, but he tells all who want to hear that he knows some secret of yours. He says he can make you give him as much money as he likes."

"Lamphere is a liar, you know that. I've been trying to get rid of him for some time, but he doesn't want to leave the farm. I was thinking of speaking to the sheriff about him."

"Yes, I figured you'd had some dispute."

"Whatever could he have on *me*? A lonely widow with three small children—"

"He said it had something to do with the way you make money." His face lit up as if he just recalled.

"What money? I have nothing but the farm and the land—"

"Of course, but Lamphere insists there's a second source of income, one that won't stand the light of day . . . I'm sorry, Mrs. Gunness, I'm just telling it like it is."

"And I'm glad that you do. It won't do at all having that madman telling lies about me."

"We have to look out for each other." The man was still clutching his cap.

"It's good to have good neighbors."

"Anytime, Mrs. Gunness." He placed the cap back on his head. "My wife would never forgive me if I didn't tell you."

"Of course. She knows how vulnerable a woman's reputation is, especially if she lives alone."

"You should get rid of him, Mrs. Gunness."

"Oh, I will."

I was fuming with fury when he had left. *Of course* Lamphere would betray me—he always did betray me. I had not forgotten the slight when he failed to purchase that insurance for me, had not forgotten how that drunken fool rejected my suggestion of marriage in effect. Now he was telling tales, suggesting that he knew some dark secret—it would not do at all.

I changed my clothes and pinned my hair, got the buggy out, and set out for La Porte. I was going to place another advertisement, looking for a farmhand this time. If Lamphere thought he could keep Belle Gunness shivering and on her knees, he'd better think again. I would not stand for it—*could* not stand for it.

I told him as much when he finally arrived that night, drunk off his feet and reeking of perfume. He had been staying with Lizzie Smith, an old whore he had been slumming with from time to time, just as fond of liquor as he was.

"You can get your things and go." I stood before him by the kitchen table, holding the cleaver to make my point. It would look strange if he disappeared just after saying those things, but no one would blame me for chasing him off. It was what any decent woman would do.

Lamphere poured himself more drink; he had been in my pantry without asking. "I don't think you get to decide that, Belle. I decide from now on."

"Is that what you believe? Have you seen nothing?"

"I have and I do. I know what you are. People would like to know too."

He was brazen and very stupid. "What makes you think you will live through the night?"

Lamphere laughed. It was a slick, ugly sound. "Well, I will have you know that I've made some arrangements in the event of my disappearance . . . I keep a safe deposit box at the bank, and now I've left the bone that the pig dug up in there, and some other bones too that I found behind the barn. I've left a note with them telling people where to look to find more, and named the one who planted them there as well. My family will find it for sure should I go missing. The sheriff might not like me much, but my father used to be a justice of the peace, so he will listen to my mother."

I planted the cleaver on the table's worn surface while shock and anger coursed through me. "What do you want, Lamphere?"

"For things to be as they were. I want to move back inside again, and then we can talk about marriage some more."

"You let that opportunity slip, Ray."

"Good thing I did or I'd be dead in the ground."

"You can *still* end up like that. Don't think some measly bones can scare me."

He smiled then—*smiled*! "You don't mean that. You're not stupid."

"Get out!" I pulled the cleaver loose and lifted it in the air. "Get out or there'll be no morning for you! I'll take my chances with the law!"

He did go, but no farther than the barn.

He was a problem then, a big one. I did not like problems at all.

I DID NOT care for my children as I ought to in those days. They often ran wild in the house and tore through the cupboards in search of sweets. I forgot which day of the week it was, and my girls lost days of school. Though I had always taken great pride in their neatness, their clothes were often stained and wrinkled. The troubles with Lamphere seeped into everything and left me in a poor state. I still gathered the children around me at night, though, to tell stories, play games, and share some warmth. Sometimes I fell asleep before they did, as I was so tired of it all.

One of these nights, when Lamphere was still in the barn, Myrtle and Lucy leaned on me as I sat up in the bed, while little Philip, freshly bathed, was sleeping with his head on my chest. He smelled of soap and milk, and his soft cheek was warm against my collarbone. Myrtle draped a quilt over us all with much ceremony.

"Tell about when you were little," she said when she had settled.

"Something scary!" Lucy shuddered against me with delight.

"Not too scary," Myrtle argued.

"A fairy tale, then?" I asked.

The girls' silence was all the answer I needed. "This happened many years ago in Selbu," I started as I always did. "There was a very strange old man living on a farm. He had a very big head and long arms—and he had been on that farm forever, it seemed. No one knew how old he was."

"Couldn't they ask him?" Philip had woken up and lifted his sleepy gaze to meet mine.

"No, they couldn't, because people didn't keep track of their age as well as we do now, and besides, this man, whose name was Paul—"

"Like Grandfather," Myrtle remarked.

"Just that. Well, he wasn't like other people, this Paul—he was a bit simple. He never worked a day of his life, but he ate like ten men his size. Still the farmer, whose name was Andor, did not show him out, because he thought that Paul was a changeling."

"Why did he think that?" Lucy's toes dug into my thigh.

"Because one time, when he was tired of Paul, he meant to strike him, but then he heard a voice that bellowed from the mountain: 'Take care, Andor, Paul belongs to me!'" The children giggled and squirmed around me.

"As it was, a girl whose name was Mali, who was a daughter on the farm many years before, had stayed alone on the summer farm, high up in the mountains. After she came back, her mother could see that she was with child, but Mali refused to give her the name of the father no matter how much she begged. Then one night, the farmer's wife woke up to hear footsteps upstairs where poor Mali lay, and in the morning, the girl was gone, but Paul was there, just a baby, all alone."

"Where did she go?" asked Lucy.

"Wait till the end and maybe you'll know," I said, and tousled her hair. "Paul stayed on the farm for years and years, though he could never do anything more useful than carrying an armload of firewood. When he had gotten older than anyone could remember, he suddenly stopped eating one day. No matter what they brought him, he didn't want any food. The farmer's wife went to him then and asked him how he could live without, and the changeling answered: 'Oh, I eat well enough. My mother and father are here every night, and they bring food to me . . .' The farmer's wife laughed, and said he couldn't possibly have parents alive, being as old as he was, but Paul answered: 'I have both mother and father, and I'm not so very old either.'

"The changeling lived for another two years, with no food or drink but some milk and some water. When he finally withered away and died, the servants said they had seen two people, old and bent, a man and a woman, crossing the yard to the house where he lay, just that very same morning. They figured it was Paul's parents. They also said that before he died, they could often see lights glimmering in the mountain, but after he died, they never saw it again—and that was the story about the changeling."

The children lay quiet for a moment, thinking about what they had just heard. Then Lucy said, "What *is* a changeling, Mama?"

"Well, in this story it was a child half troll and half human, but it usually means a child that the trolls or the hulder people have traded."

"Traded for what?" Asked Lucy.

"They take a human child and leave one of their own behind. The children left in the cradle are always difficult and ugly. My father used to call me a changeling whenever he was displeased with me."

"What happens to the children?" asked Myrtle. "The ones they take, I mean."

"Oh, they go into the mountain to live among the trolls."

"Aren't they afraid?"

"They are just babies when they are taken, and grow up with a troll for a mother. They don't remember anything else." I suddenly started sweating; the quilt was much too warm. "Perhaps the troll mother loves them just as well as their real mother would—perhaps she even loves them better."

"I didn't think trolls could love at all," Myrtle argued. "In another story you said they have no hearts."

"Trolls can be cruel, that is true, but never to their children. I think the changelings are lucky to live with the troll mother who gives them good food to eat and nice beds to sleep in. Perhaps their real mothers couldn't give them that. Perhaps they would have eaten only cold potatoes, herring, and gruel if the troll mother hadn't taken them away. Trolls are rich, you know."

"Just like you are, Mama," said Lucy.

"Yes," I replied. "Just like me."

LAMPHERE WAS NOT much at the farm after our row, but when he came, he was rude and threatening. He still wanted to come back inside, still wanted to be let into my bed. Sometimes he wanted money for another bender. I kept worrying that the children would see him, reeking of drink, screaming and shouting. I did not know if it was true that he kept that box at the bank, but I could not risk it either. He had not lied when he told me his family had some standing. If they raised the alarm, there would surely be consequences—of a kind I did not want. I could not make up my mind about what to do. I could give in, of course, and let him have all he wanted—for a while—but just the thought of his smugness if he had his way made me feel cold with shame. I could kill him and brave that box, but it jeopardized the enterprise, and I could not have that either.

In the end, I figured the best thing to do was to sow doubt about the messenger himself. Ray was a drunk, so people already distrusted him, but if I could make them think he was truly deranged, no one would believe the story in that safe deposit box. They would think it the yarn of a madman for sure, left with the bones of a sow.

When the new hand, Maxon, arrived, his first task was to clean out Ray's belongings from the barn. I dug a pit and burned it all, as I had told him I would do if he did not remove it.

He was livid when he found out and asked me what plans I had for the new farmhand, if I was to marry him too. I told him Maxon had a room inside and he could make what he wanted of that.

In truth, I had no taste for Maxon. I had no taste for company at all just then. Asle Helgelien, Andrew's brother, had sent me a note asking for his brother's whereabouts. He had found letters from me to Andrew, and his brother had not written to him in weeks. I wrote back in early March and told him Andrew had been to see me in January but had left to go to New York to look for another brother. I said he had mentioned going to Norway after but had planned to come back to me after the trip. What else could I say? Mr. Helgelien had read my letters and knew very well what plans we had made.

Then one morning, as I came out to help Maxon with the animals, I saw a dark-clad man running across the fields. It did not look like Ray, but I figured it could just as well have been, and on March 12, I filed a complaint against him, charging him with trespass. He denied ever having been on my property but was not believed as I had often told people about it. The whore Lizzie Smith paid his fine.

In late March, after countless sleepless nights, I went back to the police to file an affidavit to declare Lamphere insane. He was trespassing daily, I told them; he refused to leave me and mine alone. In truth, I had not seen the man for weeks, but that did nothing to ease my worry. It was almost worse not seeing him at all; then I knew nothing of where he was or what he said to whom. I would feel better if he was deemed insane—no one would believe him then.

Dr. Bowell would not have it, though. He refused the declaration, and that was not what I had expected. I had believed it would be easy to have him deemed mad. I was furious with Bowell but could not air my complaints, remembering only too well the inquest after

Peter died, so instead I filed another trespassing charge to gather ammunition for another try. This did not turn out as I had planned either.

"YOUR HUSBAND DIED under mysterious circumstances, isn't that so, Mrs. Gunness?" Lamphere's lawyer, Mr. Worden, was a soft-looking man in a gaudy suit with blond hair that looked much like a mop of feathers. He was a slick fish who meant to undercut my attempt at smearing Ray by smearing me instead.

"He was hit by the sausage grinder." I clutched the handkerchief in my hand. I had known ever since I took the stand that this would not be easy. The way that lawyer looked at me with something like disdain—his blue eyes glittering with cunning—I did not like him at all.

"Oh, Mrs. Gunness," Worden said. "I was not talking about your latest husband. I was talking about the one before that."

"Who? Mr. Sorensen?" I was sweating in my corset; every item of clothing on my body felt too tight. I had not expected to be questioned like this—had not expected this ambush!

"Well, yes, did you have any other husbands we don't know about?" Worden answered, and the gathered erupted in laughter.

"No . . . no . . . of course not." I dabbed at the crook of my eyes with the cotton square while my heart raced as well as my mind. "My husband, Mr. Sorensen, that is, died of a defective heart. It was hardly mysterious."

"But the insurance companies in Chicago found his death mysterious enough to have you questioned, wasn't it so?"

"I did talk to them," I admitted, "but they believed it when I told them the truth."

"Your brother-in-law had the body exhumed, didn't he? He did not believe that his brother died from illness." Worden was prancing before me.

"He was mad with grief—he did not think straight." I shifted in my seat and added some more tears. On the bench before me was Myrtle, primed and ready to support my claim. I took some comfort in looking at her, my sweet and gentle girl. Oh, how I hated Worden just then for saying such things in front of my daughter. I watched his plump lips with terror, fearing what he would say next. "I don't see what any of this has to do with Mr. Lamphere," I said. "Mr. Lamphere is not dead, just a nuisance."

"Well." Mr. Worden paused on the floor before me. "If you say Ray was there and Ray says he wasn't, it's interesting to look at who has a history of lying."

"I have never lied about anything." My voice was loud and indignant.

"Some people think you have." He smirked. "Let's look at it this way, Mrs. Gunness: if you had been a woman of impeccable reputation, I would have taken your word for anything, but you are not. You have lost two husbands under strange circumstances and been questioned more than once about those deaths—and fires too—no less than three of them in Chicago, among them one at the store that you owned."

"I have been very unlucky," I said. Before me, I could see Ray sitting by a table, looking down. On the bench behind him were his mother and sister; both of them looked at me with scorn. It was they who had paid for that horrid lawyer.

"Have you truly been so unlucky, or are you a maker of your own luck?" Worden looked straight at me, defiant and rude.

"I am not here to be interrogated by you." I looked straight back at him—who did he think I was? I was not so easily frightened, least of all by a small-town lawyer like him. "I am here to make a complaint about trespassing—*again*—and I expect to be believed—*again*!"

"Why is that? Because you have always been believed before?"

"My husbands—"

"Died in strange ways—"

"They looked into that, and they found nothing because there was nothing to find, Mr. Worden." I lifted my chin sky high.

"Then why are you crying, Mrs. Gunness?" His voice mellowed to a soft hiss.

"Because you keep bringing up my dead husbands!"

"Do you truly mourn them so terribly?" A mocking smile played on his lips.

"Indeed I do, Mr. Worden." My bad jaw flared to life. "But it has nothing to do with Mr. Lamphere."

Thankfully, the judge agreed with me—or he did not like the sight of a crying widow. He leaned forth in his chair and said, "Let's talk about Mr. Lamphere, Mr. Worden."

The lawyer did not ask more of those unpleasant questions, but the whole affair had rattled me deep. The trial reminded me that my devil's luck might not last forever, and that it was a good thing I had let my enterprise go. On the other hand, I figured that taking care of things in my own way was surely much easier than going through all these questionings and trials.

Ray was found guilty of trespassing again. His new employer, Mr. Wheatbrook, paid his fine and told everyone who cared to hear that he did not believe Lamphere was guilty.

"She is a vindictive old woman," Mrs. Nicholson heard him say. "I don't know why she has it in for Ray, but he must have done something that irked her."

SHORTLY AFTER THE trial, Asle Helgelien wrote to tell me he was still looking for his brother. He asked me to help him and offered to pay. I wrote him back, trying to appease him by saying there had been a letter from Andrew. Unfortunately, my man Lamphere had made away with it so I could not show it to him. I only knew about it because I had found scraps of it in the barn. I also told him that the same Lamphere had heard that Andrew lived in Mansfield now. I said I would aid him without any cost. Perhaps he could sell what was left of Andrew's belongings and come down here in May so we could look for him together? If everything else failed, at least I would have that then, the rest of Andrew's estate for my coffers.

A man from First National Bank in La Porte came to see me next, asking for Andrew too.

"What?" I quite lost my head. "Why? Do they think I made away with him too?" It had not been that long since Budsberg.

I told the man from First National the same as I had told Asle Helgelien, and added that I did not know anything else. Maxon was out in the yard just then and gave the man from the bank a curious stare.

"I worry so," I told Maxon, who was new to all this, as soon as the cashier had left. "My former man Lamphere is mad and was very jealous of Andrew. God only knows what has happened to him. I hope they'll find him soon."

47.

Fate washed up on my shores as a man called Eddie Hinkley. If he was a gift from the devil or the Lord, I do not know, but his arrival at the farm changed everything. He was a horse trader from Minnesota whom I had expected to arrive the year before. Now he was nearby in business, and had decided to show up unannounced to surprise the widow in La Porte.

"To make up for my negligence last year," he said, standing in my parlor, bowlegged and filthy. He was a stocky man, just shy of sixty. His mustache was unkempt and steel gray.

"I am of course delighted to see you." I tried for my best smile, but he had caught me at a bad time. My house was in severe disarray after the troubles with Lamphere and Asle Helgelien. Had it not been for Myrtle, the floors would never have been swept. Not that a man like Mr. Hinkley would know the difference. He was probably living in a shack from the looks of it. "Did your business go well?"

"For sure." He patted a bulging pocket. "I was in luck and made more than I had bargained for. I thought I'd come here to celebrate."

I itched to ask him just how much that was, but of course I could not. Instead, I insisted that he should spend the night and set out to make a room ready for him. Who was I to say no to an unexpected gift? As I shook out the linen and beat the pillows, I swore to myself it would be just that: one single night. I did not have the patience to keep a man around and was already mad at him for ambushing me. I could not afford surprises; my whole enterprise depended on me being in control of the comings and goings on the farm. Showing up unannounced was unacceptable.

Before I set to making my unwanted guest comfortable, I told Maxon to dig a rubbish pit. "A little off the way," I said. A place where no bones could worm their way to the surface. Then I asked him to go into town for feed and told him he could stay the night. He had earned it, I said, to have a little fun.

HINKLEY WAS RESTING in the parlor when I came in. His dirty boots were placed on my bottle green footrests, staining the fine velvet. I told him which room he was to stay in, in case he wanted to wash up a bit and maybe rest some before dinner.

"I have left our soap and a towel for you, a razor too, if you are so inclined."

"Bless you, Mrs. Gunness." The man grinned up at me with brown-stained teeth. "A little rest would do me good, I think."

"I hope you like a roasted chicken. It's all I can offer today."

"Of course." He still grinned and got up on his feet. "I love a good chicken—and bless you again. It has been a long time since I ate a proper meal."

With him out of the way, I went into the kitchen and found the chicken I had plucked the day before resting on the table. I had meant for my children to have it, but now it would be Hinkley's instead. It could only feed so many: three children or one grown man.

I blessed my luck that James had sent me a crate of oranges just the other week, knowing full well my affinity for the fruit. I was all out of cyanide tablets, though, so Hinkley had to go by chloral. I cursed myself as I rattled through the amber bottles in the cupboard.

Cyanide was quicker and did the job all by itself, while chloral often required the assistance of the cleaver. There was a lot I had let slip of late. The business with Lamphere and Mr. Helgelien had left me horribly unprepared.

I set to cut the oranges, and was generous with the chloral. If I was in luck, it would be enough to kill him out without the mess. It would take some time, though, for a grown man to die from it. Next, I prepared the chicken and rubbed it with butter and set the potatoes to boil. I would serve the bird with peas, as that was all I could find in my pantry. Before long, my kitchen filled with the scent of roasting meat.

The children came in, dirt-smeared and sweaty from working on the vegetable patch, preparing it for this year's bounty. They crowded around me in the kitchen and looked at the roaring range with hungry eyes. I had not been a good mother to them lately. With all my troubles, I had scarcely had time to feed them. They had eaten much porridge over the last few months and had been looking forward to the bird. The disappointment was visible when I told them they would not taste the chicken after all.

"But we are hungry, Mama." Lucy looked at me with pleading eyes.

"You can have some bread in the kitchen while we eat in the dining room."

"But we want what you're having," she said, sulking. "It smells so good." She closed her eyes and sniffed the air.

Myrtle had opened the door to the pantry. "The bread is stale and the cheese is green."

"There should be some ham in there," I told her while checking the potatoes with a fork.

Myrtle stretched to get a better view of the crammed shelves, which proved to hold nothing at all of value. "It doesn't look so good," she told me over her shoulder.

"Some oats, then," I said. "You can cook a porridge just as good as Jennie's."

"But I don't want porridge, Mama." Lucy's face was red from the heat from the range. "I want chicken, just like you're having."

"Why can't we have dinner with you?" Myrtle joined the choir of complaints.

"Because I said so." My headache was getting worse. "We are to talk about horses and you have no interest in that."

"I like horses." Philip peered up from his place by the kitchen table. He was playing with a toy train, pushing it across the table-top, between a sugar bowl and an apple core, the heel of a bread loaf and a bottle of syrup.

"Oh, oranges!" Lucy was suddenly next to Myrtle, looking up at the shelves as well. She had spotted my plate of after-dinner treats, carefully prepared and set aside.

"Those are for Mr. Hinkley," I told her. "You will have the por-ridge Myrtle makes for you." It was on days like that I truly missed Jennie. It had all been easier when she was around to keep the chil-dren occupied at delicate times.

"But we are hungry," Lucy complained again, and it cost me some not to slap her. I reminded myself it was not the girl's fault but Mr. Hinkley's fault, for arriving so unexpectedly and disturb-ing the day's peace. The chicken was meant for the children, not him, but now all they got was porridge.

It was Hinkley who was to blame.

"I am tired of porridge," Myrtle muttered in the pantry. "How come _we_ never get to eat oranges?"

"Oranges are for adults. You can have as many as you like when you grow up." I could not tell her it was because her mama could not smell the fruit without thinking about poison.

"I like oranges." Philip made a tooting sound when his train drove around a vase of wilted flowers.

"Oh, Mama, _why_ can't we have oranges?" Lucy asked.

"I told you why."

"But please . . . ?"

"It doesn't seem fair that all those are for him," Myrtle agreed with her sister.

"You are only quarrelsome because you are hungry," I told them. "You will feel better with some porridge in your bellies, and if there is anything left, you can have the cold chicken come morning."

"The oranges as well?" asked Lucy.

"No," I said. "Not those."

"Not even if we eat the porridge?"

I did not answer that. It was better if they believed there was some hope.

THE CHICKEN WAS dry and not nice at all, even if I had found some liquor to chase it down with. Mr. Hinkley did not complain, though, but kept telling me tedious stories about bargains he had made and bets he had lost. I could not wait to get to the dessert, and get the ordeal over with. I truly had lost my taste for the chase— it brought me no pleasure to ensnare Mr. Hinkley. It was as rewarding as milking a cow: hard work for a short-lived pleasure. When the last pea was finally consumed, I let out a secret breath of relief, filled his glass anew, and rose to get the oranges from the pantry.

I opened the door to the kitchen and stepped inside, then glanced at the table and froze. A wave of horror washed upon me, as I tried to make sense of what I saw: Philip's head was on the tabletop, his pale face tinted blue. His mouth was working as if struggling for breath. Myrtle's head had fallen back on the chair; her dark curls fell toward the floor. Lucy had slid down from her chair and lay sprawled on the floor like a rag doll. Her arms and legs twitched as I looked on, but her mouth was slack and there was vomit on her plaid dress: orange pulp stained the fabric. On the table, between three empty bowls with traces of porridge clinging to the rims, the china plate stood empty. They had eaten it all: every piece of poisoned fruit.

I rushed across the floor with my hand outstretched and pressed my fingertips to Myrtle's cool skin. I searched her neck for a beating vein, but my hands shook so badly I had to give up. Lucy, then! She had vomited some. Maybe it was enough to see her through? Her pallor was not good, though; she was white as a sheet when I knelt beside her. I took a hold of her dress and shook her. "Lucy!" I called. "Lucy, my girl!"

Her eyes slid open then, showing just a sliver of blue as she peered up at me. "Don't be angry, Mama . . . You said we could have them if we ate the porridge first . . ."

"I did no such thing!" I shook her again so as to keep her with me, but her eyes closed and she went limp in my arms. Her arms and legs were still—they were not twitching anymore.

Tears streamed down my face as I let her go and lifted my gaze to look at my son, but Philip's blue gaze saw nothing at all. His mouth was still open in death. I could see traces of orange on his tongue.

I rose to my feet but faltered, and had to cling to the edge of a chair so as not to fall over. I leaned over the back while sickness coursed through me in waves. Ragged sounds came pouring from my throat, sounds I did not know I had in me. How could it have gone so horribly wrong? I should have been firmer about the oranges; should have slapped them all to be sure. My jaw burned—burned and ached—as if it had just received the shattering blow, down on the ground by the lake.

Just as I stood there heaving for breath, Hinkley entered through the door. He would have heard me for sure.

"Oh goodness," he muttered when he saw the children. "God almighty," he said as he sank down to his knees by Lucy's limp body and reached for her wrist in search of a pulse.

"Don't you touch them!" I cried. I spun around and found the cleaver on the counter. With it in my hand, I moved toward the cursed man who had cost me what I cherished the most.

"Ma'am?" he tried, crawling backward on the floor. "Mrs. Gunness, please." I hit him in the head, just in the bald patch, and watched as his skin split open like a soft-boiled egg, spilling deep red yolk.

He was still alive, though, and kept crawling toward the door, sobbing now, while bleeding on my floor. Next, I hit him in the neck, then the side of the head, and there was no more sobbing after that.

Eddie Hinkley was dead.

I dropped the cleaver and looked down at my shaking hands and red-stained skirt, and then I looked at the blue-lipped children who rested by the kitchen table, their features waxen and unfamiliar in death. I looked at the open door to the pantry, where stale food crammed the shelves, and to the nook above the range, where the sausage grinder rested on the night of Peter's death, and then I stepped over Hinkley's slumped body and went outside.

I did not stop before I was in the orchard, below the naked branches of the apple trees. There I sank to my knees in the cool night air and buried my hands deep in the soil, just to feel something real. Around me, the world moved on: a crow cawed, a cow lowed, and a light breeze touched my skin—but it had nothing to do with me anymore.

It was all lost. There was nothing left for me to want.

48.

Nellie

FOUR LIVES ARE LOST

Fearful Fire at La Porte Results in Shocking Tragedy.

LA PORTE, IND., APRIL 28.—The farm residence of Mrs. Belle Gunness was destroyed by fire at an early hour this morning. Four lives— those of Mrs. Gunness, who is a widow, and three children ranging in age from 5 to 11 years—are believed to be burned in the ruins. The theory is advanced that the fire was started by a former hired man with whom Mrs. Gunness had been having legal trouble, and whom she attempted to have declared insane. Mr. Gunness died under suspicious circumstances several years ago.

Chicago, 1908

No one came to tell me that my sister and her children were dead, no officer of the law, nor a priest. It was Rudolph who learned of it first, having read about it in the newspaper at work. I was at home preparing some cabbage for dinner when he suddenly burst through the door, waving the greasy newspaper in the air. I could tell at once that my son was upset; his face was pale and his eyes were wild. When he saw me sitting there by the table, there were even tears gathering in his eyes.

"Mama." He staggered toward me. "Mama . . ." He bent down and embraced me, holding me tight to his chest, while his body shook with sobbing.

"What is it? What is it?" I patted his shoulders with nervous hands, like bird wings flapping. "What has happened to have you in such a state?"

He put the newspaper down on the table then, but of course, I could not read it. I recognized her name, though—I recognized the name, and at first, I went cold with fear, thinking that she had killed someone and been caught red-handed.

That her secrets would all come tumbling down.

"What is it?" My voice seemed to come from that cave again, that vast place built of dread. "What did she do? What did they find?" Now it was *I* who clung to my son's shoulders for support, as the world around me became hazy and spun.

"They are dead, Mama! All of them are!" Another sob shook his body. "Aunt Bella is, and Myrtle and Lucy, and little Philip, too . . . There's been a fire, Mama, at the farm. A terrible, terrible fire!"

It was too much—was just too much. I leaned on my son and keened.

WE GATHERED IN the sitting room later. John and I, Rudolph and Nora. Olga was at the house too, but in the kitchen just then, rummaging through the pantry for a bit of liquor to settle our nerves. It was all for our benefit, as she was heavy with child and abhorred strong drinks in those days.

John looked gray and old, sitting in the chair next to mine. I had never before seen it so clearly, how age had changed my husband's handsome features.

Nora was as pale as her father was gray, weeping into a hand-kerchief. When she looked at me, I could tell from the expression in her eyes that it was not as much grief as shock that had her so in tears. She had not yet embraced the truth of the ink.

Neither had I, and perhaps I never would.

"Those little children," she muttered. "How can it be? How can someone do something so *vile*?"

"It *does* happen." Her brother sat on the sofa; his hands lay aimlessly in his lap. "Men do mad things for all sorts of reasons, and Aunt Bella did not always get along with people—not to speak ill of the dead." He sent me an apologetic look. He was trying so hard to keep it together, my boy, but the thin line of his lips and the redness of his eyes gave him all away.

"But who is this 'hired man'?" John folded the newspaper and smacked it lightly against the table. "Who is he? What is this story about her wanting to declare him insane?" He looked to me, but I could not answer. I had not been there in a year. I did not know what sort of squabble they had, and I could never voice the suggestions that ran through my head: that she had tried to kill him but failed; that he had caught her in some unspeakable act . . . The worst thought of all was that she might have killed this foe of hers instead of trying her luck in court—and thus saved the children's lives—if only I had not gone there with my anger and demands . . . The guilt was almost as strong as the grief, though I knew it held no reason . . .

"Clearly Aunt Bella was right." Nora curled her feet up in the chair and clutched the handkerchief in her hand. "The man was truly insane! Who would set fire to a house full of children but a madman?"

"I only wish we knew more." Rudolph rose from the chair and started pacing the floor, back and forth in the cramped room. "I wish we knew more before—what went down between them."

"It does no good to think like that." Olga entered with a tray of bottles and glasses. "It won't change what has happened—it won't bring them back." Her voice broke a little when she said that last part.

"Jennie will be devastated when she learns what has happened," Nora muttered in the chair, and my heart skipped a beat. They would find out now, when they tried to reach Jennie Olson. They would find out that she was already gone. The thought of that would have worried me before, but now it barely touched me. The day had numbed me; I had nothing left to give—and the truth had very few left to harm.

"Those poor children." Olga's hand shook a little when she poured for us all; drops of liquor spilled down on the tablecloth. "Innocent victims in a dispute that had nothing to do with them."

"We must go there, of course," said John, still holding the folded-up newspaper. "We must go there and find out what happened—make sure that the man stands trial."

"Mama, what do you think?" Nora looked at me with concern. "You are awfully quiet tonight; did you take a few of your laudanum drops?"

I nodded to her, though I had not. I had not even thought to do so, even if they would doubtlessly settle me some. I only was quiet because I could not find my voice—because what I grieved was different from what they mourned.

In my head, I did see her one final time, that little girl from before, rushing across the moor. Her large eyes and her tousled hair peeking out from the headscarf. Her laughter, loud and carefree, rising toward the mountains—beautiful and wild.

It was over. She was dead.

There would be peace.

49.

The morning after it all went wrong, I wrapped my children in blankets and carried them down into the cellar. Brought them underground like a hulder, never to see daylight again.

Mr. Hinkley was already there by then, lying on the oilcloth. I did not put my children with him but placed them in the coolest part of the room, next to the potato bin, to preserve them the best that I could. Although I had done the work countless times, I just could not bring myself to take them apart and put them in the earth. When I wheeled away Mr. Hinkley, they were left behind.

I did not know what to do with them.

When I came back inside, the house was too quiet. It was as if all life had left with their sweet breaths. This was truly a house of death, when my angels were no longer there to call it home. Brookside Farm deserted me at last, and the walls wept with an invisible grime that tarnished the roses on the wallpaper and gathered between the floorboards like tar. It was as if rot came bursting forth, clinging to every surface. The house was no longer my sister but a foul and cold creature made of dread. Nothing seemed to matter anymore: not Lamphere, not Mr. Helgelien, not the bones that littered my yard. Those were all small concerns compared to what had struck me.

My jaw felt as if hit by lightning; the pain was so bad that it made me retch.

I wondered, not for the first time, if Anders was not done with his beating yet but reached out from the grave to pluck every child I dared called my own. That he meant to see me forever bereft.

As if he had not done enough harm, kicking me asunder by that lake.

Slowly, slowly, I cleaned the kitchen floor, and then I pulled on my boots and locked the door to the cellar. I left a note for Maxon saying that the children were ill, and I had taken them to Chicago to see our old doctor. He knew very well I did not trust the doctors in La Porte. I got out the buggy then and went—not to see a doctor but James.

When I arrived, he was not at home, so I waited in the narrow stairwell of his building, completely at a loss as to what to do if James did not come home that night. Many ugly thoughts passed through my head as I tried to make sense of what had happened. All I could see with my inner eye were those blue-lipped faces on the kitchen floor. I knew I needed James, and needed him fast, or else I might truly fall apart.

I tried but could not muster my wit to figure a way out of my predicament. I could not explain the children's deaths as natural, nor as an accident—not after what happened to Peter. I could say I had sent them away, but that too could rouse suspicions, especially so soon after Jennie left, and with no good reason at all. Just the thought of living in that house without them made me feel sick to the bone, but if I left the farm, it would only be a matter of time before the soil gave up its secrets and my handiwork was exposed. I would be hunted if that happened. Maybe even captured and tried. And no matter where my thoughts went, they always came back to a blue-lipped child.

When James finally arrived, I was in quite a state. He was not alone but had a friend with him, whom he promptly sent away. The two of them were reeking of beer and had had a grand day for sure.

James quickly sobered up, though, when he realized my state. He opened the door to his apartment and kicked it closed behind us. Without delay, he placed a bottle and a cup on the rickety kitchen table and told me to sit down.

"Tell me everything," he said, pouring with a generous hand.

He saved my life that night, James Lee, talking me through the worst of it, plying me with drink and cooking up a scheme. When I at last fell asleep in his bed, I could finally see a light. It was tiny, but it was there, guiding me through hell.

THE NEXT DAY, we entered the bustling streets of Chicago, and the noise from the carriages, streetcars, and chatter was almost more than I could bear. I felt as if I were caught in a dream, exhausted and wrung out as I was, walking next to James on the sidewalk. He had donned a fancy suit with silver buttons and his shoes were gleaming black. Next to him, I looked like a beggar, but that would not last for long. Our first aim was to get me a satin skirt, a hat, and a decent coat. A pair of shoes too, and gloves.

Then we went on a hunt.

We found Moira in a women's clothing store, drifting among rows of shirtwaists and long skirts, coats and pairs of gloves. James sat in a chair by the entrance reading a newspaper when I swung by him and nodded in her direction. She was clearly not a woman of great means, and was likely shopping for a mistress. Her coat was worn and her hat simple; her hands were as dry and hard as my own. When she riffled through the silk gloves, the fine fabric snagged in her skin. The clerk, a tall woman my age with a shirtwaist beset with ruffles, saw what happened too, and scowled.

James looked up. "She's a little small compared to you, I think."

"Well, I would have to handle her, wouldn't I?"

"Oh, but you have handled some big beasts before."

I looked at the woman again. She was perfect in age and stature and I did not think the difference in size was that notable. "She's the best we've found all morning."

"The hair color is wrong."

"It doesn't matter." I could work around that.

"Well, go talk to her, then."

I circled her a few times before I approached. "It's hard, isn't it? Finding the right color."

She looked up. Her eyes were brown, not blue like my own, and there was a gap between her front teeth. "Yes." She smiled at me. "My employer is very particular."

"I used to work in Chicago as well. I had two different employers while I was here. It was hard, I remember, living with all those demands. It did not turn around for me before I left the city behind." I was amazed at how easy it was to slip back into it. I had worried that with my grief, the lies would not come as easy to me as they usually did. But they came, like ducklings in a row, one following the other, tumbling forth. I *liked* being the woman I pretended to be, the one without blue-lipped children in the cellar.

She looked me up and down then, at the fur I wore and the bottle green hat with a plume. "Where did you go, then?" Her mouth hung open.

"I married a farmer in Indiana. My husband is dead now, bless his soul, but the farm is thriving and makes a good living."

"Oh, how I miss the countryside." She sighed. "I grew up outside Dublin and came here when I was eighteen."

"I was twenty-one when I came from Norway. It was hard at first, trading one country for another, but it paid off. I never could have made as much money in Norway."

"No?"

"We don't *have* farms the size of mine in Norway."

She laughed then and lifted her hand to hide her teeth. Some rot then, perhaps. "I don't think I'll ever escape the city." Her smile turned bitter, drooping at the edges.

"Why?"

She shrugged. "I was going to settle with my fiancé as soon as we had the money, but he died. Now I don't see how it could happen."

"It's a hard life, unless one is in luck." I reached out my gloved hand. "Belle Gunness."

"Moira Callaghan."

The soft, dark fabric of my glove swallowed her callused hand. "It appears you *are* in luck today, Moira. I'm looking for a woman just like yourself."

She instantly looked wary.

"Nothing strange, I assure you." I laughed and patted her hand. "I'm looking for a new housekeeper, that's all. The running of the farm takes up so much of my time that my house and children suffer for it—and here you are! Another woman left behind. I think I could appreciate your company."

"But I—I could . . ." She stuttered and struggled to find the right words.

I gave her another warm smile. "Come meet my brother if you like; he's waiting there by the door. We could take you for a meal and talk things over. You don't have to decide right away."

She would, though, I was certain that she would. She had that longing in her eyes for something easier—better. A glass of beer, a nice meal, and a promise to fix her teeth, and she would be mine, signed and proper.

How could she ever resist?

MOIRA LOVED THE farm, as I knew she would. I gave her a nice room upstairs and told her the children were visiting an aunt but would be back in the morning. "They'll be so happy to have someone to look after them when I can't," I told her.

Maxon was out and I was glad for it; everything would be easier then. I asked Moira to keep me company while I made soup and sliced bread. I found that while she was there beside me and had me talking as if nothing were amiss, I could briefly believe it too—that the children were merely away for a while. It was a most welcome respite.

Moira stood by the window while I cooked, and looked out in the yard at the chickens and the dog.

"He'll bark at you at first, but then he'll get used to you," I said.

"Oh, look at the cat. I love cats!"

"We have kittens in the barn too, no more than a week old."

"And so many chickens!"

"They are a menace at times, digging up my vegetables."

"All those horses, Mrs. Gunness!"

"They are a fine investment."

"Oh, I could never have done all the things you have done."

"No," I muttered, "I don't think you could."

Halfway through the meal, Moira had to excuse herself, as she was feeling ill. I wished her a speedy recovery as she made her way upstairs. Soon after, I cut her throat and let her bleed out in a bucket.

I do not think she ever woke up from that soup.

When I had her in the cellar, I cut off her head but nothing else. I dug it down behind the water pump but left the body clothed in the cellar. I brought down a log from the range next, glittering with embers, and set to singe the severed flesh of her neck. The air quickly filled with the reek of burned meat. It was not perfect but the best I could do.

The whole time I was down there, I had not looked at the children. I did not want to see those blue lips again. Every time I closed my eyes, I was there, by the hole in the dirt, next to a root. I could smell the damp forest floor and feel the slick soil in my hands. It had happened again, despite my best efforts.

Anders had hit me again.

My teeth ached and my stomach too, as if fists had just pummeled the flesh.

Then came the moment when I had to approach them. I had to go upstairs for a glass of whiskey first, had to pace those empty rooms once more and tell myself that it needed to be done. Then I went back in the cellar.

Steeling my heart, I dragged Moira's headless body to the resting angels in the corner by the bins. She was stiff and hard to move, but Philip was soft when I touched him. I had him cling to her breast just as he would a mother, and he fit neatly in the curve of her arms. Had it not been for her headless state, the scene would have looked comforting.

I placed Lucy on her left side and Myrtle on her right, leaning in on Moira's shoulder.

People would believe it was me, would they not?

Why would they *not* believe it?

THE MORNING AFTER, I went in to La Porte. I was to see the lawyer to draw up a new will. I made quite a spectacle, I believe, sitting there in his office, weeping into my handkerchief.

"I cannot put it off any longer. That man drives me mad ... There simply is no telling what he can do!"

"The police—"

"They won't put him under bonds, and they won't declare him mad. What is a poor woman to do but endure? There's no justice in this world!"

"I'm so sorry that you have to put up with this, Mrs. Gunness. I'm sure that he is harmless—"

"Harmless? If only people knew what things he's been saying to me! No Christian woman should ever be forced to hear such foul language."

"I'm so sorry, Mrs. Gunness."

"Well." I took the fountain pen he gave me. "It is no fault of yours ... Where do I sign the papers?"

My new will gave everything to my children, but should they all die without issue, it would go to the Norwegian Lutheran Children's Home in Chicago. They could surely use the money. It was not much, as most of my earnings were kept at home in my money box, but I did have a few trinkets in a safe deposit box at the bank and added some seven hundred dollars to it when I went to deposit the will. The farm would probably fetch a decent sum of money too, when it sold.

I stopped on my way home to buy a large can of coal oil.

A FEW DAYS later, I found myself on a train with James. I sat on a red velvet seat in a first-class coach and read about my ghastly death in the newspapers. Arson, it said, suspected to be the work of a madman.

Outside the window, dusk had just settled and painted the leafy woods in shadows. Soot from the train had stained the glass and obscured the view even further.

"This is old news already." James lifted his cane from the floor and tapped the newspaper in my lap. "Lamphere is long since arrested."

"I know that." I reached for the paper bag of sweets by my side and shoved a piece of anise-flavored candy in between my lips. At least I could have some sweetness, I thought, even if I all I cared for was lost—except the money. I still had that, greasy and foul in a box. "What if they don't believe it's my body?" My gaze darted to the wooden door to our small compartment, making sure that it was closed. It would not do at all to be overheard by a Norwegian, although the chugging of the train made that almost impossible.

"Who else could it be? Not to worry, Bella, they will buy it." He looked calm enough to calm me too.

"It's not Bella anymore." Not Belle either, and certainly not Brynhild.

"What then?"

"I don't know." I picked another piece out of the bag. "I'll think of a new name when we get to New York."

"You ought to rejoice! You escaped!" James tapped the cane against the newspaper again. The train kept chugging, ever faster. James smiled, but it did not reach his eyes. He worried for me, my friend. "You can have another child."

"Another child won't make up for those I lost." My mouth felt dry and the darkness that always dwelled inside me ever since that fateful day came rushing back to the surface, threatening to devour me whole. It did not mean much at all, the clever planning, the cunning escape, when I thought of the three little bodies in the cellar. "I like to think that they went to Minnesota. I think they were adopted by a family there. They have eggs and milk for breakfast every day. Myrtle plays the piano and Philip has a new kitten. Lucy is learning to make apple pie."

"If that suits you." He arched an eyebrow. "It was a damned unfortunate affair. They shouldn't have eaten those oranges."

"No, they knew well that they shouldn't."

"It isn't your fault that they chose to misbehave. Children will do that, no matter how well-raised."

"If they had only listened to me, nothing bad would have happened." I moved, uneasy on the seat, my lips pressed tightly together.

"But you would have been stuck in La Porte, and things could have gone very wrong. Instead, you are here with me, on your way to a new enterprise." He slipped his hand inside his coat and a second later, it emerged with a flask. "Here." He held it out to me. "Dry your tears now and strengthen yourself."

I had not known I was crying, but when I touched my cheek, it came away wet. It startled me, as I was not prone to tears, other than those of convenience. The whiskey tasted good, though; it burned all the way to my stomach, soothing the pain all the way. The anger too.

The only silver lining I could think of was that with my disappearing like this, my sister would not be tempted to have me hanged—and I would not be tempted to kill her, either—and that was certainly something. She would grieve me, perhaps, and then she would move on, doubtlessly relieved, maybe scarred . . . Had not my pain over the children been so stark, I might even have shed a tear for leaving Big Brynhild behind.

It was better for us both if she thought me dead. Nellie would be safe now.

"Give it a little time," James said, "and if you want another child, I will get one for you. I might even help you raise it." His lips twitched.

"You always wanted me to elope with you." I gave the flask back.

"That I did, and now you do. Good things come to those who wait."

"Aren't you afraid that I'll kill you in your sleep?"

"Yes, but that's a part of your charm, my dear."

"I never had a friend as true as you."

"We are a rare breed. We have to look out for each other." He took a swig of the flask. "When the rumors have died down and no one is writing about the fire anymore, you will feel better."

"I will still miss them, though."

"Think of Minnesota."

And I did. It is what people like me do. We learn how to survive.

When I was younger, I sometimes thought a devil had slipped inside me in place of the child I lost. Later I came to accept that there was never anyone but me in my skin, human through and through.

We are all just creatures on this earth, fending for ourselves the best that we can. There is nothing unnatural about me. I walk the same pastures as any other. I am as natural as they come. There are just not many of my kind.

Author's Note

So, what happened next?

After the fire in 1908 and the discovery of the bodies in the basement, Ray Lamphere was arrested and charged with arson. Asle Helgelien arrived in La Porte shortly after, certain that something had happened to his brother, and insisted that they dig where the earth was disturbed around the farmhouse. In a trash pit, they found Andrew's remains and other bodies under it, among them Jennie Olson's. Soon other bodies were found as well, and Belle's cunning enterprise was finally exposed.

The discoveries made huge headlines and attracted thousands of onlookers who came to watch the police dig. The visitors could buy refreshments and souvenir postcards with pictures of the deceased in their putrefied state. One Sunday, the doors to the makeshift morgue were opened, and the public was free to file past the corpses before indulging in their picnic lunches. One vendor sold pink ice cream and cake next to an open grave. A journalist dubbed the scene "An organized feast of the morbid and curious."

Because of the findings on the property, it was soon suggested that the headless woman in the basement was *not* Belle Gunness but some unknown, smaller woman. A long-winded trial was set in motion; its first task was to determine if Belle was dead or alive.

Her dentist came forward, describing the bridge of teeth he made for her, which had not been found in the basement. An old gold miner, Louis Schultz, was hired to sift through the ashes to look for them. Weeks later, his search was successful, and he pulled them out of his pocket one day, announcing that he had found what they were looking for.

Mr. Schultz did not testify at the trial; he disappeared without a trace shortly after the find.

Although many still believed Belle was alive, and reports of sightings kept pouring in from all over the United States and even from Norway, Ray Lamphere was found guilty of arson. He died in prison two years later, still proclaiming his innocence.

The mystery of Belle Gunness's fate has until this day not been solved, but it was another kind of mystery that inspired this novel. Belle was a local girl, from the same part of Norway as me, and I just could not fathom how a dirt-poor girl from the middle of Norway ended up in Indiana with a yard full of corpses—and maybe even got away with it.

I DON'T REMEMBER when I first heard about Belle. I was an avid reader as a child and probably found out about her through a lurid book or some magazine article. She existed in my mind as a vaguely Victorian, cleaver-wielding shadow who fed her victims' body parts to pigs. That was all I knew about her, which is strange, since I have always been interested in history—especially women's history—and have an ongoing fascination with vintage crime. She remained that vague shape for quite some time, swinging her cleaver in the recesses of my mind.

That changed when I made a friend who lived in Selbu. I spent a lot of time there throughout my thirties, and even lived in the valley for a year, renting a house in the middle of a field, while honing my novel-writing skills. I didn't write *this* novel while living there, but I got the idea while I sat in that house and watched the wind blow in the birches outside the windows.

I read everything I could about Belle and her murder farm, and quickly realized that I wanted more than headlines and facts; it wasn't that interesting to me just how many bones they found at her farm. I wanted to try to understand *who* she was and *why* she did what she did, even if her reasons were twisted and obscure for those of us with somewhat healthy minds.

When I finally sat down to make sense of my notes, it wasn't as easy as I had thought to get a clear picture of Belle. She was mercurial in every way. According to contemporary descriptions, she was difficult and amiable, outgoing and timid, overly religious and lewd. One person described her as talking a lot in a sugary voice; another said she muttered to herself. Some said she was stupid, others bright. Her sister said she loved children, while Jennie Olson's suitor claimed that the girl was mistreated. Farmhand Peter Colson, who made a narrow escape, said that he loved her in spite of himself, suggesting a charismatic personality.

I found that the reports of Belle's crimes were as varied as those of the woman herself. Some said she killed fourteen people, others forty. Belle's possible escape has also been the theme of much debate. In 2008, Belle's cemetery plot in Chicago was opened in an attempt to determine once and for all if Belle died in the fire. The female remains in the grave were tested, but the results were inconclusive. For years, it was almost perceived as a truth that Esther Carlson, an elderly Swedish woman on trial for murder in California in 1931, was in fact Belle Gunness. An amateur historian from Selbu was able to disprove that in 2014.

Belle Gunness remains mercurial.

This, then, is not a novel about the truth. It's an attempt to understand how someone like Belle could have happened. While the bones of this novel are facts, I opted to keep my favorite rumors and lies, and made up some new ones as well.

The biggest lie in this novel is James Lee. I came across him in a Norwegian true crime book from the 1970s that wasn't entirely accurate. Among the stories presented, I found this accomplice of Norwegian descent. I chose to keep him because there probably *was* an unknown male who presented himself as Belle's brother and ushered men to the farm. Victim Henry Gurholdt is supposed to have come to Belle through him. I also wanted to give Belle a confidant, someone she could freely discuss her crimes with, and another killer seemed to fit the bill.

The next biggest lie is Nellie. Though Belle's sister in Chicago did exist, she said she had lost touch with Belle shortly after Mads's death. There is, for the record, nothing to suggest that Belle's family knew anything about her criminal activities, and the Nellie of this novel is a fictional character with only superficial similarities to the real woman. I opted to use her in this way to add another, more empathetic voice to the story, and there was also an element of curiosity on my part: What is it like to love a serial killer? Not in a romantic way but as a sister, or a mother? When (if ever) does conscience override the instinct to protect?

Belle and Mads had foster children, but besides Jennie, it is unclear how many and for how long. They also had a son, Axel, born shortly after Myrtle, who only lived for a very short time. I also made other adjustments to Belle's family for the sake of the narrative, and must also state for the record that there's no proof that Belle was ever mistreated at home as a child. I opted to go that route after reading up on research that suggests that most sociopaths develop from a combination of nature and violent nurture.

After the fire, there were rumors about Belle and the mob. Allegedly, she disposed of bodies they delivered to the farm in crates. This is almost certainly not true, but it fit nicely with my narrative. Poor Edvard from Bergen (the one with the scissors) is entirely my own invention as well, and people familiar with the story will notice that I have taken some liberties with Belle's last days in La-Porte, and completely ignored Maxon's testimony. The men who

visit Belle at the farm are a mixture of confirmed victims, suspected victims, and my own inventions, and Myrtle's secret about
the night Peter died was allegedly told to a friend at school and not
to her aunt.

A questionable truth I embraced was the attack Belle suffered in
Selbu and the subsequent murder of the perpetrator. Although the
attack has never been proven, some people in Selbu still claim to
know who he was. What seems to be more uncertain is if she truly
killed him or if he died of natural causes.

It has often been assumed that Belle killed two of her children
in Chicago, and later Peter Gunness's younger child, but there is no
proof of that. Child mortality was high at the time, and the children
could just as easily have died of natural causes. There has also been
speculation that Belle killed her children in La Porte before starting the fire, either as part of a murder-suicide or to cover her tracks
as she fled. This seems very strange to me, as her one redeeming
quality in life was a love of children, and there is nothing to indi-
cate that the younger ones were ever mistreated at home.

As for Belle herself, *my* Belle is a tad more eloquent than the
original, judging by her letters. There are also sides to an antisocial
personality that don't translate well on the page, and the real Belle
may have had a little less compassion and depth than the Belle in
this novel. The original would also have been more concerned with
religious matters, even if only superficially.

Another thing about the original Belle is that as a mother, farmer,
and housewife at the turn of the last century, she would have worked
all the time. The perhaps most impressive thing about her endeavor
is that she found time to execute it at all.

Acknowledgments

A novel doesn't rise out of nowhere: it takes time, preparation, and countless revisions to get it just right. When it is based on real events, even more so, because life is a messy and complicated thing—and when the life in question is that of a notorious serial killer, the stakes are even higher. I owe thanks and gratitude to a lot of people, most of all to those who saw potential in the manuscript and helped me polish my words to a shine.

Brianne Johnson, my amazing agent, helped me take the story from a scraggly early draft to a solid piece of work. She has been this novel's champion all the way, for which I am immensely grateful. I also owe thanks to everyone else at Writers House who have worked on this novel's behalf.

I am also deeply grateful to my wonderful editor, Sarah Blumenstock at Berkley, for seeing just the right things and helping me take this novel to next level. Likewise, to my UK editor, Jillian Taylor at Michael Joseph. This novel would have been much poorer without the two of you, and I am so very happy that you saw the potential. Another round of thanks goes to the teams at Berkley and Michael Joseph respectively. It really takes a village to raise a proper book.

I also owe thanks to Liv Lingborn for countless late night discussion about Belle and her exploits, to Sissel Berge for introducing me to Selbu and taking me to visit Størsetgjerdet, to my cousin Øygunn Skaret for her boundless enthusiasm, and to my son, Jonah, for patience and understanding.

My mother, Sidsel Kristin Degn Skaret, who died while I was working on this novel, also deserves heartfelt thanks for raising me among well-stocked bookshelves crammed with works by feminist writers. I think she would have liked this one.

I am also grateful to all the historians and nonfiction writers who have taken on Belle and excavated her story. In addition to providing me with facts, their work has served as a huge inspiration.

There is also Belle herself, and though it feels wrong to *thank her* per se, there wouldn't have been a book without her, so I think I should at least acknowledge that fact. Writing a folkloric monster back to flesh and blood has been a challenging yet immensely rewarding experience, and though I still don't know just who Belle Gunness was, at least I feel a little bit wiser.

Discussion Questions

1. How does Belle from the early chapters compare to Belle at the end of the novel? Has her personality changed at all?

2. What part does poverty play in Belle's development? Do you think she could have turned out differently if she had grown up with financial security?

3. In the nineteenth century, the female ideal was the "domestic angel," whose main occupation was child-rearing and house-keeping. Women were generally perceived as being delicate and sentimental. How did these prejudices help Belle? How did she exploit them?

4. In the novel, Belle is described as being close to her children. Do you think it is possible to love one's children and still be a cold-blooded murderer? If so, would that love be different from the one you and I feel?

5. Belle was more than likely a sociopath. How does this come through in the text? How does she compare to her sister Nellie?

6. Although money was Belle's main motive for murder, it might not have been her only drive. Did she carry a hatred for men? If so, was the attack she suffered in Selbu the only reason for her negative feelings?

7. At one point Belle says, "Living with hatred is like living with a being, an entity made of spikes and thorns. You get used to it—you embrace and nurture it. Eventually it becomes a part of your soul." What does she mean by that? Do you think she is right?

8. Throughout the novel, Belle tells her children Norwegian fairy tales about trolls and hulder people. How does she see herself in these stories? Why do they make her uncomfortable?

9. In the novel, Nellie discovers Belle's crimes, and though the discovery nearly kills her, she chooses to do nothing about it. What would you have done in Nellie's stead? Would you have protected a loved one? Is Nellie's journey of discovery realistic?

10. Referring to the novel's title, what role does spite play in Belle's development? Did it help her to survive?

11. Motherhood is very important to Belle. Why do you think that is? Nellie once suggests that if Belle had succeeded in getting a child of her own, she would have just found another grievance to obsess about and it would not have made her happy. Do you think this is true?

12. In closing Belle says, "We are all just creatures on this earth, fending for ourselves the best that we can. There is nothing unnatural about me. I walk the same pastures as any other. I am as natural as they come. There are just not many of my kind." Do you think she is right in this sentiment? When, if ever, does a person stop being a fellow human in our eyes and turn into a monster?

LENE J. LOKKHAUG

Camilla Bruce is a Norwegian writer of speculative and historical fiction. She co-founded micro-press Belladonna Publishing, where she served as an editor on two anthologies. She currently lives in Trondheim with her son and cat.

CONNECT ONLINE

CamillaBruce.com

 CamillaBruce_Writing

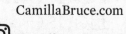 MillaCream

Ready to find
your next great read?

Let us help.

Visit prh.com/nextread

Penguin
Random
House